Haven Harbor

Haven Harbor

KATHERINE SPENCER

Next
Chapter
Press

Copyright © 2022 by Katherine Spencer
All Rights Reserved

🦉 Next Chapter Press

979-8-9871899–1-7
This is a work of fiction. Names, characters, creatures, businesses, etc. are either the product of the author's creativity and imagination or used in a fictitious manner. Any similarities between people, events, or places are coincidental.

Cover: MaryDes Designs

BY KATHERINE SPENCER

The Cape Light Novels

Cape Light

Home Song

A New Leaf

A Gathering Place

A Christmas Promise

The Christmas Angel

A Christmas Star

A Wish for Christmas

On Christmas Eve

Christmas Treasures

A Season of Angels

Songs of Christmas

All is Bright

Together for Christmas

Because It's Christmas

Christmas Blessings

A Christmas Secret

When Christmas comes

One Bright Christmas

The Angel Island Novels

The Inn at Angel Island

The Wedding Promise

A Wandering Heart

The Way Home

Harbor of the Heart

BY ANNE CANADEO

Black Sheep Knitting Mysteries

While My Pretty One Knits

Knit, Purl, Die

A Stitch Before Dying

Till Death Do Us Purl

The Silence of the Llamas

A Dark and Stormy Knit

The Postman Always Purls Twice

Murder in Mohair

Black Sheep & Company Mysteries

Knit to Kill

Purls and Poison

Hounds of the Basket Stitch

Strangers on a Skein

Death on the Argyle

Acknowledgments

As I've often said, "It takes a village to make a village." I'm sincerely grateful to everyone who helped create the village of Haven Harbor, especially my longtime editor and friend, Ellen Steiber, who is always in my corner with thoughtful direction, encouraging words, and a helpful push back in the ring when I get weary. Also, many thanks to Kate Seger, for excellent editorial and production support and her genius for problem-solving. And, Dina Santorelli and Susan Laurie, for their helpful recommendations. My goat expert on speed dial, Dana Cavaliere, generously shared her time and knowledge, so I could turn Tess Hargrove into a real farmer.

As always, many thanks to my friends and family, for their encouragement as I ventured into uncharted territory, especially my husband, Spencer, and daughter, Kate.

To everyone who asked for more books.

One

The ferry was crowded, a boatload of travelers eager to begin the Memorial Day weekend. An earlier cruise would have been more comfortable, but Carrie had been stuck in the office until five, added to that, bumper-to-bumper traffic from Boston to Rockport.

As the boat left the dock, she and her daughter, Sophie, elbowed their way through the main cabin. The best seats were filled—young parents with children handed out snacks and games from bottomless tote bags while millennials plugged into phones and laptops. A handful of passengers gazed at a book or a newspaper. Carrie admired their optimism. The flags at the station snapped in the wind, predicting a choppy ride to Haven Island.

Another reason for Sophie to be in a snit. Not that she needed one lately. Carrie loved her only child beyond description, but Sophie's adolescent angst could push Carrie's patience to the limit. It helped to recall her own teenage temperament. Compared to her sisters, Carrie easily won first prize for "most headstrong and willful," and it didn't take long to regret the choices she made, against the advice of her parents.

Like putting off college to marry her high school boyfriend, Tim Staub, weeks after graduation. She'd so thoroughly believed she knew better than anyone, and that their young love would conquer every challenge. But the realities of adult life gradually wore down her naivety and heartfelt convictions. When she and Tim divorced a few years ago, her parents had taken no pleasure in being proven right, though Carrie remembered they'd warned her.

Never one to wallow in regret, she looked for the positives. If she hadn't married Tim, she wouldn't have Sophie. Crabby, sweet, or in between, her twelve-year-old daughter made up for everything.

A rolling suitcase zoomed by, and Carrie jumped aside. "It's wild in here, honey. Let's go out on deck."

She pushed open a heavy door and a cool, salty breeze whipped her long, dark hair. Finding a hat wasn't worth the bother. Either way, her hairdo would be a mass of curls by the end of the trip.

There were two spaces on a wooden bench outside the main cabin, and she made a beeline with Sophie in tow. Just as they took their seats, the bow bounced up as the ferry smacked into a wave. Water sprayed over the rail, barely missing them.

Carrie laughed. "That was fun. Like a waterpark ride."

"The kind that makes you barf," Sophie added.

"Take a deep breath and stare at the horizon. That always helps. I'm glad we came outside. It's better to be in the fresh air on a ride like this."

"And even better if we'd stayed home." Sophie's sweet features were fixed in a pout.

Carrie slipped an arm around her daughter's shoulders. "I know you wanted to hang out with your friends this weekend. But we couldn't disappoint Grandma and your aunts. They can't wait to see you. We haven't visited since February. We had a great time, remember?"

"It was cold and wet, and we were stuck inside the *whole* week. Watching *Downton Abbey* and playing *Pictionary*."

Carrie thought the island had an uncommon beauty in the winter when the sky seemed even wider and the windswept beaches stretched without end. But she wasn't surprised Sophie didn't appreciate those qualities—yet.

"We weren't in the house the whole time. We took beach walks and helped Grandma at the café . . . and we played *Pictionary* there," she teased.

Sophie rolled her eyes, but Carrie knew she loved hanging out at their family-owned restaurant, The Blue Sky Cafe. She just wouldn't admit it, and certainly not right now. Even on a bleak winter day, when only the hardy year-round regulars stopped by.

The little eatery at the harbor had been opened by her great-grandparents almost a hundred years ago. They'd started with an open-air shack on the dock and a scant menu: clams—raw, steamed, or fried. Chowder, of course, and boiled lobster. The family still followed the original recipes precisely and won the island's coveted "Best Chowder" contest every year.

Before long, her great-grandfather, Gerald, found a shop on Front Street and opened The Blue Sky Cafe. The entrance faced the village's busiest throughfare, and the awning-covered deck in the back overlooked Haven Harbor. The single storefront expanded over the years, tripling in size, as The Blue Sky Cafe was handed down to Carrie's grandfather, then to her own father, Patrick Duffy.

By the time her dad took over, the café was an honored island landmark. As all the New England guidebooks said, "You can't visit Haven Harbor without a meal at the Blue Sky."

When Carrie's father, Patrick, passed away, there was no thought of selling the business. Carrie's mother, Gena, stepped in to carry on the family tradition.

Which was another reason Carrie thought she should visit more often. She knew her mother struggled with the job she had not expected to inherit. But her mother never complained, and right now, Carrie had enough worries about her own job—or lack of one. At the start of the week, the entire accounting department was called into a meeting and told that budget cuts at Sheridan College would result in a wave of layoffs.

Soon after, a supervisor told Carrie her position was "redundant." She was given one week's notice. Her last day in the office would be June 1st.

Carrie had done such a good job of hiding the bad news from Sophie, she was practically in a state of denial. As much as she wanted to confide in her mother and sisters, she hated to admit she was unemployed. It felt like a defeat, as if she was an undependable parent. Like her ex-husband, Tim. It was her nature to act like everything was under control even when it wasn't.

Carrie put aside her worries and focused on Sophie. "You say you don't like visiting Haven, but you never mind jumping behind the counter to make an ice cream sundae."

Sophie glanced at her. "I'd rather have a cappuccino. Grandma really needs a coffee machine."

Sophie actually wasn't allowed to drink coffee. Even if she did,

Carrie couldn't imagine a trendy, sputtering espresso machine in the Blue Sky. But stranger things had happened. "If she ever gets one, you can be her barista."

"Please stop talking about food, Mom. I'm not kidding. I'm going to be sick."

As if on cue, the boat gave another lurch, causing passengers to grab for the railing.

Rough water never bothered Carrie. Her father, who pulled off his apron and jumped on his sailboat every chance he had, always said she took after him that way. Carrie couldn't tell if the gene had bypassed Sophie or if she was trying to make her mom feel guilty for ruining her weekend plans.

A woman stepped toward them. Carrie had noticed her standing nearby, gazing at the water. Slight in build, she looked very fit. Her straight brown hair was fixed in a single, shiny braid that trailed down her back. The shadow of a baseball-cap brim and large sunglasses covered most of her face—except for a tentative smile.

She held out something in her hand. "I couldn't help overhearing your daughter say she doesn't feel well. I have an extra sea sickness bracelet if she'd like to try it."

Intrigued, Sophie quickly accepted the gift. "This is cool. Does it really work?"

"It does for me. But you should ask your mom first," the helpful stranger suggested.

Carrie nodded an okay. She'd seen the bracelets in the drugstore and saw no harm in accepting it. "That was thoughtful. Thanks."

"Yeah, thanks a lot," Sophie echoed, remembering her manners as she slipped the circle of plastic on her wrist.

"Looks like we're almost there." Carrie spotted the island emerging on the horizon. "The water in the harbor will be calmer."

"Yes, it should be." The woman offered another shy smile and headed for the boat's bow.

Dressed in worn jeans and a denim jacket, without makeup or jewelry, she carried a big backpack over one shoulder. She could have been visiting the island to hike or camp, but Carrie had the feeling she was not a tourist. Something about her seemed familiar, but that happened a lot when Carrie came home; so many faces struck a note in her memory, though she couldn't always recall the right names.

Sophie was admiring her new accessory. "Does that help?" Carrie asked.

"I feel *a lot* better, Mom."

"Good. I'll get you another for the trip back." Carrie wasn't sure if the effect was medical or psychological. A little of both, she decided with a secret smile.

Tess Hargrove found her way to the bow of the ferry and stood by the rail. The sun had slipped to the horizon, the low clouds touched with hues of gold, rose, and even lavender.

Haven Island was still a mound of brown and green rising up from the sea, like the back of a shaggy animal. As it gradually grew larger, Tess could make out the wooden pilings of the harbor, and the silhouette of rooftops on Front Street, the row of grand old hotels, the shops and restaurants.

But most of the island was empty, with a scattering of

weather-beaten buildings visible along the coast, and a good part of the shoreline rimmed by high, white clay cliffs.

On the farthest tip, a rocky spit of land, the North Light stood, one of the oldest lighthouses in New England, if not the entire country. Though she couldn't discern it clearly, somewhere in the gently sloping hills, she knew that she'd find High Meadow Farm.

She felt torn as a place deep inside instinctively called it home. But not the warm, cozy way most people mean the word.

In her mind, the island was a sort of Eden, a paradise she'd been expelled from. Despite the cold, loveless household of her childhood, the farm and the island's wild places—the long, rocky shoreline, clay cliffs, and bramble-filled woods—had been a wonderland, offering comfort and acceptance when the world between four walls was harsh and barren.

And there had always been Aunt Lila. Tess couldn't imagine what would have happened to her if it had not been for her aunt's unconditional love and support, gently but boldly contradicting her father's efforts to deny her.

But Tess had been cast out, banished, and in a very public way. She hadn't returned in ten years and wouldn't have come back now except to please her aunt. She had to remember that her father was gone, though his memory cast a long shadow. Along with her well-known disgrace.

There was only Lila left. The dearest person in the world, who longed to see her, even for a few days. "To talk about things that must be sorted out, Tess. Face to face," she'd said over the phone.

As the island grew larger, a sense of dread expanded inside her. But, no matter how hard it was to return, Tess couldn't refuse her aunt's invitation.

Two

"Oh my gosh, will you stop growing? Is she taller than me? Please say it isn't so." Carrie's younger sister Brooke stood side by side with her niece, appealing to Carrie to judge.

Brooke had picked them up at the ferry station and quickly hopped out to grab the luggage from the hatch when they arrived at the house.

"Sorry, Aunt Brooke. I think I *am* taller than you now... Not that it takes much," Sophie added with a sly grin.

"Hey, I might be small, but I'm mighty," Brooke said, grabbing a suitcase in each hand.

"Don't mess with your Aunt Brooke," Carrie warned with a smile. "No matter how big you get."

Patrick Duffy had often likened his daughters to a set of nesting dolls, especially when they stood side by side for holiday photos. Rebecca, the oldest, was the tallest, with Carrie next in height and age, and Brooke, the youngest, had the same petite build as their mother.

Carrie's mother called them her three graces—a comparison Carrie preferred. Their coloring did resemble images she'd seen of the trio of lithe maidens. Rebecca with her rich, red hair; Carrie with coffee-colored tresses and Brooke, a honey-gold blonde. Though Carrie was ever thankful her mother hadn't named them Faith, Hope, and Charity.

Her mother waited at the top of the porch steps, the open doorway silhouetting her slim figure in a golden light. She greeted Sophie first with an octopus-like hug.

"I'm so happy to see you, sweetie...I could burst."

"I'm happy to see you, too, Grandma." Sophie giggled at her grandmother's hyperbole.

Gena gave Carrie a hug, too, then ushered everyone inside.

Carrie followed last, lingering on the porch. Just across the street, a winding path led to the soft, sandy beach. Carrie could barely see the water in the darkness, but she took a deep breath of the salt air and listened to the steady rhythm of the waves, like a familiar heartbeat, welcoming her back.

Inside she was met by the appetizing aroma of her mother's cooking.

"Drop those bags by the door. I bet you're all starving. Wash up. Everything's ready."

Carrie was happy to follow her mother's gentle orders. She did feel tired and hungry. And it felt good to be home.

A short time later, she sat in her usual place at the kitchen table, enjoying her mom's famous spaghetti and meatballs. It was Sophie's favorite and Gena made it to please her. Famous because it was the only Italian dish on the café's classic New England menu, and because it tasted so good.

The recipe had been passed down from Gena's mother, Stella, who had grown up in Boston's Little Italy. She and Carrie's grandfather, Michael, had met in college and lived most of their married life in Bedford, a pleasant village not far from Boston, where they raised Gena. Grandma Stella had been a teacher and Poppa Mike, an engineer.

Carrie visited her grandparents often and recalled their fun-filled stays on Haven Island throughout her childhood. But both of her grandparents passed away when Carrie was in high school; a great loss for Gena, especially since she was an only child. She'd always told her daughters that as a little girl, she'd stuff all her dolls at once into her toy stroller. She was determined to have at least three children, and so she did.

"How was the trip?" Gena passed Carrie a green salad. "I bet the ferry was crowded."

"Crowded and bumpy. I almost barfed," Sophie reported.

Gena offered her a sympathetic look. "It's a good thing *almost* doesn't count."

"A lady gave me a motion sickness bracelet." Sophie held up her wrist. "It really works."

Gena smiled. "It's nice when a stranger does a good deed out of the blue. Now, it's your turn."

Sophie's forkful of spaghetti hung in midair. "Write her a thank you note, you mean? I don't know where she lives."

"I'm sure you thanked her." Gena sounded confident of Sophie's manners, though Carrie knew no reason why she should be. "Next time you see someone who needs help, you can pass on the good deed. Even if it feels awkward."

Carrie knew what her mother meant. Sometimes it seemed everyone in the world walked around in their own private bubble, herself included. It was easier to ignore a stranger's distress and walk on, or stare at your cell phone and tell yourself someone else would help. Especially in the city, where life rushed along like a swiftly moving river, and there barely seemed time to take care of herself and her daughter.

A slower pace was one of the things she loved about Haven Island and even strangers said hello. But it took a certain type of courage to step forward and offer a helping hand or even a kind word.

"Okay, Grandma, I'll try. Even if I feel weird."

"Good, let me know how it goes," Gena replied with a smile.

While they finished dinner, they caught up on each other's news. Brooke was officially home for the summer. Carrie's youngest sister lived in Providence, Rhode Island, where she'd studied writing and literature at prestigious Brown University on a scholarship. After graduating a few years ago, she'd settled there. She earned some money writing for newspapers and magazines, but fiction was her first love. Her short stories had been published in literary journals, and Carrie suspected she was secretly working on a novel.

But Brooke couldn't earn her entire living from writing yet and was often juggling two or even three part-time jobs—waitress, dog walker, delivery person, or shop clerk. She'd try anything if the pay was decent. "A writer needs to see the world from different perspectives," she'd say.

She came home every summer for her favorite job, driving a taxi on the island. Most visitors left cars at home, and while they enjoyed walking, biking, and renting scooters, the island's taxis were always filled, carrying tourists to beaches, inns, and sights.

Brooke loved talking to visitors who came from near and far. Sometimes she even picked up a celebrity. Or someone who was *almost* famous. When Brooke hit the jackpot with a prominent fare, she'd try to get an interview for the local newspaper, *The Haven Island Observer*. She wrote news stories as well. On the road all day, she kept watch for emergency vehicles on the move and followed a siren if her cab was empty.

"I was crazy busy today," Brooke said between bites of spaghetti. "I think this place is becoming discovered. I don't mind sharing. I just hope the island won't be spoiled by the time I bring my kids here."

Brooke was twenty-five and claimed she wouldn't marry until she was at least thirty. A true free spirit. Carrie knew that any man who hoped to win her heart had to appreciate that.

"Glad to hear I'll have more grandkids to spoil someday." Gena smiled wistfully. "I think Haven will be very much the same whenever that turns out to be."

Haven Island wasn't a popular and pricey destination like Martha's Vineyard or Nantucket. It was lesser known and more tranquil. Year-round residents still outnumbered the tourists, one reason Carrie's parents had loved raising a family there. But Haven attracted more visitors every summer, and Carrie knew change was inevitable, though it seemed to her the island should be exempt from that rule, and always remain unspoiled, a place apart from time.

"People have worried about preserving the island's atmosphere for as long as I can remember," Gena added. "The village council debates the question once a month. Then again, I'm still a newcomer. I've only lived here...thirty years?"

Her daughters laughed, but it was true. Most islanders had deep roots, with family trees that stretched back for generations. The Duffys, among them.

"Any room for chocolate cake?" Gena's tone was deceptively innocent.

"Was that really a question?" Sophie stared at her grandmother in disbelief.

"It's never a question you need to ask me," Carrie said.

While Carrie cleared the table with Brooke and Sophie's help, her mother set a delectable-looking cake on a glass stand. She seemed short of breath, Carrie noticed, but she'd worked at the café all day and come home to cook a big dinner. She'd probably rushed around the last few days to get the house ready for their visit, too. Who wouldn't be tired?

"That was a great meal, Mom. You didn't have to go to so much trouble. I thought you'd bring home something from the café. You know how Sophie loves the crab cakes. Especially the way Victor makes them."

"She'll have plenty while she's here," Gena predicted. "By the way, Victor isn't working this summer. I'm not sure if I told you. He fell and broke his shoulder, poor man."

"No, you didn't tell me. When did that happen?"

"A few weeks ago. Guess I forget to mention it." Gena shrugged as she set the kettle to boil. "So much going on."

Her mother sounded overwhelmed, and it was only Memorial Day. "How's the new manager working out? Is she settling in?"

Gena set a stack of dessert dishes on the table. "I had to fire her. She was stealing from the till."

"That's awful. How distressing." Carrie didn't know what else to say.

There had been one or two troublesome employees under her father's long watch. But Carrie suspected that quite a few people found her mother an easy target. Gena was so sweet and trusting. She'd been a presence in the café when her father needed an extra hand, but she'd never been a boss there. She never wanted to be. Carrie feared her mother didn't have the firm, detached attitude it took to manage a staff, and employees sensed that.

"I meant to tell you, but I knew you'd be here soon. And—" Gena paused. "I guess I feel foolish for being hoodwinked."

"You can't blame yourself, Mom," Brooke said.

"A dishonest person will find a way," Carrie added. "How did you figure it out? The books didn't balance?"

Gena placed the cake in the middle of the table. "If that was the case, I'd have to fire everyone." She smiled, and Carrie took her quip to mean sometimes the café's bookkeeping didn't add up. Maybe, never?

"Jack told me. He noticed right away."

Carrie was lost. "Jack who?"

"The new cook," Brooke filled in. She set a container of vanilla ice cream on the table along with a scooper.

"Temporary cook, I'd guess you'd call him," Gena explained. "He's working for the summer, until Victor recovers."

"I see. How did you find him?"

"I put an ad in one of those trade papers your father subscribed to. I was lucky to sign him so late in the season. He was the first to reply, and I hired him on the spot."

The kettle whistled, covering the sound of Carrie's sigh. She wouldn't call that lucky, exactly. Unprofessional? Maybe even naïve? Certainly not the best way to fill an essential position. Carrie was slowly but surely working on a degree in the hospitality industry, focusing on restaurant management. Classes were squeezed into nights and weekends, but tuition was practically free for Sheridan College employees, another reason she'd liked working there.

From what she'd learned, hiring the first and only person who answers an ad was number one on the "Don't" list of how to find qualified staff. But her mother had been in a tight spot. By late spring, it was hard to find any kind of cook, no less one who could handle a busy kitchen. If this Jack was so wonderful, why did he need a job at this time of year?

"How were his references?" she asked.

"Couldn't be better." Her mother sounded so certain, Carrie was instantly suspicious. She was tempted to ask more questions but decided to let it go. Her mother was doing her best at the café, and Carrie didn't want to spoil their homecoming dinner.

Gena sliced into the cake. "I can't take any credit for this masterpiece. Evaline Finch baked it. She decorates with real flowers, but she promised that they're edible."

Evaline had been delivering her baked goods to the Blue Sky for years, so Carrie knew the cake would be delicious. Evaline not only baked, but in the warmer months, she had a roadside stand where she sold fresh-cut flowers, fruit and vegetables, preserves, baked goods, and honey from her own hives. She also made herbal teas and served tea and confections at little tables set up near her cutting garden. When she was in the mood, she would even read the leaves at the bottom of the cup. Carrie didn't put much stock in such things, though Evaline's predictions were known to come true from time to time.

The cake was not only pretty but a fitting choice to celebrate the first summer weekend, the swirls of icing dotted with pale yellow and lavender blossoms.

The rest of the conversation touched on lighter topics, like the weather forecast, the tide schedule, and how sweet the lobsters were this summer.

Carrie was savoring the last bite of cake when her mother pushed back her chair. "It's been wonderful catching up, girls, but I'd better get to bed. I'll be out early tomorrow. The breakfast shift will be mayhem."

"Go on up, Mom. We'll clean the kitchen," Carrie offered.

"Thanks, honey." Her mother paused in the doorway. "I won't be stuck at the café all weekend, I promise. Let's go to the beach tomorrow when Rebecca gets here."

Carrie's older sister Rebecca was due to arrive sometime on Saturday. Knowing Rebecca, that timetable could be stretched into the evening or even Sunday morning. Rebecca was so devoted to her law practice, they were happy to see her at all.

"Good plan, Mom. Wake me up tomorrow. Sounds like you can use some help," Carrie said.

Rolling out of bed at dawn to face a herd of hungry customers was the last thing Carrie wanted to do tomorrow morning. But a wave of sympathy for her mother inspired the idea and she couldn't stop herself from offering.

"Don't be silly," her mother said. "It's your vacation."

That was true. Though Carrie knew that without a job, she'd soon have plenty of chances to sleep late, like it or not.

"Your room is ready, and Sophie is in the guest room. Make yourselves comfortable." Gena blew kisses as she left. Carrie smiled but couldn't help worrying about her.

Three

While Carrie and Brooke cleaned the kitchen, Sophie retreated to the living room to watch TV and text her friends. Carrie was glad to have her sister alone for a private chat.

"What do you think of the cook Mom hired? Sounds like she signed the first guy who could fog a mirror."

Brooke stood at the sink, washing the pots, while Carrie stored leftovers and wiped down the counters and stove.

"Jack is all right. The kitchen crew like him, which says a lot. You'll meet him soon enough. Mom gave him the guest apartment over the garage."

"She what?" Her father had turned the loft space of the detached, two-car garage into a cozy studio for his in-laws, so they could visit anytime. And her family often hosted overnight guests, especially in the summer. But a café employee had never lived there. Carrie wasn't sure her father would have approved.

She was getting a picture of the new cook, and it wasn't flattering. He sounded like a kitchen nomad who hopped from gig to gig with no zip code to call his own. Easy to hide bad references that way. No wonder he liked a free apartment.

"Why did she do that? Is this guy some sort of con man? Maybe he thinks Mom has money or something."

"Calm down, Carrie. You've been watching too many true crime TV shows." Brooke squirted dish liquid on a burnt pan. "He's a perfectly ordinary guy. Well…not ordinary, exactly," she clarified, piquing Carrie's curiosity again. "He went to some fancy cooking school, and Mom couldn't afford the salary he asked, so she offered the apartment as a perk. Besides, where would he find a decent place for the season this time of year?"

It was a valid point. But Carrie was determined to Google "Jack the temporary cook" as soon as she had more specifics.

"It's too bad the new manager didn't work out. Does Mom seem tired to you?"

Brooke rinsed a pot and nodded. "I was going to bring this up when Rebecca got here, but we might as well talk now. I think she's having problems running the business. I'm not sure the café broke even last summer, though the place was crowded every day. Mom has many wonderful qualities, but she's not a boss. She could barely manage us," Brooke reminded her.

Carrie was concerned to hear the café was in trouble, but not surprised. "She needs some help to turn the place around."

"But she'd still need to manage the manager, if you know what I mean," Brooke replied. "She could sell the business and get a good price on the reputation alone."

Carrie stood speechless, her mouth ajar, then said, "Are you crazy? We can't sell the Blue Sky."

Her sister shrugged, slowly scouring another pan. "I know it's our family legacy and all that. But what good is it if Mom is unhappy and overwhelmed? She's almost sixty, Carrie."

"Fifty-eight in September. Don't rush her."

It was hard to believe her mother was in her fifties. She seemed so much younger, still attractive, and full of energy.

Though her light had dimmed after Carrie's father died; they'd all noticed that.

"You know what I mean, Carrie. Is this how she'll spend the rest of her days—at a difficult, demanding job she never wanted or asked for? She loves the café. We all do," Brooke continued. "But she was never involved in the business side. Dad didn't even like her filling in as an extra waitress."

"Because she's so bad at it," Carrie nearly whispered. "She did like displaying her paintings there." *My private art gallery*, her mother used to call it.

Gena had studied fine art in college; she was a talented painter who worked in watercolors and pastels. She had a job as an illustrator for a famous magazine lined up after graduation but married Patrick Duffy instead. She kept her easel and supplies ready in a little room on the third floor that she called her studio and had entered her paintings in local competitions. She often won acclaim for her work, too. But while raising three children, she'd rarely had time for the vocation she loved best.

"Mom always said when we left the nest, she'd return to her artwork," Brooke reminded her. "That was her plan for this chapter. To capture a sunset over the ocean. Not getting up at dawn to fill syrup bottles and saltshakers."

Brooke was exaggerating. But not by much. Carrie didn't know what to say. She hated the idea of selling the Blue Sky but wanted what was best for their mother.

"I'll talk to Mom and find out how she really feels. You know how she puts a happy face on everything."

"Tell me about it." Brooke set the last shiny pot on the drainboard and sprayed the sink. "When I try, she brushes me off. I'm still 'the baby.' She listens to you, Carrie. Rebecca gets too bossy."

Carrie laughed. "But we love her anyway."

"Sure we do." Brooke dried her hands on a towel. "In small doses," she added.

Carrie smiled, though she wasn't sure if Brooke was entirely joking.

"Looks like you made a friend." Aunt Lila watched Honey, a border collie mix, lick leftover bits from Tess's hand.

"She's sweet," Tess remarked.

"Yes, she is," Lila agreed. "She's usually runs from strangers. She can tell you're a dog lover."

"Maybe so." Dogs were sensitive and had a certain canine ESP, Tess thought. Or perhaps it was just their keen senses.

This dog had good manners. She'd rested on a rug some distance from the table during dinner, though Tess could tell the feast Lila served—roast chicken with gravy, string beans, and potatoes—had tantalized her.

Tess admired her fluffy coat and bright eyes. Mostly white with patches of toffee-colored fur, she had pointed, mismatched ears, one light brown, the other white. A sprinkle of freckles on her muzzle suited her sweet personality.

Honey gave Tess's hand one more lick, then sat back, panting, maybe even smiling. "She reminds me of Buddy." Tess recalled the farm dog she'd had while growing up.

"Honey is one of Buddy's pups...maybe a grand pup?" Lila laughed. "She's got the same calm temperament, but she keeps the goats and chickens in line."

Tess stroked her soft fur. "I'd love to have a dog again. But I'm at work all day and move so much. It wouldn't be fair."

Lila didn't answer at first. Then said, "It doesn't have to be that way, Tess."

Tess glanced at her, then down at Honey, acting as if she didn't understand what her aunt meant.

"I thought you'd move back to the village after Dad passed," Tess said.

"I did, too," Lila admitted. "But I like it out here, more than I expected. I like to keep an eye on things. I feed the animals every morning, collect the eggs, and do what I can. Owen Jessup comes by a few times a week to help with the heavy work. He'll hardly accept pay, but I try. I've told you that."

Tess knew the neighboring farmer had been hired to help keep the farm in order while her father was still alive. Lila had moved in to care of him last fall, a few months before he'd passed, in February. Her aunt hadn't complained, but Tess knew those days must have been difficult.

Lila had grown up on High Meadow Farm, along with Tess's father. When she and her husband Will were married, they moved into a cottage in the village where she made a fine home for her husband, and their son Richard. White clapboard with a peaked roof and blue shutters. The window boxes overflowed with flowers all summer. The house was full of light and colorful paintings, bookcases, and comfortable furniture.

The very opposite of the drab farmhouse where Tess was raised. She hadn't expected her aunt to stay one minute longer than necessary, even though her father had left the house and property to Lila in his will.

"Owen thinks I should plant some vegetables. He says it's not too late and Evaline Finch would sell them at her stand."

"There's still time to plant plenty of things—tomatoes and zucchini. Potatoes, cabbage, pumpkins," Tess replied.

Then squashed her interest. Why should she care if her aunt cultivated the land? She had a job lined up on a farm in Vermont. She was expected there in three days, the first of June.

That was the rhythm of her life since she'd been released—working as a farmhand from June into the fall, followed by jobs as a supermarket cashier or in a factory over the winter.

"By the time I hire helpers and pay a good wage, I don't know if it's worth the bother," Lila said.

Tess sensed her aunt edging up to a conversation about "things that needed to be addressed face to face." But she wasn't sure she was ready.

"Listen dear, I have a pension and social security, and your father left enough to cover taxes for a while. But I doubt I can watch the place for you much longer. Though I want to."

A lump stuck in Tess's throat. It was hard to talk about her father and the choices he'd made.

"The farm is yours, Aunt Lila. If you want to move back to your real house tonight, I'd gladly help you," Tess said sincerely. "Please don't feel stuck because of me. I know you mean well, but I rarely had a minute of happiness here."

Tess suddenly realized she had been content tonight with her aunt and Honey—until this part of the conversation.

"Oh sweetheart, I understand why you don't want to come back. But if I sign the deed over, you'll have choices. And security. I can leave the farm to you in my will. But why wait? If you don't want to work the land, you can lease it to another farmer. Or sell. I bet Owen knows someone who'd be interested."

Tess guessed he did, too. Though if her name was ever on the deed, it would be very hard to turn her back on the wide fields and the barn full of animals.

But how could she stay? The idea was preposterous. Her aunt meant well, as always, but she wasn't thinking clearly.

"What about Richard? Have you discussed it with him?"

Tess got along well with her cousin, though they'd never been close. He hadn't offered much help when Tess got in trouble, but he was only a few years older and young at the time, too. Tess never held it against him. She'd often felt he envied the love Lila had showered on her. In his place, she might feel the same.

"My son will understand. He'll have to," Lila said. "He won't go empty-handed when I pass, believe me. Richard knows this farm should have passed to you directly—if your father had any sense of doing right."

More like any heart, Tess wanted to say.

"If you stay, we could make a go of it. I bet you'd have some grand ideas once you settled in."

Tess already had ideas. It was a good spot for micro-farming, organic crops that could be sold to specialty markets and restaurants. Or even a goat farm, expanding the small herd here with more females and making use of their milk. Each time possibilities rose in her imagination, the shadow of her past loomed larger, eclipsing her optimism. Eclipsing everything.

"Aunt Lila, you know I want to. But how can I come back?

Even with my father gone."

"May he rest in peace," her aunt interrupted. Tess knew her aunt had no great love for her younger brother, but pitied him because he'd been such a sad, angry man. One who never knew the true joy of living. At least, not that Tess had ever seen.

"—There's still the Croft family," Tess added. "And the entire village. How can I *ever* live here again?"

"I haven't forgotten how you were treated. How could I? My heart broke for you." Lila paused, then said, "Time has passed. People move on. Time may not heal all wounds, but it puts things in perspective."

"I know what you're saying, Aunt Lila. But—"

"But what? You were very young and made a grave mistake. You've paid your debt…one that wasn't even yours to pay. I'll tell anyone who goes against you. You have a right to live your life. A handful may not like it, but once they see you're here to stay, they'll give up. Most people are too focused on their own lives to care one way or the other."

Tess wondered if that was true. Most people *were* wrapped up in their own concerns. Then again, a small but vehement group had been very vocal after her arrest.

"What if you went to the Crofts and told them the truth? And made them really listen. Once they decide to let it go, everyone else will follow," Lila assured her.

"What makes you think the Crofts would even speak to me? They've heard my side. I wrote them a letter when I went into detention. I doubt they'll suddenly believe me."

The Croft family had been in court for her sentencing. Their faces were a blur in her memory. Except for Ben, Andrew Croft's younger brother. He looked so angry and bitter, hollowed by his sorrow. He stared at her as if she were a monster. She felt like one, too. Even though she was innocent. But she pleaded guilty and accepted punishment for a crime she had not committed.

"Whatever happened to that Zach Webster?" Lila continued. "It's been ten years. He probably wouldn't have trouble now if he told the truth."

Tess wasn't sure if the statute of limitations had run out. And Zach would have to be found and persuaded. It was a long string of ifs. Even her optimistic aunt had to see that.

"I doubt he'd ever do that. Besides, I have no idea where he is. And I don't want to know."

"Probably in jail," Lila said. "He was a bad penny, that one. I hope it caught it up with him. But people wrongly accused clear their names all the time. I've seen it on TV."

Tess had seen those shows, too. "They never talk about people like me who don't have new witnesses or new evidence. Or the resources to find those things."

Lila sighed and dropped her gaze. "I fault myself for not fighting harder for you. For not finding a better lawyer."

That's what her father should have done. Instead, he used the trouble to confirm the many shortcomings he saw in her, an excuse to turn his back, once and for all.

Tess reached across the table and took her aunt's hand. "Don't say that. You were the only one who tried to help me. It was my own fault. I should have told the truth straight off."

"You would have, too. Zach Webster made you lie. He persuaded you somehow."

Tess didn't answer. Yes, Zach had pressured her to lie. But she faced a choice and chose wrong. By the time she realized what she'd done, it was too late.

Four

Zach said they had to run. His car was wrecked, and they had to take off through the woods before the police arrived. He knew a fisherman who would take them to the mainland, no questions asked. When Tess refused, he got angry.

If she wouldn't run, she had to lie. She had to tell the cops she'd been behind the wheel, not him. Nothing bad would happen, he promised. It was a rainy night, and the accident could have happened to anyone. She was still a minor, with no marks against her and no alcohol in her system. He was twenty-one with enough priors to be thrown in jail for a long time.

She wouldn't send him off to rot for years, would she? *Of course not; she loved him*, he'd answered for her. Besides, it was her fault. She'd made such a fuss. *You made me lose control of the car. You caused this mess, and you need to own up to it.*

Tess hadn't realized Zach had been drinking when she got in the car. They began to argue and she wanted to get out. She didn't care if she had to walk in the rain. She was afraid of him when he got like that. Other times he could be so sweet, and he always felt sorry the next day.

They'd been talking about their plans to leave the island. She'd just graduated high school and was free to go. But Zach said they couldn't leave until she got some money together, her share, he called it. He'd never mentioned that before.

Get a job, you mean? Tess was disappointed. She could work all summer at some low-wage job and not save much.

Your father has plenty. I bet there's loads of cash in the house.

Her father did keep money on hand to pay workers or buy supplies. She knew where he hid it, too. But she refused. No matter how she felt about her father, she would never rob him.

It's not really stealing; it's taking what he should have given you all these years. And what he owes you for being so mean.

Tell me where he keeps it. If you won't get it for us, I will. Then we can leave, right away.

When Tess told him to stop the car and let her out, he yelled and swore; and the car drifted to the opposite lane. She tugged his arm and screamed at him to pull over. He shook her off and they sped around the curve. Suddenly, another car was in their path.

Just say you were driving. If you do that one little thing, we'll get through this mess and go away, like we planned.

Wasn't that what she wanted? To get away from her father and start a new life? Wasn't that what they both wanted?

It would never happen if she didn't help him. If she didn't tell the police that the accident was her fault. *Which is the truth, and you know it,* he insisted.

Panicked, terrified, trembling with shock, Tess stupidly

believed him, and believed she loved him and needed to protect him. She wondered if it was her fault, just as Zach explained.

Back then, she'd do anything he asked, terrified that he might leave her, and secretly fearing what he'd do if she crossed him.

She could still remember his grip on her arm as he made his appeal, his desperate, savage expression. The car they'd hit had flipped and spun like a top. The twisted, smoking wreck blocked the road. Broken glass was everywhere, the smell of gasoline rising from the wet pavement.

Zach's car had slammed into a tree. She felt blood in her hair and a fierce pain in one arm, shooting into her chest. But she unhooked the seatbelt and opened her door. She heard a call for help and stumbled toward it.

Her sneakers slipped on the wet pavement and puddles of oil. Zach yelled at her to stay back. The other car was smoking, it might explode, but she was desperate to help the passengers if she could. She heard the voice again, a boy's voice.

She found him, thrown from the car, his leg badly bleeding. Tess pulled off her belt and made a tourniquet. Her hands shook, her vision blurred by tears.

"My brother, Andy," the boy mumbled. "He was driving. How's my brother? Can you see him?"

Shrieking sirens drew closer, making it impossible to answer. She didn't want to, anyway.

Uniformed officers led her away as EMTs took her place beside the boy. Others carefully removed the boy's brother from the driver's seat and whisked him into an ambulance.

The police began their questions immediately. She and Zach stood on opposite sides of the road. But he looked past the officers interrogating him and caught her eye, and Tess knew what she had to say.

* * *

"Tess? Did you hear me, honey?"

Tess blinked. She felt her cheeks grow warm. She'd drifted off, remembering too much. The worst night of her life. A black hole that could pull her down into a dark place. She'd learned to push away the memories and regrets and keep her vision forward. Reliving the past couldn't change it.

"I'm sorry. I was just thinking."

"I said that boy Zach had some mysterious hold over you. I know you were afraid of him. You were so innocent. You didn't know any better about boys. Or how you should have been treated. You can't blame yourself for giving in to him."

Her aunt had said this all before. As always, Lila was too easy on her.

"I see it clearly now, Aunt Lila. He was my first boyfriend, and too old for me. He wasn't a good person and easily manipulated me. But I chose to take the prosecutor's deal. Zach Webster was nowhere in sight."

"That's my point. That coward ran off and left you with all the blame."

Soon after the accident, Zach disappeared. The police did little to find him since they had Tess's confession. Andrew Croft, the driver of the car Zach hit, died in the hospital a few days after the crash. Ben Croft, his younger brother, was seriously injured but survived.

Tess was charged with vehicular manslaughter, and the district attorney promised she'd be sentenced to the minimum time in jail if she entered a guilty plea. She'd never been in any sort of legal trouble before and was technically a minor, so she'd be sent to a detention center that wasn't as harsh and punitive as a jail that held adults. But it was still a prison, and she'd be locked away there for five years. Her court-appointed attorney, fresh out of law school, was no match for the prosecutors seeking justice for the Crofts, a well-known and influential family. If she opted for a trial, she'd be found guilty, and the sentence would be even longer than the one they offered.

Her aunt wanted to prove her innocence in court, but Tess saw no hope without witnesses. Despite the truth, she gave in.

"I know you'd love to tap me on the head with a magic wand so my past would be forgotten. But I doubt that can ever happen, Aunt Lila," Tess said gently.

Lila squeezed her hand. "I'm sorry. I didn't mean to bring up weighty matters the first night you're back."

Tess met her aunt's soft blue gaze with a smile. "You never need to apologize. I know that whatever you say and do, it's because you care about me. I just don't agree that taking over the farm is a good idea."

Honey walked over and poked Tess with her nose.

"Your new friend wants a walk," Lila said. "It's her time to get some fresh air."

Tess smiled and rose. "I could use some, too."

"I'll clear the table and put out some dessert."

"Chocolate chip cookies?" Tess asked hopefully. Her aunt made the absolute best she'd ever tasted—crisp on the edges and perfectly soft and chewy inside—but wouldn't tell anyone her secret.

"When will you give me that recipe?"

"When you take over the farm, I'll toss it in for free." Lila winked. "Think about it."

Tess had to laugh. Aunt Lila wasn't giving up. But Tess was not surprised by that, either.

Tess stepped into the front yard and Honey ran ahead. The air smelled sweet as they followed the path that led past the barn and down the hill.

The farm was set on one of the highest points of Haven's terrain, a flat stretch atop the island's hilly interior.

Tess often recalled the impressive view, but it was stunning to see it again. Especially at night.

She looked down at the scattered lights of nearby houses and, in the distance, the street lamps in the village, the peaks of the old hotels, and the church steeple on the curved road near the cliffs. She could see the harbor lights, too, and even a blinking buoy beyond the jetty.

As her eyes grew accustomed to the dark, the night sky filled with a million stars. She leaned her head back, trying to pick out constellations, then just enjoyed the sight, recalling a quote of Amelia Earhart's, "The stars seemed near enough to touch and never before have I seen so many."

Her problems seemed insignificant compared to the awesome sight. She could have felt unimportant. But she felt honored to be part of it, with her own place in the wide, beautiful universe.

Tess heard Honey sniffing in the tall grass. The dog suddenly took off, chasing something. A mouse or a rabbit, Tess guessed.

Tess followed and found herself near the barn. She heard the animals stir, tucked in for the night. The chickens in their coop, huddled in feathery bundles, and the goats in their hut next to the corral. She inhaled the earthy smells and felt peace seep into her bones. One that lifted her cares like a gentle wind and carried them far away.

She was tempted to stay longer than she'd planned. But she knew it was best not to give her aunt false hopes. Or herself.

Honey's sharp bark broke the stillness. Tess called and she came running. "Time to go in, Miss Honey-Pie. There must be a biscuit in there somewhere. Should we look for it?"

The dog dodged around Tess in a playful, herding dance. Then jumped up and licked Tess's nose.

Tess laughed. "You were easy to win over. If only the humans around here could be halfway as accepting."

The Duffys' rambling old house was spacious enough for Carrie and her sisters to have their own rooms while growing up. Rebecca had first dibs and chose the largest on the third floor. Once part of the attic, it had a low, eave ceiling and a window seat. But at her full height, Rebecca literally outgrew it and happily traded with Carrie for a room on the second floor.

Carrie still loved the cozy space. The shelves were cleared of her souvenirs, and her posters had been exchanged for her mother's paintings. A bookcase above a secretary-style desk still held many of her favorites, and she chose one before she slipped into bed. She'd read *Pride and Prejudice* many times, but Jane Austen's sharp wit and keen observations of human nature never failed to entertain.

Though she was exhausted, she was still wound up from the busy day and her jobless state. Worries about her mother added to her list. Luckily, the Bennet sisters proved the perfect distraction. She soon shut the light and drifted off.

She woke with a start, with no idea of the time or how long she'd been asleep. The sound outside was not loud but persistent. As if someone or something was intentionally creeping very quietly.

She sat up as her heartbeat quickened. Then laughed at herself. Probably a foraging raccoon or stray cat. But the sound was different than that and coming closer. She stepped to the window, pulled the curtain aside, and looked around the property.

A half-moon hung low in the sky, bathing the scene in a silvery blue light, the lawn and shrubs, the brick path to the garden, and the sloping stone drive. The sound had stopped, she realized, and nothing seemed amiss. She was about to go back to bed when a figure came into view.

A man stood by a motorcycle, a helmet dangling from the handlebars. Carrie could only see him from the back; dark hair and wide shoulders outlined in a white t-shirt.

He leaned over the bike, pushing it slowly up the drive, and causing the ominous noise. His muscles strained against the weight, outlined by the shirt's thin fabric. This was no prowler. It had to be Jack, the new cook. She recalled Brooke's indifferent description. He rated more than a shrug in her book.

It was late, well past midnight. Where was he coming from? Partying in town? That didn't bode well, though a lot of people in the restaurant business worked hard and played hard, too. She hoped he wasn't that type and wouldn't be late to work tomorrow.

He paused and glanced up. Did he sense he was being watched? She ducked behind the curtain, then felt silly, spying.

As Brooke said, they'd meet soon enough.

Five

Carrie had set her alarm for half past five. She usually didn't get up that early for work, and she was on vacation...sort of. But helping at the café was a good way to find out what was going on there. She and her sisters would surely visit once or twice over the weekend, but they wouldn't go behind the scenes, where the real action–and dramas—played out.

She quickly dressed in jeans and a t-shirt, barely taking time to comb her hair and brush her teeth. Heading downstairs, she peeked in on Sophie, sound asleep in the guest room. The way her daughter slept on the weekends, there was a good chance Carrie would be back before Sophie was out of bed.

When she got downstairs, her mother was just on her way out the back door. "What are you doing up? Go back to bed, silly."

Carrie was tempted but fought the urge to follow her mother's instructions. "I'll take a nap later. I want to come. Honest."

Her mother shook her head and grabbed her keys. "Then we'd better get over there and prepare the troops for battle."

Carrie could tell she was nervous from the lilt in her tone. It was the first weekend of the summer, when the number of visitors on the island tripled. But their business depended on tourists, and the season was short. "We have to make hay while the sun shines. And pancakes," her father always said.

By the time they arrived in the village, the sun was rising over the rooftops on Front Street and the café was almost filled. "The boat tours and cycling groups," her mother murmured. "And plain old early birds."

Dory Sloan, a waitress who'd worked for the family for many years, was the first to greet them. She didn't look happy, Carrie noticed. "Shelia called in sick and Joey is late. I'm running my Nikes off, taking orders and busing at the same time."

"Good thing Carrie's here," her mother replied in an even tone. "She'll fill in the blanks this morning."

Grabbing an apron, Carrie jumped in. A group of seniors waved her over, and she forced a smile, heading to their table without even stopping to grab a pad and pen. "Ready to order, folks?"

"We've been ready for an hour. I'm about to walk out," a silver-haired man said. He wore a green baseball cap and a t-shirt that read, "Eat Chicken. Save a Lobster's Life." His wife touched his shoulder and he simmered down.

The café hadn't been open an hour yet, but Carrie didn't point that out. "What can I get you, sir?" Carrie's tone was so syrupy, he could have poured it on a waffle.

The group gave their orders, and she repeated each dish so she wouldn't forget anything.

"I'll put that order right in and bring everyone some coffee."

"Thank you, that sounds great," one of the women said.

"She didn't even write it down. Who knows what we'll get," Carrie heard the other man say. "I used to love this place. I think it's really gone downhill."

"Hush, Arnold. She'll hear you," the woman said.

"So what? Someone should tell them," the man with the baseball cap said.

Carrie shivered with annoyance but resisted the urge to defend the café. She reminded herself that some people loved to complain; for them, nothing ever seemed right.

But what if was true? Was the Blue Sky going downhill?

The cranky seniors were served their breakfast without further complaints, though her excellent service was not reflected in the meager tip, she noticed.

She was not so lucky a short time later when an order for poached eggs on a rye toast came out fried with a side of bacon, as the irate customer pointed out.

She hopped back to the counter and peered through the pass-through. The new cook stood at the stove, dressed in kitchen whites and a black baseball cap turned backward. She could have asked a helper to fix the eggs, but he was the first in view.

"This dish was poached. Can you fix it, please?"

Jack glanced over his shoulder, then back to a small sauté pan where he deftly swirled the mixture for an omelet. The energy around him was hectic and noisy with all hands-on deck. He barked a few orders but somehow remained in his own zone, cool as a cucumber, totally focused on the task at hand.

"Hold your horses. I'll be right with you."

Annoyance simmered. She had tables to check and food to deliver, cooling down while he took his sweet time.

She was about to snap, when he slipped the omelet into a dish, sprinkled fresh herbs on top, and set the plate at the window with its proper ticket.

He met her gaze. "What's your problem?"

"These eggs. The order was poached."

He took the plate and checked the ticket. "I'm a little rusty reading Egyptian hieroglyphics. This is the symbol for English muffin, butter on the side, right?"

"Funny. Maybe you should do your stand-up routine out here and someone else should cook."

He cracked two eggs to poach, his eyes fixed on the task. "Who are you again?"

Before Carrie could answer, a deep, gravelly voice said, "Try the boss's daughter, wise guy."

Carrie turned to find Finnbar Mulligan in his usual seat at the counter. The old fisherman and her father had been good friends. He often sold his catch directly to the café, and her father always said Finn's conversations made his workday fly. Especially his exaggerated fish tales.

"Good to see you, girl. Gracing us with your presence this weekend?"

"Something like that. Good to see you, too, Finn."

Jack set the correct order at the window. "So, you're working here now?"

Carrie had the impulse to tell him she was the new manager. That would wipe the smug expression off his face. Where had that idea come from? She picked up the dish and set it on her tray. "Helping out."

"Glad to hear it," he murmured as he turned to the stove. "This place could use some help."

The comment irked her, but she didn't ask him to clarify. He was obviously a pro who'd seen his share of eateries. Well run and not so well run. He knew where the Blue Sky fell.

She'd only seen him from a distance last night. Up close and personal, he was darned good-looking. She had to give him that. If you went for the tall, dark, and cranky type, which she definitely did not.

It was nearly eleven when Brooke brought Sophie in. They took a booth near the window, and Carrie gave them menus. "Good morning, ladies. What can I get you two sleepyheads?"

Sophie smirked. "A real waitress wouldn't say that."

"I'm not a real waitress. I'm your mom. You want some orange juice?"

"Okay, and the silver dollar pancakes, please. With extra bacon?"

Carrie jotted down the order, calculating the nutritional value. "I'll bring you some fruit salad on the side instead."

"Good idea. We can share," Brooke suggested. "I'll have a yogurt parfait. And coffee, please."

"Oh, some coffee for me, too." Sophie echoed her aunt's casual tone.

Carrie kept her eyes fixed on the pad. "Sure thing, lady... Not. But you can have chocolate milk."

Brooke laughed. "Looks under control. I expected worse."

"The calm after the storm. Or should I say, in between the breakfast and lunch storms?"

"A good time for you to take a break and sit with us," Brooke suggested.

Carrie hadn't thought of that, but she had been on the floor since six, without stopping.

"I think I will. Save my seat." She put their order in, adding one for herself. She'd only eaten a few bites of toast.

A few minutes later, Carrie removed her apron and turned into a tourist. Seated with her daughter and sister, she relaxed and tasted her cheese omelet.

Light and airy, it was expertly folded with just the right dash of fresh herbs. Which was extremely annoying. Now she had to admit Jack was a good cook.

They chatted as they ate. Rebecca was due on a ferry that arrived at one o'clock, giving them just enough time to get to the beach in the afternoon.

"Grandma's coming with us, right?" Sophie asked.

"I hope so," Carrie replied. "Why don't you tell her the plan?"

Her mother had been working non-stop since they'd walked in, seating customers, watching over the staff, serving at the counter, and working the register.

Once Sophie ran off, Brooke leaned closer. "Everything okay? You seem a little off."

"Nothing a few more hours of sleep wouldn't cure. But I'm glad I came. Two employees didn't show, and I don't think Mom scheduled enough staff to begin with."

"Oh." The single syllable was filled with concern. "What else did you notice?"

"Plenty." It was clear to Carrie the restaurant wasn't running smoothly. Aside from the staffing glitch, customers were annoyed at long waits for tables, which weren't cleared fast enough. Many items on the menu had run out. Some people got up and left. If her father were around, he'd be beside himself.

"Let's talk later, when Rebecca gets here."

"Good plan. I still think you should speak to Mom. You've seen the problems, and you know what you're talking about."

Carrie felt nervous about broaching the topic with their mother, but she was the logical choice.

Carrie and her sisters had all worked at the Blue Sky while growing up. It was a rite of passage in the family. Carrie was the only one who had enjoyed it and took a real interest in the business. She knew enough to see the café's problems and have some idea of how to address them.

She hoped her mother wouldn't feel criticized by the intervention. Though how could she *not* feel that way? Carrie dreaded the conversation, but it couldn't be avoided. The survival of the Blue Sky Cafe depended on it.

Six

Tess had always been an early riser. Or maybe it was force of habit. Her father required her to work on the farm every morning before school. In the detention centers where she'd lived for years, she'd risen at dawn to start her day and her assigned work.

Her aunt came out to tend the animals at half past six but found most of the morning chores done. Tess had fed the goats and milked the cow, mucked out stalls, and laid down fresh hay, Honey following at her heels, the perfect helper.

Lila met Tess at the hen house, where they collected eggs. She used the bounty to cook a hearty breakfast, including biscuits, with fresh butter and plum jam she jarred last summer.

"I'll clean the kitchen and pick up the house a bit." Aunt Lila paused to lick a bit of jam off her spoon. "Then we can take a ride somewhere, to the beach or the North Light?"

Tess was touched that her aunt remembered how much she loved the lighthouse on the island's rocky, northern tip. The site didn't tempt her today. There'd be far too many tourists and even locals showing visitors around. Someone was liable to recognize her, and she wasn't ready for that.

The beach seemed a safer bet. Not the public beach near the village but one of the stretches of shoreline that were always deserted.

"The beach sounds good. Can I help around here?"

"You relax. You'll work hard enough in a few days. I bet you don't get much time off on a Vermont farm."

"There's some," Tess replied, though she was usually too tired to do more than take care of laundry and rest in her bunk. But she didn't take that job to socialize, that was for sure.

While Lila did morning housework, Tess wandered outside. It had been so dark last night, and even in the early morning, she hadn't noticed the condition of the barn and house. Both buildings were badly in need of paint and some TLC.

Her father had his faults, but he was an orderly man who always kept his property and belongings in good repair, his equipment clean, his tools lined up on his workbench. It was all a shambles now. Loose boards in the barn walls had been hastily patched. The wide swinging doors hung at odd angles, like two big, white loose teeth. Random pieces of machinery were strewn about. She examined a small rusty tractor and wondered if it would start—or could, with fresh oil and new spark plugs?

It would take hard work and enthusiasm to get the farm in order. It wasn't her aunt's fault. Her father had grown weak as the years passed, even before the cancer was discovered, but he hated to admit he needed help. If it hadn't been for Owen, Tess wasn't sure there'd be much of a farm left. He was a good neighbor and a good man. When he'd noticed that her father was failing, he somehow tricked or persuaded him to accept a hand.

She left the damp, shadowy barn and stepped into the light. The sight and scent of the spring day drew her to the fields. She knew her aunt hadn't planted, but sprouts were still popping up from the rich earth, determined little plants that had self-seeded. Tess could identify a few and wondered which were strong enough to overcome the weeds that outnumbered them.

She came to a berry patch and spotted a few ripening strawberries the birds had missed, the long vines tangled with the useless but prolific weeds.

She crouched down and tugged out some grassy clumps. It had been a rainy spring and the earth was soft. She walked back to the barn for gloves, some tools, and a wheelbarrow, then began the task in earnest. There was no sense leaving the beautiful berries for the birds and bugs when Lila could enjoy them.

Her aunt found Tess hard at work and halfway through the patch. "I brought you some water."

Tess was surprised to see an old-fashioned thermos in her aunt's hand. She poured icy water into the plastic cup on top and handed it to Tess. Waste not, want not had been her father's motto. No plastic water bottles or even reusable, personal containers for him. Or her aunt, it appeared.

Tess drank gratefully. "Ready for the beach? I'll run inside and clean up."

"I'm not in any rush. It will be hot this time of day. I have a few things to catch up on if you want to finish this job."

"I do." Tess assessed how much she'd cleared so far. "It would be a shame to let the fruit go to waste. Strawberry vines will grow whether you want them or not."

"Who says I don't want them?" Lila answered with a laugh. "I'm just too lazy to rescue them."

Tess knew her aunt was far from lazy. But this was not a job for an old person, despite Lila's fitness for her age.

"Here are some to bring inside." She handed her aunt the basket of berries she'd picked so far.

"It's early for strawberries, but you're bound to find a few that ripen quickly. If you find more, I'll make a pie or maybe some shortcake," her aunt promised.

"Both sound good to me." Tess leaned on the rake and wiped her arm across her brow.

Aunt Lila walked toward the house. "Don't work all day. I bet it's been a long time since you sat on a beach and did nothing."

It had been a while. Tess couldn't recall the last time.

* * *

Sophie sat at the table, wearing a big t-shirt over her bathing suit, huge sunglasses Carrie had never seen before, and a straw hat with a floppy brim.

"I'm incognito," she confided in a hushed tone.

"I noticed. Avoiding the paparazzi?"

Carrie set a tote bag on the counter and packed it with cold drinks, a bag of chips, and a few pieces of fruit. Brooke would eat the fruit. She'd eat the chips. Rebecca would talk about eating the fruit but eat the chips anyway.

Sophie answered with a world-weary sigh. "I try. But they're everywhere. Like ants at a picnic."

Carrie fought to keep a straight face. "That's the price a celebrity must pay."

"Tell me about it." Sophie sighed and checked her phone.

"Don't you look cute," Gena said as she walked in the back door. Carrie was happy to see her. She had returned with Brooke and Sophie and worried her mother would stand them up.

"That hat looks familiar. Did you find it in my closet?" her mother asked Sophie.

"Aunt Brooke said I could wear it." Sophie knew she was on shaky ground. "I really need it, Grandma. I'm incognito," she explained.

"Well, that's different. In that case, of course, you can borrow it," Gena replied decisively.

She took a pitcher of iced tea from the fridge and poured a glass, then sat at the counter and sifted through the mail.

Carrie zipped up the tote bag. There was a beautiful beach right across the road, down a winding path that cut through some brush. But on a holiday weekend, it could get crowded.

"Sophie and I will set up before Brooke and Rebecca get back."

"Good idea," her mother answered. "How long will you stay? No rush. I'm just not sure what to make for dinner."

Carrie stared at her. "Aren't you coming?"

Her mother met her glance, then looked down at the mail. "I don't think so, dear. It's almost the first of the month. There are bills and the payroll to take care of."

"Come on, Mom. Just for an hour or so? You can walk back to the house any time you like," Carrie suggested.

Gena touched her arm. "I'd love to, honey. But I'll be thinking about all that paperwork and won't relax a minute."

"Don't we have an accountant to do that? I don't remember Dad slaving over bookkeeping."

"We did. But a bookkeeper is expensive, and it's just a lot of check writing and adding numbers. Well, subtracting numbers, lately," she added with a frown.

Carrie decided to let it go. It was clear her mother could not be persuaded. Though her reason for hanging back made Carrie feel a discussion about the café was needed more urgently than she'd thought.

"All right, Mom. Do what you gotta do. But don't worry about dinner. We'll take care of everything."

Gena looked pleased by the offer. "Grab some takeout. You know me, I'm not fussy."

Carrie knew very well her mother wasn't fussy, but she wanted to do better than takeout for the first dinner the family would enjoy together in months. Also, a special meal would be a way to show her mother that they appreciated how hard she worked to keep the cafe afloat.

Right before they lowered the boom.

"You two should get going," her mother said. "It's after one. Brooke and Rebecca will be back from the ferry any minute."

Carrie sensed her mother was eager to start her paperwork. It didn't make sense, but she let it go.

"And Rebecca will give us grief if the umbrella isn't set up perfectly by the time she arrives. You know how her majesty claims to be the fairest in the land . . ." Carrie's lilting, la-di-da tone made Sophie laugh.

Gena frowned but seemed to be fighting a grin. "Your sister burns easily. She can't help it. Have fun, my lovelies. I'll see you later."

Seven

"I'm going to sit out here awhile," Tess called to her aunt from the porch. "I don't want to get dirt all over the house."

Aunt Lila soon appeared at the screen door with a tall glass of iced tea. Tess had stumbled into a wicker chair, achy but satisfied, dirty from head to toe. She sipped the cold drink and tossed a few ice cubes to Honey, who quickly crunched them up. The dog had stayed with Tess the whole day, watching from a damp, shady space under a hydrangea bush.

The grit under her nails, in her hair, and even behind her ears certified a solid day's work. She'd liberated the strawberry patch and moved on to a raised bed that had last yielded vegetables.

"I should have dragged you inside hours ago but you were enjoying yourself so much, I didn't dare."

Tess was grateful for her aunt's consideration. As usually happened when she worked outdoors, once she fell into a rhythm, she lost all track of time. One minute the noon sun was beating down, and the next time she looked up, the day was done.

"You'll find plenty of berries this summer. The plants look healthy. I pruned all the runners. Tomorrow I'll cover the bed with netting so the critters don't pick them before you do."

"Thank you, dear," Lila said sincerely. "What patience. That's the most important trait a gardener can possess. You've got heaps of it, God bless you."

Tess sipped her tea; she didn't reply. Sometimes she was too patient. But she knew her aunt meant the comment as a compliment.

Lila had brought out a cup of hot tea for herself, which she drank year-round. She claimed that in the summer, it cooled her off, which Tess found totally illogical.

"Who's going to pick all those berries is the question. I can still get down low enough," Lila insisted. "The only glitch is getting up again. Maybe I'll get one of those alarms that old people wear in case they get into trouble. Can you imagine the police racing up here to pull me out of a berry patch?"

"They might fall for that once, but don't make it a habit." Tess knew her aunt was joking. Lila was still capable and independent. But she was older, a fact Tess could not deny.

"I'm sorry I made you wait all day to go to the beach, Aunt Lila. There's plenty of time before sunset. I'll just take a quick shower."

Her aunt looked pleased. "Late afternoon is my favorite time at the ocean anyway."

"Mine, too." Tess drained her glass and headed into the house.

She'd done her aunt a favor today that would result in weeks of sweet strawberries to enjoy, share or even sell. But Tess knew it was important to spend quality time with Lila, too. She would leave on Monday and their reunion was quickly passing.

Lila sat behind the wheel, and Honey jumped into the back seat of the cab. As they set off, the dog stuck her head out the window and her ears flapped in the wind.

"How about the beach at the clay cliffs?" Lila asked. "There are a million steps down to the shore, but we can just sit and take in the view."

The plan was fine with Tess. Except for the public beach near the village, most of the beaches on the island required stairs. Or walking down a long sandy trail. Or both. She had to admit, she'd had enough exercise for one day.

Lila turned off the road at the cliffs, found a space, and parked. There were only a few cars and Tess felt no fear of being recognized.

She jumped down from the truck and Honey followed. They sat side by side on a bench facing the sea, the dog between them.

"Sometimes I think I could travel the world and never find a more breathtaking view," her aunt said.

It was a stunning sight, especially on such a clear day. Tess thought if the sound of a ringing bell could transform into a color, it would be the bright blue of the sky above them.

The ocean was calm. Sunlight glittered on long waves that gently rolled to the shore. Tracks of bright green showed above the shallow places where fish fed at sandbars.

"It will be a clear night for the tall ships," Lila remarked. "There'll be the usual re-enactment. We can see it fine from the farm with field glasses."

Haven Island drew its name from a colorful history. Originally inhabited by the Wampanoag tribe, the native people did not meet European settlers until the early 1600s, when a gang of mistreated sailors who had mutinied on a trading ship landed on the island's shore. From their safe haven, they launched attacks on cargo ships traveling in and out of Boston Harbor.

Now with both drama and comedy, an ambush on the pirates by the British Navy was recreated in the harbor every Memorial Day Weekend. Somehow the daring fugitives always evaded capture and sailed south to the Caribbean.

"Are they still putting on that show? It will be fun to see," Tess agreed. They both knew she wouldn't join a crowd in the village even if they couldn't see the show from High Meadow.

Lila's gaze settled on the old church farther down the shoreline. At this distance, the white-steepled building seemed balanced at the very edge of the cliff, as if to test the forces above that watched over it.

A cemetery stood on one side, surrounded by an ornamental wrought-iron fence, rusted and bent in places. Many stones marked the resting spots of the first settlers. Beaten by the rain, wind, and sun for centuries the carved letters and numbers had all but worn away.

Her father hadn't wanted to be buried there. He'd asked Lila to scatter his ashes at sea without ceremony, which she did days after his death. There was no marker for her mother there either. Tess had never really been told where she rested.

"Your uncle used to say if that cemetery was a hotel, they'd charge a fortune for the view." Lila laughed at the dark humor. "My room is reserved. They'll save it till I'm good and ready, too."

"Which won't be a for a long time," Tess quickly added.

Lila smiled. "I pray it won't. But you never know, dear. He can call you home any time. That's why you need to live life to the fullest. Make the best of every day."

Tess didn't answer. She'd lost five years, important years in a person's life. Time that should have been spent in college and gaining a foothold in a career. After her release, it had been hard to find direction and catch up. She wasn't sure if she ever would.

"I'm not going anywhere," Lila asserted. "But I think about you. I'd rest easy if you were settled."

"Oh, don't worry about me. I can take care of myself," Tess assured her. Though she wouldn't go as far as to say she'd live a conventional life, the kind she knew her aunt wanted for her, with a husband and children. That rosy picture was unavailable to her now. Tess had resigned herself to the fact. What worthwhile man would want to be with a former convict?

"I know you're independent. But that's not what I mean."

Lila sighed and stood up. She smoothed her cotton dress. "I don't know why, but every time I pass a cemetery, I crave a hot fudge sundae. Maybe because no one's final words were ever, 'I ate too much ice cream'?"

Tess laughed. "I think you're right. No one *ever* said that."

The late afternoon sun was sinking toward the sea, painting the horizon a palette of colors. Tess took one more look at the sweeping vista, then headed for the truck, calling Honey to her side.

"Let's pick up some ice cream on the way home," Tess said, "and all the trimmings."

Eight

It was Carrie's idea to cook lobsters. It was their mother's favorite meal and sure to please her. She offered to drive over to Bolton's, the fish market side, and pick up a few.

"You guys," she said to Brooke and Rebecca, "can go to the supermarket and grab a few potatoes or corn, and stuff for a tossed salad."

"Can you make fries?" Sophie, the local celebrity, asked.

"If you want fries, we can get a bag of frozen."

Carrie thought Rebecca was asleep, until she raised her hand like a police officer directing traffic. "Stop right there."

Stretched out in a reclining beach chair, most of her body was protected by the umbrella's shade, with only her long legs, smeared with sunblock, exposed to the light. Wraparound sunglasses covered her eyes, a pair that likely cost at least one of Carrie's weekly paychecks.

"—We'll get the lobsters and all the sides cooked and ready to go at Bolton's, the restaurant side. Baked, fries, corn, whatever. Then all we'll need is paper plates."

"That will cost a small fortune. Except for the paper plates," Brooke said.

"My treat, I forgot to add."

Carrie and Brooke insisted she couldn't do that, but their older sister easily overruled their objections.

"Don't be silly. I want to. How often do we get together? Besides, cooking lobster makes a mess."

"If you want to make an omelet, you have to break some eggs, Becca," Carrie said lightly

"I wouldn't know, but I'll take your word for it." Rebecca slipped the glasses down her nose and offered Carrie a sassy grin. She was kidding, of course. Even Rebecca scrambled a few eggs once in a while—didn't she?

Rebecca had been right. As usual. It was much easier and more fun to buy the lobster feast cooked and ready to serve. Their mother was very pleased by the surprise and eager to make the evening festive. They found a bright tablecloth and strung colorful lanterns across the deck. Rebecca placed tea candles on the table, along with a vase of bright flowers.

They'd splurged on shrimp cocktail, and Brooke made a fruity summer drink in the blender. Sophie picked a playlist from the music on her phone, and Rebecca produced a tiny speaker that amplified the sound ten times.

It felt like a real party and must have looked like one, too, Carrie thought, judging from the expression on Jack's face as he rolled his motorcycle down the drive.

Carrie acted as if she didn't see him. But her mother bounced up from the table and waved. To Carrie's dismay, he waved back.

Okay. Decent manners. Your mother taught you well. On your way, Mister, she silently urged him.

He looked about to do just that. Until her mom called out, "Hey, Jack! Come over a minute and say hello."

Carrie hoped he'd make some excuse. But he smiled, parked the bike, and headed their way.

She sipped her frothy drink, her gaze cast down. Freshly shaven, with his dark hair combed back wet, he looked very handsome in a black polo shirt and jeans. She recalled an illustration from a book about Greek mythology, a big, dark satyr encountering a party of frolicking nymphs. That's what his arrival suddenly felt like.

"My daughters made me a wonderful dinner. Lobster with all the trimmings," Gena told him. "Wasn't that sweet?"

"Bolton's made it. We just brought it home," Rebecca clarified.

"We made the cocktails. Want to try one?" Brooke held up the pitcher of pink foam.

"Looks good, but I'll pass."

"For goodness sakes," Rebecca cut in. "He's not going to drink that unicorn juice. Find the man a beer. I'm Rebecca, by the way. I don't think we've met."

"Jack Dubensky. Nice to meet you. You must be the lawyer."

Her mother must have bragged about her daughters, Carrie surmised. She wondered how she'd been described.

"Good recall. Ten points," Rebecca replied.

"I didn't realize anyone was keeping score." He smiled straight white teeth against tanned skin and a set of champion dimples.

Carrie hadn't noticed that before. He could turn on the charm when he wanted to. That's how he must have persuaded her mother to give him the job...and the apartment.

Carrie compared the civilized banter to their first encounter. Maybe the guy she'd met was locked in the garage, and this pleasant George Clooney version was let loose at night to socialize.

"I'll pass on the beer, thanks. I'm headed into town."

"Going to see the nautical parade and tall ships?" Gena asked. "The re-enactment doesn't start until eight, but it's smart to get there early. The waterfront will be jammed."

"They act out a British frigate attacking a pirate ship. It's really fun," Sophie explained.

"You can see it from a few points on the island. You don't have to fight the crowds," Rebecca advised.

"But when everyone oohs and aaahhs at once, it does make it more fun," Brooke added. "Like riding a roller coaster when everyone screams at the same time.

"I didn't know there was a show in the harbor. Thanks for the tip."

So, he was headed to town for another reason, a date probably. Or soon would have plenty of female attention, Carrie thought.

"We're going to sneak into the café and watch from the deck," Gena said. "You can join us if you like."

Carrie gritted her teeth to keep from objecting out loud. *Mother! Are you kidding? We barely know this man. Please don't say yes*, she silently pleaded.

She'd come to the bottom of her drink without realizing it, and the straw made a rude sucking sound.

"Excuse me," she mumbled. Her cheeks felt warm and she hoped no one would notice in the dim light.

Sophie giggled and Jack struggled not to laugh, though it showed in his dark eyes.

"Thank you, Carrie. It's about time you contributed to the conversation," Rebecca remarked in a dry tone.

Carrie could hold her own, trading witty barbs with her older sister. This time, she decided to get Rebecca back later.

"It's getting late. I think we should clean up and head to town," Carrie said.

"We were having so much fun, I lost track." Her mother checked the time and glanced at Carrie, who had begun gathering the paper plates.

Jack stepped back, sensing a shift in the mood. "Maybe I'll see you later. Have a nice evening."

With a brief wave, he turned and walked toward the drive.

A few moments later, they heard the motorcycle roar away. Her mother went into the house with Sophie while Carrie and her sisters bagged the trash.

"Why didn't you want him to watch with us?" Rebecca asked.

"He's an employee, not a house guest. It's bad enough that he lives in the apartment. We know nothing about him. Mom barely checked his references."

Rebecca looked concerned. "Okay, I get it now. I didn't have all the intel."

"Mom just told me last night. I'm going to check him out online when I get a chance."

"Leave that to me. We have an entire department of snoops who can dig up more dirt in five minutes than you could in five hours...No offense, *Cara-mia*. I bet you're very good at it."

Rebecca always used the cute nickname she'd made up for Carrie when she wanted something, or stepped on her toes.

Carrie was glad to hand off the task. It was going to be hard enough to speak to her mother about the café's problems. She and her sisters had strategized at the beach, but she was unanimously elected to be the messenger.

Carrie had decided to do it tonight. She'd get it over with, and they'd have Sunday and Monday to help sort things out in the office and place another ad for a manager.

That was another reason Carrie didn't want Jack hanging around. She had enough on her mind without the surly, six-foot distraction.

* * *

Aunt Lila had put together a light dinner of green salad with fresh goat cheese and sliced beets, preserved from last year's garden. There was also freshly baked bread, fragrant and warm from the oven.

Tess's hard work had sharpened her appetite, and she ate her fill, then took Honey out for her evening romp. But a few steps from the house, the first cannon boom of the mock pirate battle sounded. The dog stood stone still, then ran back inside, nearly knocking over Lila, as she stepped out to the porch, carrying a tray with their dessert.

"Come join me in my private box, Madam. First class all the way. They even serve ice cream."

Lila sat in a fan-back wicker chair, and spread a fancy linen napkin on her lap, then picked up a large bowl of ice cream, drowned in fudge sauce and smothered with whipped cream, sprinkles, and even a cherry.

Tess sat beside her and picked up her napkin and ice cream. Her aunt had even given them silver spoons, Tess noticed.

The next volley of cannons boomed. Tess could see the ships clearly, the wooden frames outlined with lights. She lifted the field glasses and watched the fake pirates swing on long ropes, waving silver swords.

"Who's winning?" her aunt asked around a mouthful of ice cream.

"The pirates, of course," Tess reported. She handed her aunt the binoculars. "These *are* the best seats in the house, Aunt Lila."

Lila turned and squeezed her hand. "They are if you're here. I'm so happy you've come back, Tess. I can't tell you how much it means to me."

Her aunt seemed teary, and Tess felt teary too, though the echo of the explosions made it impossible to answer. When she caught her aunt's eye, they started laughing. Maybe because it seemed so silly to be crying and eating ice cream and watching pretend pirates, all at the same time.

Or maybe just because she felt happy. Happier and more at peace than she'd been in years.

They thought they'd left in plenty of time but found themselves stuck about half a mile from the village in a line of traffic that barely moved an inch per minute. Carrie heard the cannon's boom. If they didn't get out soon, they'd miss the show.

They'd piled into Brooke's taxi, a van with three rows of seats. Rebecca sat in the front, claiming the spot for the leg room. Her mother was in the next row with Carrie and Sophie had jumped in the back.

"You'd think, living here most of our lives, we would have gotten here in time to find parking," Rebecca observed.

"Let's just pull over and watch from the road," Brooke said.

The suggestion made sense, but Carrie didn't like missing their family ritual of watching from the café's deck. Since her father had passed away, she always felt he was there in spirit. But she wouldn't have that sense if they watched from some random spot.

"Wait, I have an idea. We can't make it to the café but I'll bring us around to the village green." Brooke took a sharp right turn into a neighborhood and drove through the winding streets as the second round of cannon fire exploded.

"We're missing the *whooole* thing," Sophie grumbled.

Before Sophie could finish complaining, the green came into view. It wasn't empty by any stretch, but there was plenty of room to set up their chairs and watch the show. Brooke found a space for the taxi on a grassy patch, and they piled out.

Carrie was first to exit her side and noticed her mother hesitate. Carrie stretched a hand to help. "Are you okay, Mom?"

Her mother smiled and hopped to the ground. "I think that pink drink went to my head." She laughed. "But it was worth it."

Carrie smiled but took her mother's arm. It was dusk and she didn't want her to stumble on the uneven ground.

They took beach chairs from the hatch and wandered on the green to find a spot. Brooke, Rebecca, and Sophie led the way. But her mother hung back, to catch her breath.

"I'm fine here," she said.

"Are you sure?" Carrie hadn't grabbed any chairs. Her sisters had all of them. "Let me get you a chair, Mom. I'll be right back."

"I'm fine. You go with the others. We can meet later at the car."

Carrie didn't want to leave her mother alone. All the benches were filled, but maybe someone would get up before the show was over. She'd keep her eye out.

"I'm fine here, too," Carrie said. "I'll watch with you."

The show was better than ever, Carrie thought. The pirates and British sailors fought with daring and acrobatic agility. The explosions were deafening, but the crowd's cheers were just as loud.

She turned to her mother to share the fun but found her staring at the ground, her hand pressed to her chest.

"Mom? Are you okay?" Carrie gripped her mother's arm, panic rising in her chest.

Gena raised her gaze and seemed about to answer but took a deep, gasping breath. Her eyes closed and her head rolled back as she crumpled toward the ground. Carrie held on tight, barely able to manage a soft landing.

Carrie knelt beside her, cradling her mother's head in her hand. "Mom? Can you answer me? What's happening?"

Her mother's eyes flickered. She seemed about to speak, then winced with pain.

Carrie looked up, feeling frantic. Before she could scream for help, someone knelt on the other side of her mother and felt her pulse.

It was Jack. Where had he come from?

"Stay with her. I'll call 9-1-1." He stood up and pulled out his phone. "Where are your sisters?"

Carrie waved at the crowd. "Over there somewhere. I'm not sure."

"Don't worry, I'll find them." Carrie heard him talking to an emergency operator as he ran to find her family.

She looked back down at her mother, who had a hand pressed to her chest, her breathing labored. She stroked her mother's brow, alarmed to feel her skin cold but damp with sweat.

"It's going to be all right, Mom. An ambulance is coming. Just hang on..."

Rebecca and Brooke appeared. They gasped as they took in the scene and immediately knelt beside their mother.

"Mom? Can you hear me?" Rebecca's tone was unusually gentle, edged with panic.

Her mother's eyes flickered open, and she nodded. Carrie offered silent thanks.

"She was short of breath and didn't want to walk anymore. She touched her chest and sort of fainted," Carrie explained.

"What's wrong with Grandma? Is she going to be okay?" Sophie's voice trembled, and she started to cry.

Carrie put an arm around her daughter's shoulder. "An ambulance will be here any second. They'll take Grandma to the hospital and doctors will take care of her."

"I hear the siren, Sophie," Jack said. "They're almost here."

Carrie had forgotten about him. He looked deeply concerned. He was either a con man with a compassionate side or, despite her suspicions, a good person.

"Thanks for your help. I didn't even see you in this crowd."

"I saw you," he answered quietly.

Before she could reply, the ambulance arrived, followed by a police car. Both parked on the green, and EMTs ran toward them.

Rebecca explained what had happened to one EMT, while the other attended to her mother.

"Did she have a heart attack?" Rebecca asked.

"It's possible. You can follow us in your car to the medical center."

Lying on a gurney, her mother was wheeled to the back of the ambulance and lifted inside. Her sisters headed for the van with Sophie, but Carrie felt glued to the spot.

Someone touched her shoulder. A light touch, but a strong, heavy hand. "Hey, are you okay?"

She turned and met Jack's gaze. "I'm a little stunned," she admitted.

"Don't worry. Your mom will be all right."

He had no way of knowing, but it was nice of him to say.

"Yes, she will be," Carrie echoed, though she was anything but sure.

She simply has to be, she silently added.

Nine

By the time her aunt left for church, Tess was mending the fence on the goat pen. Ever optimistic, Lila invited her to the service but wasn't surprised when Tess declined.

Tess had attended church every week while growing up. Her father, who saw himself as a faithful man, insisted. Though Tess often wondered why she saw no hint of love and kindness at home when there seemed to be so much talk about it on Sunday. Her usual prayer back then was that God would let her live with her Aunt Lila. But sometimes she prayed for other things, like nicer clothes or a best friend.

The girls in her grade school classes were not always mean, but they whispered about her when they thought she couldn't hear, and sometimes when they knew she could. She wore strange clothes, and her hair was never right. She gave the wrong answers in class and, sometimes, no answer at all; she was so shy.

She felt she was invisible to her father, who was either working outdoors or lost in his own thoughts when they sat together at the supper table. He made sure her needs were taken care of—food, clothing, keeping up with her homework. But he didn't seem to notice her most of the time. Except to remind her of chores around the house and farm.

She didn't try to attract his attention either. There were worse things than being invisible, she learned. Her father had an awful temper that could explode without warning. He usually kept it hidden, but she'd seen enough of it to keep her guard up. When he got angry, often about some task on the farm, he called her stupid and clumsy and worse, insisting she'd been only trouble to him since the day she was born.

Tess tried hard to change, to somehow win his approval and affection. A quest that proved futile.

Much later, she understood it was not about her at all. Her mother had died soon after giving birth. He never said the words outright, but from the way he explained it, Tess knew that he blamed her for his loss.

There was only one picture of her mother in the house, taken on their wedding day. It sat on a chest of drawers in her father's bedroom, where Tess was not allowed. She'd wait until he was out to sneak in and study it.

She could hardly recognize the well-groomed, smiling man in the photo as her father, who was at least ten years older than her mother. Her mother was so beautiful, with bright blue eyes, soft brown hair, and a radiant smile. She looked like a princess, Tess thought.

If she gazed at the photo long enough, a warm, comforting feeling would settle over her. A sense of being protected and cared for. Of being held close in a gentle embrace, even the recollection of a flowery scent. Tess knew it was impossible for her to have any memories of her mother. Still, she cherished the feelings and the fantasies the photo evoked.

Some nights when she couldn't sleep, she imagined that her mother had survived and was hiding somewhere, watching and waiting, and finally, whisking her away to a place her father could never find them. She knew it was sheer fantasy, but for a few sweet, hazy moments, she allowed herself to imagine that meeting, what her mother would do and say. The joy and relief that would fill her heart, and her mother's, too. How her life would change forever.

In the real world, when Tess asked her aunt questions, Lila would either repeat the few bits her father had revealed or say she didn't know. "Your mother was beautiful and kind and you're just like her," Lila would say. "She loved you with all her heart."

"How could she love me? She didn't even know me." The logic was painful but true.

"She did," Aunt Lila would insist. "Never, ever doubt it." Tess didn't argue. She felt her aunt knew more than she'd ever say.

Books were Tess's first and most loyal friends. As a little girl, Aunt Lila would take Tess into her lap for storytime, instilling a love of reading at an early age. Once she was able to read on her own, Tess discovered that opening a book was like slipping through a secret doorway, and entering a magic world for hours at a stretch. Later in life, Tess knew if she hadn't had books while locked up, she would have lost her mind.

She got on a better track at school and met two girls who were also ignored in the lunchroom. The loyal trio helped each other navigate the rapids of high school.

With the encouragement of her science teacher, Mrs. Conklin, and her aunt, Tess applied to college. Mrs. Conklin assured Tess if she worked hard, she'd have plenty of choices. To her amazement, Tess did. She brought the admission letters to her father, feeling for once he'd be proud.

But he brushed off the idea with a wave of his hand. "Those schools will take any kid if they pay. You're not the type for college. You wouldn't last a week."

Her aunt promised they'd persuade her father and they'd find the money somewhere. Tess was doubtful. She would be eighteen in August, free to do anything she wanted. She had no money or plans but could hardly wait to leave the farm and Haven Island. Though she had no idea how she'd manage it. She'd rarely been off the island and never any further than Boston.

She was an easy mark that summer for a guy like Zach, who showered her with the attention and affection she craved. And offered a way out of her father's house. If she couldn't go to college, she would run away with Zach. Even though she'd often felt uneasy about things Zach did or said, she stuck with him. He was her ticket out, and she couldn't see any other way.

The fencing wire stuck Tess's finger through her glove. No more than a prick, but enough to bring her back. It wasn't good to sift through the ashes of her past, but hard to stop once she started. Especially in this place.

Her phone rang and she answered quickly. It was Betty Nidds, who owned the farm in Vermont.

"Glad I got you, Tess. I didn't want to leave a message."

"Is everything okay, Betty?" Tess thought of Betty's husband, Jim, who had some health issues.

"We're fine, thanks. But we decided to sell and found a buyer faster than expected. No planting this season. We bought a big RV, and we'll visit our grandkids and see what we've missed all these years—giant Redwoods, Yosemite, the Grand Canyon. The whole bucket list. Before we're too old to have fun."

Tess was not surprised. Of course, they wouldn't farm forever.

"Best of luck, Betty. Please tell Jim I said hello and wish you both very happy adventures."

"Good luck to you, too, dear. We've hired a lot of hands, but you were always my favorite. So hard working and responsible. I don't say that to everyone."

Tess was touched. "Thanks. That means a lot to me."

Now what? Tess wondered as she ended the call. It was late to find a spot on another farm. Or employers as nice as the Nidds. She'd had bad experiences as seasonal help, and there was no way to tell what you were getting into.

Don't be an idiot. There's plenty to do right here. On your own farm. It could be yours after a few documents are signed.

She remembered what her aunt had said. There would be people who remembered the accident and objected to her returning, who would snub her, or worse. But most have forgotten or are too immersed in their own lives to care.

Some of those angry voices were in her own head, Tess had come to see. She'd carry them wherever she ended up. On Haven Island, Vermont, or anywhere.

Tess was in the barn, working on the tractor, when her aunt's truck pulled up. Honey barked a greeting and ran out, and Tess followed.

"Looks like you've had a productive morning," Lila said, hopping down from the cab. A polite way of noticing Tess was dirty from head to toe, with mud stains on her jeans and grime from the tractor engine on her hands and t-shirt.

"You could say that. I got some news. No job in Vermont this summer. The farm owners decided to sell their land and go cross-country in a camper."

"Oh...that is news." She felt Lila trying to gauge her reaction. "You must be disappointed."

"For a minute or two. Until I realized I'd be an idiot to look for another job as a farmhand when I can work right here."

"Does that mean you'll let me put the deed in your name?" Her aunt's tone was cautious.

"I'm sorry, Aunt Lila. I can't think that far ahead. Let's see how it goes. We'll know soon if this will work."

"Fair enough." Lila looked pleased. "I prayed you'd stay and try. Otherwise, you'd punish yourself more for something you didn't do."

Her aunt's words rang true. She'd almost done just that.

"I don't mind saying God answered at least one of my prayers quickly," Lila added. "I'm sure He'll sort the rest."

Tess smiled but didn't reply. She knew what Lila meant.

"How about lunch? You must be starved. I'll bring some sandwiches out here."

Tess was grateful for the offer. She washed up with the hose at the side of the house, then sat on the top of the porch steps with Honey beside her. There was so much to do. She wasn't sure where to start. She had to make a list. A few lists, she decided.

She took a deep breath, overwhelmed by all she'd taken on. Once the bout of nerves passed, she felt a sense of purpose and direction, one she'd rarely known. This was her place, to manage any way she liked. The realization filled her with giddy happiness.

The grit under her nails and mud stains on her jeans proved it was no fantasy. Though it certainly was a turn she never imagined when she arrived two short days ago.

"'God works in mysterious ways,'" her aunt would say. Tess had to agree that today at least, the proverb rang true.

Ten

Carrie had no trouble finding her mother's room in the island's compact medical center. She silently gave thanks that her mother had been moved out of intensive care, and that her condition had never been dire enough to require an airlift to a hospital on the mainland.

Still, her mother looked awful. Propped on pillows, her wavy brown hair framed her pale face. She looked weak, barely able to sit up. An IV tube trailed from one arm, and wires connected to monitors were strung in all directions.

Her sisters, along with Sophie, circled the bed and greeted Carrie in a chorus.

"Sorry it took me so long. It was hard to leave."

"Was there a problem?" Her mother sounded alarmed.

"Everything's fine. We had a lot of customers this morning. That's a good thing, right?"

"I don't know why the doctor is keeping me. I'm perfectly

fine. He'd better let me go home today. I need to get back to work."

"Sorry to break it to you, lady. I doubt you're going anywhere." Rebecca's tone was firm but kind. "Relax and get used to the idea."

"For goodness sake, I felt a little lightheaded. It was very muggy last night, and there was such a big crowd," her mother continued. "I was probably just dehydrated."

"Yes, you were," Brooke agreed. "But more importantly, Dr. Croft said something is going on with your heart. He's waiting for the test results before he can say for sure."

"He also said you need more tests at a larger hospital. We'll go to Mass General." Rebecca named a prestigious medical center in Boston. "I found an excellent cardiologist."

"Mass General? Cardiologists? Don't be silly. I'm not fussing with all that." Gena waved the hand that wasn't attached to the tubes. "I can't waste time in Boston for a lot of useless medical tests."

Carrie had staked out a corner of the bed and sat quietly. She'd been at the café all morning and knew little of her mother's diagnosis.

Rebecca's agenda was alarming, and so was her mother's blatant denial of the situation.

Sophie tugged her sleeve. "Can I get something to eat, Mom? There's a cafeteria downstairs."

"Sure, honey. Get whatever you like." Carrie fished in her handbag and gave Sophie a few bills.

Sophie had been terrified last night to see her grandmother so ill. She'd been on her best behavior ever since, which made the situation easier. Carrie made a note to praise her.

"See you later, Grandma." Sophie kissed her grandmother's cheek. "Want anything from downstairs? Cookies or chips?"

The offer seemed absurd, all things considered, but was very sweet. Her mother smiled. "No thanks, honey. Maybe later."

Once Sophie was gone, Carrie said, "You know I love you, Mom. But last night, you scared us to death. It was more than a dizzy spell. I bet you haven't felt well for a long time."

"I've been tired, that's all. A little short of breath here and there, and my heart beats fast sometimes. It's part of the territory at my age. Once these doctors get their teeth in the bit, they run away with themselves," she declared.

"I'm sure by that you mean we investigate all possible causes of a patient's condition, Mrs. Duffy. Which is our job," a deep voice answered from the doorway. Everyone turned as Dr. Benjamin Croft entered the room.

Ben Croft was not a stranger. He'd grown up on the island and gone to the same high school as Carrie and her sisters, his age falling somewhere between Carrie's and Brooke's.

Ben's brother, Andy, had been a year ahead of Carrie, student body president and the school's star quarterback. He'd gone to Penn State on a football scholarship and was drafted by the New England Patriots soon after his senior year. Carrie had been living in Boston, but the news of his triumph reached her even there, and not long after, news that the hometown hero's life had been cut short in a car accident. A loss mourned by the whole community.

It surprised her to see Ben back on Haven. There were so many sad memories for him here. But the Crofts were a large and close-knit family, an influential family who had played an important role for generations in the island's history. They'd donated the funds for the hospital's new Emergency and Trauma Center. She'd learned last night that Ben Croft had specialized in that area of medicine and had returned to be on the staff.

Her mother had been treated with first-class equipment and technology that may have saved her life. Dr. Croft had given her expert care and sincere concern. If he could only give her a common-sense pill, they'd all be a lot happier.

Gena looked embarrassed to realize the doctor had overheard her snide remark. Color rose in her cheeks, which Carrie thought was a good thing.

"I'm sorry, Doctor. I didn't mean *you*. It's my daughters. I know they're concerned, but they get carried away. Please tell them there's nothing to worry about."

Dr. Croft stood at the foot of the bed, a folder in hand. He was tall, with wide shoulders, and his white coat hung off a lanky build. His thick brown hair was combed to one side but slipped down over his eyes. He impatiently pushed it back with his hand, the expression on his wide mouth serious and thoughtful.

"Your condition is stable, Mrs. Duffy, and so far, the tests show no damage to your heart—"

"See? I told you, girls. You're all worked up for nothing," her mother cut in.

"—But you're not out of the woods. We see signs of atrial fibrillation."

Carrie and her sisters sat up, on high alert. Her mother frowned. "Is that serious?"

"It can be. Most people call it A-fib. Feeling tired and light-headed and the shortness of breath you report are common symptoms. The most obvious are chest pain and the irregular, rapid heartbeat you experience." He glanced at the paperwork in the folder. "This wasn't the first episode. Is that true?"

"Well, yes. But it always goes away quickly. I never fainted before," she added, still downplaying her situation.

"What causes the condition?" Rebecca asked in her cut-to-the-chase way. "What's wrong with my mother's heart?"

"Basically, the signal that tells the heart to beat gets confused. Let's say this is your heart," he sketched out a circle on the back of the folder. "There are four chambers, two upper and two lower," he added, making four even sections. "During a normal heartbeat, the signal for the muscle to contract starts in the upper chambers and travels to the lower through a pathway of nerves. But during A-fib, the signals are chaotic. The upper chambers quiver, and the lower chamber is overloaded, which causes a rapid and irregular heartbeat."

"That doesn't sound good." Carrie knew she shouldn't have voiced the first thought that popped into her head but wasn't able to stop herself.

"It's not what we want to see," Dr. Croft agreed. "But it's a common and treatable condition. When it's ignored," he paused and met Gena's gaze, "it can lead to serious problems—blood clots, a stroke, and other complications." His gaze swept over the group. "I know this is a lot to take in. In most cases, A-fib can be controlled with drugs, or a reset that gets the heartbeat on the right rhythm."

A "reset"? He made it sound like there was a button in her mother's heart he could push to restore the factory setting, the way Carrie fixed the WiFi network in her apartment.

"Our cardiac specialist, Dr. Singh, will stop by tomorrow and explain in more detail."

"Tomorrow? I can't go home today?" Her mother was upset.

"I'm sorry, Mrs. Croft, but it's best if we watch you for a little longer. You've had a serious episode." He smiled. "But I admire your spirit. It bodes well for a quick recovery."

Her mother looked deflated, finally accepting his orders. "Thanks, Doctor. Please call me Gena."

Rebecca turned to Dr. Croft. "I've already contacted Dr. Fischer at Mass General. She's a world-class cardiologist. I have some pull and can get an appointment with her next week."

"Then you're set. Dr. Singh will send your mother's records to her office." He turned back to his patient. "For now, Gena, you need to rest. Stress is a risk factor."

Carrie's mother suddenly looked contrite. "I'll try. But this is the busy season for people like me. I don't know how I can let it all go. Even for a few days."

Before he could answer, Carrie said, "How long do you think my mother has been walking around with this condition without realizing it?"

Without admitting it to herself or anyone else, she wanted to say.

"It's impossible to guess. Sounds like your mother had symptoms a person her age could easily ignore. Don't be too hard on her. I think she's learned her lesson."

"The jury is still out on that question," Rebecca said. "Please be clear about any restrictions, Doctor."

"Like, she shouldn't jump out of bed and run back to the café? Even when you send her home," Carrie added.

Dr. Croft's gentle smile disappeared, his expression suddenly severe. "Not for a few weeks, at least. When her specialists give their approval. Possibly not for the rest of the summer."

Now it was her mother's turn to look shocked. Carrie thought she'd protest, but she held her tongue though tears welled up in her eyes.

The sight was distressing. Carrie took her hand. "It's going to be all right, Mom. We'll figure everything out."

"It's a good thing we were all here when this problem caught up with you, Mom. Sounds like it could have been a lot worse," Brooke said.

"She was lucky this time," Rebecca added.

Jack made the same observation last night. This morning at the café, Carrie had thanked him again for his help; for some reason, feeling shy and awkward. He seemed uncomfortable too, brushing off her gratitude and quickly returning to work. They barely knew each other, but had shared an intensely emotional moment. Now it was hard to remember he really was a stranger.

"Your only job now is to rest and let us find out what's going on with your heart, Gena."

Her mother nodded, suddenly solemn. "Thank you for spending so much time with us, Doctor. You must have a lot of patients to visit today besides me."

"And you're all important." He smiled and squeezed her hand. "See you soon."

Carrie's mother leaned back and closed her eyes. The diagnosis had been a blow, and Carrie guessed she was exhausted from putting up a positive front.

Brooke smoothed the covers. "Do you need another pillow, Mom? Or a drink of water?"

Gena shook her head without opening her eyes. "I'm just tired, girls. I think I'll sleep awhile."

"We'll go downstairs and give you a break." Carrie checked the time. It was eleven, usually a lull at the cafe. She wanted to return before lunch was in full swing.

"We'll be back. You're not rid of us yet," Rebecca added, following Carrie to the door.

They all knew it was time for a sisters' meeting, beyond their mother's earshot.

Eleven

"What do you mean you lost your job? When did that happen?" Rebecca stared Carrie down as if she were in the witness chair.

They sat in the hospital's small cafeteria, sipping iced coffee. Sophie was outside, getting some fresh air. She sat on a bench wearing headphones, and Carrie was thankful today for the cell phone's amusements.

"You make it sound like I was fired. I was downsized. There's a difference."

"It's completely different," Brooke said. "And so unfair. Why didn't you let us know?"

"I meant to tell you, but there was never a good time." Her voice trailed off. She wondered if she really would have told her sisters. It wasn't her fault. Still, she was ashamed.

"So managing the café awhile is convenient for you," Rebecca reasoned aloud. "You'll get paid, of course."

"Absolutely," Brooke agreed.

Carrie could not find fault with the plan, and she did want to help her mother. But something inside her balked. Coming home to run the café felt like a defeat, as if she were waving a white flag to the whole world. Or at least to everyone on the island who recalled her brash, self-assured talk when she was young and didn't know better. When she had no idea how hard it was to make ends meet and raise a child on her own while trying to finish a college degree in her spare time, which could be measured with a teaspoon. Ending up back here was proof that she'd clearly failed to build a successful, stable life in the city.

Skulking home, tail between her legs, and working in the family business. *That's what losers do*, a cruel voice taunted.

Rebecca and Brooke were staring at her, their expressions questioning. "It's a good solution for everyone," Rebecca repeated. "Isn't it?"

"For Mom especially," Carrie agreed. "For me, it's a pit stop while I find a new job. And a real manager for the café. Mom needed help even before she got sick."

Rebecca looked relieved. "All true. You know the business best. We trust you to hire someone qualified and trustworthy."

"What about your apartment? Maybe you can sublet a few weeks, since you're so close to the college," Brooke suggested.

Carrie didn't answer. Her apartment posed another pressing problem she was reluctant to admit.

Her lease was up in two weeks, and her landlord had raised the rent. She'd been looking for a cheaper place even before she lost her job. But she didn't want her sisters to know her life was a complete mess.

For one thing, it made her look irresponsible, especially with Sophie in her care. Carrie knew she was a good mother and did it all with little support of any kind from her ex-husband. She'd hit a rough patch, and asking for help had always been hard for her.

"The apartment won't be a problem," she said, without going into details. "I'll go back this week and get our things."

It suddenly hit her. "The problem will be Sophie. She'll have to miss all of the end-of-the-year events at school."

Brooke's expression was sympathetic. "The social scene is important for kids her age. That will be tough."

"Tough for me, too. She's going to hate me for this." Carrie sighed. "I'll talk to her teachers and get assignments for the next few weeks. She needs to keep up with her schoolwork." Carrie wondered how she was going to manage the café and homeschool her daughter simultaneously.

She imagined Sophie at the counter with her laptop and schoolbooks as coffee pots and plates of eggs flew by, and Finn Mulligan told his fish stories.

It didn't fit well together.

"Kids don't learn much at the end of the term. You already said, it's all parties and events," Rebecca replied. "All she needs is a tutor. It will be fine. Find someone, and I'll pay," she offered. "And please don't argue. I'll cover any moving expenses you have, too. I can't be here to help Mom much or help in the café. It's the least I can do."

Carrie didn't refuse the generous offer, as she normally would have. Tutors were expensive, and Rebecca was honest to admit she wasn't available for a "boots on the ground" contribution to their plan. Of the three, Rebecca had least enjoyed wearing the blue apron. She wasn't about to start.

"It's settled. More or less. We appreciate this, Carrie," Rebecca said.

"We really do," Brooke echoed.

"Let's tell Mom. She'll be relieved."

"After she stops insisting it's not necessary," Rebecca added. "Don't forget, Carrie. Put a bright spin on it. As if you've been aching to come out here and work at the Blue Sky. Otherwise, she'll feel too guilty to accept the help."

Carrie knew that was true. It did solve the problem of finding a job and a paycheck, at least temporarily. She'd live rent-free at home for a few weeks and save to sign the next lease. She had to concentrate on the plus side and stop feeling sorry for herself. Most of all, she'd lift a huge burden off her mother's shoulders. That was the most important thing.

As they left the table, Carrie said, "You go ahead. I need to talk to Sophie."

"She's bound to be disappointed, but she'll come around," Brooke said.

That was how Carrie hoped it would go, while bracing herself for other possibilities.

Carrie stepped outside into a blast of warm air and sunlight. It was a beautiful day, with a clear sky and a light breeze, typical of the island. A few weeks of this weather wouldn't be bad, as opposed to summer in the city.

She met Sophie at the bench, and her daughter pulled out her earphones. "Time to see Grandma again?"

"Your aunts just went up." Carrie paused. "But I need to speak to you. Hear me out, and then you can ask questions, okay?"

Sophie looked alarmed. "Uh-oh. What did the doctor say? Is Grandma going to die?"

Carrie gave her daughter a hug. "Not for a long time, God willing. The doctor said she has something wrong with her heart that's causing it to beat too fast. But the condition is common and can be treated easily."

Sophie leaned back, and Carrie stroked her cheek. "I got worried for a minute."

"We're all worried about her, sweetie. And we need to do whatever we can to help her get well, right?"

Sophie nodded. "Of course."

"When Grandma gets out of here, Aunt Rebecca will take her to Boston for more tests. After that, she needs to rest. She won't be able to work and needs someone to watch over the café until she's healthy."

"I understand," Sophie said calmly.

Carrie took a breath, bracing herself to deliver the punch line. "Your aunts and I decided the best way to help Grandma, so that she doesn't feel stressed and make herself sick again, is for me to run the café. Just until I find a real manager to take over. That means that you and I need to stay a few weeks."

At first, it looked as if Sophie didn't understand. Then something clicked. Her eyes widened.

"Live here, you mean . . . forever?"

"A few weeks, a month at the most. Just until I find a good manager and the person settles in. Grandma can't do that anymore. It's too much for her."

"Why can't Aunt Brooke run the café? She lives here for the summer anyway."

"Aunt Brooke would if she could. But she doesn't know how to run the business. Neither does Aunt Rebecca. They're helping in other ways. This is the best way I can help."

Sophie's expression turned sullen. "Okay, but why do I have to stay? I'll miss a lot of school. Aren't you worried about that?"

"I'll get your assignments from Ms. Chang and find a tutor to work on them with you."

"A tutor? Ugh..." Sophie rolled her eyes. Then her expression crinkled, and Carrie knew she was going to cry. "This is horrible, Mom. A complete disaster. I'm going to miss *everything*—sports day and the class picnic..."

"I can get you back to Boston here and there. I'll do my best to make it work, honey." Carrie wasn't sure how she'd do that but hated to see Sophie cry. The news had blindsided her, and Carrie didn't blame her for being upset.

"How about when school is over? My friends will be hanging out and having fun. I'll be all alone. What will I do all day?"

Carrie hadn't figured that out yet. She was still wondering how to get the apartment packed up and most of it put in storage in record time this week. Though it was just as well that Sophie wasn't hanging out with friends once school ended. Medford wasn't an awful neighborhood, but kids Sophie's age got into trouble quickly. Haven was a much safer environment.

"There are tons of kids your age here in the summer. We'll find a camp or activity, and you'll make some new friends."

"I don't want new friends. I want my *real* friends." Sophie was angry now. "I'm not going to a dumb day camp, either. That is so-o-o not happening."

Carrie clung to her patience. "We don't need to figure it out right now. Please remember we're doing this for Grandma. I know you want her to get better. This is how you can help."

Sophie stared at the ground; it was hard to catch her eye. Carrie bent closer.

"I know this is a lot to spring on you, sweetie. We can talk about it more tonight. We need to check on Grandma now."

Sophie nodded and brushed some hair off her face.

"And try not to look so glum if she asks what you think about staying, okay?"

"I get it. But you owe me, Mom. Big time."

Carrie had to smile, though she hardly approved of being blackmailed. "What do you mean by that, young lady? You should be agreeable about this out of the goodness of your heart."

"I know...I am. Sort of. But this deal is worth at least a new phone. Or a dog?" Sophie asked hopefully.

She'd been asking to adopt a dog for ages. Even though Carrie loved dogs, she had to refuse. For one thing, Carrie knew the mom ended up with all the extra work, no matter what the kids promised. A pet in the mix would also make finding a new apartment harder. But maybe Sophie was old enough to take on the responsibility, and she'd learn a lot.

"We'll see," Carrie offered her standard reply.

Sophie scoffed, but at least she smiled. "I hate when you say that."

"I know it's annoying. But I have to say it a lot. It's part of my job," she teased.

At the elevator, Sophie pushed the button. Carrie felt a flutter in her stomach, just nerves. The last twenty-four hours had swept through like a tornado and sent her life spinning in a completely unexpected direction.

A temporary direction, she reminded herself. Just like Sophie, she had to remember, she was doing this for her mother.

Carrie had intended to get back to the café sooner, but by the time she returned, lunch service was almost over. The dining room was quiet, and only a few customers lingered.

Dory was behind the counter, filling glasses from the fountain machine. "How's your mom doing?"

"The doctor said she's stable but needs to stay in the hospital a day or two more."

"Do they know why she fainted?" She set the glasses on a tray and added a handful of straws.

"It's a heart problem. She needs more tests. When you're done, come to the kitchen. I'll fill everyone in."

"Good idea." Dory grabbed the tray and headed to her table.

A few minutes later, the staff assembled in the kitchen, the waitresses, busboys, kitchen helpers, and Jack. She explained her mother's condition, going light on medical jargon.

"The bottom line is, even when my mom recovers, she can't continue to manage the café. I'll be here to run things until we find someone to fill that job."

Most of the staff looked pleased, which was a relief. A few looked surprised, which was to be expected. Sheila, a waitress who'd started a few weeks ago, looked annoyed.

Sensing I'll be a tougher boss than my mother, Carrie guessed. *You're right*, Carrie felt like telling her.

She met Jack's dark gaze. His expression was unreadable. Maybe he didn't like the idea of having her as a boss, either. Carrie wasn't looking forward to managing him, so that playing field was even.

"I noticed schedules posted for the next two weeks. We'll stick with those for now. I have to go to Medford for at least two days, so someone needs to cover for me here. She turned to Dory. "I thought you could supervise while I'm away."

Dory looked surprised at the request. Then shook her head. "I'd love to help, Carrie. I would. But I'm no good at telling people what to do. Honestly. Sorry."

Her mother had suggested the older waitress, who sometimes closed out when she needed to leave early. Carrie just assumed Dory would agree. She realized now she should have asked privately. Five minutes into her new role, and she looked like she didn't know what she was doing.

"I'll do it." Jack's deep voice broke the silence. He was very sure of himself in the kitchen, but how could he handle the dining room, too? He didn't have four arms and extra eyes behind his head.

"No offense, Jack. But you have enough going on back here, especially when it's busy."

"I can manage the kitchen and chew gum at the same time." The comment made the others snicker. "If I liked to chew gum, that is, which I don't."

"He'll be fine," Dory said. "He kept us in line today while you were at the hospital."

"The place will still be here when you get back, don't worry," Jack promised. "You can give me the details later."

"All right, I will." Carrie kept her tone businesslike. "Thanks, everyone. I'll let my mom know you send good wishes."

Carrie headed to the dining room without looking back. Jack had solved her problem, though she felt as if he'd hijacked her authority. The staff seemed satisfied; that was a good sign. He was clearly the Alpha Dog back here. If it had been anyone else, she would have been grateful. But something about Jack stepping up, and the way he'd done it, irked her.

She had to remind Rebecca to do the background check when she returned to her office. With all the excitement about their mother, it was easy to forget. Despite the way he'd swooped in to help her with her mother last night, there was still something about him she didn't trust. She got the feeling he was hiding something. Her intuition insisted Jack Dubensky wasn't what he seemed.

Twelve

It was hard to find a parking space on Front Street. The village was crowded. Tess had forgotten what the tourist season was like, or maybe there hadn't been this many summer visitors while she was growing up. It was just an ordinary Wednesday in the middle of June. What would it be like in July?

She'd barely come to town since she'd arrived. Quick stops at the post office or the hardware store. She'd stuck to the farm, working from sunrise to sunset. With the help of Owen Jessup and a few of his hands, the fields were ready to be planted. A major victory, considering how late she'd started. She was lucky that the time to sow on Haven was just about now, the third week in June.

Owen had been pleased with her decision. He hated to see the land sit fallow. He dropped by almost every day to offer help and advice, from starting the old tractor to tips on the hardiest and most valuable crops.

Her father had stuck to potatoes and cabbage, rotating the

fields. That's all she recalled, apart from a vegetable patch that mainly supplied their own table.

Tess had read books and periodicals and explored the question online. If she stayed, maybe she'd turn the land into a lavender farm. She could easily imagine a sweeping violet ocean as far as the eye could see. Or plant crops that would turn a good profit, like garlic. Or microgreens.

Maybe she wouldn't plant at all; so much depended on the weather and battling insects. She'd read a lot about goat farming and making cheese and other products from their milk. She hoped to experiment on a small scale in the next few weeks.

She'd still plant a vegetable patch and bring any extra yield to Evaline Finch to sell at her stand and at the farmer's market on the village green. Tess imagined that if people knew where the vegetables were from, they wouldn't buy them. And if she applied for her own booth at the market, she might be denied.

So far, this was just her feeling — her fear, to be more precise. She had no evidence that people knew she was back. Maybe what her aunt said was true: time had passed, and no one would bother her.

But she didn't want to put herself in situations that would test the theory.

She'd made a visit to the agricultural store on Mariner's Point that morning to pick up bales of hay and seedlings for the patch—tomato, zucchini, peppers, and lettuce—along with herbs. And fencing to keep the deer and other critters from staking out the garden as their private salad bar.

She'd left Aunt Lila in town a few hours ago for her book club meeting at the library and lunch with Evaline. She'd tried calling, so Lila could come out and meet her, but only reached voice mail.

Her aunt either couldn't hear the phone in the noisy café or had forgotten to charge it again.

Tess finally parked in the lot near the ferry station, behind the town's main street. She spotted the deck of the café that overlooked the harbor, the white tables covered by a blue awning. She walked up the hill to the entrance on Front Street.

The café was crowded. Lila and Evaline sat at a booth near the door. Her aunt waved her over, and Tess could see they hadn't started their lunch yet.

"I didn't expect you so soon, Tess. We're still waiting for our order."

"Take your time. I'll do some errands and come back." Tess didn't have any errands to do, but she didn't want to spoil her aunt's visit with Evaline. Evaline had grown up in Cape Light, a coastal village not far from Gloucester and Marblehead. Her marriage to Harold Finch, a science teacher and inventor, had brought her to Haven Island in her early twenties. Lila and Harold taught at the same school, and Lila was Evaline's first friend on the island. She had also turned out to be her closest.

"Don't run off, dear. Sit with us," Evaline coaxed her. "I want to hear what you've been up to."

"When the waitress comes back, you can order a bite or at least get a cold drink," Lila added.

"All right, something fast." Tess sat down beside her aunt. Waiting in the truck would be hot and sticky, and eating lunch now would save time at home.

"I haven't been up to much, Evaline. Just getting the fields ready. I picked up plants for a vegetable patch at the agro store."

"She's been going nonstop since she got here. I never saw such a hard worker, neither has Owen. He told me the other day," Lila interrupted.

Tess blushed. "All farmers work hard, Aunt Lila."

"That's true, I guess...except for the lazy ones," her aunt replied, making Tess and Evaline laugh.

A waitress approached carrying a tray. "Here you go, ladies. Sorry for the delay." She set a plate with a crab cake sandwich in front of Lila and served Evaline a salad.

"Can you bring a menu, please?" Lila asked. "My niece would like to order something, too."

"I don't need a menu," Tess said. "Just a grilled cheese, please, and some water?"

The waitress stared at her. Tess thought she was annoyed to have to put in another order. Then Tess watched her lift a glass of ice water from the tray—and calmly, deliberately pour it into Tess's lap.

"Here you go. How's that for service?"

Tess jumped up. A puddle washed out of her lap, and cold water soaked into her shirt and jeans. She thought it was an accident at first, then met the waitress's gaze and knew it had been anything but.

Words swirled in Tess's head, but she was dumbstruck, intimidated by the triumphant light in the woman's eyes.

"What in the world! What did you do that for?" Her aunt tried to dab at the spill with a wad of napkins.

The waitress didn't seem the least bit sorry or ashamed. "She killed an innocent boy, with his whole life ahead of him. You think anyone could forget?"

"How dare you speak to her like that? She has a perfect right to be in here, like anyone else," Evaline said.

"She's done nothing wrong. She's never hurt a soul," Lila insisted.

"Never hurt a soul? Are you crazy?" The waitress flicked her scornful glance to Tess.

Tess was still too upset and shocked to answer. But under that, not surprised. She ignored the waitress and tried to catch her aunt's eye.

"I'll bring the truck around and park out front."

Without waiting for Lila's reply, she grabbed her sunglasses and ran out. She paused on the sidewalk and took a deep breath, then quickly headed for the truck.

Carrie was on the deck, helping to clear tables when she heard shouts in the dining room. As she ran in, she saw a slim woman in jeans run out, the front of her clothes dripping wet. Sheila was arguing with two older women. Carrie quickly recognized Evaline Finch and Lila Norton.

"Is there a problem here?"

"This woman slandered my niece. And poured ice water all over her," Lila insisted.

"She was covered, poor thing. She ran outside. Mortified." Carrie knew Evaline Finch well and Lila Norton, who had taught at the elementary school.

"Her beloved niece is a monster. She killed my neighbor's son, Andy Croft."

Carrie knew only the basic details of the story. Sheila's outburst confused her. "Killed him? What are you talking about?"

"You don't remember?" Sheila asked her boss. "Drunk

driving. She slammed right into the car. He didn't have a chance, poor kid."

"You don't know the first thing about it. She wasn't even behind the wheel," Lila Norton argued. "You should be ashamed, treating an innocent person like that."

Mrs. Norton was red-faced with emotion but stood her ground. Carrie felt bad for her.

Sheila laughed. "Whoever let her out of jail should be ashamed. Tell your *innocent* niece to catch the next ferry if she knows what's good for her. Isn't that right?"

She gazed around the café, looking for validation.

Carrie cringed when she saw some people nod. Some looked away, embarrassed at the scene. Some even got up from their seats and left their meal, annoyed and disturbed.

Carrie didn't care if the customers took sides. Even if what Sheila claimed was true, her actions and words were totally disrespectful and unacceptable.

"You're done, Sheila."

"Someone had to say it. A lot of people recognized her but didn't have the guts."

"Or the decency?" Carrie paused. "I mean, you're done working here. Punch out. I'll call when your check is ready."

Sheila looked shocked, then angry. "Taking her side? Wait till that gets around. Let's see how many customers you have left. . .I mean the *real* people. For someone who grew up here, you act like a tourist, Carrie Duffy."

Carrie brushed off the insult, though it secretly stung. She turned to face the pale and shaken women, who were busily gathering their handbags and shopping totes.

"That behavior was inexcusable. I sincerely apologize to both of you, and your niece, Mrs. Norton," Carrie said. "Please come back any time as my guest," she added, though the offer sounded weak, even to her own ears.

Lila nodded. "I know it wasn't your fault."

People whispered as they passed. Lila didn't seem to notice. She held her chin high and stared straight ahead as she walked out.

Joey, one of the busboys, was already cleaning up, about to mop the floor. "Hey, Carrie, someone left a phone."

He reached down to the seat and handed Carrie a black cell phone. Carrie turned it on, looking for a hint of the owner. The screensaver was a photo of a big herding dog, white with brown markings. In the background, she saw a barn and the sign High Meadow Farm. It belonged to either Lila Norton or her niece, she surmised.

"Thanks, Joey. I think I know who left it."

She slipped the phone into her apron pocket. The scene had shaken her, and she stepped into the kitchen to take a break.

Jack was cleaning the grill but turned to glance her way. "Pretty hot out there. Did you come into the kitchen to cool off?"

"Funny...and true." She picked up a clipboard and pretended to leaf through bills from the deliveries. "Is Sheila gone?" she asked quietly.

"She disappeared in a puff of smoke. Or should I say obscenities? I had to turn the exhaust fan on 'high.'"

She smiled again. "I'm not surprised."

"You did a good job. Those scenes aren't easy."

What did he know about quelling a scene in a dining room? The question reminded her that she knew very little about him. About his past, who he was, and where he'd come from.

By all accounts, he'd handled the café—dining area and

kitchen—smoothly while she'd been gone. That was over two weeks ago. With all the attention on her mother, neither she nor her sister Rebecca had remembered to follow through on his background check.

She set the clipboard on the stainless table where she'd found it. "Thanks," she said finally.

"I mean it. You kept your cool. But you still called out Sheila for her bad behavior. What was the dustup about?"

"A car accident on the island. It happened a long time ago. A boy in the car that was hit died. The woman who ran out was in the other car. I think she went to jail, but I really don't know the details." Carrie paused. "Aside from acting totally unprofessional, Sheila was very cruel. I never fired anyone before," she confessed. "Is that grounds?"

"If her lawyer calls, let him know I caught her swiping Dory's orders a few times."

Carrie was not surprised. Sheila was late to start, the first to leave, and never pitched in with prep tasks, like refilling ketchup bottles.

"I'm well rid of her. But now we're down a waitress."

Jack returned to scouring the grill. He'd removed his cooking jacket and wore a gray t-shirt underneath. The muscles in his shoulders and arms bunched as he pushed the scouring brush across the metal surface in a straight path.

She felt herself staring and turned her gaze away.

"You'll figure it out."

His vote of confidence made her feel good, but she was glad he couldn't see her smile.

"I'll start with a 'Help Wanted' sign in the window. There's one in the office, somewhere. Catch you later," she said, in a "Nice to chat, but I'm still the boss" tone.

She headed to the tiny office that doubled as a storage closet, her spirits lifted. Because she'd been able to vent about firing Sheila, she told herself. But she knew it was more. She was attracted to Jack. Plain and simple. That didn't often happen, and she wondered why it had to happen with this guy.

She suspected he felt it, too. Though he was difficult to read. Either way, it wouldn't do her any good to get mixed up with Jack Dubensky. Now or ever.

She'd only be here a few more weeks. It shouldn't be hard to keep this simmering pot on the back burner—with a tight lid on top.

Tess and her aunt drove back to the farm in silence. Tess couldn't wait to take off her wet clothes but didn't want to squirm and attract her aunt's attention. Lila looked so upset when she got in the truck, Tess worried about her aunt's blood pressure.

They rode with the windows open and the light breeze ruffled wisps of her aunt's gray hair. Her phone rang, and she checked who was calling. "It's Richard. I'll call him back."

Tess kept her eyes on the road. Her aunt had to be awfully upset not to talk to her son. When she did call back, Tess had no doubt she'd report the scene at the café. Richard would voice concern, but she knew he viewed his cousin as damaged goods and didn't believe she'd been treated unfairly, as his mother did. But there was no way she could ask her aunt to keep the incident from her son, and it wouldn't be the first time she'd felt embarrassed in front of Richard.

"I'm sorry you had to go through that. Some people are so nasty. I don't understand it."

Tess shrugged. "I told you they'd remember."

Tess had met many belligerent people looking for a fight while living in detention centers. Getting doused with ice water was nothing compared to the skirmishes she'd found herself dragged into. But this was different. It was the public shame that cut her to the core.

"And I told you it would take a while to convince them you intend to stay," her aunt replied. "Even a horrible waitress."

One down, twenty to go. Possibly more, Tess silently noted.

"At least that woman lost her job because of what she did," Lila remarked.

Tess knew her aunt was trying to make her feel better. But Tess didn't like the idea of anyone losing a job because of her, not even the malicious, ill-informed waitress, who might be a single mother supporting a family.

If only she could disappear whenever she pleased, like Harry Potter, wrapping himself in his invisibility cloak. That would solve her problems. Short of that, from now on she'd be very careful about leaving the farm.

As soon as they reached the farm, Tess checked the back of the truck filled with flats. The delicate plants had done well on the ride. No stems were broken.

Tess was eager to start planting but had to fix the fence first.

She decided to move the flats into the barn where they'd be out of the hot sun and protected from nighttime nibblers.

Honey ran out from behind the house, her tail wagging like a flag. She put her paws on Tess's chest and licked her face.

"Oh dear, don't let her jump up like that, Tess. She's liable to knock you down."

Tess usually discouraged such enthusiastic greetings, but the affection was welcome today.

Her aunt had just hopped down from the cab when her phone rang again. She fished through her purse to find it, an old-fashioned flip model that Tess found amusing, though it suited Lila well.

"Hello? Yes, this is she," Lila answered. "Oh, hello Carrie. She did? Here, I'll put her on …"

Lila held out the phone. Before Tess could figure out why, she heard Carrie Duffy's voice. "Hi, Tess, we found a cell phone at the table where you were sitting. I called Evaline Finch and figured it out."

Tess patted her back pocket. In all the excitement she hadn't realized the phone was missing. "Thanks so much. I can pick it up later. What time do you close?" She fought back a stab of irritation at having to ride back to the village. She had already lost most of the day.

"I'm usually here until five. But I'm coming that way tomorrow morning and can drop it off if you like."

"If it's not any trouble," Tess said.

"No trouble at all. It's the least I can do."

After the scene with the out-of-control waitress, Tess knew she meant. "That would be great."

"I'll see you tomorrow then," Carrie replied.

Tess ended the call and turned back to her aunt. "She's going to drop the phone off tomorrow morning."

"As I always say, 'All's well that ends well.'" Lila smiled, offering a favorite motto.

Tess smiled but didn't reply. Driving to the farm to return the phone was a nice gesture. But maybe Carrie didn't want to risk another scene by having Tess return to the café.

The possibility brought a fresh wave of doubts about staying on the island.

Thirteen

When Carrie got home, she found her mother and daughter standing side by side at the kitchen counter, surrounded by spices, bowls, and cooking utensils.

"Mom, you're not supposed to be cooking," Carrie said.

Gena turned briefly. "Sophie is showing me how she makes guacamole. That's not really cooking."

The way Sophie made it was as complicated as building the Taj Mahal, but Carrie didn't dare comment. Her daughter had recently taken an interest in the culinary arts. So far, her trademark dishes were brownies, smoothies, and the guac.

"I told Grandma to sit down, but she wouldn't listen," Sophie explained.

"I've been sitting all day. It's bad for my circulation. The doctor said I can 'resume normal activities.' Acting like a couch potato is not my style."

"I know, Mom. But your Energizer Bunny days are over. We don't want you back in the hospital, right?"

"I know." Gena sat at the table and sipped her water bottle, lifting it in a silent toast. "Staying hydrated. See?"

"Very good. It keeps your—"

"—blood pressure down," her mother finished. She rolled her eyes. "My new mantra."

Carrie smiled. No one would guess her mother had made it through a serious health episode a little over three weeks ago. When Rebecca took her to Massachusetts General Hospital for follow-up tests, a specialist discovered a blocked artery that had contributed to, or even caused, the erratic heartbeat. Gena had an angioplasty that day—a cardiac procedure that opened the artery with a tiny balloon—and she left the hospital twenty-four hours later.

But she was still limited by what she could do and where she could go. Her doctors agreed she shouldn't return to the café for at least four more weeks and had to cut back her hours and duties drastically. If it were up to her daughters, she wouldn't return at all and only stop in now and again to oversee a new manager.

Carrie thought the weeks her mother had spent at home recovering had provided a long overdue rest. There had never been time for her to recover after Carrie's father died almost two years ago. But now, the shadows under her mother's lovely blue eyes had begun to fade, along with lines on her face, caused by constant stress and pressure.

Sophie set the bowl of guacamole on the table along with a basket of chips. "Voila!" she said.

"Wow, this looks yummy." Carrie took a chip and scooped up a bite. It really was good. She wasn't just saying that.

Her mother took a chip and tasted the dip, too. "How was your day?" she asked, deflecting attention from herself in her typical way.

"The usual. And those are too salty for you. Sorry," Carrie added, moving the chips away.

"For goodness sakes, when did you turn into the fun police?"

"She's always like that. You never noticed?" Sophie turned from the counter, giggling.

"I *am* not. Everyone knows I'm fun. Super fun," Carrie defended herself. "Ask your Aunt Brooke."

"She is *absolutely* fun," Brooke came in from the patio. Her hands were grimy, and Carrie guessed she'd been starting up the grill. "Most of the time."

"She won't let me eat chips," Gena complained, eyeing the basket with longing.

"Too salty, Mom," Brooke agreed. "We're having burgers. Turkey," she clarified. "Better for Mom's cholesterol. I hope that's okay?"

"Perfect." Hardly Carrie's first choice, since she smelled and served the dish all day, but she was happy to have someone else cook and wasn't about to complain.

"How can I help?"

"Just relax and keep Mom away from the chips. How's life at the Blue Sky?"

"Something strange happened during lunch. There was a scene in the dining room, and I had to fire Sheila Tatum."

"You did?" Her mother looked surprised, then shrugged. "She was always difficult."

She'd snuck another chip but nibbled on the edges like a mouse. To make it last longer, Carrie suspected.

"Why did you fire her?" Brooke asked.

Carrie told them about the confrontation that had erupted between Sheila and her customers.

"I don't know the full story of the accident. But treating anyone the way Sheila bullied Tess Hargrove is inexcusable."

"I'm proud of you," Gena said. "Your father would be, too. Our family doesn't turn a blind eye to that kind of behavior."

"What's the real story, Mom?" Brooke was at the counter, shaping burgers with Sophie's help.

"Lila Norton claimed Tess was innocent. Is that true?" Carrie asked.

"It's complicated, and it was so long ago. I'm not sure I remember the details." Her mother sat back and was quiet for a moment. "It happened in the summer, about ten years ago. There was a car accident near Mariner's Point. It was a rainy night, and the cars collided at a bend in the road. It's always been a dangerous spot. The Croft brothers were in one car, Dr. Croft and his older brother, Andy. Andy was driving and ended up badly injured. He was airlifted to a hospital on the mainland but died a few days later."

"What about Tess Hargrove?" Carrie asked. "Was she driving the other car?"

"Tess first said she was the driver, but later claimed that her boyfriend—I don't remember his name—was driving and she was only a passenger. I don't think the police found any alcohol in her bloodstream. But empty beer cans were in the car, and her boyfriend was over the limit, which confused things. By the time she professed to being innocent, her boyfriend had run away, and there was no one to back up her story. Her aunt was very vocal about Tess's innocence and being treated unjustly."

"She's still sticking up for her," Carrie reported.

"When all was said and done, Tess did plead guilty and went to jail," her mother concluded. "I'm not sure anyone will ever know the truth."

"What about Tess's parents? Didn't they fight for her in court?" Brooke asked.

"I think her mother died when she was very young, and she was raised on High Meadow Farm by her father, Walter Hargrove. I only knew him from a distance, but he seemed a withdrawn, severe man. I don't think he helped her at all when she got in trouble." Her mother finished her single chip and licked a crumb off her fingertip. "She only had her aunt, Lila Norton, who is a very good-hearted person."

"Mrs. Norton was my third-grade teacher. She's a peach," Brooke said.

"Just don't cross her about Tess. That peach turns into a tiger," Carrie reported.

"Perhaps with good reason," Gena added. "Now that her father died, maybe Tess came back to live on the farm."

Carrie had thought of that, too. "From what I saw today, it won't be easy."

"That's too bad. Whether she was behind the wheel that night or not, she served her sentence, and has the right to live where she wants," Brooke said.

"Not if people like Sheila Tatum have their way." Recalling the scene made Carrie upset all over again.

"Then people like us need to speak up. Like you did today, Sis." Brooke turned with the tray of burgers and headed for the door. "These babies will be perfectly grilled in five. Sophie will take cheese orders."

"I'll set the table." Carrie headed for the cupboard.

She still didn't know the truth, but from what her mother said, only Tess and her vanished boyfriend knew for sure. The details of the story cast a different light on her visit to the farm. Her mother was right. Some people would try to chase Tess away if others didn't stand up for her.

It was a beautiful summer night, and after the meal, Carrie lingered at the table with her sister and mother while Sophie went inside to video chat with friends on her laptop.

"How's Sophie handling the end of school?" Brooke asked.

"She's torturing me. I know it's hard, but I hear about it every minute. I feel so guilty. I can't wait for the events and parties to be over."

"I'm sorry, honey," her mother said sympathetically. "She seems perfectly content when she's with me."

Carrie was glad to hear her mother wasn't subjected to Sophie's crankiness.

"I took out some art supplies today, and we did charcoal sketches," her mother added. "She drew one of me. It's excellent. She has a good eye."

"She's got that natural talent, just like you, Mom."

Her mother smiled. "I think she's talented, too. We had a lovely afternoon."

Carrie was relieved to hear that. Sophie had flown through the lessons with her tutor, a college student whom her daughter found acceptably cool. Now she was bored. Apart from time with Brooke and her grandmother, Sophie had nothing to do but think about her friends and all the fun she was missing back home.

"A friend of mine has an art studio and gallery at Mariner's Point. The Firefly Gallery," Brooke said. "She runs a program for kids in the afternoon. Maybe Sophie would like it."

"Nadia Popova, you mean?" their mother asked. "She's a good teacher. I've taken classes there."

"Text me the info asap. I'll sign Sophie up tonight." Carrie wasn't joking. She needed Sophie occupied as much as possible, as soon as possible.

"There are all sorts of programs for kids Sophie's age going on in the summer. Check the flyers on the community bulletin board in the café. There are notices in the *Haven Island Observer*, too," Gena said.

Carrie knew she could find activities for Sophie that way but hadn't found the time to research. The art studio seemed a good place to start.

Brooke had gone inside and returned with a bowl of fresh berries. She filled a dessert dish and passed it to Carrie. "Any replies to the ad for a café manager?"

"A few more résumés came in. The candidates were either underqualified or had red flags. I did call one woman with great experience who sounded very professional over the phone. But she can't move until the fall. I've put the ad all over the place, in trade magazines and professional sites online. I even got in touch with an agency that specializes in restaurant staffing. They charge a hefty fee, but I'm not sure what else to do."

"We know you're doing your best," Brooke said.

"I had the same problem, honey. It's very late in the season to find anybody worthwhile. Unless they've been fired from another job," her mom said.

"Have you given any thought to staying?" Brooke tried for a casual tone, but Carrie sensed her interest.

"Not really," Carrie replied in a thin voice.

Their mother gave Brooke a look. "I would never ask you to do that, dear. You don't need to babysit me and the café all summer. I'm getting stronger every day. You go back to your own life whenever you want. We'll manage fine."

"I'm in no rush, Mom. Believe me. I need to find a new job and an apartment. I think you're stuck with us for a while," Carrie said, purposely flipping the situation around.

"I'm glad to help any way I can. You know that." Gena smiled and patted her arm. "I'll head up to bed, girls. I suddenly feel sleepy."

Her mother had always been a night owl, working on her painting, paying bills, or even baking while the rest of the family was in dreamland. It was shocking to see her head to bed so early, but a sobering reminder that she had a long way to go before she was strong again.

After her mother went up, Carrie helped Brooke. "I guess I should stay," Carrie said as she loaded the dishwasher. "We can take our time finding a manager and hire someone solid."

"I didn't mean to pressure you. I know you have a life in Boston, like Mom said. Even if you forgot, Sophie certainly hasn't. If you don't want to stay, we'll all understand. And we'll manage. I'll give up the taxi this summer and take over at the café. You can show me what to do, and Mom will be looking over my shoulder, I'm sure."

It was generous of Brooke to offer. She was a very good waitress, but running the business took a lot more than that. Carrie wouldn't know where to begin instructing her, and before long, their mother would step back in. Which was exactly what she and her sisters didn't want. As of today, there were other factors to consider.

"Thanks, Brookie, but you stick with your taxi. I know you love it. I do see a good case for staying," Carrie admitted. "I did a deep dive into the bookkeeping this week. It's not pretty."

"Really?" Brooke frowned, looking alarmed. "How bad is it?"

"I don't want anyone to panic, but you need to know what I discovered. The accounts are a shambles—and the café is hanging on by a thread."

Brooke shook her head in disbelief. "We all know bookkeeping isn't Mom's strong point. How bad is it?"

Carrie sighed. It was hard to face this squarely and say the words out loud.

"We're overdrawn and have almost depleted our credit line. I had to juggle things around to pay suppliers and meet this week's payroll. We managed to squeeze by," she added, trying to offer hope, "and more money will come in with the summer rush to make up the slack. But the accounts need to be in much better shape before we hand things over to a new manager. It wouldn't be fair, for one thing."

Brooke was upset. "That's awful, Carrie. I had no idea. Mom never mentioned any problems, though that part of the job is her least favorite. I can't understand it. The place is always so busy. Like it's always been."

"We draw our fair share of customers, but there's more competition this year. New places, like the Farmer's Table and that fancy coffee shop. They've started serving breakfast," Carrie noted.

"People don't mind paying five dollars for a cup of coffee over there, either. Our prices haven't gone up for years, though the cost of everything has. We need a better profit margin if we want to stay afloat."

Brooke's expression was solemn. "Thank goodness you're here to sort all this out. Sounds like you caught it in the nick of time, too." Carrie wasn't sure, though she certainly hoped so. "Does Rebecca know?"

"We spoke this afternoon. She was concerned, of course, and insisted on loaning the business money so we don't have to rack up more debt. I didn't want her to, but you know how she gets."

Brooke looked relieved. "That was good of her. We'll pay her back, of course."

"No question," Carrie agreed. "Right now, it's a lifeline. Going forward, we need to trim costs, increase profits and bring in more customers." As Carrie outlined the prescription for the café's recovery, she felt the full weight of its success on her shoulders.

No one would blame her if the business did not survive the summer. But Carrie knew she couldn't bail now. She would have to stay longer than planned, maybe even until September. It wouldn't feel right to desert a sinking ship.

"I'll help any way I can," Brooke promised. "Waitressing, kitchen help, whatever. I don't even need a salary if that would be a savings."

Carrie touched her sister's shoulder. "That's sweet of you, Brookie. It hasn't come to that. At least we know what we're dealing with and what we need to do. Let's go forward and hope for the best."

"You know what you're doing, Carrie. We all trust you."

"Thanks, pal." Carrie wished she could feel half as sure as her younger sister sounded. "Not a word of this to Mom, of course."

"Of course not. With any luck, she'll never know the Blue Sky had such a close call."

Carrie also hoped that's how it would go but knew it would take more than luck to put this near-miss behind them.

***

On her way up to her room, Carrie passed Sophie's door. It was open a crack, and Carrie saw her daughter sitting at the edge of her bed. Sophie looked as if she'd been crying.

"Hey, honey. Can I come in?" Sophie replied with a glum expression, and Carrie sat beside her. "What's the matter? Did you have a disagreement with one of your friends?"

Girls could be so mean at Sophie's age; even the closest friendships ran hot and cold. But as easily as they fell out, they made up again, Carrie noticed. To Sophie, though, it always felt like the end of the world.

"Everyone's having so much fun. Monday is the last day of school. Kayla is having a party Saturday, and that's all my friends talk about." She turned to face Carrie. "You said you would get me back home for all this stuff, remember?"

Carrie did remember. She'd said *some* stuff. And only that she'd try. It had been next to impossible to keep even that vague a promise, as much as she'd wanted to.

"I know I did, honey. I've just been so busy at work, especially on the weekends."

"I guess that means I can't go back for the party, right?" Her tone was a mix of disappointment and defiance, catching her mother in a broken promise.

Carrie felt torn. "Let me think about it. Maybe Aunt Brooke can take you."

Carrie doubted her sister's schedule was any more flexible, but felt pressed to say something. Sophie's father would have helped, but his band had been hired as the opening act for a more famous group, and he was about to go on tour around the country for most of the summer. Another reason their marriage had not worked out.

Tim did keep in touch with calls and FaceTime. It wasn't his fault his daughter lived so far away right now.

"I can take the ferry by myself. I'm not a baby."

"I know you're growing up, Sophie. You've been so reasonable and mature since Grandma got sick. I really appreciate that. But you can't take the ferry to Rockport all alone. How would you get into Boston? You're not ready yet," she said firmly.

Sophie sat back, pouting. "I'd take a bus or something? It's not exactly rocket science. I'm bored to death here. You said we were only staying a few weeks. When are we going home?"

Carrie sighed. "I don't know," she said honestly. "I haven't found a manager. I need to stay until that's settled. One way or the other."

Sophie's eyes widened. "That doesn't sound good."

She was sharp. Her keen intelligence and persistence would serve her well as an adult. Right now, the gifts were challenging to manage.

"The short answer is, we need to stay longer than I expected. I haven't had any time to look for a job or a place for us to live. That has to be settled, too."

Carrie didn't want Sophie to worry about practical matters that were not a child's concern. On the other hand, she felt it was important to be honest and give her the whole picture.

"I'm sure I can find a new job and a great apartment. You don't need to worry. But it will take time, honey."

Sophie didn't answer at first. Finally, she said, "Okay, I get that. But why do I have to stay? I can live with Dad."

"Your father is about to go away for the whole summer, remember?"

"I could go with him. I bet he'd say 'yes' if I asked. I never go anywhere. Except this dumb island. Before you know it, we'll end up living here forever."

She looked about to cry again. Carrie put her arm around Sophie's shoulder, and her daughter didn't resist.

"It won't be forever. I don't want to stay any longer than we need to, either. You've been a really good sport. Let's find fun things for you to do, where you can make friends."

She stroked Sophie's dark, smooth hair and tucked it behind her ear. "It's going to be all right. I promise."

"Whatever." Sophie sighed, tired of arguing.

"I love you, Nugget. More than anything. I hate to see you unhappy, even for a minute."

"I know," Sophie replied in a singsong tone. "Love you, too."

Carrie kissed her cheek. She nixed her plan for a bath and her mystery novel. "Pjs and a show? You choose."

"*Gilmore Girls*," Sophie said, cheered by the suggestion.

"Perfect." The classic mom-daughter series was not her first choice, but Sophie loved it.

"Meet you here in five. I'll make popcorn." Sophie was already halfway in her sleepwear.

Carrie gave a thumbs up and headed for her room. The mediation had been exhausting, but her daughter seemed soothed and back on track.

Forget restaurant work. I should apply for a job at the United Nations, Carrie decided. *I'm a natural.*

Fourteen

Honey woke Tess from a deep sleep. The big dog jumped up from her spot beside the bed and ran to the top of the stairs, barking loud enough to be heard in the village. A herding dog's alarm that a predator was near.

Honey raced down the staircase to the front door. Tess followed with sleepy, stumbling steps.

"Calm down, Honey. It's only a raccoon." Or some other creature, Tess guessed, turning over the trash or scampering too close to the house for the dog's comfort.

But as Tess reached the foyer, she heard tires spinning and headlight beams swept across the dark sitting room.

She ran to the window just in time to see a car race out of the front yard and speed toward the gate. Honey growled low in her throat, and Tess calmed her.

"It's okay. They're gone." She stroked the dog's head with a trembling hand. She was afraid to open the door and look outside, but she knew she had to.

"Tess? What's all that racket? What's going on?" Aunt Lila stood at the top of the steps and flipped on a light.

"Nothing, Aunt Lila. Honey heard an animal. You can go back to bed."

Her aunt didn't budge. "I thought I heard a car. Didn't you?"

Tess considered lying but couldn't. Not even for the sake of saving her aunt worry. "I did. Maybe someone was lost and turned around in our yard."

Her aunt came downstairs and met her at the front door. "Let's make sure everything's secure. I'll get flashlights."

Tess didn't argue. She also wanted to look around, though she wished her aunt had slept through the noise.

It was a few hours before dawn; a damp chill hung in the air. Tess had pulled a sweatshirt over her pajamas and stuck her bare feet in her work boots. Her aunt wore an old barn jacket over her nightgown and sturdy walking shoes.

Honey shot out into the darkness as soon as Tess opened the door.

On the porch, Tess flashed her light around, the thin beam illuminating the front yard. Everything looked in order. She walked down the steps toward the barn, and her aunt followed.

"Seems fine out here. It's chilly, Aunt Lila. Maybe you should go back in."

As she turned to her aunt, a red chicken trotted by and clucked. Another followed. Her aunt pointed her light at the coop. The gate was open.

"The chickens are loose. Oh, dear…"

Tess didn't answer. She chased the big red hen. Most people didn't realize how they loved to roost. Tess knew she'd find most of them perched in the trees between her farm and Jessup's tomorrow.

"I'll get the white one," her aunt said. "She's slow."

As Tess followed the chicken, her flashlight caught the barn. She stopped in her tracks. Streaky, neon-green lettering covered one side. Scrawled in spray paint, the words said, KILLER! MONSTER! GO AWAY OR YOU'LL PAY!

Tess stared at the message, speechless. Tears welled up, but she didn't want to cry in front of her aunt.

"What have they done to the barn? Cowards—sneaking around here in the middle of the night," Lila declared.

"I can paint over it," Tess said quickly. She turned to her aunt, glad to leave the ugly words in the dark.

"Of course you can." Her aunt touched her arm, her calm, steady self again. "I'll check the goats and get the chickens locked up. You'd better look inside the barn."

The barn doors stood partly opened. Tess was sure she'd left them closed. She pushed at a big sliding door and flipped the light on, afraid of what she'd find.

Clover, their cow, rested peacefully in her stall. But a few bales of hay had been pulled from the stack, cut open, and strewn about. She turned toward the flats of vegetable plants, and her heart sank. The rows of small plants had been torn from the containers, the stems broken and smashed, dirt tossed in all directions. She knelt and gently picked one up. Just a cracked stem and one leaf left, the thin white roots exposed. It wouldn't last long like that.

She felt a panicky tightness in her chest. As if she wanted to give the little plants CPR or something. She was helpless to save them, but it was hard to leave the pile of dirt and vegetation without doing something.

Lila stood behind her and made a *tsking* sound. "Our vegetable garden. How can people be so mean?"

"They're ruined. Or they will be by the morning." They both knew that the roots would dry up, and that would be that.

"We can't let that happen if we can help it." Lila walked to the workbench and found two hand shovels and gloves. "As long as there's some greenery above ground and a few roots below, they have a chance."

Her aunt was right. They had to try. She took a shovel and got started, carefully replacing the damaged plants in the flats and small pots they had arrived in. Anything that survived the night would be planted in the vegetable patch tomorrow. She could usually identify plants by their leaves, but there wasn't much left to decipher.

"I might not know what's growing where, but something in this mess should take root."

"That's how they do it in England, flowers and vegetables all mixed up. We'll have a *victory* garden," Lila declared, drawing on an old phrase from World War II. She'd already filled two small pots and set them aside. "We should call the police, Tess. Whoever did this should be found and punished."

"No police. I don't want any attention." Any more attention, she could have said, recalling the café.

Were the same officers who had arrested her years ago still on the island's force? It was possible. Things changed so little here. She'd hate to face any of them again.

"Tess, please. We need to call. It could have been worse."

"Thankfully, it wasn't. It was just...mischief. Annoying but nothing that awful." She downplayed her real reaction, though she doubted her aunt was convinced.

She wondered if the police would even care. Maybe they'd be happy to see a notorious jailbird harassed. Some of them.

"It's bad enough in my book," Lila said.

"Maybe I'll call in the morning. There's nothing they can do now, except delay us from saving these plants."

Lila sighed and stood up. "In that case, I'll make some coffee. We'll be out here for a while."

Coffee was a good idea. The wave of adrenaline that flooded her senses when she jumped out of bed had subsided. Her body urged her to go back inside and slide between the covers.

"Can you bring some donuts? That will pep me up," Tess called out. She heard only a chuckle in reply.

Despite working several hours in the middle of the night, Tess rose at the usual time to take care of the cow, goats and any chickens that had been captured. The angry words scrawled on the barn looked even uglier in the daylight. She wondered how much paint it would take to cover the ominous message.

Tess went into the barn to hunt for brushes and pans. She hoped to find some old primer and paint, too. She was wary of venturing into town again to buy anything.

"Hello? Is anyone here?"

Tess turned and saw a woman framed in the doorway. With the sunlight at her back, Tess couldn't see her face but guessed it was Carrie Duffy.

She wiped her hands and walked out. "Hi, I'm Tess. Thanks for coming up here. I hope it wasn't a bother."

"Not at all. Happy to help." Carrie handed Tess the phone and said, "I think we've met before. On the ferry around Memorial Day? You gave my daughter a sea sickness bracelet."

Tess remembered, too. "That's right. I came for the weekend ... but I'm still here."

"It's a long story, but the same thing happened to me," Carrie replied with a laugh. She paused, then said, "Maybe it's none of my business ... but it looks like you had some nasty visitors."

Carrie's gaze swept up to the graffiti, her expression concerned. The sight was hard to ignore.

"Just some annoying kids. I can paint over it."

"They got at your plants, too." Carrie noticed. "That's awful."

"They'll be all right once I get them in the ground." She did her best to make light of the sight. Carrie's concern and sympathy made her feel self-conscious.

"What did the police say?" Carrie asked.

"I haven't called. I don't want to make a big deal of it. It was just teenagers, I'm almost sure. They had their fun. I doubt they'll be back."

Carrie considered her words, her expression thoughtful. "I understand. It's your decision."

"Maybe it's a good thing I didn't come back for the phone. You might have had another scene to deal with...Or, maybe that's why you brought it up here?"

Tess wasn't sure why she'd been so blunt; it wasn't like her, and Carrie was being so friendly.

Carrie's smile faded, her eyes wide with surprise. Tess wondered if she was offended. "Come back any time. If anyone dares to bother you, I'll show them the door. I owe you a free meal—or two—after yesterday."

Tess had to smile. "I'll take you up on that. The Blue Sky always had the best food in the village."

"I agree." Carrie's expression turned thoughtful. "I don't know the whole story." About the accident, Tess knew she meant. "But I hope you don't let people like Sheila Tatum, or whoever came here last night, chase you away."

"That's kind of you to say," Tess replied quietly.

"Will you stay and run your father's farm?"

"I'd like to. I'm trying to see if it will work out."

Her reply was vague, but she could tell Carrie understood. Would people leave her alone so that she could work the land? That was the question.

"Evaline said she'll be selling your produce."

"That's right." *If I don't get chased away,* Tess silently amended. "Strawberries and eggs for now. We'll have vegetables and blueberries in a few weeks, too."

"I'll buy them from her. Or from you directly. Let's talk about it."

"That would be great." Tess was surprised by the offer. The extra income could really help. Evaline could only take a limited amount. She had her own products to sell. Tess doubted any restaurants on the island would knowingly buy her goods. She felt intimidated now to contact them.

"Farm-to-table is all the rage these days." Carrie rolled her eyes, making Tess smile again.

The women said goodbye, and Tess watched Carrie drive away, then returned to the barn, feeling brighter.

Carrie Duffy had arrived at the right moment, a reminder that for every nasty waitress and cowardly vandal, there were people on the island who believed she had a right to live here.

Tess knew she had to remember that.

* * *

"I was up at High Meadow Farm this morning to drop off Tess Hargrove's phone." Carrie spoke so quietly, Brooke had to lean over the counter to hear her above the café's midday din. "The scene with Sheila Tatum wasn't the half of it, poor thing."

"What do you mean? What else happened?"

"The farm was vandalized last night. There was graffiti all over the barn. Icky, Halloween-green spray paint. Really vicious stuff." Carrie was reluctant to repeat the ugly epitaphs. "Some plant seedlings in the barn were torn to shreds, too."

"That's awful." Brooke frowned.

"What did the police say? Do they have any idea who did it?" Brooke had been wolfing down a bacon, lettuce, and tomato sandwich, along with a pile of French fries. She'd always eaten anything she wanted without gaining an ounce. Carrie and Rebecca called her Greyhound when they were growing up, because she had the same metabolism.

Carrie's, on the other hand, was more like a lazy Labrador whose figure showed every treat. She'd come to love her curves—that was who she was and would always be. A woman didn't need to be broomstick-thin to be beautiful, she often reminded herself. But she sometimes envied her little sister, especially when she washed down her lunch with a gulp of a chocolate shake.

"Tess didn't call the police. She was really downplaying it. She didn't even sound angry," Carrie realized. "But waking up in the middle of the night like that had to be frightening. And finding that graffiti painful. We talked a bit," Carrie added.

"Turns out, we met on the ferry. She's the woman who gave Sophie the sea sickness bracelet, remember? Whatever mistakes she made in the past—or didn't make—she seems like a good person."

"Check for table twenty-three." Dory handed her a table check and a bunch of bills. Carrie put the slip of paper through the register and handed her back the change.

The café needed a computerized system to place orders for the kitchen and ring out charges, Carrie had decided. At the risk of moving into the twenty-first century.

"I hate to see a bunch of hooligans get away with something like that," Brooke murmured. "It doesn't seem fair."

"Not one bit. I hope this is the end of it."

Brooke sat back. "Time to cue up for the one o'clock from Rockport. Can I have a cup of coffee to-go, please?"

Carrie filled a paper cup, smacked a lid on it, and slid it to her sister. Brooke drank so much coffee Carrie wasn't sure how she fell asleep at night. Then again, Brooke was often up past midnight working on her writing, so perhaps staying awake was the point.

"Thanks, Sis. See you later." Brooke grabbed her knapsack with one hand and the coffee with the other. "Hey, am I picking up Sophie today at the art studio?"

"No, that's tomorrow," Carrie replied. "You'll need to take her there too if I can't sneak out of here around noon."

Carrie had signed Sophie up for the afternoon art classes Brooke had suggested at the Firefly Gallery. Sophie had not been thrilled by the news but hadn't argued. Perhaps because she'd barely been awake, staring sleepy-eyed into a bowl of cereal. Carrie hoped she liked the group but had other ideas if this one didn't stick.

"Don't worry, I'll remind you. I appreciate the help, Brookie," she added.

"Hey, 'it takes a village to raise a child,'" Brooke replied with the famous quote. "In our case, an island."

"That might be true," Carrie agreed, though most of the time, she was flying solo. That was another hidden blessing of being here, all the help she had with Sophie from her family. Sometimes, she wondered how she'd ever managed without it.

* * *

Brooke pulled up to the station just as the one o'clock ferry passed the jetty and entered the harbor. A line of taxis waited for the passengers who would walk off the dock. She took her place at the end of the queue with a few minutes to spare.

As she watched the ferry's progress, she pulled out her phone and called the *Haven Island Observer*, a direct number that bypassed the receptionist.

"News desk, Whalen."

The Observer's news editor, Jeremy Whalen, had a few years on her, including experience as a reporter on the *Boston Globe*. He acted as if he'd knocked around the world for decades, with a curt and crusty newsman act. Brooke secretly laughed but pretended to buy it to boost the odds of seeing her work in print.

"Hey, Jeremy, it's Brooke Duffy. I have a good story for you. And it wasn't on the police blotter."

She knew that detail would snag his interest. The public record of police activity was a primary source of leads, doled out to reporters each morning like bits of worms to baby birds.

"Go on." She heard his keyboard clacking; his tone telegraphed, "Get to the point."

"A farm on the island was vandalized last night. There was graffiti left on the barn and property damage."

"Where was this?" He stopped typing—a good sign.

"High Meadow Farm. In the hills, central island. Do you know who Tess Hargrove is?"

Fifteen

Tess didn't return from the hardware store until nearly three. But she was determined to start the job and wanted to get the graffiti covered with primer before dark.

Her aunt watched her unload the truck. "Did you get my message, Tess? I called a few times, but it went to voice mail."

"I'm sorry, I didn't hear my phone ring. The service on that side of the island is spotty." A paint can dangled from each hand as Tess turned to face her.

"Is something wrong?"

"No, dear. Well, I hope not," Lila amended. "Brooke Duffy stopped by. Carrie's younger sister? She was one of my students. I had her in third grade."

"What did she want?"

"She heard what happened here last night, from her sister, I assume. She thought it would be a story for the newspaper. She always loved writing, even when she was young. I told her we didn't want any attention, but she kept asking questions. I think she took some photos, too, with her phone."

Tess nearly dropped the heavy cans. Her heart raced as her mind jumped ahead to the consequences of Brooke's visit.

She couldn't blame her aunt. A clever girl like Brooke knew how to get a woman like Lila chatting, and her aunt was far too polite to chase her away.

"I'm sorry, Tess. I didn't know what to say. I didn't know how to get rid of her."

"It's not your fault, Aunt Lila."

It wasn't Carrie Duffy's fault either, Tess realized, though it would be easy to blame her. She'd told Carrie she didn't want attention, but she'd never told her to keep the situation confidential.

"It's a tight community. People are bound to hear about this sooner or later," Tess added.

"There aren't many secrets around here, that's for sure," Lila agreed quietly.

Tess slammed the gate on the truck bed closed, then got back in the driver's seat. Her aunt ran over and spoke to her through the window. "Where are you going now?"

"To the newspaper office. Maybe I can stop them from printing the story."

Lila looked doubtful. "I suppose it's worth a try."

The newspaper office was in an old building near the harbor that had once been a small warehouse. Whitewashed and unadorned, a sign above the porch painted in bold, black lettering read, "Haven Island Observer – Serving the community since 1820."

Tess swung into the first space she spotted on the street and cut the engine. She'd driven like a mad woman and realized she looked like one, too—her wavy hair falling loose from the clip at the back of her head, her jeans and t-shirt soiled from the work she'd done today. She could have washed her face and found a comb, she realized as she caught her reflection in the glass panes of the door.

She pulled the door open anyway and stepped into a dimly lit area with a high ceiling and a creaky wooden floor. There was a staircase straight ahead and a desk to her left. A computer sat on top, but no one sat behind it.

Through an archway past the desk, she saw an open space that covered most of the first floor, filled with desks and partitions. Most of the desks were occupied, but no one glanced her way. People seated there tapped quickly on keyboards, talked on the phone, or did both simultaneously. She couldn't decide where to start with her questions.

"The receptionist should be back in a minute," a voice behind her said.

Tess turned and saw a man seated on a bench across from the desk. She was in such a state, she hadn't noticed him. He paged through a newspaper, *The Haven Island Observer*, of course.

"Thanks. I guess I'll wait."

He looked up briefly, then looked back at the paper. He wore a light blue tailored shirt, the sleeves rolled to his elbows, and khaki pants. His thick brown hair fell across his forehead, and he swiped it aside.

A young woman trotted down the stairs, a long blond ponytail swinging behind her. She sat at the desk and adjusted black frames of her glasses.

"Your aunt asked if you could please wait five more minutes," she said to the man. "She's in a meeting about the front page."

"Yes, of course." He answered without looking up, then turned a page.

The receptionist finally turned to Tess. "Can I help you?"

"I hope so." Tess tried not to speak in a rush but couldn't help it. "Someone wrote a news story about me. Brooke Duffy. There was some trouble at my farm last night. But I don't want it to be in the paper. I have some say about that, don't I? I mean, can I speak to the person who decides these things?"

The blonde stared back at her. Tess guessed she didn't hear the request often. Maybe, never?

"You need to speak to the news editor. He's in a meeting. Can I have your name, please?"

Tess moved closer, her bold tone tuned down to a whisper. "Tess, Tess Hargrove."

The receptionist made a note on a pad. "Did you say Bess?"

"Tess. With a *T*," Tess replied just as quietly.

A phone buzzed. "Excuse me." The young woman seemed impatient now. She picked up the receiver and listened. "Yes, he's still here. I'll let him know."

She hung up and smiled at the man on the bench. "That was your aunt, Dr. Croft. She'll be right down."

Tess froze. Her heart pounded so hard, the sound echoed in her head. She heard a newspaper crinkle behind her and couldn't breathe.

Ben Croft. Andrew's younger brother. Sitting two feet away.

The receptionist looked up again. "I'm sorry. I didn't get your last name. Could you spell it for me, please?"

Tess took the pad from her hand and quickly jotted her name and phone number. "I have to go. Please, *please* have someone call me."

She dropped the pen and pad and raced to the door, not daring to look back at the stunned girl or Ben Croft, though she felt them watch her hasty escape. The newspaper fell from his hand and fluttered to the floor.

Tess was so flustered, she forgot where she'd parked her truck. She walked in circles on the sidewalk in front of the newspaper office for a moment too long. She heard the door open and knew she should have just run.

"Tess Hargrove." He said her name in a deep, low tone. A wave of fear crashed over her as she turned to face him.

"Someone said that you were back. I didn't believe it."

Tess met his gaze but had to look away. "I'm sorry. It must be hard for you to see me."

"Hard doesn't come close." His tone took on a colder, keener edge.

"I understand. I'm sure you must hate me...I'll just go."

She turned, but he blocked her path.

"Hate is a strong word. My parents told us to never say it."

Tess didn't reply. She didn't dare look up at him. Even if he didn't say the word aloud, she was sure he felt it.

"I've imagined meeting you," he confessed, "and what I'd say and do. But this is . . .unreal, seeing you . . .out of the blue."

Tess felt the same. She swallowed and nodded. "I shouldn't

have come into town, to a busy place like this. I should have called."

He answered with a curious expression. His eyes were a golden, hazel color. She suddenly remembered the way he'd stared up at her that night.

"Can you see my brother? He was driving. Is he okay?" she heard him say.

"You sounded upset in there. What sort of news report do you want stopped?"

She searched his expression, wary of his motives. He was curious, and she didn't see any harm in telling him the truth.

"There was vandalism at the farm last night. Spray paint on the barn, that sort of thing." She spoke quickly, avoiding the details. "We didn't report it. But word got out, and someone thought it was a good story for the paper. I don't want that," she said sincerely. "It will only make things worse."

"That must have been frightening. Why didn't you call the police?"

She shrugged, unwilling to admit how frightened she'd been. "It was just a prank. Kids, probably. I don't think the police can do much about it. Or would even bother."

"You've come back to take over your father's farm?"

"I hope so."

"Even though people will make it hard for you?" He seemed interested in her answers, not just badgering to make her admit she wasn't wanted.

She shrugged. "I need to stick it out. If I can."

He frowned, looking upset. "I hope you don't think my family had anything to do with the vandalism."

"That never occurred to me," she answered honestly. "But

there was this waitress at the Blue Sky..." Her voice trailed off. "There are places in the village I shouldn't go," she said instead. "I had a feeling this would happen sooner or later."

"What do you mean, 'places you shouldn't go'?"

"Places where people recognize me." She felt frustrated, trying to explain it to him, of all people. "I don't want any trouble. I just want to work the farm for the season. See how it goes. People might not like to see me back at first. But maybe they'll get used to it in time. That's what my aunt says, anyway."

The theory sounded unlikely now, far less than it had a few days ago. Ben Croft probably thought that, too.

"Which is why you don't want this incident reported in the newspaper."

"Yes. Exactly." She nodded, still afraid to raise her gaze to his. "I just want to be left alone, to work the farm. I won't get in anybody's way if I can help it."

She was ready to get back in her truck. But Ben didn't seem ready to let her go yet. He stared at her, and then it happened, what she'd expected since the conversation began. He suddenly looked angry, his reasonable attitude pivoting one hundred and eighty degrees.

"If you really feel that way, why come back here at all? In the whole wide world, Tess Hargrove, there must be *someplace* else you could have gone. Someplace where no one knows you, or what you did." He pinned her with his fierce expression, and Tess didn't dare to answer. "You claimed you were innocent. But you stood in front of a judge and entered a guilty plea. You can *never* deny that. A lot of people loved my brother. And still do. I understand why they're upset, myself included."

Tess backed away and took a breath. "Sometimes I wonder

why I came back here, too," she admitted. "I don't want to argue with you ... I think it's best if I go."

She turned and headed for her truck. She'd given Ben Croft plenty of time to speak his mind. How long was she supposed to stand there and be berated?

It had been one of the hardest confrontations of her life. And she was no closer to having the article stopped, she realized.

* * *

"Ben, glad I caught you." Ben's aunt, Frances Croft flew through the door, sounding breathless. She held a scrap of paper, and Ben recognized the note Tess had left.

"Did you see Tess Hargrove?"

Ben knew his aunt, the editor-in-chief of *The Haven Island Observer,* was not surprised by much but pure shock showed in her pale complexion and sharp blue eyes.

"I did." He nodded, unable to say more as a wave of emotions unexpectedly surged up.

"Are you all right, dear?" His aunt touched his arm, her tone softer.

"Still stunned. I've imagined facing her down a million times." He shook his head. "It was nothing like that. And she wasn't anything like I'd pictured."

"How do you mean?" Aunt Frankie's gaze narrowed. The breeze off the harbor mussed her short, silvery blonde hair.

"I thought she'd be tougher. Defiant about what she'd done. She was a scared rabbit. Apologizing to me every other word."

"She knew you were angry. More than angry. Maybe she was afraid of what you might do."

He looked back at the street, where Tess had raced away in her truck. "I thought if I ever saw her again, I would lose control. But it never came to that. Maybe I don't hate her after all."

His aunt was silent, then lightly touched his shoulder. "That's a good thing. It means you're moving on."

He knew she meant well, but he didn't agree. So much of his life had been shaped by that single night, even his choice to become an emergency room doctor. He missed his brother every day and had come to accept those dark memories would shadow his life forever. Part of him didn't want to get past it or give up his sorrow and anger. It felt disloyal to think he ever could.

His aunt glanced at Tess's note. "There was vandalism at her farm last night. A story came in about it."

"Yes, I know. She seemed to take the intrusion in stride." He didn't want to feel impressed by that or feel sorry for her. But he knew some part of him did. "She was more upset about the incident being publicized. She thinks that will give other people ideas. I tend to agree."

His aunt shrugged. She tucked the note in the pocket of her dress, a slim linen shift, deceptively stylish. He doubted it had been purchased on the island. Although Frankie had been raised on Haven, she'd lived in Manhattan most of her life and had made a name for herself as a top-ranking editor for a national news magazine. She was the proverbial big fish in a small pond at *The Haven Island Observer*. More like a whale in a kiddie pool, Ben thought. But she seemed to like it and claimed she'd been ready for the change. She'd come home five years ago after she lost her husband, Charles Frasier, to a long battle with cancer. Charles had also been a power player in New York publishing, and they'd moved among the city's intellectual elite.

Haven was a sleepy backwater compared to her former stomping ground, but she still took the small island's news seriously. Like today.

"Even if we don't run the story, the word will get around. People are already talking about it," his aunt said.

"I'm sure they are. I'm only relating what Tess said. She wants to be left alone to work her farm." Ben caught his aunt's blue-gray gaze and held it.

"Some people might sympathize with her and feel she's being treated unfairly," she pointed out.

"Others might be emboldened to intimidate her more. They might even think the Crofts were behind the vandalism. Or that we condone bullying Tess Hargrove or harming her property. Or that we're using the newspaper to chase her away."

His aunt looked annoyed; her dark brows came together in a frown. "We present the facts as objectively as possible. How people react and what they read between the lines is *not* our responsibility." She paused and looked out at the harbor, weighing the two sides of the question, he guessed. "But any story about Tess Hargrove is a slippery slope for us. I'll grant you that. A blatant conflict of interest."

She looked back at him, her head cocked. "I'm surprised to hear you advocate for her. Maybe if her lawyer was half as persuasive, she wouldn't have gone to jail."

"I'm thinking of our family. You said it yourself; it's a slippery slope. No matter what I think of Tess Hargrove, I don't believe that kind of behavior should be encouraged. Even unintentionally."

"Okay, case closed. I get your point." His aunt slipped her phone from her pocket and checked the time. "Brooke Duffy will be crushed when she hears her first front-page story was scrapped. Our lunch date is scrapped as well. I need to stay and figure out the front page. Again."

Ben smiled at her impatient tone. "Lunch next week. Check your schedule."

"Sure, kid. Bolton's, the dining room. You're buying."

He laughed, and they hugged goodbye. His aunt turned on her heel and sailed back into the office, chin held high. As if she ran the show and everyone inside knew it, which they did.

Ben walked toward the dock where his car was parked. The water in the harbor was dark blue today with a light chop, despite the bright sun. Sea birds swooped into the white peaks, squawking and flapping their wings. One held a wriggling fish in its beak, and the others fought over the prize.

His aunt had been persuaded to drop the story. But Tess Hargrove still faced a hard time. Even without a newspaper article, gossip about her would travel. He wondered if she could hold out. She seemed so timid and vulnerable. But he also sensed something steely and resolved at her core. An unusual combination.

Sixteen

It was almost noon on Friday when Tess finished covering the graffiti with a coat of gray primer. She'd returned from town the day before, rattled after her confrontation with Ben Croft. Once she set up the ladder and supplies, she'd worked furiously until sunset.

She came down from the ladder to survey her progress. Up close, she could still spot a patch or two of that garish Halloween-green. But at a distance, the vile words had been erased. As if someone had come along with a giant bottle of white out. The sun would dry the primer quickly, and she would apply the red paint that matched the rest of the barn in an hour or so. And no one would ever guess what was hidden underneath.

Just like I can't guess what's hidden in the hearts of people I meet. Until they lashed out, like the waitress at the Blue Sky. Or trespassers who came in the dark of night.

As for Ben Croft, he probably did hate her but was too well-brought-up to say it to her face.

At least he'd helped her. Tess had been on the ladder painting when her phone rang, and she missed the call. But his aunt, who ran the paper, left a message to let her know they would not print the story. She didn't give a reason, but Tess surmised Ben had persuaded her against it.

To protect his family's reputation, Tess thought. It wasn't concern about her or her property. She felt sure of that.

Facing Ben had been a shock, but she'd gotten through it, and would be careful to avoid all the Crofts from now on. Which wouldn't be hard. From what she could see, they didn't rub shoulders with farmers or folks like her and Aunt Lila. They were doctors and newspaper editors—wealthy people who belonged to the golf and yacht clubs. Running into Ben yesterday had been a fluke. She'd make sure it never happened again.

Tess was cleaning the paintbrushes when her aunt pulled up in the truck. She headed to the house, a tote bag of groceries hung from one hand, a bunch of mail and the newspaper were clutched in the other. Tess ran over to help.

"I thought you'd like to see *The Observer*. I bought a copy in town." Her aunt opened the newspaper to show Tess the front page. "'High School Honor Student Wins State Science Award,'" she read aloud in a happy tone. She quickly turned the pages. "Lots of interesting articles. But not a word about our farm."

Tess had no reason to doubt the message from Frances Croft but seeing with her own eyes that the paper did not include any mention of the incident was a great relief.

"We dodged that bullet. Due to your quick thinking," Aunt Lila said.

Her aunt had felt terrible yesterday for talking to Brooke

Duffy. Tess was glad to see her smiling. "Very true, Aunt Lila. In a few hours, the paint will dry on the barn."

"And we can put this unfortunate episode behind us."

Tess nodded, though she would not forget. She needed to remain vigilant. To be mindful of where she went and who she spoke to if she really wanted to stay here.

* * *

Gena had made Sophie a grilled cheese sandwich. She shut off the burner and covered the pan. Then called to her granddaughter from the bottom of the staircase.

"Lunch is ready, honey. Come down before it gets cold."

"I'll be right there," Sophie called back.

Gena returned to the kitchen, where Brooke sat at the table, paging through the island's newspaper, still feeling glum that an article she'd written and expected to see on the front page had been cut at that last minute. She would publish hundreds of other articles, of course, Gena was sure. And short stories and even books someday. But she'd been so excited about her scoop; Gena knew that a pep talk wouldn't cheer her.

"Did your editor give any reason for dropping it?"

She shook her head without looking up. "Jeremy Whalen doesn't need to give a reason. He's like the all-powerful Wizard of Oz."

Gena smiled at the comparison. "But the Wizard was just a clever little man behind a flimsy curtain, remember?"

Brooke glanced at her. "Very true. I hope he feels so guilty, he gives me a plum assignment soon."

"You'll find more good stories. You don't give up easily. None of my daughters do."

"We're all stubborn. Just like you, Mom."

"I meant persistent, but I suppose it's a different side of the same coin."

Sophie appeared, a big purple backpack hooked over her arm. The bag looked about to explode, and Gena wondered what was in it, but didn't ask. At Sophie's age, she needed privacy.

"Hope this is still hot." Gena slipped the sandwich on a plate, then added pickle chips on the side, the way Sophie liked it.

"Thanks, Grandma. Looks great." Sophie took a huge bite.

Gena guessed she'd changed her outfit ten times, worried about making the right impression on the first day of art class. She looked adorable no matter what she put on. But kids were so self-conscious at that age, especially girls.

"What are you up to this afternoon, Mom?"

"I might walk across to the beach with my sketch pad."

"As long as you bring a water bottle and don't sit in the sun. I'll set up a chair and umbrella before we go," Brooke decided. "Leave it there when you go home. I'll get it later."

"Thanks, honey, but I can manage." Gena glanced at her daughter's expression and decided to give in. "If you really want to go to all that trouble, I won't argue."

"It will take two minutes. Sophie will help. Eat up, kiddo."

Sophie downed the rest of her lunch, and they left in a flurry of activity, locating car keys and cell phones.

Brooke kissed Sophie's cheek as she headed for the door.

"A nap would do you good, Mom," Brooke said. "The house will be quiet."

Too quiet, Gena thought. "I'm not taking a nap in the middle of the day. For goodness sake. You act like I'm ninety years old."

"Sorry. We just want you to reach ninety."

Gena laughed. "I do, too. But no need to treat me like I'm there already."

She stood by the door and waved as they drove away. She hoped her granddaughter enjoyed the class and made a friend. She'd been moody the past weeks, and Carrie bore the brunt of it. Sophie was sweet as sugar with her, especially after she got sick. Time with her only grandchild was the silver lining of this health problem, that was for sure.

Unfortunately, since her diagnosis, her daughters watched her every move. She wished her life would get back to normal, but the doctor said six weeks of recovery, and she was barely halfway there.

She went upstairs to the little bedroom she called her studio and packed a canvas tote with her sketch pad and the case containing charcoal and soft pencils. To entertain Sophie, she'd unpacked her art supplies and started using them again. Maybe she would have eventually, anyway.

Like most children, Gena had loved to draw and paint. But the interest stayed with her all through her school years. Whether studying a landscape, a still life, the human form, or face, she'd lose all sense of time and place as she struggled to capture the image. Teachers had always praised her work, but it came so easily, she didn't value it. She could see that now.

She'd been ambitious when she was young, her sights set on a career as an illustrator for magazines or books, perfecting her own paintings in her spare time. She'd imagined a sophisticated city life but ended up on Haven Island. Much to the dismay, and even disapproval at first, of her parents.

The summer of her junior year in college, a group she hung around with rented a house on Haven. Guys and girls, though it was all friendly. Of course, there was some flirting. Gena was shy but so pretty she attracted her fair share.

There was one young man she'd always liked who was just as shy as she was, Jonathan Borden. He finally built up his courage to ask her out, and they went to the beach and had lunch at the Blue Sky.

The waiter who served them was about their age. He had a dazzling smile and a teasing light in his dark eyes. He was perfectly polite, but Gena felt sparks zing between them.

Her "friend" tried hard to hold her attention, but her gaze wandered. She felt rude and insensitive. So unlike herself. She didn't spare the bold waiter another glance.

That night, when they all went to the movies in town, there he was, the waiter, taking tickets as they walked in and selling popcorn. Gena pretended she didn't recognize him, but he knew she did.

The next day, he was up on the lifeguard stand at the public beach. She couldn't resist teasing him about having so many jobs. He shrugged and smiled into her eyes in a way that made her feel lightheaded. "You won't get rid of me now. Wherever go, I'll be there. You ought to tell me your name. Mine is Patrick Duffy."

Gena thought Patrick Duffy was very brash and pushy. She never liked that type, but he made her laugh and forget her shyness, and they saw each other every day while she was on the island. She'd tried to put him off at first, but he wouldn't give up. And she soon stopped refusing.

When she returned to college, they spoke on the phone a lot but also wrote each other long letters. Gena had saved all of them.

Looking back, she knew how important part that correspondence had been to their courtship, how they had confessed their deepest feelings, fears, and dreams to each other. Patrick encouraged her ambitions and praised her artwork. He was earning an engineering degree. His older brother was in the Navy and would return to take over the café at the same time Patrick would finish school. Patrick would look for a job in Boston and already had connections at a few firms.

Life rarely works out the way we plan, Gena reflected as she sifted through a stack of watercolor paintings that she'd saved. That wasn't always a bad thing, though the change in direction might feel like a catastrophe at the time. Patrick's father grew ill and had to retire early. And his older brother never returned from California. He'd met a girl in San Diego, and when they married, her father gave him an executive job in the family's electronics firm.

She and Patrick graduated and married, but he was stuck holding together the Duffy's family business, the Blue Sky. His parents could not bear the idea of selling the café, and while solutions were proposed, time passed. As they lived on the island, believing it was temporary, Patrick grew accustomed to his role. Gena had a baby, and then another, and another. Haven was a wonderful place to raise a family, and eventually, their youthful plans seemed unimportant. Even childish.

Gena had no doubt they'd shared a happy, fulfilling life. It just wasn't the one she'd envisioned. But in so many ways, it was better than anything she had expected or imagined. Losing Patrick two years ago had been a blow. She wasn't over it and wondered if she ever would be.

After his death, she'd hit the ground running and only now

had a chance to reflect upon the past, and work through her loss. A hard job but one that couldn't be brushed aside or stuffed down any longer.

A photo of Patrick was perched on a shelf among pots of brushes and cups of pencils. She picked it up and dusted it off. He sat at the rudder of his sailboat, *Far Horizons,* a lofty name for a little boat that wasn't built for long trips. When they retired, he'd say, they'd get a larger boat with a nice cabin and take long sails up and down the Atlantic Coast. But Gena knew the class of the sailboat didn't matter. Out on the water, he felt free. As if he was already voyaging far and wide.

He'd been a fun-loving, generous man with a talent for appreciating life's simple pleasures. Everyone in town adored him, and many considered him the village's unofficial mayor. He could have easily been elected the real one.

Patrick looked back at her from the photo, tan and smiling.

He would have wanted her to enjoy the years she had left. But, tossed off the café merry-go-round, the future was unclear. Gena wished he was here to share this time. Or at least tell her what to do. She missed him so much; a piece of her was lost forever.

She placed the photo on her worktable and slung the tote strap over one arm. She was sure to find a chair and umbrella at the bottom of the path, as Brooke had promised. But she had another destination in mind, a cluster of boulders some distance down the shoreline. The tide was low, and the light was perfect for capturing the glistening beads of seawater on the stone, the varied mosses and seaweed that clung to the rough edges, and the tiny creatures that thrived in the watery shadows.

She set off for that spot, knowing that her artwork was always the best medicine.

Seventeen

As her day at the café wound down, Carrie often found herself alone with Jack, or almost alone, while one or two of their helpers finished cleaning the kitchen and dining areas.

At that time, Jack checked the stock in the cold box and then the storeroom, where her desk was crammed against one wall, surrounded by shelves of giant, commercial-sized cans of tomatoes, twenty-pound bags of pancake flour, five-gallon containers of syrup, and other supplies.

It was a tight space, even for one, and she usually left when he came in. Otherwise, they ended up standing so close, any conversation was awkward. Everything was awkward. For her anyway. She'd come to accept she had some absurd attraction to him and did her best to ignore it.

As the weeks had passed, Jack's rough edges smoothed out. Or, maybe she didn't notice them as much. She often recalled how helpful he'd been when her mother fell ill at the village green.

Keeping his head, calling the ambulance, and watching the café while she went to Boston.

The best thing about Jack was that he saw what had to be done and did it without having to be told. It was also a drawback, since he often took the initiative without asking and did things she didn't want him to do—especially with the menu. The kitchen was his domain, but she still expected him to clear changes in recipes with her.

"Recipes that have been handed down for generations," she'd often remind him.

"Which is why they need updating," he'd argue. "They were eating these dishes on the *Mayflower*."

When he messed with the café's beloved baked macaroni and cheese, adding fontina and even truffles, Carrie hit the roof. Secretly she thought the tangy combination was delicious and scarfed down an entire bowl before protesting. But the updated version was definitely not suitable for their loyal customers. Business at the café was not booming. There were a few new eateries on Front Street that were drawing away customers. Diners came to the Blue Sky with clear expectations, and Carrie was afraid to make drastic changes.

After the mac and cheese debate, Jack was careful to clear all inspirations with her. The end of the day was his favorite time to seek her out and offer a taste test of a new creation. If Sophie was around, she'd taste test, too, offering her opinion with the flair of a TV cooking show judge. Carrie rolled her eyes while Jack took her comments very seriously.

Brooke would spend time with Sophie at the beach or in town during the day, but often had to start work before she could drive her niece home. Dropped off at the café, Sophie would go straight to the kitchen to see Jack. Carrie had often told him it was all right to tell Sophie he was busy, but he always greeted his tweenage friend cheerfully. He'd patiently answer questions or teach her cooking tricks, like how to crack an egg with one hand or flip a burger. Jack listened to her ideas and opinions respectfully and never condescended. Not even about mixing green olives with peanut butter. He'd never mentioned children, but Carrie wondered if he was a father. He had a way with a certain ornery adolescent, and that was a small wonder.

But Sophie would not be dropped off this afternoon. She was at her first art class. Brooke was picking her up and bringing her home. Carrie was eager to find out if Sophie had liked the class but had a few tasks to take care of before she left the cafe.

She stood behind the counter, the salt and pepper shakers lined up on trays, ready to be filled, when Jack emerged from the kitchen. He headed down the narrow lane behind the counter with a determined step, a dish in hand.

He set it down in front of her and stepped back. It looked like a burger. A fringe of lettuce and the edge of a tomato slice peeked out from under a toasted bun.

"If you say you don't like this, I won't believe you."

"What a charming tag line. We should print that on our menus."

A begrudging grin tugged one side of his mouth. The side with the dimple. A five o'clock shadow outlined his strong jaw, but the scruffy look suited him.

"What is it, a burger with a special topping?" She tried to peek under the bun top, but he caught her hand.

"I'm going to blindfold you next time. Just relax and taste. Stop thinking so much."

Carrie knew she had that tendency. He was observant to call her on it.

"I'll close my eyes, see?" She did just that, trying to be a good sport. Then lifted the bun and took a bite.

"Hmmm ... good!" she exclaimed around a mouthful. She tasted melted cheddar, avocado, tomato, and something else that was not meat but had a yummy, charred, satisfying flavor.

"Portobello mushroom?"

"Ten points. Marinated and grilled. I want to call it a Zen Burger. Aiming for the hip, non-meat eaters."

"Oh yeah, that crowd is banging down the door to get in here." The hip, "anti-burger" people, as she called them, favored The Farmer's Friend down the street, with a selection of twenty herbal teas, side orders of seaweed salad, with chia-seed and alfalfa-sprout topping on everything.

"Maybe more would come if we served dishes like this."

"Possibly," she conceded, taking another bite. "But in the restaurant biz, as in life, you can't be all things to all people. You need to know who you are and perfect that."

"Well said," he tilted his head, looking impressed by her reply. "So your philosophy nixes the Zen Burger, is that it?"

He did work hard on his creations, and she was reluctant to disappoint him.

"Let's try it as a special on the weekend when the urbanites invade?" Jack usually acted uncaring about praise, but he looked pleased, and she knew she'd said the right thing. He took pride in his work and was an excellent cook, employed well below his potential and skills at the Blue Sky. She loved the place, but she knew that.

She still couldn't figure out what he was doing here. She'd searched for his resume once but couldn't locate it. Her mother's files were disorganized, and Carrie hadn't found time to investigate online. Rebecca had forgotten to have her office snoops check into Jack, as she'd promised. Carrie still suspected that Jack had an undisclosed story in his background but had to admit she felt less and less motivated to catch him out.

She felt him watching as she filled the shakers. Musclebound arms crossed over his chest. She kept her gaze down, warmth rising in her cheeks. She hoped he didn't notice.

"Need some help?"

"Thanks, I'm okay," she replied without looking up.

"A waitress should do that, not the boss."

"If I shouldn't, you shouldn't either. You're the cook."

Her reply made him laugh. He picked up a pepper shaker and removed the top, then filled it, despite what she'd told him.

"Did you find anyone to replace Sheila?"

Carrie had been covering the job along with her own. No easy feat. But a good applicant had finally appeared.

"A college student named McKenzie. She starts tomorrow."

"You should have saved this chore for her." He picked up another shaker. It looked small in his big hand, but he had a light, precise touch and barely spilled a grain of salt.

"I won't give her grunt work right off. I want her to like it here. At least for a few days."

He grinned but didn't counter with another comment. "How's the search for a manager going? Find anyone for that job yet?"

She shook her head. The situation was frustrating. The café's finances were finally moving in the right direction, but every penny still had to be watched closely. There was a long way to go before the books were back in the black, and she couldn't hand off the business until they were home free. On the other hand, if she didn't keep looking for someone to fill the spot, she might be stuck here after September.

She was tempted to confide in Jack about the dilemma but decided it was best to keep this problem in the family. She didn't want rumors spreading around town that the Blue Sky was going out of business.

"I re-did the ad, and we're trying another employment agency. This one specializes in restaurant staffing."

"I'm not surprised it's hard to fill the spot. All the good ones are snatched up before the season even starts."

She was tempted to ask why he'd been available, but she decided not to. He probably wouldn't tell her the truth anyway.

"Why don't you stay for the summer, Carrie? You've made good changes. Your mother is a lovely woman and great to work for. But you know the business a lot better."

She appreciated his compliment. She'd made the work flow in the kitchen and dining room more efficient so that food got out to their hungry customers faster. And she'd cut costs of supplies considerably and gently pushed up the menu prices. But she wasn't ready to confide the reasons she'd decided to stay the summer to him. Why was he asking? Would he miss her if she left?

"I'll see. I haven't given up on filling the job yet."

"And you're a diehard optimist and not the type that gives up easily," he added.

"I am ... and I don't." She met his gaze a moment and looked away. Was he teasing her? He was smiling but not in a teasing way. A way that sent a chill down to her toes. She focused on the shakers, trying not to show how much he affected her.

Her persistence was usually a positive trait, but a few times—like sticking with a bad marriage—it hadn't helped. Persistent people could be blindly stubborn, too.

They worked in silence, shoulder to shoulder, hands brushing as they reached for the big containers at the same time. Carrie felt oddly breathless standing so close. She didn't dare look up and give her feelings away.

Jack was calm as toast. He could have been standing beside a mop in a bucket. Which made her feel like even more of a dolt for thinking he might be flirting. Even Sophie would act cooler.

For goodness sake, get a grip. It's salt and pepper shakers.

Her phone rang, and she quickly answered. "Hey, Brooke. What's up? Did you meet Sophie?" she asked, noticing the time.

"I wish you hadn't said that." Brooke sounded upset. "I'm calling to see if you forgot and picked her up yourself."

Carrie felt a jolt. The box of pepper in her hand slipped to the floor. Jack retrieved it and stared at her.

"What do you mean? Isn't she at the art studio?"

"She's not here, Carrie. Nadia said all the kids scattered at the end of the session. She thinks she saw Sophie leave with another girl, but she's not sure if they kept walking toward town or got in a car..." Brooke's voice trailed off. "Carrie, I'm so sorry. I got here on time, I swear. I must have just missed her."

"She knew you were coming. She should have waited." Carrie was horrified but struggled not to panic. "Maybe she made a friend, and they went for ice cream or something, and she forgot to call."

"That must be it. I'm driving around Mariner's Point, the streets near the studio, looking for her. She couldn't have gone too far, right?" Brooke's voice sounded shaky. "I kept calling, but she didn't pick up. Maybe she'll answer for you."

"I'll call right now. I'll let you know if I get through. She's going to get a piece of my mind for not waiting."

"Don't be hard on her. She's having a rough time. Just let me know that she's all right, okay?"

"I will, don't worry."

Carrie knew she sounded a lot calmer than she felt. Her hand was shaking as she tried Sophie's number.

"What's the matter? Wasn't Sophie at the art studio?" Jack asked with concern.

"The teacher thought Sophie left with another girl, but she wasn't sure. I guess the first day was confusing, and she doesn't know the kids yet..."

Carrie's voice trailed off as she listened to Sophie's phone ring and ring. She wasn't picking up. Which was extremely annoying and worrisome. Carrie left a message and hung up.

"Did Brooke try the house? Maybe she made it home on her own." Jack's expression was serious, his trademark smug grin stashed in his apron pocket, she guessed.

"Good idea, I'll call my mom...but I might worry her." Carrie hesitated. "She'll get upset. It's bad for her heart."

"I'll find out. Leave it to me."

Before Carrie could agree, he'd dialed her mother's number.

"Hi, Gena, I'm just leaving the café and Carrie's gone, too. I think Sophie left a jacket. I can bring it back for her."

"Thanks, Jack. That would be great."

"Is she around? I'll make sure it's hers if you can put her on the phone."

"She started an art class today. I expect her back any minute with Brooke."

Carrie's heart sank. She let out a massive sigh and hoped her mother hadn't heard. Jack met her glance. "I'll drop it off. See you later, Gena."

Once the call was over, Carrie said, "I'm worried now. Where could she be? She never wanders around the island by herself. Why didn't she call me?" she asked, dark thoughts spinning out of control.

Jack rested his hands on her shoulders and looked into her eyes. "Sophie is fine. She messed up and just hasn't checked in yet to let you know where she is. Maybe her phone battery died."

Carrie nodded, suddenly glad that he was there and she wasn't dealing with this nightmare alone. She hoped with all her heart his theory was correct.

"I'm going to look for her. I'll start in Mariner's Point." Carrie pulled off her apron and raced to her office to grab her purse.

"I'll close up and look for her in town," Jack offered. "Someone should call all the kids in the class. One of them must have seen where Sophie went."

Carrie knew she should have thought of that herself—would have, if she hadn't been so crazed with worry and dread. "Brooke knows the teacher. She can get a list and start calling."

He'd followed her to the back door, and she paused to look at him. He reached out and touched her shoulder again. "She's all right. Don't worry. She's probably having fun with a new friend and lost track of time."

She couldn't speak and nodded. "Sure. I'll let you know if I hear from her."

Carrie headed to her car and slipped behind the wheel, but before starting off, she whispered a short prayer.

"Please let me find Sophie very soon. And help me keep my temper when I do? Amen."

Eighteen

Hours later, Carrie's prayer had boiled down to a desperate plea to find Sophie safe. She even offered God a deal or two while driving from one end of the island to the other.

Brooke and Jack also searched along with Finn Mulligan and several police officers. Sophie's new art teacher blamed herself, though Carrie knew that Sophie was old enough to realize she should have waited for her aunt or at least let someone know she'd gone off with a friend. Nadia called all the students in the class, but none could say for sure where Sophie had gone after they were dismissed.

It was after two in the morning when Carrie decided to go home. The adrenaline rush fueling her for hours had drained off, and she was crashing. Her eyes drifted closed as she steered her car around the island's back roads. Driving into a tree wouldn't help her find her daughter, she decided. She needed rest, at least an hour or two before she charged out again.

The house was dark and quiet. Her mother had left a note on the kitchen table. She'd gone up at midnight but hoped Carrie would wake her if there was news.

Brooke texted to say she'd be home soon, and Carrie put the kettle on. She set up a mug for tea, then sat at the kitchen table. She hadn't eaten a bite since the Zen burger but wasn't the least bit hungry.

She stared into the dark. She felt like pulling open the door and shouting Sophie's name at the top of her lungs, as if her daughter had gone out to play in the neighborhood.

Where was her little girl? Why hadn't she called? Considering the possible answers, Carrie pulled her thoughts back from a dark place. Sophie could call or even appear at any minute. Safe and sound. Just a huge misunderstanding.

She heard a light tap on the back door and jumped. Jack peered through the glass. She sighed and let him in.

"I didn't mean to startle you. I was going up to my place and saw you here."

"That's okay. Making some tea. Want some?"

"No thanks. You sit. I'll make it for you."

Carrie was about to protest, but the kettle whistled, and he quickly stepped to the stove and poured water into the mug she'd set out.

"I'm glad you came home. You look exhausted. The police are still searching, right?"

"The officers on duty promised to do a double shift. They circulated Sophie's photo around the department and sent it to the mainland." She paused. "The harbor master and the ferry crews have been informed to watch for her, too."

"Do you think she'd leave the island? Is she that precocious?"

"She's complained a lot about staying here. I said we'd only be a few weeks, and it's dragged on. She even asked if she could take the ferry on her own to get to a party with her school friends this weekend. I said I would try to take her, but she must have guessed I couldn't manage that."

"Kids get crazy ideas, that's for sure." He shook his head, thinking back to his own childhood? "What about her father? Where does he fit in? If you don't mind me asking."

It was a personal question, and Carrie was a private person by nature. But for some reason, she didn't mind telling him. Her defenses were worn down by worry and fatigue, and the night's ordeal had brought them closer.

"I called him a few hours ago. He's very upset, of course. He's also called her without result and even wanted to come here, but it's better if he stays in Boston. She had a wild idea she could stay with him over the summer. And that he'd take her on tour with his band. I don't know. Maybe she'll turn up at his place."

"That is a wild idea," Jack said. "She's resourceful."

"Too much at times," Carrie agreed. "Tim isn't a bad guy. He loves Sophie, and they have a good relationship, but he's not around much. He leaves her upbringing to me, which usually makes me the villain. He always did, even when we were married."

"That's not exactly fair."

"It isn't, but that's how things work out sometimes." She took a sip of tea. "You have a way with Sophie, Jack. I've noticed."

"Thanks. She's a sweetheart. I love spending time with her."

Carrie thought he would have mentioned by now if he was a father, but she decided to ask anyway. "Do you have any children?"

He shook his head, staring at the table. "I was married for a while and wanted to start a family. But my wife was never ready. Which turned out to be a good thing in the long run. When you get divorced, kids complicate things, right?"

"It was messy at first," she agreed, thinking back to all the times she and Tim disagreed about sharing weekends and holidays, or even child support, which was rarely on time. "But we both want the best for Sophie and can usually put our differences aside."

"The police will find her, Carrie. They're professionals. And you're persistent, remember? You're a positive thinker."

His reminder echoed their conversation over the salt and pepper shakers. It felt like years ago, instead of a few hours.

"Easy to say, harder to do right now," she admitted. She took a sip of tea and met his gaze over the edge of the mug.

"I'm sure." His dark eyes filled with concern and understanding. "While driving around, I remembered all the dumb stunts I pulled as a kid. My father would tear his hair out, what was left of it."

"Did you ever disappear for hours without letting anyone know where you were?"

Jack nodded with a solemn expression. "Ashamed to admit it, but yes, I did. I was about Sophie's age, maybe a little older. I took a train into the city with my buddies, and we lost track of time and didn't have enough money to get home. We were too scared of what our parents would do to call for help. After that, my folks didn't let me out of my room until I was like …twenty-five?"

"That explains a lot." She smiled briefly, and he smiled back, looking grateful to have distracted her for a moment.

"Will you get some rest after you finish that tea?"

"I'll get comfortable down here somewhere. Brooke will be back soon. And Sophie might be, too."

Her prediction sounded hopeless, even to her own ears, but he answered with a gentle smile as he headed for the door.

"Hold a good thought."

Carrie followed him. She wanted to believe him, but for some reason, her eyes filled with tears.

"Hey, don't cry. It's going to be okay." Jack put his arms around her, and she stepped into his warm embrace. He held her tight, in a sweet, solid, comforting hug, the type she hadn't felt for a long time. From anyone.

Carrie rested her cheek on his solid shoulder, squeezing her eyes shut, willing herself not to cry.

She felt his hand on her hair, the touch light and comforting. "I know you can't help worrying, but don't let the worst scenarios run away with you. Okay?"

He pulled back to look into her eyes, and she nodded.

"You're right. I'm not thinking straight anymore."

He caught her gaze and held it. They were barely a breath apart. She felt sure he was going to kiss her, and she wanted him to. She closed her eyes and felt him move closer. He dropped a soft kiss on her forehead, then stepped back.

Carrie opened her eyes, and he smiled softly. "I'd do that for real, but there must be some rule about kissing your boss under adverse circumstances?"

His explanation made her smile. As a gentleman, he wouldn't take advantage of her vulnerable state. Which she found sweet.

"There might be a rule, but I won't hold it against you."

"Good to know." He laughed softly and stepped outside.

Carrie was reluctant to see him go. She felt a chill from the night air and the absence of his nearness.

"Call me if there's news. Or if you want company. And close your eyes a few minutes, even if you're sure you can't sleep?"

"I'll try." She closed the door and watched him disappear into the darkness.

She sighed and headed for the living room. There was nothing to do now but wait. Wait and worry.

The phone rang, startling Carrie awake. She'd fallen asleep in an armchair in the living room. She grabbed the phone and nearly rolled onto the floor.

The number was unknown to her, and she prayed it was news of Sophie. *Good* news.

"This is Carrie Duffy," she answered breathlessly.

"Sorry to bother you so early, but your daughter is here. She wants to talk to you."

Carrie pressed the phone to her ear, her hand shaking.

"Hi, Mom," Sophie greeted her in a meek tone.

"Sophie? Thank God! Are you all right? Where are you?"

"At a friend's house. A girl from art class. Can you come pick me up? Please?"

"What a question. I'm on my way." Carrie ran into the kitchen, her bare feet padding on the wooden floor. "Where am I going? Give me an address."

She hopped on one leg, jamming a shoe on her foot and holding the phone with the other hand.

"I'm not sure. Here's Hannah's dad. He'll tell you."

Carrie heard the man's voice again. Had he given his name? She was foggy-headed and couldn't remember.

"I can bring Sophie home if you like. It's no trouble."

"Thanks, I'm almost out the door. Can I have your address, please?"

She grabbed a pen and pad off the counter as he gave an address on the north end of the island. An area known for old, expensive houses on waterfront properties.

Sophie had landed in the lap of luxury, hadn't she? The little squirt.

"I'll be right there," Carrie spoke as she located her car keys and purse. "We can talk about this later, of course. But how did Sophie end up there? Did she sleepover and no one remembered to tell me?"

She hadn't meant to blame him, but after she finished, she knew it sounded like she did. She was tired and half-sick from worry. For goodness sake, why hadn't someone called her last night and put her out of her misery?

"I had no idea she was here. Honestly. The girls cooked up a scheme, and Hannah hid Sophie on my boat. I just found out a few minutes ago when I caught Hannah sneaking out with some food."

"I'm sorry... I sounded so sharp. Please forgive me."

"Of course. I can only imagine what you've been through," Hannah's father said. "No apology necessary. I'd feel the same."

"Thanks for understanding," Carrie said sincerely. They said goodbye, and the first thing she did was send a quick text to her ex-husband, Tim, to let him know Sophie was safe. Then she left a note for Brooke and her mother. With any luck, she'd be back with Sophie before they woke up.

She started her little SUV and headed for the address jotted on the slip of paper, giddy with happiness, relief, and gratitude. Luckily, the roads were empty. It was hard to focus on driving.

She'd once heard that if you only say one prayer, it should be, "Thank you." She kept repeating the words in her head, like a chorus. A happy chorus, as opposed to one the last night, which was almost as brief, "Please, God, let Sophie be all right."

Nineteen

Sunrise tinted the horizon with a golden glow, though most of the landscape she passed—stretches of marshes, tall, golden grass, and the rocky cliffs that rimmed the coast—remained in deep shadow. Carrie took a breath of cool morning air, feeling she might burst into tears again from sheer relief.

Sophie was safe. That was all that mattered.

She had gone off with a new friend, apparently. Hannah Something. And, for some reason, had hidden overnight in a boat. She was trying to run away, as Carrie had speculated. The realization made her heart skip a beat. Thank heaven she'd been found before her plan went too far.

Carrie found the address and turned down a private road, brambly woods on either side. A big house came into view, a classic colonial with high columns and a wide front porch that overlooked a sloping lawn and a magnificent ocean view.

A private beach edged the property, and Carrie saw a large cabin cruiser tied at a dock. The type of boat with a full galley, couches for socializing and entertainment, and several sleeping areas. Sophie had spent the night in style, hadn't she?

A shiny convertible was parked near the house, alongside a fancy SUV. She noticed the name "Bolton" on a brass marker at the foot of a brick path and realized Sophie's new friend belonged to one of the island's wealthiest families.

Carrie had no time to ponder that revelation. A man came out the front door, followed by a girl about Sophie's age.

His reddish-brown hair was cut short and his blue polo shirt and khaki shorts looked a bit rumpled. He held a coffee mug and squinted into the sunlight. It was barely six a.m. She suddenly realized she'd slept in her clothes and had to look like a dog's breakfast. With good reason, Carrie knew.

"That was fast," Hannah's father said.

"I'm lucky I didn't get a ticket," she agreed. "But it's early for the police to hide in the bushes with speed guns."

Which was a common practice on the island, especially near the public beaches, much to the consternation of tourists who didn't know the trick.

"I'm sure the police would have given you a pass this time," he said with a kind smile.

As Carrie walked up the porch steps, Hannah's father stepped out of the shadows. She met his bright blue eyes and realized she knew him. They'd been in the same year at school.

"Doug Bolton...I'm sorry, I was so distracted about Sophie, I didn't recognize you."

"That's okay. Sophie said her last name was Staub. When you answered the phone this morning, I thought you said Duffy. I was a little confused but had a feeling it was you."

"Here I am, in all my anxious, exhausted mom glory." Carrie

shrugged, feeling even more self-conscious about her bedraggled appearance.

She'd never been friends with Doug Bolton in school, but they'd been in a few classes together. He was in the popular group. The guys were all athletes, and the girls, cheerleaders. They were the kids who got cars as soon as they could drive and gave rowdy parties at their fancy houses—mostly when parents weren't home.

Carrie and her friends, rungs lower on the social food chain, would hear the gossip in the hallway, but were never invited. She was surprised at his warm greeting, but they were grown-ups now, and all that silliness was in the past.

"Would you like to come in for coffee?"

"It's nice of you to offer. But I'll just grab Sophie and head home. We've bothered you enough, and I need to lecture her for about three hours before I go to work."

She wasn't sure if she should smother Sophie with kisses or take away her every electronic device and ground her for life. A little of both, she decided.

He smiled at her wry humor. "Some other time then. The girls are in the kitchen, making smoothies. Come in a minute. I'll tell her you're here."

He politely held the door open as she stepped into a large entranceway with a high ceiling and a tiled floor. A long staircase led to the upper floors, and a balcony hallway circled the space above.

He headed down a hall where Carrie glimpsed a kitchen and heard a blender whirr. "Sophie's mom is here. It's time for her to go," she heard Doug say over the noise.

He quickly returned, though the noise had not stopped. "She'll be right out. Hannah insists on sending her with breakfast." He rolled his eyes. "I'm very sorry for my daughter's part in this. It was very irresponsible, to say the least. She'll be lectured, too," he promised.

Carrie thought it was nice of him to say. Some parents would have blamed it all on Sophie. "Of course. But please don't forget, it was really Sophie's fault."

Before he could answer, the girls appeared. Hannah led the way, wearing a big t-shirt that said "Super Woman"; pink pajama shorts underneath hung on her lithe build. Her honey-blond hair was piled on her head in what Sophie called a "messy bun." She met Carrie's gaze with a shy smile.

Sophie walked behind her new friend but couldn't hide for long. Her head was bowed as she avoided her mother's gaze.

"Hey, Soph'. What's up?" Carrie greeted her daughter in as calm a tone as she could manage.

"Hi, Mom ... I'm really sorry."

"I hope so. Please thank Mr. Bolton for having you here. Even though he didn't know it," she added in a sharper tone.

"Thanks, Mr. Bolton," Sophie mumbled.

"You're welcome, Sophie. We'll see you soon, okay?"

Carrie was relieved to hear him say that. He could have decided she was too troublesome to be friends with his daughter.

"Thank you," Sophie repeated. She gazed at Hannah as if she was being dragged to a firing squad. "Bye, Hannah."

"Text me." Hannah hugged Sophie and handed her a travel mug. "Don't forget your smoothie."

Carrie steered her to the door. "Thanks again, Doug. I appreciate your help."

"It was great to see you. I hope we can catch up soon."

She smiled but didn't reply. She didn't think there was much she and Doug Bolton needed to catch up on. He was just being polite. But she had to admit, he'd turned out a lot nicer than she would have predicted.

* * *

They drove home in silence. Sophie sipped the smoothie and gazed out the passenger side window.

"Ready to tell me what happened? And why you disappeared and made us crazy with worry all night?" Carrie said finally.

"There's not too much to tell."

"Humor me," Carrie coaxed.

"Let's see...I met Hannah at the art class. You told me to make new friends, right?"

Carrie could have laughed out loud. "I did," she agreed.

"Hannah was like the coolest girl there, and she sat next to me when she came in." Sophie sounded proud of the honor. "She's stuck here, too. Visiting her grandparents. I told her I wanted to see my friends this weekend, but you won't let me take the ferry."

Take the ferry alone, Carrie nearly interrupted with all the reasons she'd made that rule but held her tongue.

"We figured if I hid on her dad's boat overnight, I could get a ferry today and find a bus or something from Rockport to the city. I knew you'd be mad, but I'd be with my friends by the time you figured it out. I was going to ask Dad if he'd take me with him this summer. Instead of being dragged back here."

The last part made it sound like she was an escaped prisoner being returned to a maximum-security jail.

"Your dad was sick with worry, too. You need to call him as soon as we get home." Tim would have never agreed to it, but the thought of Sophie traveling with her father's band was mind-boggling. "I guess I spoiled your plan."

"Yeah, you did." Sophie's tone was glum. "Mr. Bolton did, actually."

"True. I've got to send that man flowers or something." She glanced at Sophie. "Didn't you realize how worried I'd be? And your aunts and Grandma and your father? The police were looking for you all night. I didn't sleep one minute. I thought something awful happened to you."

Carrie had not wanted to get overly emotional or pile Sophie with guilt. That was the wrong way to encourage her to open up and talk honestly. But part of her couldn't help it.

Sophie avoided her gaze. "I guess I wasn't thinking of all that, Mom. I just want to like...go home. I miss my friends, and it's so boring here. It's like being stuck on a desert island."

Carrie nearly jumped in with all reasons why they were lucky to be on Haven Island, surrounded by the blue ocean and beautiful landscape. Instead of dirty, noisy Medford. But Sophie didn't appreciate any of that and didn't realize many people would have switched places with her in a heartbeat.

"I'm sorry you've been so upset. I knew that you missed your friends, but I never thought you'd go to such extremes. I know I've been very busy with the café since Grandma got sick. I should have paid more attention to your feelings," she admitted. "I thought you'd get used to the island."

Sophie listened to Carrie's apology with a contrite expression, but suddenly exploded. "That's just it, Mom. I don't want to get used to it. I don't want to live here forever. But you sound like we're going to, whether I like it or not."

"Is that what you're afraid of?" Sophie met her glance and nodded in reply, her arms crossed tightly over her chest.

"Oh, honey—that's not the plan. Not at all."

Carrie paused, weighing out the pros and cons of putting her cards on the table, and decided it was best to be totally honest with Sophie.

"You know I haven't been able to find a manager, and we need to stay until I do. But I'm also looking for a new job. Hopefully it will be in Boston," she clarified, knowing she might need to widen the search. "But we won't stay here any longer than the summer. That's my deadline. I promise you."

"What if you don't find a new job by then?"

"I'll find something. It may not be perfect, but we will leave and get back to our own lives. If something unexpected pops up, we'll talk it through." Too little talking and not enough listening had caused this problem, Carrie realized. "Does that make you feel any better?"

"I guess so." Sophie tugged at the hem of her hoody.

"One more thing," Carrie added in a serious tone as they pulled into the driveway and she parked the car.

"Yes?" Sophie was alert, expecting to be scolded again, Carrie suspected.

"Do you know that you are absolutely the most precious thing in the world to me? I know I'm not perfect, but I'd do anything for you."

Sophie slowly smiled and met her glance, then looked away. "I'm not perfect either," she admitted. "I love you, too, Mom."

"Then how about a hug? Feels like it's been ages." Carrie turned and opened her arms, and Sophie eagerly hugged her tight. Carrie stroked Sophie's hair and kissed her cheek, savoring the feeling. And brushing aside fragments of the horrifying worries that had plagued her.

"Before we go inside, we need to call your dad. He's already left three messages. And there will be consequences for this stunt. Your father and I will figure it out."

Sophie sighed. "I was wondering when we'd get to that."

Tim was elated to hear his daughter's voice. Carrie doubted he'd have any suggestions for appropriate "consequences," but they agreed to discuss it that night. He was leaving in a few hours for the tour and sounded relieved that he didn't need to change his plans and come to Haven instead.

Carrie was also relieved, though part of her wished she had a partner who was more involved in raising Sophie. Maybe a crazy stunt like running away wouldn't have happened.

Carrie led the way to the back door. "Grandma and Aunt Brooke probably have a brass band in there to greet you. Not that you deserve it, young lady," she added quickly.

Carrie's mouth twitched with a grin. She knew she should act sterner, but she couldn't help being indescribably relieved.

There were no musicians, but Brooke and Carrie's mother swamped Sophie with hugs and kisses as she walked into the kitchen, flapping around her like two fussy hens.

"I bet you haven't eaten for hours. How about some French toast?" Gena said, naming Sophie's favorite breakfast.

"She just had a smoothie in the car," Carrie replied.

"I'd love some French toast, Grandma," Sophie replied with dramatic flare. "I'm absolutely starving."

"You poor thing. Were you out in the cold all night? Brooke, run Sophie a hot bath while I make her breakfast," her mom called as she set a skillet on the stove.

"It's eighty degrees out, Mom. She doesn't need a hot bath," Carrie said.

"I didn't sleep outside, Grandma. I slept on a boat."

"A boat?" Her mother turned from the refrigerator, her arms filled with ingredients—eggs, butter, milk. "For goodness sakes, how did that happen?"

"It's quite a story." Carrie glanced at her daughter. "Need any help, Mom?"

"I'm fine, honey. You sit. You look awful," Gena said cheerfully.

"Gee, thanks," Carrie mumbled.

Her mother had not cooked since her heart procedure, except to make a sandwich or such. French toast was a step up in effort, but Carrie was too tired to take over.

Brooke brought Carrie a mug of coffee and set it down under her nose. Carrie thanked her, thinking she'd need the entire pot to wake up. She was even too tired to add her two cents to the story Sophie told about her adventure.

When Sophie finished, Gena set a heaping plate of French toast in front of her. "I'm sure it seemed like a harmless idea. Maybe even fun. But you had us all worried sick. I hope you learned a lesson, dear."

Sophie's expression was contrite. "I did, Grandma. Totally. I won't do anything like that again."

"You were lucky to end up in a luxury cabin cruiser," Brooke said.

"Wasn't she?" Carrie sipped her coffee, ready for another cup. "Guess who owns it—Doug Bolton."

"A Bolton. That makes sense." Carrie's mother sat at the table next to Sophie. "I don't remember a Doug."

"He was in my year at school. Captain of the lacrosse team, and all-around Mr. Popular," Carrie recounted. "I was much lower on the food chain."

Sophie laughed. "Funny, Mom."

"It's true. Everyone knows the pecking order. But he turned out to be a really nice guy. He didn't even seem annoyed at the stunt Sophie pulled. I thought he'd discourage the girls from seeing each other, considering all the trouble they cooked up. But he was very understanding and gracious."

Sophie looked alarmed. "Not see Hannah? She's like my new best friend."

They'd already exchanged a few texts, Carrie had noticed. At least the nightmare had a silver lining.

"I'm glad you made a friend. Next time, do it the normal way. Like invite the girl for a sleepover," Carrie said.

"I know who Doug Bolton is," Brooke cut in. "He doesn't live on the island full-time. I bet his house is spectacular."

Carrie peered at her over the rim of her mug. "Let's just say the cabin cruiser didn't look out of place docked there."

Gena raised her eyebrows. "Oh, I know who he is now. I heard he just got divorced. Did he remember you from school, Carrie?"

It wasn't the question; it was the way she asked it. Carrie sat back and smirked. "What's that supposed to mean?"

Her mother shrugged. "Just curious."

"Yes, he remembered me," Carrie answered reluctantly. "Though I don't know why. We barely said two words to each other there. And we didn't discuss his marital status this morning, or have any reason to," she said pointedly. "Please don't get ideas, Mom."

Her mother offered an innocent look. "What ideas would I have ... about an eligible, successful man your age from a wealthy family who you say is a 'nice guy'? Oh, and has a daughter the same age as Sophie. You didn't say if he was good-looking, but if he was so popular, he must be, right?"

Carrie gave her a look. "I liked it better when you were too overworked and stressed to poke around in my social life."

"I'm merely pointing out a possibility. Right, Brooke? You always say you'd date more, but you can't meet anybody nice."

Her sister looked put on the spot. "We get the point, Mom."

"Yes, we do," Carrie added. Her phone sounded, and she was glad for the interruption.

It was Jack. Seeing his name on the screen pleased her. She wanted to talk to him but hoped he wasn't calling to report a crisis at the café. If that were the case, her hair might go on fire.

"Hey, Jack. What's up?"

"I heard Sophie is safe and sound. I stopped by before I left for work. How is she doing?"

"She's perfectly fine. Stuffing herself with French toast."

Sophie perked up, noticing that she was being talked about. "Is that Jack? Can I say hello?"

"Do you have a minute? She wants to talk to you."

"Absolutely, put her on."

Carrie handed Sophie the phone. She could only hear half the conversation, but it was easy to figure out the rest. "Yes, I'm fine, no worries... I slept in a boat. It's sort of a long story." He said something that made her laugh, and then she looked serious. "Yes,

I know. I didn't mean for everyone to worry. It was a dumb move...All right, see you later, Jack."

When Carrie took the phone back, he said, "She slept in a boat? Very resourceful."

"Wasn't it? I'm still a basket case. Thanks for checking in about her."

Carrie realized she should have texted him when she got the news. He'd been so sweet and supportive last night and sincerely concerned about Sophie, riding around the island for hours on his motorcycle, looking for her. She recalled how he'd made her a cup of tea and, afterward, their warm embrace and chaste kiss. Intended to comfort her, of course, though she knew other emotions were brewing there, too.

He'd stayed up as late as she had and must be tired today, too. But he'd still opened the café on time and was watching over things.

"It must be crazy there," she said, remembering it was Saturday. "I'll be in soon."

"Everything is under control. The new waitress jumped right in. She's sharp, too."

Carrie felt a jolt. "Mackenzie! I forgot all about her. She can't start without me there—"

"She's doing fine," Jack cut in. "Dory is showing her what's what. Take the day off. I bet you didn't get any sleep last night."

Maybe she had caught an hour or so, against her will, but nothing more. Her head felt foggy, despite the coffee.

Her mother had overheard the conversation. "You look like a zombie, dear. Get some rest. Jack can handle things."

"Since everyone is ganging up on me, I guess I will catch some sleep. I'll see you later. Thanks for covering."

"Not a problem. Sweet dreams," Jack added in a teasing tone.

As she ended the call, she wondered why that made her smile. Their relationship felt different today. She wasn't sure why, or even if it was a good thing.

Like it or not, the pot on the back burner was starting to boil. Carrie wasn't sure how much longer she could keep a lid on it and was too tired to figure that out.

Twenty

"Oh, blast...The pie isn't half done, and I still need to change my clothes and comb out my hair. Richard's ferry will be in soon."

Aunt Lila closed the oven door and stared at Tess in dismay. Tess's cousin Richard was coming. He'd called last night and told his mother he'd arrive on the midday ferry. Lila had been both elated and stressed by the surprise. He visited so rarely, she wanted everything to be perfect. She got up at dawn to prepare the house and cook.

Tess helped, cleaning inside and out, and changing the linens in the guest bedroom. Then she headed to the convenience store near the village for a few ingredients her aunt didn't have on hand, including a container of heavy cream to top the strawberry rhubarb pie she was baking, Lila's son's favorite.

"I'll pick him up, Aunt Lila. You'll have plenty of time to get dressed and do whatever you need to do."

Her aunt looked relieved and set the oven timer again. "Thank you, dear. That's a big help. You'd better leave right away. I don't want him to wait."

Tess had more than enough time to reach the ferry station but appeased her aunt by heading back to the truck. Honey wanted to come with her, but she told her to stay. "You keep Lila company. I don't think Richard likes dogs," she recalled.

As she drove toward the harbor, Tess tried to remember the last time she'd seen her cousin. He'd come with her aunt once on visiting day while Tess was in a juvenile detention center.

He'd hardly looked at her and offered only a word or two. He'd mainly come to escort his mother. But those visiting sessions were unnatural and tense for everyone. Tess usually felt more depressed after seeing her aunt than she did before. No one could be blamed for acting awkward under those circumstances.

The truth was, she'd never had a close relationship with Richard, though they'd been tossed together while growing up. If it wasn't for her aunt, she doubted he'd have anything to do with her. Not out of malice, but because their lives were different and their ties were not strong.

If she stayed at the farm, she'd see him often, on weekend visits like this one and on holidays, when her aunt loved bringing people together. Perhaps they could have a better relationship now that she was starting a new chapter in her life. They both loved Lila, and maybe Richard drew some comfort from knowing Tess was looking after his mother. Tess was curious to see him and find out if they could get to know each other on new terms.

Though she hadn't seen Richard in years, her aunt had plenty of photos of him around the house, and Tess recognized him easily, coming down the walkway from the ferry. She waved and walked toward him.

"Tess, it's been a long time. Good to see you," Richard leaned over and gave her a brief hug.

He was a tall man, with fair, wispy hair already thin on top, though he was only in his early thirties. He had his mother's pleasant, round face and blue eyes.

"Good to see you, too. How was the ferry ride?"

"I caught calm weather, luckily." Once inside the truck, he said. "You look well. Visiting the farm agrees with you."

"It's been great." *And more than a visit,* she nearly added.

She wondered if her aunt had told him she wanted Tess to take over the deed. Tess got the feeling he was unaware of his mother's wishes.

"I'm sorry about your father," he said. "I meant to call or send a card. I know you were never close to him, especially after you left Haven. But it's hard to lose a parent, no matter what."

Tess glanced at him. "It was hard. In a different way for me than most people, I guess."

It was the day she had to give up any remaining hope their relationship could ever change.

"Are you still in the insurance business?" Last she'd heard, Richard was an executive at a well-known firm based in Hartford, Connecticut. He'd graduated with a Master's in business and started there right after college, climbing quite a few rungs up the ladder in the years since.

"Yes, still in the race. Bigger offices, better titles, more meetings..."

"Sounds like a lot of pressure." Tess searched for the right response. The first word that came to mind was "soul-crushing." She'd go mad if she ever had to live that life.

"It's fine, for now. But I won't stay there forever. I've been thinking of going into real estate."

"That sounds...exciting." She knew even less about real estate than insurance, but he sounded excited about the idea.

"I'm ready for a change. I mean, why not make a heap of money while you're still young enough to enjoy it? Instead of waiting for investments and all that when you retire?"

He smiled, and Tess smiled back. It wasn't that she disagreed with his theory; she just didn't think that way, in terms of making "a heap of money."

"There's your mom," she said as the farmhouse came into view. "She's so happy to see you, she's jumping out of her shoes."

Her aunt waved from the porch as they pulled up. Lila wore her best dress, along with earrings and lipstick. Tess had found her at the stove that morning with her hair pinned up, but it was combed out now in a fluffy hairdo.

Richard smiled fondly. "I'm happy to see her, too. I don't come home often enough."

Tess watched their reunion from the truck. She wasn't sure why she hesitated. To give them a few moments of privacy, she told herself. But more because Lila's eyes were so bright with love, it would be hard to stand there feeling like a third wheel while they embraced.

Not that Lila loved her one atomic particle less because of Richard. Tess wasn't jealous. But even the warmest and most wonderful aunt like Lila was not her mother, and Tess felt a hollow place inside, reminded of that.

***

As Carrie expected, her ex-husband Tim failed to offer any creative suggestions for disciplining Sophie, except to say she should be grounded, and her phone and laptop should be taken away for a few days. Carrie agreed, and Sophie stayed at home on Saturday—without her devices.

The truth was her daughter was exhausted and napped most of the day. She read a Harry Potter novel, then wheedled her way into watching a movie that evening, snuggled with her grandmother on the couch.

It was a touching sight, and when Carrie found them there, she couldn't order Sophie back to her room. As Sophie pointed out, the TV was her grandmother's electronic device and, therefore, acceptable. Carrie knew when she was beaten and cuddled on the other side of her daughter for the rest of *Forrest Gump*, an amusing film with a worthy message, she thought.

As the credits rolled, a text appeared from an unfamiliar number. She was surprised to see a message from Doug Bolton.

Sorry to bother you so late, Carrie. Hannah would not let me rest until I got in touch. We're going out on the boat tomorrow morning, and we'd love to have Sophie join us.

While Carrie composed a polite decline in her head, Sophie read the invitation over her shoulder. "Can I go, Mom? Please? I know I'm grounded, but if you say I can't go, Hannah might think I don't want to be her friend and never ask me again…"

"I doubt that, Sophie. I'm sure Hannah and her dad will understand."

"Can't I *please* go with them, just a little while, and I'll stay grounded for the rest of the week, and even extra? For *two* weeks," she added, doubling the term Carrie had assigned.

"You don't even like boats. You get seasick, remember?"

"That was the stupid ferry. Mr. Bolton's boat is super cool. I bet it just glides on the water."

Carrie had a feeling she was right but didn't agree aloud. Her mother returned from the kitchen, carrying a mug of tea. She glanced from Carrie's stern expression to Sophie, who was kneeling on the couch in a begging pose. "What's gliding on the water?"

"My friend invited me to go on her dad's boat tomorrow. It's my only chance, Grandma. She may never ask me again."

"The problem is that she's grounded," Carrie stated flatly.

Sophie flopped on the couch and hugged a pillow to her chest. "The one time I get invited to do something fun around here, I can't go." Her eyes were glassy, tears about to fall.

Gena met Carrie's gaze. She looked about to say something, then sat down in the armchair and sipped her tea. Carrie knew she sided with Sophie. Carrie was putting up a stern front, but she *had* told Sophie to make new friends, and Sophie did seem sorry for the stunt she'd pulled.

And she was missing all the end-of-the-year parties with her classmates this weekend. At least the outing would give her something to brag about when she spoke to her friends back home.

"All right, I guess you can go. Consider it a 'get of out of jail free' card for the day. You're still grounded for the rest of the week, plus one," she added.

Sophie sprang up from the couch, her tearful expression transformed into a huge smile. She squeezed Carrie in a hug. "Thank you, Mom. Thank you *sooo* much."

Carrie laughed at the mood flip. "I'm sure Mr. Bolton wants to leave early. Go up and get ready for bed."

"Goodnight, Mommy. Thank you again," Sophie gave Carrie a kiss on the cheek. "Night, Grandma," she added, kissing her grandmother's cheek, too.

Gena smiled. "Sleep tight, sweetie. Don't let the bedbugs bite."

Sophie shivered. "Did they really have bedbugs in the old days, Grandma? Ugh…"

Carrie and her mother laughed.

Twenty-One

It was late afternoon and the café was quiet when Carrie spotted Sophie and Hannah walk in, followed by Doug Bolton. The girls looked worn out but happy. Doug looked windblown, tan, and very much the seasoned boater in a white polo shirt, khaki shorts, and dark sunglasses.

Carrie made her way across the dining room to greet them. "Ahoy, sailors. How was your day?"

"It was awesome. We even went tubing," Sophie reported.

Not nearly as demanding of athletic ability as water skiing, tubing delivered the thrill of being dragged through the water by a motorboat while sitting in, or hanging on to, a big inner tube.

"Wearing life jackets the whole time," Doug assured her.

Carrie was happy to hear that. Sophie was not the best swimmer, but maybe that would change this summer.

"Let me find a table. You can have a bite to eat," Carrie offered.

"That's all right. I gave the girls lunch on the boat. I dropped Sophie off so you wouldn't have to drive out to my place again."

Considerate, she thought. Especially since it was hard to get Sophie from A to B while she was working. He'd been so thoughtful. Carrie wanted to reciprocate.

"Please stay. Even if you don't want lunch, the girls can have ice cream. I insist."

"Want to meet Jack, the cook? He's really cool. He'll let us make shakes or something," Sophie told Hannah.

That was all Jack needed, two tween-agers bugging him.

Carrie rested her hand on Sophie's shoulder. "The kitchen is a little too busy for you to go back there, honey. Let's find a table, and I'll put the orders in."

Carrie led the group to a table on the deck with a view of the harbor. Despite the afternoon sun, it was shady and cool beneath the awning.

The girls decided quickly, two chocolate shakes

Carrie met Doug's glance. "Can I get you something, Doug? Would you like a menu?"

He smiled and slipped off his sunglasses. His eyes were very blue. She hadn't remembered that. "An iced coffee would be perfect."

"I'll send it right out."

"Thanks...and I hope you have a minute to join us?"

She was surprised at the question but decided he just wanted to be friendly. When kids made new friends, she also liked to get to know the parents a bit.

"I'll try," she promised as she headed back inside.

A few minutes later, Carrie saw Dory serve the shakes and iced coffee. Carrie glanced at her watch. She had a few minutes before the staff started the daily closing-up routine, so she returned to the table.

Doug sat alone, sipping his coffee. Sophie and Hannah had already drained the fountain glasses, and stood at the deck railing, huddled together and giggling.

"They've been like that all day," he reported. "I've never heard so much giggling."

"Sophie doesn't usually make friends this quickly," Carrie confided. "But she misses her school friends. It's good to see her with a girl her own age."

"The same for Hannah. She's here for the summer visiting my family. We live in Marblehead," he said, naming an exclusive town on the Cape Ann peninsula, west of Rockport. "I handle the accounting for the family business, and I'm back and forth in the summer to my office in Boston. This is the first year Hannah is staying for the season. She was horrified to leave her friends at home. I'm so happy she and Sophie found each other."

She heard the relief in his voice. He seemed a concerned, involved father. "Sophie mentioned her grandmother's heart problem and how you decided to stay. How is your mother doing?"

"Very well. Some days, you'd never know she was so sick. She needs to take it slow a few more weeks, but she should be good as new by the end of the summer."

"That's great. I'm sure you've been a big help here. I know the Blue Sky and Bolton's have always been rivals," he added.

"Like the Red Sox and Yankees," she agreed with a grin.

"But I always loved this place," he replied. "It still has that special charm. I've always loved the food here, too. But don't tell anyone in my family I said that. They toss traitors in the fry vat."

"Your secret's safe," Carrie replied with a smile.

The girls returned. "Ready to go, Hannah? We're due at Grandma's soon. Family barbeque," he explained. She imagined there were many; he had a few siblings, she recalled.

Hannah stood close to Sophie and nudged her. "Just ask her. Before I go," she whispered.

Before Carrie could ask what was going on, Sophie said, "I know I'm still grounded. But could I please go to sailing camp with Hannah? You're trying to find something for me to do. And I don't like art class…And neither does Hannah."

Carrie and Doug glanced at each other. Carrie felt put on the spot, though the idea made sense. "I'll look into it."

Sophie smiled. "Is that better than, 'We'll see'?"

Doug laughed. "Good question." He met Carrie's gaze. "The sailing group is based at Bolton's dock. It's been there for years. It's very safe and well run. Here's the link to the website," he added, his phone in hand. "I want Hannah to learn how to sail, but I don't have the time to teach her."

"I haven't been on a sailboat in years. Since my father died, I guess. He taught all of us, but I loved it the best. I never thought Sophie was interested," she said, glancing at her daughter.

Her father loved to be on the water whenever he could untie his apron and escape the café. He'd owned two boats, a small daysailer and a skiff with a motor for fishing. Both now sat behind the garage on wooden horses, covered with tarps. Sailing was a good skill for Sophie to master. It would give her confidence, Carrie thought.

"It looks fun. I really want to try," Sophie said.

Carrie smiled at her. "I'm on it. You'll have an answer soon," she promised, already half-sold on the idea.

"Thank you, Mr. Bolton, for taking me on your boat," Sophie said with perfect politeness.

"Any time. We'll make a sailor out of you before the summer is done."

"I hope so." She looked at Carrie, hands folded in a prayerful pose.

Carrie rolled her eyes and laughed. "Oh brother…"

Doug laughed as well and said goodbye while Sophie and Hannah bumped fists in victory and made plans to text all night.

"See you soon, Carrie." Doug waved as he and Hannah left.

Carrie waved back, wondering why he was so nice to her. *Trying to prove that he isn't that stuck-up, popular guy from high school? Maybe you never really knew him back then, and this is what he's always been like?*

She hadn't noticed Jack standing behind the counter until she turned to face him. "Was that the guy who owns the boat where Sophie hid out?"

"That's him. Sophie and his daughter became instant BFFs. They were out on the boat today. She might take sailing lessons with Hannah, too. It will give her something productive to do."

Jack nodded. "He seemed very friendly."

"We were in high school together. He was in the preppy, popular group. I was not," she admitted.

"Not surprised. Polo shirt with a flipped-up collar? Give me a break."

Did Doug flip up the collar of his shirt? Carrie hadn't noticed . . . then wondered why Jack had. He fussed with the soda machine. Dory reported it was on the blink. He was so grumpy this afternoon. Tired, probably.

She'd offer him some time off. But she'd wait until he was in a better mood. He had a bee in his bonnet about something.

* * *

Richard was grateful for his mother's efforts to cook his favorite dishes and fuss over his every need. They urged Tess to come with them to the beach and the village, but she gave them time on their own to visit. Richard had come to see his mom, and she was sure Lila loved having him to herself, even if she'd never say it. Tess had plenty to do on the farm and was happy to steer clear of public places.

On Sunday morning, Richard took his mother to church, and the rest of the day passed quickly, with a big midday meal Lila had prepared. Richard had to leave on an early evening ferry. Lila tried to persuade him to stay longer, but he needed to be in the office Monday morning.

"I'll be back soon, Mom," he promised.

Lila looked doubtful.

"I hope so. It's so lovely here in the summer. I can't think of any place nicer a person could be."

Tess could tell she already missed him, and her heart went out to her aunt. After helping in the kitchen, Tess went outside to check the animals with Honey at her heels.

She was at the hen house when the dog barked. She turned to find her cousin approaching. "Calm down, Honey. It's just Richard," she scolded the dog. "I don't know why she's acting like that. She's usually very friendly."

"Dogs don't like me. I don't know what it is," he admitted in a humorous tone. "Maybe they can tell I'm a cat person."

"That would do it," Tess agreed with a grin.

He watched her secure the coop and lock the gate. "It's so peaceful here. I wish I could stay longer."

"Your mother would be happy to hear that. You'll have to come back soon, like she said."

"I will, but it's good to know you're here with her now. I can see you take good care of her."

"I think she takes care of me," Tess said honestly. "I guess we watch out for each other."

"She's getting older, Tess. I saw it this visit. She's not as strong as she used to be." Tess headed for the goat pen, and he followed. "She told me that she wants to sign the deed to the farm over to you, but you're not sure if you should take it."

Tess was surprised by the sharp pivot in the conversation. She kept her eyes on her tasks. "I want to see how the summer goes."

"I think that's wise. And realistic," he added. "She also told me about the vandalism. I wondered why the side of the barn was painted two shades of red," he said, striking a lighter note.

The fresh paint Tess bought had covered the foul words, but it was hard to match the old color that was faded and weathered.

"I'll fix that when I have time," she explained.

"I'm sure you will. You've made some real improvements to the property in a short time. But we can already see that staying is not safe. Maybe it's unfair, but people are still angry, and that puts you at risk. And my mother." His tone was concerned. "I'm not blaming you, Tess. But it is what is."

His tone was matter-of-fact, and Tess knew what he said was true. She worried about her aunt, too.

"You think I should leave? Is that what you're saying?"

"I can't tell you what to do. But I know how persuasive my

mother can be. She thinks people here will accept you someday. But they won't. They'll make your life miserable. And hers. Is that what you want, after all she's done for you?"

"Of course not," Tess said quickly. "She's done more for me than anyone. Of course, I'm concerned about her."

"I think she still feels she could have saved you from going to jail. As impossible as that sounds now." Did that mean he believed she was guilty? Tess thought it did. "Giving you the land is her way of making up for that failing, real or imagined. Personally, I wouldn't feel comfortable accepting such a grand gift under those circumstances."

Tess caught his gaze, her body tense with the instinct to defend herself and remind him that her father should have left her, his only child, the farm. Lila wanted to set that wrong right. It had nothing to do with feeling like she'd let Tess down. Well, maybe a little, Tess had to admit. But it wasn't the main reason. She looked back at Richard, annoyed that she'd let him get into her head and twist things all around.

He touched her shoulder. "I'm sorry, Tess. This is coming out all wrong. I'm just worried about my mother. I know this situation isn't fair, and I know how hard my mother will try to make it right. We both love her for that. But sometimes life isn't fair. You, of all people, should know that." He tried to catch her gaze, but she wouldn't look at him. "I'm sorry to pull the plug on this hopeful fantasy my mother's spun. But I know in my gut if you take this farm, it isn't going to end well."

Tess stared at him, then looked at the ground. His words reminded her of the ice-water dousing in the café, the feelings of shame and embarrassment.

"Are you done?" Her tone was sharp.

"I think you get my point," he replied.

She turned and headed toward the house. Honey ran out of the shadows and followed. "And I think it's time for you to go. You don't want to miss your ferry."

Richard smirked. He thought he'd hit a bull's eye. A few points he'd raised were true. She wasn't a fool. She knew the harassment could happen again. Mostly, he'd confused her, but that was his intention. To make her doubt herself and her plans and take away the one thing she believed rightfully belonged to her.

Aunt Lila stood beside the truck, keys in hand. "We'd better go if you want to make that six o'clock boat. I put your bag in the backseat. Is there anything else?"

"No, that's it." He pulled open the passenger side door and Lila climbed into the driver's side. "Are you coming, Tess? There's room."

"I still have things to do. Goodbye, Richard." She was about to add, 'it was good to see you,' but she couldn't lie that boldly.

"Take care of yourself, Tess. And my mom." His tone was warm, but the message between the lines was not lost on her.

Twenty-Two

It was nearly closing time on Monday when Carrie's older sister called. "How's it going? Any new crisis to report?"

"It's been extremely boring for at least twenty-four hours. I'm knocking on wood with my fingers crossed," Carrie replied.

Rebecca had been in touch during Sophie's disappearance with sound, supportive advice and wanted to join them that night but, fortunately, didn't need to.

"I have news. I hope it doesn't set off another drama."

"Something about Mom? Did her cardiologist call?"

"No worries. He's thrilled with her recovery. It's about Jack Dubensky. Remember I asked an investigator in my office to check him out?"

Carrie did remember. It seemed ages ago, though only three weeks or so had passed. She braced herself. "Out with it. He was arrested for scamming old ladies, or something just as awful, right?"

The first man she'd been attracted to in ages. Of course, he had to be hiding some dreadful secret. She had the worst luck with relationships, always drawn to the wrong kind.

"He has a secret past, but I don't understand why he'd hide it. Ever heard of Jackson Gardeaux, the celebrity chef? He ran one of the hottest restaurants in Manhattan, called, not surprisingly, 'Gardeaux's.' The wealthy, beautiful, and famous were lining up for a table. He was on all the cooking shows, too. Chopping and flirting with the female culinary stars. I never watch daytime TV," she added, "but I checked out clips on YouTube."

"I've heard the name and about that restaurant." Carrie felt her stomach drop, as if she were in an elevator that missed a floor. "Are you telling me Jackson Gardeaux and Jack Dubensky are the same guy? I don't believe it."

"I sent you an email with links to the articles and the YouTube clips. Gardeaux is his mother's maiden name, so the pseudonym makes sense, sort of."

"Where does the Jackson come from? Did he just make that up?"

"No, it's his given name," Rebecca answered. Carrie heard papers shuffling. "I guess his mom read a lot of romance novels."

"Possibly." Carrie thought the no-frills 'Jack' suited him better.

"He used to have a little hipster beard. But it's the same guy. He looks much better without it, if you ask me."

Carrie could easily picture Jack with a beard. He practically had one by the time their workday was done. She thought he'd look fine either way but didn't share that with her sister.

"Why did the restaurant close? It must have been making tons of money."

"Truckloads, I'd bet. A few articles mention the closing. It sounds like a train wreck. Jack's wife ran off with a business partner, and the restaurant was caught in the crossfire. Sounds like Jack was left in the cold financially, too. It was all over the gossip pages in the New York newspapers. Right above the bits about Prince Harry and Megan."

Carrie felt sad for him, imagining the painful and public betrayal of the two people he trusted most. "What a nightmare. On top of the world one minute and on the street the next."

"No wonder he's hiding out," Rebecca said.

"Incognito," Carrie added, recalling Sophie's new favorite word.

Carrie's intuition had always insisted that Jack had a secret. Once she got to know him, she didn't want to imagine what it was. Now, it turned out he was a celebrated, wildly successful chef, who'd chosen to flip crab cakes for the summer rather than head a kitchen in another Michelin-star restaurant.

She didn't understand it but felt surprisingly relieved; there was no dark stain on his past after all.

"Sounds like his wife and partner siphoned off all the cash from the business," Rebecca speculated. "He needs to earn money, and he's too proud to work in a place where he'll be spotted."

"Maybe," Carrie replied. "I guess we'll never know."

"We won't?" Rebecca sounded surprised. "If you don't ask him about all this, I certainly will."

Carrie didn't like that idea. Rebecca would give him the third degree. On the other hand, Carrie doubted she had the nerve.

"Do we have to? I was worried he was putting something over on us...and he is, in a way. But nothing that would cause me to fire him. We're lucky he's here, and I'd rather he didn't know we snooped."

Rebecca sighed. "All right, handle it any way you like. Just don't slip up and call him by his stage name."

Carrie smiled, knowing that might happen if she wasn't careful. After Rebecca hung up, Carrie considered opening the email her sister had sent and reading all the articles—then decided to look at it at home where she wouldn't be disturbed.

Jack had left by the time she emerged from the office, which was a relief. She needed this revelation to sink in before she saw him again.

As Carrie locked the café, Brooke drove up with Sophie.

"Here's your delivery, ma'am," Brooke called out.

"Perfect timing," Carrie said as Sophie jumped out of the taxi. "Ready for our shopping trip?"

"What a question, Mom. I've been waiting all day."

Sophie wanted some new clothes for camp. Carrie thought the clothes she had were fine but agreed to buy a few new things, the type of t-shirts and sports shorts Hannah said all the other kids would wear. Including boat shoes, too.

There were all sorts of shops on the village's main street-- galleries that featured the work of local artists and artisans, with paintings, ceramics, and jewelry; a beanery, with fresh roasted coffee on one side and jars of loose-leaf tea on the other; and more than one store that sold homemade fudge, ice cream, and chocolates. There were boutiques with bright, airy fashions for women and no-frills shops, like Lenhardt's Marine Supply, with foul weather gear for fishermen and boaters, like thick yellow storm jackets and tall, green waders.

Sophie was drawn by a yellow slicker displayed in the window, enough protection for a hurricane. Carrie doubted she'd be on the water if there was the least sign of rain. They decided to concentrate on the fair-weather outfits first.

They arrived at Surf's Up!, a store Hannah had recommended, and Sophie led the way. A short time later, her arms filled with choices, they staked out a dressing room.

Her little girl was almost a teenager, Carrie realized. She knew what she liked and chose her favorites quickly. The sales clerk rang up several pairs of shorts and tops, short sleeve and tank style, in "cool colors," along with a new sweatshirt and a red windbreaker.

"Thanks, Mom. I love my new clothes," Sophie said as they left with two full shopping bags.

"You're welcome, honey. We can look at the boat shoes if you want—" Carrie's offer was interrupted by a greeting shouted from down the street.

"Hey, Soph'! Wait up!"

They turned to see Hannah charging down the sidewalk. An older girl was with her but walked at the usual pace. Sophie and Hannah greeted each other as if they'd been parted for months.

"Did you get new clothes?"

"Loads. Want to see?" Sophie opened the bag, and Hannah peered inside.

"I love that top. I'll get one, too. We'll be twins. I'm hanging out with my cousin. We're going to get ice cream. Want to come?"

Hannah's cousin had caught up. She looked about sixteen, and Carrie guessed she was "hanging out" as a babysitter, but Hannah considered the term embarrassing.

"Hi, I'm Emily. You must be Sophie. The girl who hid in Uncle Doug's boat."

Sophie beamed at the recognition. "That's me." Then to Carrie, she said, "Can I get ice cream, Mom?"

"Don't worry, I'll keep my eye on them," Emily promised.

"Sure, I'll wait on the green."

Carrie gave Sophie some money, took the shopping bags, then crossed Front Street and strolled into the green village, a shady, cool oasis set on the harbor.

She walked along a path at the harbor's edge lined with benches and found a spot beneath a big tree. She was about to check her phone for messages, a mindless reflex, then stopped. How often did she get to sit and do nothing? Carrie leaned back and gazed at the wide harbor filled with boats of all shapes and sizes. A flock of seabirds squawked and swooped over the docks, searching for tasty bits of bait or fish. The green was busy, as people walked towards the dock and their boats, or strolled along, taking in the fine weather. Many walked with dogs, reminding her of Sophie's constant pleas for a puppy. She'd also love to get a dog but they couldn't take on the responsibility until she knew where they'd be living in the fall.

Sophie was distracted by sailing camp for now, and Carrie put the dog question aside. She savoured her solitary moment, breathing in the cool, salty air and closing her eyes.

"Hey, Carrie..." Someone tapped her shoulder, and she turned to see Jack. He wore his black baseball cap, as usual, along with a faded Red Sox t-shirt, shorts, and worn-out sneakers. There was a tackle box in one hand and a fishing rod in the other, a pricey model too, she noticed. A souvenir from the days when Jackson Gardeaux could afford the best, she guessed.

The first thing she thought was—*if only gossip columnists could see him now. He's gone totally native.*

He took her in with a shocked expression. "Wait...are you running away from home now, too?"

"You got me. Dang." She had to laugh at the accusation. "I didn't know you were a fisherman, Jack."

"I had a rod and reel in my hand before I could walk," he said as he sat on the bench beside her. "We lived in Niantic, down on the Connecticut shore, just south of New London. My father was a professional. Sometimes he left us for long stretches. That was hard for my mom. But he was a good father. He taught me how to catch a fish and cook it too. He had his own boat, *Oh! Susanna*. That's my mother's name. He'd sing the song so much she almost lost her mind."

Carrie laughed. "I probably would, too."

"What was it like growing up here? I mean, after all the summer people go home."

His warm, interested expression was distracting. Carrie could hardly get her thoughts together. "The summers were wonderful, as you can see. We were always on the beach, swimming, boating, clamming. Some fishing, too," she added.

"I don't think I wore shoes from the day school ended until it started again." Carrie smiled, feeling wistful as she recalled her childhood summers.

"But it got very quiet in the winter. I didn't mind when I was a kid. I read a lot and belonged to clubs at school. Around Sophie's age, I got restless. My parents took us to Bedford every few months to visit my grandparents. We'd always go into the city while we were there and check out the sights. By the time I was in high school, I was determined to leave the island and live in Boston."

"And, so you did," he said.

"And here I am again." She shrugged and gazed at the harbor. "Just to help my mother," she added. "But it does feel deflating." She wasn't sure why she admitted that to Jack. The fact that he was so successful made her defeat seem even worse. At least in her eyes.

He turned toward her. "Don't think of it that way. It's not how many times you get knocked down, Carrie. It's how many times you get up." She glanced at him. He did know something about that, didn't he?

"You're going to score a great job. I can see it. In the meantime, you're making big changes at the café. The kind that will keep the place thriving after you've moved on."

"That's nice of you to say, Jack. I appreciate it." Even more, knowing he wasn't the rambling short-order cook she'd taken him for, but a seasoned restaurateur who knew much more about the business than she did.

"I'm not saying it to be nice...well, maybe a little," he admitted with that grin that made her breath catch. "It's just true."

She tried to pull her gaze away but couldn't. "Fishing off the dock tonight?" she asked, breaking the spell.

He smiled and sat back. "I'm going out with Finn. He wants to show me where the sea bass are hiding. I'd love to catch a nice twenty-pounder."

"Catch a few, and we'll run a special. There's a skiff behind the garage if you want to use it. I bet the motor is still good. It was my Dad's, but I'm sure my mother wouldn't mind if you borrowed it."

Jack looked excited by the offer. "Thanks so much. I'll pay you back with what I catch."

"Good deal. I'll take it." Carrie felt the wind lift her hair. It was so relaxing to talk to Jack like this. But not when she remembered he wasn't plain old, down-to-earth Jack Dubensky. He was Jackson Gardeaux, chef to the stars.

"Hey, something wrong?"

"I just remembered...The chowder contest. You know it's coming up, right?"

"There are signs all over town, and I can read. Of course, I know."

"It's a big deal around here, Jack. The Blue Sky always wins Best Chowder on the island. I mean, *always*, since the contest began in the 1940s. Last year, I'm ashamed to say, we were knocked out by Bolton's. We came in second, but—"

"Nobody ever says, 'Let's eat the *second*-best chowder on the island.'"

"Exactly. I know it seems silly. It's just a little local contest. But a big sign out front that says, *'Best Chowder' on the Island!* confirms our reputation."

"I understand," he assured her.

He had to think this contest was well below him, but he was putting on a good show of believing it was important.

"Just follow the recipe we always use. It's been in the family since my great-grandfather opened a shack out on the dock. I'm sure you think it's horribly bland, but people love it."

"Keep it bland as baby food. That's what you're trying to say, right?"

"I know you're creative, Jack. The Zen Burgers and truffled mac and cheese really perk up our list of specials. But the Blue Sky's award-winning chowder is family history."

"I'll follow the recipe as if it was written in stone." He raised his right hand, his dark eyes devoid of irony.

Before she could stop herself, she said, "I know this sort of cooking is minor league. But I appreciate that you take it seriously."

He stared back curiously. "Minor league? I'll forget you said that. The Duffys will disown you."

Carrie laughed, knowing that was true. Should she confront him about what she knew? Or maintain the status quo? He might be upset to know his cover was blown and leave them high and dry. Then where would she be?

Loose lips sink ships. She decided to forget the revelation Rebecca had discovered. At least for now. Once she acknowledged his fame, it would be even harder to be his boss.

"I meant because...you're so creative," Carrie fudged as an answer. "You like to put your own mark on the food you serve."

She could see he was relieved. "I do. But there's a time and place."

"Exactly," she summoned an innocent tone.

"Jackie, my boy—sorry to keep you and the little fishes waiting."

Carrie had never been so pleased to see Finbarr Mulligan in her life.

"No rush, Finn. I haven't been here long." Jack glanced at Carrie. "Time flies when you're in good company."

Carrie liked spending time with him, too. They were usually surrounded by so much noise and activity. They rarely shared a quiet moment like this.

When they'd first met, she'd felt intimidated and suspicious. She felt foolish to admit it now, even to herself. They still disagreed but always worked through the rough patches. Jack was as sharp as the elite set of steel knives he brought to work each day.

He kept her on her toes and laughed at her jokes. That was always a plus.

Their time today felt more personal than business. Too personal, perhaps. Jack's true identity, his success and fame, only added to a list of reasons why getting involved with him was pointless. A celebrity chef lived on a different planet than she did. When he wasn't hiding out on Haven.

Carrie came to her feet. "I better catch up with Sophie. It's getting late. Good luck. I hope the fish are biting."

"Luck has nothing to do with it, young lady," Finn told her, sounding rather stern. "I find the nooks and crannies where they're hiding. And without all that high-tech radar and whatnot. Just a boat and this old contraption." He tapped on the side of his sizable nose.

Carrie almost laughed, but she knew the claim was true.

Jack gathered his gear. "I'm like Ahab searching for my Moby Bass. Only I plan to sauté it in brown butter, lemon zest, and capers."

"Sounds delicious. But I don't think that story ended well," she reminded him. "Not with a gourmet dinner."

Jack grinned, with deep dimples and bright eyes. "I did the quick notes for that one. I was probably studying a cookbook."

"Sounds about right." Carrie could see it, too.

"Shake a leg, Jack-o. Tide's going out." Finn led the way toward his boat. Jack followed with a parting wave.

Carrie waved back, then followed a path out to Front Street. *Jack Dubensky...or Jackson Gardeaux...or whoever you are...Why do you have to be so dang attractive? I wish I didn't like you half as much as I do.*

Twenty-Three

"Harold Woods is back from visiting his new grandbaby in New Hampshire," Aunt Lila reported, mentioning her attorney. "I made an appointment for tomorrow at ten. You'll have time for morning chores, but it won't cut into your workday."

Her aunt had thought of everything. It was hard for Tess to object. They sat on the porch, the click of her aunt's knitting needles in synch with the chirping crickets.

Aunt Lila was determined to sign the land over, despite Tess's plan to put off the paperwork. Her aunt thought Tess should hear what the attorney had to say about the pluses and minuses of taking over the property. A reasonable suggestion, but Tess guessed she hoped Mr. Woods would convince her to go through with it—the sooner, the better.

Tess sat in a wicker chair with Honey at her feet. She looked up from a thick book on goat farming. Richard's parting words had gotten under her skin, kindling her doubts all day. She kept reminding herself she deserved the land. Her aunt had no doubts about that or about giving it to her. Richard probably wanted it for himself when his mother passed on. Or wanted to take it over even sooner.

Even when she put her cousin's motives aside, Tess still couldn't see her way clear to accepting the gift. Her aunt seemed to read her thoughts and said, "We're just going to talk to him, Tess. More information might be helpful No one will pressure you to do anything you don't want to do."

"I understand, Aunt Lila." Tess rose and closed her book. "Guess I'll head up to bed."

"One more row and I'm going in, too. Good night, dear."

Tess said good night and went into the house. She did have questions. But not the type a lawyer could answer.

Tess woke Tuesday morning before the alarm. She was nervous about visiting the attorney, though she knew there was no logical reason to feel that way. As her aunt had said, no one was going to force her to sign the deed. The attorney probably already thought she was crazy. Or at least awfully eccentric.

"Just one more person in the world who thinks I'm strange. Join the club, buddy," she said aloud.

Honey glanced at her, then back out the open bedroom window. She sniffed the air, her pointed ears standing up sharp. She whined and looked at Tess.

"I know you want to go out. Just let me get my shoes on." Tess quickly finished dressing and led the dog downstairs.

The weather forecast had predicted a hot sunny day, but the cool, thick mist that had settled on the landscape like a length of sheer, silky fabric was typical of a summer morning on the island. Tess could barely see down the hillside to the next farm, much less the harbor. She could see the horizon, just above the dark rim of the water, tinged with pink and gold, where the sun was just about to rise.

She made her way to the goat pen, rubbing her bare arms for warmth, and didn't realize the gate hung open until she stood steps from the corral. An *empty* corral, she quickly realized, running around the foggy enclosure to make sure.

She raced out, Honey at her heels, and called the goats by name. "Lucy! Ethel!... Daisy? Milo? Duncan?"

There were ten, but she gave up after the first five. She ran into the field, despairing at the fog. The goats might be lingering there. She should be able to hear the little bells they wore *jingling*. But she couldn't hear or see a thing.

Of all the mornings for the goats to get loose. Anything could happen to them. They could get hit by a car in this weather or get hurt in the woods. Someone could find one and keep it. They were marked, but such things happened.

Tess wandered in the foggy field, not knowing what to do. She heard Honey bark, and the dog soon emerged from the mist, nipping at Milo's heels.

Tess grabbed the goat by its scruff and led him back into the enclosure. "Good job, Honey. One down, nine to go." Honey soon alerted her to another escapee, Ethel. But as Tess ran to catch her, a rooster flew out of the mist, squawking and flapping his wings.

She ran to the coop and found it deserted as well. Without bothering to look for the birds, she headed for the barn and stopped short outside. Across the fresh paint, she found only two angry words, written in big, white letters – GO AWAY!

The truck was parked nearby, and Tess noticed it tilted at an odd angle. All four tires were flat, and when she looked closer, she found slashes in the rubber, leaving them beyond repair. She hoped there was no other damage she couldn't see.

The barn doors were ajar, and she gingerly moved forward and slid one open. The sight nearly made her cry. She'd stacked at least ten bags of feed for the goats and chickens against the wall, and the sacks had all been slashed open, the feed flung in all directions.

Even if she could collect it with a shovel, scoop by scoop, it was ruined. The feed had cost good money and would have lasted months. But that wasn't the reason she felt so distressed she could hardly breathe.

She'd find the goats. She'd buy more feed and new tires, which the truck had needed. She'd even paint the barn again. But the message was clear. The next time would be worse.

The intruder must have been careful to move quietly. Honey hadn't even heard them this time. Richard was right. She and Aunt Lila were not safe here. She was taking a great risk, not only with her welfare but her aunt's too. How would she feel if Aunt Lila was harmed? Or got so upset it made her sick?

She would never forgive herself. And Richard wouldn't either; she knew that already.

Two bright eyes stared out of the shadows. It was Daisy. She was expecting a baby any day, and Tess was taking extra special care of her. She must have smelled the food and wandered in. Tess hoped the pregnant goat hadn't eaten too much. There would be a call to the vet later.

Tess grabbed a thin tether that hung on the wall and moved

slowly. "Hello, Daisy." She held out her hand. "I'm just going to put you in a stall."

She nearly had the loop over Daisy's head when the little goat kicked out. Tess jumped backward, and her feet slipped on the grain. She fell hard in the pile, twisted to one side, and landed on something sharp. The pain was white hot, and she grabbed at her arm, then realized she'd been cut. She looked down and saw a pair of shears the intruder had used to slice open the feed sacks.

She sat with her hand pressed against the wound. It throbbed wildly, and blood seeped through her fingers. She blinked back tears, feeling too miserable for words.

"Tess, are you in here?"

Tess slowly came to her feet. "Right here, Aunt Lila."

"Oh, Tess...what in the world?" Her aunt's mouth hung open as she took in the mess. "Not again."

Tess met her gaze. There was nothing to say. She wondered how she'd ever clean it up. Every mouse for miles would be here by noon.

"What's wrong with your arm?" Her aunt rushed to her side. "Did you hurt yourself?"

"It's nothing. I was trying to catch Daisy, and I slipped. I just need a bandage."

"You go inside. We'll call Owen. He'll help find the goats."

Daisy was attracted to the food again. Her aunt picked up the tether from where it had fallen and slipped it over the goat's head.

"Come along, young lady. You've had enough of that," she scolded as she led the goat out of the barn.

Tess headed to the house. She couldn't round up her own shadow in this state. She'd try a bandage and an ice pack, and come out later after the fog burned off.

Owen would be happy to help. But she felt ashamed to call him. What sort of a farmer lost her animals every week and injured herself? For so long, she'd dreamed of running the farm, so sure she could do it on her own. Now it felt like she was only playing at it. She heard her father's voice; he was not surprised. *You're plain useless, Tess. No two ways about it.*

Get a grip. You had a rotten morning, and you're in pain. You don't need to figure out everything right now.

Tess managed to slap some gauze pads on the cut and wound first-aid tape around it. She made coffee one-handed and was looking for a box of cereal when her aunt came in.

"A few more goats wandered back," Lila reported. "Lucy and Ethel. And Milo. They know what side their bread is buttered on. Animals are creatures of habit. Including us humans."

Her aunt poured a cup of coffee and sat at the table. "Owen is coming this afternoon. He said we should call the police, and I agree."

Tess glanced at her. "You know what I think."

"I do, and I also know you're very stubborn sometimes." Her aunt shrugged and sipped her coffee.

"Let me think about it." She'd barely kept the last incident out of the newspaper and doubted she'd be that lucky again.

She shook some cereal into her bowl and grabbed the milk. It was awkward to use her left hand, and the container nearly tipped over. She caught it and winced with pain.

When she opened her eyes, her aunt stood by her chair. "That bandage isn't holding up very well. I think you need stitches and probably a tetanus shot. I'm taking you to the emergency room. And don't argue."

"We can't use the truck, remember?"

Her aunt already had her phone out. "I'm calling Evaline. If she can't give us a lift, we'll take a taxi. Get yourself ready."

Tess was so worn out and uncomfortable she didn't have the energy to argue.

* * *

Tess disliked visiting doctors and visiting the emergency room even more. An admitting nurse had asked a few questions, and Tess was directed to a small, curtained cubicle where another nurse asked her more questions and took her vital signs. She looked at the cut, made some notes, and put a fresh bandage on it.

"The doctor will be in soon."

Tess thanked her and sat on the edge of a gurney, though she'd been encouraged to lay back and relax. At least she hadn't been told to put on a paper gown. That was the worst.

Though it was barely eight o'clock, the events of the morning suddenly overwhelmed her. She felt her eyes drift closed but still refused to lay back on the soft, crisp pillows. The throbbing in her arm from the cut had quieted, only because she sat completely still. How could she work like this?

She couldn't. That was the long and short of it. She felt like she might cry but wouldn't let herself. Once she started, there was no telling when she'd stop.

"Tess?" She opened her eyes and realized she'd fallen asleep. She expected to see her aunt. Instead, she blinked at the sight of Ben Croft. He wore pale green scrubs and a stethoscope draped around his neck.

She shook her head and nearly laughed. "This is so not my day."

"Good to see you, too." He sounded amused. Or at least, as confounded by the situation as she was.

"It's okay if you want me to see another doctor. I can wait," she offered.

"We're short on staff today. I've got this. Unless that's what you'd prefer?"

She wasn't sure what to say. She didn't want to give the impression that she didn't trust him to treat her correctly.

"Let's get it over with. Just a cut. No big deal."

"I'll decide that. Let me take a look."

Tess stared straight ahead as he removed the bandage. His touch was gentle, but the spot was so tender, she still winced.

He paused. "Sorry, I didn't mean to hurt you."

"I'm fine," she insisted. She glanced at him briefly, then forced herself to stare straight ahead again.

"I need to clean this up a bit. It will sting," he warned. Tess answered with a nod, then tried to hold still as he dabbed the wound with cotton soaked with antiseptic. "It's a clean slice but deep. How did it happen?"

"I fell in the barn. I landed on some shears."

"Did you trip on something or feel dizzy and lose your balance?"

"I was chasing a goat, and I slipped on some grain. There was a tool on the ground, and I fell on it. End of story." Tess had given more detail than she'd intended and abruptly stopped.

He pressed the cut with a mound of clean gauze. "Except for the part about your farm being vandalized again."

She sat up straight. "Who told you that?"

"I was at the front desk and overheard your aunt talking to Evaline Finch."

"I'm sure my aunt made it sound a lot worse than it is. More of a big mess than anything else."

"Isn't that bad enough?" When she didn't answer, he added, "I hope you'll call the police. You can't ignore this and hope it goes away. It's not safe."

His concern surprised her. She didn't mean to look at him, but couldn't help it. Her gaze caught and held by his. The green scrubs made his eyes brighter.

Of all the days to meet up with him again, she looked like she'd been dragged on the back of a tractor. Her t-shirt and shorts, dirty and stained, her hair in a messy ponytail. There were probably bits of grain stuck in it, too.

It didn't matter what he thought of her. It was best to face that.

"I might take the advice painted on the barn. That will make it stop," she said quietly.

"The advice?"

"'Go away.' What else would it say?"

He stepped back and looked down at her. "I understand you're upset right now, Tess. Anybody would be. But don't make a rash decision. One person could be causing all this. Just one, out of the whole island."

She'd never thought of it that way. Still, if one person was willing to go through all this trouble, others must feel the same.

"That could be true, but I'll never know for sure."

"The police might figure it out if you let them do their job. Or you could get a security camera. They're inexpensive and hook up to a phone or computer. At least you'll know who it is if it happens again."

"Owen Jessup said to do that, too," she admitted. "But I spent so many years surrounded by cameras and alarms; I don't want anything like that on the farm."

His expression turned thoughtful. "I'm sorry. Of course not. I wasn't thinking."

"That's all right." At least he didn't see her as a former inmate all the time. "I thought you'd be glad to hear I might give up and go."

"I thought so too. But I don't feel that way. I will say, I thought you'd fight harder to stay."

His words stung. And surprised her. He almost sounded as if he was on her side...but how could he ever be?

"You need some stitches. I'll find a nurse to help and be right back."

Tess sighed. "I'm not going anywhere."

"Good to know." He smiled as he left, and she felt he'd interpreted that to mean she wouldn't let herself be chased off the island. Not just yet.

When he returned, Ben closed the cut with surgical staples and covered it with a bandage wrapped around her arm. He gave her instructions for home care and added, "Keep this clean and dry and come back in a few days to get these out. The receptionist will give you an appointment. Don't forget."

"Thank you...Dr. Croft."

He smiled so swiftly, she nearly missed it. "I think we're on a first-name basis by now. For better or worse?"

"That's a good way to put it." They'd shared an event that had defined both of their lives.

As soon as Ben left, Aunt Lila appeared. "They said I couldn't come back while you were being treated, dear. I made some phone calls while I was waiting. The truck will be towed to Hartman's in a few hours. Brad can get a set of tires by tomorrow. And I canceled our appointment with Mr. Woods."

Tess had forgotten all about it, but now felt a wave of relief. At least there'd been one lucky break today.

Twenty-Four

On Saturday morning, long tables were lined up along the sidewalk in front of the café and covered with blue and white checked tablecloths. A bright banner read, "Annual Chowder Contest! Vote for The Blue Sky Cafe! Best on the Island!"

The official start was eleven, and it was only half past ten. But chowder lovers already roamed Front Street, eager to taste test and cast their votes. The crowd would build slowly, but at a certain point, Carrie knew the bowls would be flying.

It was tricky to keep the café running smoothly during the crawl. But all hands were on deck today—Carrie, Brooke, Sophie, and her mother. Her mother had visited during her recovery, but this was her first time working. Carrie had to make sure she didn't overdo it.

Sophie was excited about helping and asked to give out the crackers. The first week of sailing camp had been a success, which was a relief to Carrie. Every day it seemed clearer that they needed to stay for the whole summer.

"Blue Sky Cafe, your booth looks very bright, as usual. It touches my heart to see you keep up the family tradition, Carrie."

George Lenhardt, the mayor of Haven Harbor, was visiting all the contestants. He greeted Carrie with a broad toothy smile. His huge white mustache compensated for his bald head, and then some. George owned the marine supply store on Front Street and rarely wore a suit and tie. Never the quaint, seersucker type he'd donned today, along with a bright red and white polka-dot bowtie and flat straw hat, a fashionable summer style for men in the early 1900s. A big pin on his lapel read, "Haven Island Official Chowder Crawl – Judge."

It was an election year, Carrie recalled, and the mayor was making the most of his chance to mingle with the community. A young man, who seemed to be his assistant, walked beside him.

"Let's get a nice photo." The assistant raised his phone as she and the mayor stood shoulder to shoulder.

"Big smile. Everyone say, 'Chowder!'"

"Chowder!" Carrie grinned, feeling foolish. How many times would he do that today? Carrie couldn't imagine.

"I assume you know the rules by now?"

"I was born reciting the Chowder Crawl rules, Mayor."

He answered with a chuckle. "You were always the funny sister. Haven't changed a bit, have you?"

She could have taken days to answer that, but forced a pleasant smile. "Why mess with perfection?"

He laughed again and handed her a flyer with a list of the contestants, the rules, and the schedule. Chowder lovers signed up at a booth on the village green and were given a map of the Crawl and a ballot for voting. Chowder could be served from eleven in the morning until four in the afternoon. All ballots had to be turned in at the village hall by five, and the winner would be announced on Sunday morning.

"Good luck. May the best chowder win!"

"That means the Blue Sky Cafe, so thanks in advance."

"Bolton's is hard to beat, but if any recipe can, it's yours."

He meant the words kindly, but the comparison irked her. "Bolton's took the title by a fluke last year. No pun intended. We'll be back on top this summer. I have no worries."

"That's the spirit." With another wide, walrus smile, Mayor Lenhardt headed for his next stop.

A crowd of early crawlers stood at the table, staring at her. Carrie checked the time. Five minutes to eleven, already?

"Chowder will be right out, folks." She smiled and speed-dialed Jack. "Where's the chowder? People are waiting."

"It's heating. Thoroughly. No one likes cold soup."

"I don't need a cooking lesson. Just bring it out."

While Carrie was scolding her cook, Brooke, Dory, and Sophie appeared, along with Carrie's mother. Brooke set up a mini-speaker and lively, soft rock to lend a festive mood.

As Carrie assigned them each a job, Jack arrived with the first pot, pushing it on a cart. He set the pot on a burner and stepped back.

"Just holler when you need more."

"And you know how good I am at that." She suddenly felt bad for losing her temper on the phone.

"I'm a cook. I can take the heat. You'd better start serving. The voters look hungry."

Carrie had already grabbed the ladle and begun filling a row of bowls. Her mother served, with a gracious smile for each customer. "I hope you enjoy it. Please don't forget to vote for the Blue Sky," she reminded them.

"Sophie, make sure everyone gets crackers," Jack murmured.

"I'm on it, chef."

Jack smiled at Sophie. Then he stepped back to watch the crawl.

"The chowder smells delicious, Jack. You must have worked hard," Carrie's mother said.

"Thanks, Gena. I tried to make it extra special."

His reply sounded a distant alarm. Carrie stopped ladling and turned. "But not any *more* special than our *very* special, historic family recipe, right?"

"I followed the recipe to the letter." He seemed miffed she would doubt him.

"Fine. Then we're sure to win."

He didn't reply, and she glanced over her shoulder again, wondering why. But he was gone.

* * *

"Spying on us, Doug? I think that's against the rules. I might tell the mayor," she teased.

Doug Bolton stood at the table, a bowl in hand and a guilty grin on his handsome face. Carrie had been in the café and found him there when she returned. She was glad she'd combed her hair and put on a dash of lipstick. She was going to smell of clam chowder for a week, but that couldn't be helped.

"It's very good," he mumbled around a mouthful. "Very... zesty. It's good to change things up once in a while."

Carrie's stomach knotted. "We didn't change a thing. It's the recipe handed down from my great-grandfather."

While answering Doug, she ladled a bit of chowder into a bowl and took a sip. Her tastebuds reported faster than a NASA computer. This was *not* her great-grandfather's recipe. Or the recipe of anyone even distantly related.

Jack lied to her. He'd changed the chowder!

She tried a second spoonful to make sure, then set the bowl down with a shaky hand.

Doug leaned toward her. "Carrie, are you all right? You look pale. It's hot out here. Maybe you should sit down."

She stared back, feeling so upset she didn't know whether to cry or scream. But she couldn't melt down in the middle of Front Street for everyone to see. She gazed at the crawlers, spooning up their soup, knowing each would soon cast a vote. She could barely stop herself from snatching the bowls out of their hands.

There was no way to fix it. Nothing she could do. Except yell her head off at Jack.

"I just remembered," she stammered. "I need to check something in the kitchen. Thanks for stopping by, Doug."

"I just wanted to say hello. And wish you luck."

"You too," she returned politely.

Was she imagining things, or did she spot a glimmer of satisfaction in those blue eyes, a silent message that he knew this "zesty" version would not beat Bolton's?

Carrie pushed the thought aside. She sailed through the door and headed for the kitchen. Doug Bolton was a nice guy. She was just being paranoid.

She had bigger fish to fry. One named Jack Dubensky.

Jack stood at the big stainless steel stove, where he could be found most of the day. He didn't hear her approach until she was inches away

"What in the world did you do to the chowder? You promised you wouldn't change the recipe. It's right here, in black and white." The recipe was tacked to the bulletin board, and she yanked it down, tearing the paper.

He turned and wiped his hands on a cloth hanging off his apron. "I followed the recipe to the letter. But it tasted like paste. I wanted to keep my promise. I really did. But how could I serve that mediocre mush? I barely changed it, for goodness sake. A few dashes to bump it up, give it a little ... character."

"Dashes of what, exactly?" She braced herself. Did the details matter? But she had to know.

"A little ginger and curry... a dash of coconut milk?"

Her ancestors were turning over in their graves. "Stop...I've heard enough."

She gripped her forehead, a doozy of a headache rolling in like a dark storm. Of course, he couldn't serve the Blue Sky chowder family recipe. He was Jackson Gardeaux, award-winning chef, honored alumni of the Culinary Institute of America. She wanted so much to blow his cover, while a reasonable voice insisted it was neither the time nor the place.

"We'll stop serving. Joey and I will take the pots inside."

That got her attention. "Are you mad? That will make it a complete disaster. It's only—" She checked the time, and her spirits sank lower. "Two o'clock. We can't stop serving until four."

He looked contrite, arms crossed over his chest. "Do you want to fire me? I'll go right now. I get it."

She felt so exasperated, she could hardly breathe. "You don't get it, Jack. *Obviously.* Yes, I want to fire you. Badly. But losing a cook right now would make this nightmare even worse. You're definitely *not* fired, and don't you dare quit ... or I'll ...I don't know what I'll do, but I promise it won't be pretty."

"I only tried to *improve* the menu. People might like this chowder as much or more. Palates have changed since the 1950s."

True enough, but she was still mad as blazes at him. "We'll have to see about that, won't we?"

Before he could reply, she stomped out of the kitchen.

Twenty-Five

It was hard enough to help a mother goat with a difficult labor, but almost impossible with only her left arm since Tess was right-handed. She'd covered her stitches with extra gauze and plastic wrap, but it was still tender and, more or less, useless for this job.

Early that morning, she'd found Daisy in the corral and knew her time had come. She'd watched and even helped her father deliver plenty of baby animals over the years but had never done it on her own. Last night, she watched some online farming videos that seemed helpful, and she had a plan. She brought Daisy into the barn, and the little mother started out fine. Tess expected a swift and easy birth. Then the process stalled, and Daisy struggled. Tess tried a few remedies, but nothing helped.

She called both veterinarians on the island, but neither could come for hours. Dr. Gerald Brooks coached her over the phone and told her to keep him posted. As Daisy bleated and struggled,

Tess feared the baby was stuck, and both the kid and mother were in danger.

There were ways to pull the baby out, but she needed someone to hold Daisy steady. Aunt Lila had gone to town. She'd volunteered to run the church bake sale on the green. The village was bustling today because of the chowder contest. Even if her aunt got back in time, which was doubtful, she wasn't strong enough to handle Daisy. Owen would have come in a heartbeat, but he was off the island, visiting family.

"Oh, Daisy, please push. I won't give up on you. But I don't know what else to do..."

Wide-eyed, Daisy looked frightened and confused. Tess wanted to cry but soothed her and tried to move the baby.

"What's going on? Is that goat all right?"

Tess looked up. Ben Croft stood in the barn doorway. Despite everything, she was incredibly happy to see him.

"Daisy is in labor, but she's struggling. The baby is stuck, and I can't do much with this arm and no one to hold her."

"Let me have a look. You hold her head."

He knelt beside the goat and pulled a pair of gloves from his pocket. Then Tess held Daisy as he examined her.

"The kid is facing the wrong way. Its head is stuck. Hold her tight. I might be able to put things right..."

Tess braced Daisy and squeezed her eyes shut, silently praying the baby would emerge alive and well. "She's been pushing awhile. I hope her kid survives."

Ben didn't answer, his expression totally focused. Daisy let loose a long, surprised bleat, and Tess saw her push again.

"It's coming now." Ben's voice was quiet but hopeful; he leaned back as Daisy—and nature—took over.

A few seconds later, the little goat appeared and rose on shaky legs. Daisy licked her baby all over.

"Congratulations. It's a boy." Ben cut the cord and made sure the afterbirth was expelled. Then Tess moved Daisy and her newborn to a special stall prepared with fresh straw.

Tess was exhausted but so relieved and happy, she had an impulse to hug him. Until she realized how crazy and impossible that would be.

"I can't thank you enough. I hate to think what would have happened if you hadn't shown up." She met his gaze and looked away, busying herself with cleaning up. "I know farmers shouldn't get emotional over livestock. But I would have felt terrible to lose the baby and maybe even Daisy."

Ben shrugged. "I got an A-plus in goat pregnancy."

The unexpected joke made her laugh. He'd so far been so serious. "What made you come here?"

"I checked with the clinic. You missed your appointment yesterday," he said, sounding like a doctor again.

Tess felt caught out. "I meant to keep it. I couldn't leave Daisy."

His expression softened. "Let's go inside, and I'll check your progress."

It was hard to act calm while Ben examined her arm and even held her hand, looking at one side and then the other. His touch was gentle and caring. She knew it wasn't personal. He was a good doctor and a compassionate one. He'd treated Daisy the same, she reminded herself.

"This looks fine. You're a good healer."

Tess had to smile at the odd compliment. "Gee, thanks?"

He smiled back. "I'll remove the staples now. Ready?"

"Please do. I can't wait to have my arm back."

She hardly felt a thing as he snipped. He was good at his work.

"Your arm will still feel tender. You also sprained it a bit. I'd say, 'don't overdo,' but I'm sure you will anyway."

"I'll be careful." It did ache but she wouldn't admit it. She guessed he knew that, too.

He dabbed the newly healed skin with antiseptic. "Have you made a decision about staying on the island?"

The question surprised her. "I'm still torn. My aunt can't wait to transfer the deed. But her son, my cousin Richard, is against it. He says it's selfish to stay and put my aunt in danger. He's worried about her, especially after all the vandalism. That's only natural. He says it would be a mistake to accept the land. He could be right."

Tess wasn't sure why she shared her worries with Ben Croft, of all people. Maybe because she had no one else to talk to about the dilemma. Not even her aunt.

Ben had finished and began to clean up, his handsome face set in a frown. "Sounds like your cousin wants the land."

Tess had thought of that. If Lila kept the deed in her name, Richard would be in line to inherit. She recalled his remarks about having money while he was still young enough to enjoy it and a newfound interest in real estate. But Tess gave him the benefit of the doubt, maybe because so few had ever given her one.

"That might be part of it, but I think he's mainly concerned about his mother. He says it's not safe for her to live here with me."

"And his solution is telling you to leave," Ben summed up.

Tess nodded and met his gaze, his eyes greenish-gold in the soft afternoon light.

"Is that what you want to do?" he asked.

"No, not really. But I'm worried he'll make trouble and my aunt will be in the middle of it. That would be awful for her."

"What sort of trouble? Your aunt has the right to transfer ownership to anyone. I'd be happy to affirm her sound mind and judgment."

Did he expect this to become a legal tangle? Tess wanted no part of lawyers, courts, and judges ever again.

"I hope it doesn't come to that." She paused, then said, "I've asked you this already, but I still don't understand. Why would you, of all people, help me keep this farm? You should be the first one telling me to go."

"I've told you before, I'd hate for anyone to think I approve of the harassment or take any pleasure seeing you and your aunt treated this way."

"You did." Tess grew silent. His encouragement and support meant more to her than she could say. She watched him put the supplies away and then snap the medical bag shut.

She was starting to have feelings for him, which was the most insane thing that had ever happened to her. It seemed like a cruel trick. Of all the men in the world to feel attracted to. The realization made her want to laugh out loud. He was the last man on earth who could ever be interested in her that way.

Tess came to her feet. "I'm sure you need to get back to work. Thanks for stopping by. It was perfect timing for Daisy."

For herself, too, though she'd never say.

"After years in emergency medicine, not much surprises me.

But, I admit, today sure did. And it was fun." His sudden smile made her breath catch. "What will you name Daisy's baby?"

"I don't know. Any suggestions?"

He thought for a moment as they walked outside. "How about Elvis? He looks like a rebel, and he has long, wiggly legs."

Tess laughed. "That's perfect."

Tess watched him walk down the porch steps and was about to say goodbye when he turned to face her again. "Listen, I have an idea that might help you."

"Really?" She couldn't imagine what he was going to say.

"I was thinking, what if we were seen together in some public place? Like, have some coffee, or take a walk on the village green? Then people would know I don't object to you being here. So why should anyone else?"

His suggestion surprised her and knocked her off balance.

"I guess I have to think about it. I barely stepped foot in the Blue Sky and caused a scene. I don't want to go through that again."

"And you don't think being in my company would prevent it?"

"It might. But who could say for sure?" She certainly couldn't. And neither could he. The last thing she wanted was for Ben Croft to be harassed the way she had been.

He answered with a thoughtful look. Tess hoped he'd given up and was ready to go. "Well...what about a church? I know your aunt attends Old First Church, on the bluff. Would that feel safe to you?"

"I'm not much of a churchgoer. And I'd still be reluctant for the same reason."

Even though it is the last place a person should be judged and spurned, Tess thought.

"My family belongs to that church, too. If you come Sunday, I'll make it a point to be there, and we could sit together. I think that will show everyone I don't approve of the way you've been treated. If I don't approve, why should anyone come here and bother you? Or try to avenge my family?"

The gesture would send a big message. Maybe more than Ben intended.

"It will also give the impression that you forgive me. Are you all right with that?"

He lowered his gaze and didn't answer. She held her breath, trying to act calm.

"I can't honestly say I do forgive you, Tess," he finally replied. "But I know I don't hate you. I know that frightening you and your aunt, destroying your property, and causing you to injure yourself—it's simply reprehensible and cowardly. I agree with your cousin about one thing; if it isn't stopped, it will get worse. And it won't change anything. Whether you live here or not, it won't bring my brother back or erase that awful night. I hope that's the message people get, because I'll say it outright to anyone who asks me."

His heartfelt reply made it hard for her to speak. He had so much integrity and courage. More than anyone she'd ever met, except for her aunt, perhaps. She wondered what his family thought. She knew his father had passed away, but his mother still lived on Haven. He had a younger sister named Jillian, a teacher. She lived on the mainland but returned to the island in the summer.

"What about your family? What do they think of this idea?"

"I wanted to ask you first. If you'll come, I'll warn them. I hope they'll understand. I can only do what I think is right. I can't decide for them as well."

Tess wondered if Ben's plan would move the needle of public opinion. It might make things worse. But it seemed he'd given it some thought and not only wanted to help her but show he didn't condone any efforts to chase her away. It was a small request, all things considered.

Before she agreed, she had to ask, "Do you think whoever is doing this damage even goes to church?"

Her point made him smile. "Probably not. But people who are there will spread the word. You can count on that. So…will you come Sunday?"

People would "spread the word"; she hated the idea of being talked about. Again. Even for a good reason. Still, it was impossible to refuse when he looked at her that way.

"Okay, if you feel that strongly about it."

"I do, Tess." Her answer had made him happy, which felt like more than enough reason to agree.

Twenty-Six

The café was closed, the front door locked, the chairs stacked, and the floor freshly mopped. The kitchen was spotless, and the staff had dispersed to enjoy their Saturday evening off.

Carrie lingered, shuffling papers around her desk but unable to focus. Her mother and Sophie were preparing dinner, but she wasn't ready to go home. Brooke had just texted the results of the chowder contest; she had a source at the village hall. It was bad news, and Carrie needed time to collect herself.

The door to her office was open a crack, and she heard a light tap. "It's me. Can I come in?"

Carrie took a breath. She hadn't exchanged a single word with Jack since her meltdown. Now she felt partly embarrassed and partly vindicated. Though the proof was cold comfort.

"Come in," she called back.

He pushed the door open but remained in the hall. He'd

changed from cooking whites to a t-shirt and jeans. His expression was wary—for Jack.

"I'm leaving. Everything is locked."

"Okay, see you," she answered without looking up.

"Any word?"

She slowly turned. "As a matter of fact, I just got the results. Bolton's won first place. We came in...third."

"Third? Are you sure?" He was shocked. "Can you ask for a recount?"

"Like they say in baseball, there's always next year." Carrie tried for an offhand note but couldn't hide her anger.

He dragged a hand through his thick hair. "I'm sorry I messed with the recipe. I was trying to do you...I mean, the café...a favor. Waking up palates and luring people in for a meal. I should have kept my promise...or at least asked before I tampered with the family tradition."

"I understand." She'd so far kept the café's financial problems from him. But suddenly, she felt too drained to keep that secret ... or his secret either. "We do need more business. More than you know. But maybe not the type of customers you're used to luring."

He looked confused. "What do you mean by that?"

Carrie took a breath and avoided his gaze. "I know that in your corner of the culinary universe, our chowder *does* taste like paste. I know this place is beneath you. What I don't know is what you're doing here."

"Of course, it's not beneath me. Why do you say that?"

"You know exactly what I mean. You're seriously overqualified to be cooking at the Blue Sky Cafe, Jack Dubensky. That's why you couldn't resist messing with the chowder recipe. Or should I say, Jackson Gardeaux?"

She watched as her words sunk in. He squinted at her, seemed about to laugh, then shook his head. "How long have you known?"

"Only a few days. But I suspected you were not what you seemed from the start."

He leaned against the doorjamb. "Who is?"

"Don't get philosophical with me. I doubt many people operate under an assumed identity. I'm just curious why you're hiding out here. Of all places."

"Just needed a rest from the real world, I guess."

"Why not take a vacation?"

"This is a vacation for me. I can't sit under a palm tree and read a book. I get too bored and antsy. I need to cook like a shark has to keep moving."

Carrie understood. She was the same way.

"I'm here for the same reason you are, Carrie. To hit the reset button."

"Don't try to change the subject. We're talking about you. You can't compare my situation—an out-of-work single mom who's trying to help her family—with a celebrity chef who's all over TV and social media. I think you had other options."

"Maybe I did. But I like this place. My family took vacations here when I was a kid. I knew it was quiet and off the beaten track. I saw the ad and applied on a whim, and your mother hired me ten minutes later. I don't think she even checked my references. Not that I lied," he quickly added.

Carrie sighed, reminded of what a pushover her mother was.

"All in all, Haven Island and the Blue Sky Cafe not only worked out but pleasantly surprised me." He caught her gaze, and she looked away. Was *she* the pleasant surprise? Is that what he meant?

"Are you going to blow my cover?" His tone was light, but she sensed his concern.

"Not if you don't want me to. So far, only my sister Rebecca knows. I'll ask her to keep it confidential."

"I'd appreciate that," he said sincerely.

"I have my own reasons. I don't want you to disappear because you were unmasked, Super Chef."

She couldn't think straight when he smiled at her—a flash of straight white teeth and dimples in his scruffy, bearded cheeks.

She forced her boss tone. "Just don't fly the coop before September, as we agreed. Even if a zillionaire offers to bankroll a new restaurant in London, say? Or Paris?"

"Give up the Blue Sky Cafe for *that*? I'd be crazy." His deadpan expression made her laugh. "We made a deal, and I'll stick to it. I promise."

"I want to believe you, Jack. But you just lied to me this morning about the chowder."

He took a step forward. "That wasn't exactly a lie. It just wasn't the whole story. I'll never do it again."

She had no choice but to trust him. Her heart told her she could, though her logical side said, *stay vigilant. What else is he deceiving you about?* But it was hard to be mad at him. Especially when he looked at her that way.

"Don't worry, Carrie. Awards are nice, but they don't affect the bottom line that much. We'll make up for blowing this contest."

She'd liked hearing him say "we," as if he felt they were a team. It encouraged her to explain why winning had been so important.

"The café's finances are on shaky ground, Jack. Everything affects the bottom line. If I don't turn things around this summer, we may need to close our doors."

He looked even more concerned than she expected. "I noticed that you keep an eagle eye on costs and changed the menu prices. I thought you were just being attentive, as you should be."

"Unfortunately, it's more than that."

"I see ... and that makes my screwup even worse," he admitted.

Carrie wasn't trying to make him feel guilty, but at least he understood the full consequences now.

"Let's just call it chowder under the bridge," she said. "I do have a strategy to draw more customers, at least for the Fourth of July weekend. But Jack Dubensky will be sarcastic, and Jackson Gardeaux will laugh his head off."

"I won't do either. Try me."

Carrie was sure he would but plunged ahead.

"Blueberries. The island is famous for them. July is National Blueberry Month, and we could have a blueberry menu with specials for each meal? And really bear down and focus on winning the Best Blueberry Pie competition. That's on Fourth of July weekend, the perfect time for the Blue Sky Cafe's salute to America's favorite berry."

She watched his expression, waiting for a reaction.

"Blueberries? The café is going under, and *that's* your strategy?"

"I knew you'd say that." She fiddled with papers on her desk. "Sorry if it's too small-town and corny for you."

"I can't deny it's corny. But it might be fun, and I do owe you one, all things considered."

Carrie stood up and faced him. "You owe me at least one."

He raised his hands in a gesture of surrender. "Blueberries it is. There's a lot I can do, sauces and such." She heard the wheels in his head spinning. He was amazingly creative. "Let me think about it."

She grabbed a folder of schedules she needed to bring home. "Don't think too long. July Fourth is next weekend. And, this is a collaboration," she added. "You create the dishes, and we'll taste test and make any necessary changes."

"You know what they say, 'Teamwork makes the dream work.'"

Carrie had heard that motivational phrase before. Why did it sound like flirting when he said it? She pulled her gaze away and brushed aside the feeling.

"As long as we understand each other." She moved toward the door, expecting him to move aside. But he came closer.

"I think we do. In fact, I'm sure of it." He wore a small smile mostly in his eyes. She was confused. What was so amusing?

"Good then." Her words came out softer and breathier than she'd intended. She suddenly realized they were standing very close. He seemed taller and bigger, filling the doorway. He gazed down, catching her gaze and holding it.

"It's time to go," she managed.

"I know. I was just thinking about...blueberries," he said quietly. He lifted his hand and brushed a strand of hair from her cheek. "It is a good idea. And I like it a lot better when we're not arguing."

Before she could reply he bent his head and kissed her, softly at first, a questioning kiss. She tried not to react and told herself to pull away. But soon felt her body moving closer as his arm wrapped around her waist. The kiss deepened, and she couldn't resist. His hold was both strong and tender. As if she was fragile and prized. She'd rarely felt that way with anyone.

She wasn't sure how long the kiss went on. It could have been a few moments or a few hours. When she heard her phone buzz with a text, she felt herself drop from a sweet cloud. She pulled away from Jack and checked the message.

"It's Sophie. I need to call her. You go ahead."

He looked surprised. "I can wait. I'll walk you out."

"That's all right. I'll see you tomorrow," she added. Which seemed an impersonal thing to say to someone who'd made her feel as if she'd been struck by lightning. But it helped hide her reaction and put distance between them.

Jack looked confused. A curtain dropped on his expression. "Sure, see you." He left with a curt wave.

Carrie waited to hear the door close and dropped into her desk chair. *Carrie Louise Duffy—how did that happen? Again? You promised not to get involved with him.*

Number one, you're his boss, and it's totally unprofessional; and numbers two, three, four, and five—in a few weeks, he'll morph back into Jackson Gardeaux, and return to a planet that's lightyears from your own. He might be interested in a summer fling, but it could never be more.

And, she reminded herself, *he knows that, too.*

Twenty-Seven

On Sunday morning, Tess got cold feet about meeting Ben at church, but she'd told her aunt about the plan and knew Lila would never let her back out.

When she came downstairs, Lila was already waiting in the truck. Tess gave Honey a biscuit as she left. "Wish me luck," she whispered. "I wish you could come."

Honey seemed to understand and licked her hand.

"You look very pretty," her aunt said as she steered down the lane to the main road. "I can't remember the last time I saw you dressed up."

"It's just an old summer dress I had handy," Tess said, trying to downplay her appearance.

Up in her bedroom, her hands shook as she applied a bit of makeup and brushed out her hair. She thought about leaving it loose or making a ponytail but finally fixed her usual long braid. She had no idea what to wear. Everything she tried on seemed wrong. Then she remembered a floral print summer dress in the bottom of her pack. It wasn't new, but she wore it so rarely, it still looked fresh. She found some small hoop earrings and her good sandals, which looked fine but didn't have a heel. *You're not walking down a fashion runway. It's just church,* she reminded herself.

"I did my best," Tess said

"You look lovely," her aunt assured her.

"I hate the idea of everyone checking me out." *To see what the jailbird looks like now,* Tess added silently.

"You will be noticed, but that's sort of the point, isn't it?" her aunt said. "Besides, once the service starts, all eyes will be on Reverend Hopkins."

They drove in silence for a few minutes, then her aunt said, "I know that scene in the diner was upsetting, but nothing like that will happen today, Tess. You don't need to worry."

Tess wasn't so sure. Most people would be far less likely to act like that in a church. But it wasn't impossible.

"And you'll have Dr. Croft there," her aunt added.

Tess turned to her. "How will that help?"

"He didn't have to do this. He wants to stick up for you." Lila's gaze remained fixed on the road. For some reason, Tess felt her aunt wanted to say, "protect you."

Was Ben "sticking up" for her? It was true in a way. Though his motives—even after his explanation—were still a mystery.

Tess saw Ben waiting outside the white clapboard building. Reverend Hopkins stood nearby, at the big arched doors, greeting everyone who entered, as he did every Sunday. The minister had been at the church for as long as Tess could remember. She wondered if he'd be surprised to see her, though she guessed her aunt had told him she was back.

"You go ahead while I park. Dr. Croft is waiting." Lila stopped the truck at the bottom of the path and practically pushed her out, though Tess would have liked to delay her arrival even longer.

She felt Ben's gaze as she approached. He'd been checking his phone, then seemed to forget it was in his hand. The way he stared made her uneasy. Was he having second thoughts, too?

"It's getting late. I was worried you wouldn't come."

"Not a chance. My aunt would have tied me up and brought me in a sack."

Ben smiled. "Luckily it didn't come to that."

"Lucky for me." She shrugged, trying to hide her nerves.

"You look very nice." His tone was polite, but she felt his gaze take her in from head to toe.

"Thanks. I have real legs under my jeans. Hope that doesn't shock you."

"You're full of surprises. I'll grant you that."

"Are you still sure you want to do this?" she asked, hoping he'd say no.

"Yes, I'm sure. Are you?"

"Not entirely. But I told you I would. So, here I am."

Lila joined them. She looked so happy. Tess decided the effort was worth it just for her.

"Shall we go in? The service is about to start," her aunt said.

They followed the flow of churchgoers. If Reverend Hopkins was surprised to see Ben Croft accompanying her and Lila, he didn't show it. He greeted them warmly and offered Tess a special smile. "It's good to see you, Tess. Your aunt told me that you were home."

"For the summer. I'm not sure after that."

"I hope it becomes clear. Summer is probably the perfect time of year to figure it out." His voice was comforting. She remembered that about him now.

Ten years hadn't changed the minister much. His white robes fluttered in the breeze around his tall, rangy frame and rifled his sandy hair that had gone white. A few more lines crinkled around his brown eyes when he smiled, but he still looked fit.

"I hope you enjoy the service, Tess. Thank you for coming."

His gratitude confused her, and she didn't know what to say. Bells sounded in the steeple. It was time to find a seat.

Inside, Aunt Lila led the way up the center aisle while Tess wished she could slink up the side and sit in a back row. So much for Ben's plan.

The sanctuary was not crowded but full enough to make Tess wonder how many recognized her. Answering the question, she heard low voices nearby. "Isn't that Tess Hargrove and her aunt with Ben Croft?"

"I think you're right," another whispered back. "I guess the age of miracles hasn't passed after all."

There was muffled laughter. Tess stared straight ahead. She couldn't blame them and even found the comeback clever. She had to tell her aunt later.

Lila found a place in a middle row, and Ben politely allowed the ladies to walk in first. Tess landed with her aunt on one side and Ben on the other. She forced herself not to look at him, which was nearly impossible. A program had been left on each seat, and as soon she opened hers, it fluttered to the floor. She and Ben nearly collided as they both leaned down to pick it up.

He handed it back and whispered, "Good try. But you won't get out of this by knocking me unconscious."

"Too bad, that usually works."

When he smiled back, Tess couldn't have felt more dazed then if they *had* struck heads. An organ sounded the opening note of the first hymn, and everyone rose. She watched the choir walk up the center aisle singing and then take their places on the risers.

Reverend Hopkins followed and walked to the front of the sanctuary. Her aunt and Ben had both found the page in their hymnals. Tess searched the wooden pocket in front of her seat, but it was empty. Before she could spot an extra, Ben held his out between them. He had a deep tenor and sang on key. They stood so close, their shoulders brushed, and she could feel his breath stir her hair. She wondered if he noticed their nearness the way she did. Of course, he didn't.

She forced herself to focus on the service, wondering why she'd ever agreed to do this.

"It's so good to see everyone on this bright summer morning," the Reverend began. "Especially our visitors. We welcome you warmly."

His gaze swept the sanctuary, but Tess felt as if he looked straight at her when he mentioned visitors. Had she imagined that?

She read the responses to the opening prayers printed in the program. Then Evaline Finch rose and walked up front to read a scripture. Her flowery dress looked as if she wrapped herself in her garden. She met Tess's gaze, nodded a silent greeting, and then read from the open Bible on the lectern.

Reverend Hopkins stood at the pulpit and read another Scripture. He closed his Bible and began his sermon, speaking about the verses and the essential messages of the church community, loving one another and forgiving each other for wrongs and mistakes. "As God forgives us," he added.

He made it sound simple. But Tess knew it was not.

"—Asking for forgiveness and giving it is something we do for ourselves, as odd as that might sound," he continued. "We're the ones carrying that toxic emotional load, being poisoned by it, every day. We're the ones being hurt by resentment. Not the object of our ire."

He paused and looked out at his listeners. "I'm not advocating that we accept it when someone treats us badly. We can recognize wrongs and still forgive. We can release the burden of anger and pain and truly move on."

Tess thought of her father and the countless Sundays she'd sat in this sanctuary by his side. For years, she'd denied her painful feelings and told herself, *What's done is done*. Nothing could change that relationship, and there was no use fretting about it. Living here again, it was hard to keep that box closed tight and carry that load, as the Reverend had just said. Maybe someday, she'd understand her father better, and forgiveness would come. But she still felt a long way from that moment.

She glanced at Ben. He sat so still, staring at the hymnal in his hands. Was he listening to the sermon, or was his mind wandering, too? Perhaps he was thinking of how he could never forgive her for the accident. Even if he wanted to.

It was too much to ask of Ben; he believed she'd been driving Zach's car. She understood and didn't blame him. Despite the reverend's optimistic advice, Tess thought there were some things a person could never absolve.

When the sermon was over, the congregation shared their

news during "Joys and Concerns." Reverend Hopkins called on each raised hand. There were happy announcements of babies, birthdays, weddings, and all the triumphs of ordinary life. Also, requests for prayers for the sick and dying, and those who faced hardship or had lost their way. The minister gave each speaker his total attention.

Tess remembered the kindness he'd shown her. Reverend Hopkins had come to visit her when she was arrested, and later when she was in detention. He must have known she only had Lila in her corner.

She was very young, frightened, and frustrated. She hadn't been nice to him, she recalled. Hadn't appreciated his patience and understanding. Maybe someday she could thank him properly.

There was another hymn with an upbeat tune and lyrics, "Down by the Riverside"—one she remembered and liked to sing. It must have shown; in the middle of the song, she caught Ben smiling at her.

The minister said a final prayer, and the service ended.

Tess felt relieved as she came to her feet. The center aisle was crowded as the pews emptied. Tess felt people stare at her and heard more muffled whispers. Even if they didn't recognize her, everyone knew Ben and his history.

Did anyone object to her being there? If so, they had the decency to keep that opinion to themselves. So far, anyway. Would this stop the vandalism at the farm? It was impossible to tell, but she knew Ben felt better, showing everyone here he disapproved of Tess and her aunt being treated that way.

At least they'd accomplished that much. The rest remained to be seen.

Twenty-Eight

The sunlight was bright and sharp in the churchyard. Tess shielded her eyes with her hand. She looked up at Ben, preparing to say goodbye.

He seemed distracted, gazing out at the crowd, chatting in small groups or heading for cars. "I thought my mother and sister were here. I guess not."

He sounded disappointed, but she felt just the opposite. Before she could thank him, a woman approached. Her sophisticated blue and white dress complimented silvery blond hair, cut in a short, choppy style. She wore little makeup except for a dash of bright lipstick. Something about her was effortlessly chic, down to the pedicured toes that peeked out of low-heeled sandals.

"You did warn me. But I had to see it with my own eyes," she greeted Ben.

"I'm not surprised." He turned to Tess. "This is my aunt, Frances Croft. She's the publisher of *The Harbor Observer*."

"For goodness sake, you make me sound like the late Queen of

England. No, the replica of her in the wax museum." She turned her focus on Tess and offered a hand. "It's Frankie. That's what everyone calls me."

Tess shook her hand. "Tess Hargrove. But you already know that. Am I about to be a news story?" she asked in a wary voice.

Ben looked shocked. His aunt laughed. "I *could* get some copy out of this situation, now that you mention it. But I know you prefer to avoid the spotlight."

Tess realized this was the person to thank for dropping the news article Brooke Duffy wrote. "Thank you for that. And for not printing the story about our farm."

Frankie Croft glanced at her nephew. "A very persuasive advocate pleaded your case. He's the one you ought to thank."

Tess felt her cheeks get warm. She had an urge to glance at Ben but didn't dare.

"It was brave of you to come here," Frankie said.

"A very persuasive person talked me into it."

Frankie smiled. "Yes, I know. And I hope it helps," she said sincerely. She glanced at her nephew. "You still owe me lunch, pal."

"I didn't forget."

"Obviously, you did because you never rescheduled. Call Jennifer tomorrow. She knows my calendar better than I do." She smiled at Tess again. "It was good to meet you. I will confess, I've been curious."

At least she was honest, though the admission made Tess feel like an exotic animal in the zoo.

Frankie must have read her expression. "Not for the reason you're thinking." She glanced at Ben and grinned. "You two have a nice day. It's gotten off to an interesting start."

That was one way of putting it, Tess thought as Ben's intimidating Aunt Frankie walked away with a graceful, confident gait. She was sharp, but she had the wrong impression. Tess had no intention of spending the day with Ben, nor he, with her.

Aunt Lila stood nearby with Evaline and her church friends. Tess wondered what the group thought about Ben sitting with them. No doubt, she'd hear about that later.

"Ready to go?" Tess asked.

"Yes, I am." Lila turned to Ben. "Would you like to have lunch with us, Ben? You must be hungry. It's nearly noon."

Tess cringed. "I'm sure he's busy, Aunt Lila. He probably has plans. Or needs to go to the hospital."

Tess expected he'd take this easy out, but he looked amused by her discomfort. "I'd love to have lunch at the farm, Mrs. Norton. I don't need to be at the hospital until four."

Her aunt's grin spread from one sunflower earring to the other. "You know the way. We'll see you there. And please call me Lila."

Tess walked to the truck in silence. Once they were on the road, she said, "I don't know why you invited him."

"He made an effort to help us. Showing some hospitality is a small gesture of thanks."

Tess couldn't argue. He had made a bold gesture. Whether it would make any difference was another question.

Tess watched the passing scenery. The road home followed the cliffs; all she could see for miles was the clear blue sky and the rocking blue sea. "I guess we should stop at a store. There's nothing in the fridge to feed him."

"I baked a cheese and tomato pie this morning while you were upstairs. There's green salad and pound cake with strawberries and whipped cream for dessert."

Tess was partly annoyed by her aunt's machinations, but also amused. "Nice menu, Aunt Lila."

"I didn't want to serve something heavy like a roast, even though it's Sunday," Lila said, oblivious—or just ignoring?—the sarcasm. "Folks don't eat like that these days."

"No, they don't." Was her aunt matchmaking? Tess shuddered at the thought. She'd get through the meal, and that would be that. The idea of spending more time with Ben made her happy, but another voice asked, *What's the point? It will only encourage your feelings. Feelings that could only be one-sided.*

Her aunt set the table with her best dishes and cloth napkins, but they ate in the kitchen, to Tess's relief. She was nervous about having Ben there. The formal dining room would have put her over the top. Flowers from the garden filled a vase, and her aunt's cooking was very tasty, as always. Ben complimented Lila with every bite.

"This is delicious. A quiche with tomatoes and herbs?"

Lila laughed. "I wouldn't tack any French words on it. My mother called it cheese pie. She'd add bacon, but vegetables are healthier."

"Don't let it get around, but even doctors eat bacon once in a while."

Tess smiled but didn't contribute much to the conversation. She couldn't treat Ben as if he was just any visitor. Like Evaline or Owen. He wasn't. Not to her.

Her aunt was her usually chatty self, asking him enough questions for both of them. Tess learned he'd gone to Colby, a small college in Maine, and then to medical school in New York City at Columbia University. He'd done a residency in California but eventually found his way back to New England. His family finally persuaded him two years ago to work at the new emergency medical unit at the Haven Island Health Clinic.

"Do you think you'll stay here long?" Aunt Lila asked.

He finally looked put on the spot. "I don't know. The department is still being developed, so that's interesting."

"It's been an enormous help to the island. Your family was very generous to sponsor the project," Lila said.

Ben seemed uncomfortable. Tess had noticed that he didn't like to draw attention to the Croft wealth and influence.

"My family has a deep commitment to Haven and the people here. We saw the need and wanted to help."

Before her aunt could interrogate him further, Tess rose and gathered empty dishes. "Let me clear the table, Aunt Lila. Then I have to take care of a few chores outside."

Her aunt looked surprised by the abrupt end to their meal and conversation. "But there's still dessert."

Tess put the dishes in the sink. "I'll have mine later. You two go ahead. The animals don't know it's Sunday."

Ben laughed and picked up a few plates that were left. "I couldn't eat another bite right now, either. I'll help Tess, and we'll be back in a little while for the next course."

Tess caught his glance. She was trying to make it easy for him to leave. Why didn't he take the hint?

"I'll wait for you outside, Tess?"

"Sure, I'll be right down." She headed up to change, not knowing what else to do.

A few minutes later, she met Ben on the porch, her flowered dress exchanged for jeans, a worn t-shirt, and work boots.

He looked her over and grinned. "Feel better now?"

She did feel better, much more herself, but brushed off his attention. "I didn't want to scare the hens dressed like that. They might stop laying."

He smiled and shook his head. She walked past with Honey at her heels, headed for the barn, and Ben followed.

"How can I help? Just tell me what to do."

She wasn't used to delegating and didn't know what to say. "You can give the goats fresh water. There are some buckets in the barn. But if you don't want to dirty your clothes, please don't bother."

"I'll be fine. Where are the buckets?"

Tess slid open the door, and Ben stood back. "What's that?" he asked.

She'd set up a contraption with pulleys and a rope to help her stack bales of hay in the loft. "My invention to move the bales. I hook the rope to the tractor, but it's still hard to steer them into the right spot."

"Resourceful of you. But two could do it much faster and easier. I have off tomorrow. I'll come back and give you a hand."

What he said was true, but Tess could think of a list of reasons why she wouldn't accept his offer.

"You don't have to keep coming back. You've done your best to show people you're not against me. I appreciate that. But you don't have to feel sorry for me."

He stood back, his arms crossed over his chest. The afternoon light in the barn was dim. She could hardly make out his expression. "That's not why I come here."

Tess wasn't sure what he meant but felt afraid to ask Ben why he kept returning.

"Have you thought any more about taking the deed to the property?" he asked quietly.

"I'm still not sure. The more I mull it over, the more confused I get. What do you think I should do?" Tess was surprised to hear herself ask his advice. Once she did, she knew his opinion was important to her.

"I think deep down, this is what you really want. What's rightfully yours. If you don't accept it, I think you'll always regret it."

Something in his words rang true. Tess felt it in her bones. Still, she questioned her reaction. "Even though my cousin is against it?"

"That's another reason to do it and not to wait."

His tone held a note of urgency that Tess took to heart. "Richard is worried about my aunt. Well, mostly about her," she conceded.

"You're very trusting, Tess. Considering all you've been through."

She knew what he meant. Her experience would have hardened a lot of people, but she tried not to be bitter. Still, she'd always felt at a distance from most people, behind an invisible wall even. One she'd built herself from the time she was young, hiding there for her own protection.

"I like to give people the benefit of the doubt." Maybe because she didn't get it herself when she'd needed it the most.

"I can see that. I just hope your cousin doesn't disappoint you." Ben stood back and rubbed his hands together, ready to get to work. "So, where are these thirsty goats? Let me at 'em."

Tess smiled and handed him the buckets. "There's a spigot near their pen. I'll show you."

As they headed outside, Ben's phone rang. He pulled it from his pocket and spoke quickly, then put the phone away and turned to her.

"That was the hospital. There was a boating accident, and they need help." He set the buckets on the ground and rolled his sleeves down. "Please thank your aunt for me. Tell her I'm sorry to miss that dessert. It was a perfect afternoon."

His gratitude seemed excessive, but his expression was sincere. The way he looked at her, as if he regretted being called away, made Tess feel off balance.

"Don't worry. I'll tell her what happened."

He touched her shoulder as they walked to his car. "Goodbye, Tess. See you soon."

He started his car and waved as he drove off—leaving her with a lot to think about.

Twenty-Nine

Carrie had asked Jack to have the special menu planned by Monday, calculating that if there were any glitches—say, he presented her with jalapeno and blueberry corn muffins—there would be time to adjust before the weekend.

When the café closed, it was time to taste test the dishes he'd created. She also needed to work out the cost of each and figure out pricing. She hoped he hadn't used a lot of exotic ingredients that cut into the profit. She wanted this idea to make money for the café, not put them even further in the red.

A herd of butterflies fluttered in her stomach. Their argument about the chowder fiasco had shaken her. Along with the revelation of his real identity and status.

She reminded herself she was the boss and had the last word on the menu. But she knew how creative he was and how seriously he took cooking, and all of that made her dread judging his efforts.

Please don't let him serve me a Zen burger topped with blueberry sauce, she silently muttered.

Jack appeared with three covered dishes and a typed list on a tray. He set the tray down and sat beside her. "Here are the new dishes, in categories: breakfast, lunch, and dessert. I've also come up with a few beverages."

Carrie scanned the catchy names and descriptions. No red flags, like "curry," "cilantro," or "siracha sauce," jumped out. That was some relief.

"We'll start with Blueberry Baked French Toast and Berry-Medley Crepes. If you really want pancakes, I'll do that instead."

Carrie nearly laughed at his intonation, which said, "Plain old, mundane, boring pancakes." She shrugged and hid her smile. "Show me what you got. I'm ready."

She eyed both dishes as a warm, buttery scent enticed her. She added a bit of syrup and took a bite of the French toast first. Thick slices of bread had been soaked with a rich mixture of cream and eggs and tasted like a delicious bread pudding studded with fruit.

"Mmmm...this is good. I like the crumb topping," she mumbled around a mouthful. Her simple words of praise were expressed in an awed tone. "Perfect amount of cinnamon."

"I used rolled oats in the topping, gives it some crunch." Jack looked pleased by her review, but also as if he'd expected no less. "Now the crepes."

She cut a bite with her fork and chewed slowly. The paper-thin pancakes were filled with a sweet cheese filling mixed with blueberries and more fresh mixed berries on top in a light sauce that wasn't too sweet. There was a dollop of fresh whipped cream on the side of the plate, with a mint-leaf garnish.

"These crepes are amazing. Thin as tissue and the filling is sublime." She took another bite, savoring the flavors. "There's something else, I can't quite—"

"Orange zest," he said. "Balances the cheese."

"Yes, it does." She was getting an advanced lesson in ingredient blending. "Where did you learn to make these? In cooking school?"

"Grand-mère Babette. She had me standing on a stool at the stove to help stir sauces when I was in kindergarten."

Carrie could picture the scene. Jack must have been adorable at that age, though she wondered if he was exaggerating just a bit? "That's very young to be cooking."

"Maybe I was in first grade by the time we got to sauces," he admitted. "My father's clan is from eastern Europe. Kielbasa and dumplings were early lessons, too. Perfect dishes for Octoberfest."

Carrie agreed with a nod. The thought that he'd be gone by then, and she would be, too, stung. She pushed it aside. "Let's just get through the Fourth of July. Both dishes are a go. But I think the word 'crepes' will throw our customers off. How about ...Stuffed Berry-Medley...Pancake Pillows?"

Jack nodded. "Catchy. By the time anyone orders that, the kitchen will be closed."

"You know what I mean. Something in that direction."

"I'll work on it." He smiled at her in a gentle way, crinkly lines at the corners of his eyes and a deep dimple appearing in one lean cheek.

"You've got whipped cream on your cheek, boss."

"I do?" She felt embarrassed to be caught being such a messy eater. Before she could figure it out, Jack dabbed the spot with a napkin. "There you go. Perfect now."

He caught her gaze and held it, and she couldn't look away. "I like cooking for you, Carrie Duffy. From blueberries to bouillabaisse."

Carrie wanted to break the spell with a clever comeback but felt breathless. She could barely think straight.

"I like bouillabaisse," she managed, trying to keep up the pretense that this was still a normal conversation. "If the sauce doesn't have too much saffron."

"Remind me when I make it for you." His warm gaze mesmerized her as his hand gently cupped her cheek. She knew he was going to kiss her again but couldn't move away. She felt herself turn toward him on the counter stool as he lifted her face to his. She closed her eyes and their lips met, softly at first, then the kiss deepened, and his mouth moved over hers, savoring the moment. She had her hands on his strong shoulders and felt his arms wrap around her, pulling her into a warm embrace.

Her cell phone rang, jarring her to her senses. It was set to vibrate and hopped around the counter next to her plate. Carrie pulled back and checked the screen.

"It's Sophie . . . I need to take this."

She turned away from Jack, feeling lightheaded. "Hi, honey, what's up?" she asked, her tone falsely bright.

Jack set the dishes back on the tray and headed to the kitchen, though she felt he was listening to the conversation.

"Why aren't you home yet, Mom? We're going out for Hannah's birthday tonight. Did you forget?"

Carrie checked the time, shocked out of her pleasant fog. It was late, and she'd totally forgotten about their dinner with the Boltons.

"I'll be home in five minutes. Don't worry."

She ended the call and slipped off the stool. Jack had returned with a tray of scrumptious-looking lunch entrees. He'd gone to so much trouble, she hated to leave him flat.

"Something wrong?"

"I'm so sorry. I've got to run. I somehow got roped into going out to dinner with the Boltons. It's Hannah's birthday, and she was allowed to invite a friend, so she asked Sophie."

"And a friend's mom?" His tone was joking but questioning too.

"Her father asked if I'd come along. I think he just wants another adult at the table for some sensible conversation. It's tough to be alone for hours with two adolescent girls."

Jack forced a smile, but she could tell he was disappointed that the tasting was cut short.

"Can you save these dishes?" Carrie grabbed her purse. "I'll try the rest tomorrow."

"Sure. But they won't taste as good."

"I'll get the idea." She picked up the sheet he'd printed out. "I'll take this list and make some notes. We'll settle it all tomorrow. If the rest is anything like what I just tasted, we're in great shape," she called from the front door.

"Right. Have fun." He wiped down the counter and didn't look up.

He was pouting. She thought it was cute. He'd been excited about presenting the specials and was miffed to see her run off. Jack did not fit the cliché of a moody chef, but today it rang true. Or was he annoyed that their romantic moment had been shut down, as if some unseen hand had flipped a switch?

Carrie was thankful that Sophie's call had saved her from another step in the wrong direction, but also felt her daughter's interruptions were uncanny. Was that merely a coincidence, or was the universe trying to tell her something?

The truth was, she wished the call had come just a minute or two later.

* * *

Tess had worked in the fields most of the day, checking the progress of the seedlings and pulling weeds. The job required focus and effort, and the hours passed with her barely noticing the sun moving from the east to the west. Though each time she took a break to gauge her progress or sip some water, she noticed Ben had not come by as he'd promised. Or even called.

Her hope that he'd appear dwindled with the passing hours. She felt silly for expecting him. She knew he had good intentions and meant well, but he'd made the offer impulsively.

He was a good person. He liked helping people. That's why he'd become a doctor. But something else had come up, and he hadn't thought much about it. Or he'd had second thoughts about seeing her again. She shouldn't have taken it to heart.

Even if he'd really meant it, it was only because he felt sorry for her. She wanted his forgiveness, someday. But she didn't want his pity, and she'd told him that, too.

She gathered her tools and headed to the barn. It was just as well he hadn't come. Every time she saw him, she liked him more. Where would that get her? Nowhere, except hurt and disappointed. The way she felt right now—only ten times worse.

"Tess, are you all right? You've barely touched your dinner."

Tess looked up, caught in her wandering thoughts. "I'm sorry. I'm just tired. The sun was strong today."

Her aunt had made a tasty pot of chili, one of Tess's favorites. But she didn't have much appetite.

"You look tired, dear. You ought to go to bed early." As her aunt carried dishes to the sink, Tess's phone rang. Tess ignored it and took a few last bites of her meal.

"Aren't you going to get that?"

"It will go to voicemail. Probably someone selling something at this hour." She couldn't imagine who it could be and didn't feel like talking.

The phone was charging on the counter, and her aunt stood in view of the screen. "Did Dr. Croft take an extra job in telephone sales?" she asked mildly.

Snapped out of her daze, Tess rose and caught the call just in time. "Tess? It's me," he greeted her.

"Hello, Ben." She kept her voice even and neutral, careful not to betray she'd been waiting for him all day. "How are you?"

"Fried to a crisp. I've been at the hospital since I left your place. I even slept here, a few hours anyway. It's been crazy. Maybe it's a full moon."

She smiled, relieved to hear his explanation. "It's only a half-moon tonight, but maybe that's enough."

She sensed that her aunt was listening, though her back was turned as she did the dishes. Tess went out to the porch for privacy.

"I'm sorry I couldn't come by today like I promised. I just realized I never got in touch to let you know."

At least he was honest and didn't make fake excuses. It felt good to know keeping the promise mattered to him. But she still thought it was best if he didn't come back. Best for her anyway.

"I understand. There's no need to apologize. Your job is so

demanding. If you have time off, you should go to the beach or get some extra sleep. Not spend the day doing farm work."

"Are you saying that to let me off the hook, or do you really not want to see me? I have off on Wednesday. I thought I'd come then."

Tess was torn. Of course, she wanted to see him. It was impossible to lie.

"I'll be here on Wednesday." She tried to sound indifferent and was glad he wasn't there to see she felt anything but. "If it doesn't work out, I understand."

"I'll see you then. I'll wear work clothes this time."

"That's probably wise." He always looked fine to her, but she didn't dare say that.

They said goodbye and ended the call.

She told herself not to get her hopes up. New emergencies might demand his attention, and he wouldn't come after all.

But at least he cared enough to call.

Thirty

Hannah had her choice of any restaurant on the island, Doug had explained, but she chose Bolton's. Carrie didn't blame her. She was treated like a rock star there or maybe a princess. Or maybe both. At twelve years old, that counts for a lot.

The fine dining side of Bolton's, built on the other side of the fish market warehouse, offered water views from almost every seat. The tables were set with linen and china, and the service was always attentive.

That went triple for the Bolton family. Doug and his guests were immediately escorted to a corner table, where waist-coated waiters swarmed, bringing ice water and baskets of warm bread while another took drink orders. Hannah and Sophie delighted in all the attention.

Doug tried his best to act as if nothing unusual was going on. For him, it wasn't, she realized.

Carrie would have been happy with a dish from the regular

menu, but Doug insisted that she have a lobster platter special. She didn't like it when a man ordered for her but knew he had good intentions. It was almost as if they were dining at his house—with a platoon of servants. She was his guest, so she smiled graciously as he dealt with the waiter.

Once the food arrived, they were left in peace to eat, but their conversation was still fractured, and most of their attention was spent on the girls, talking about their favorite music, subjects they liked in school, or their adventures at camp.

Just as their places were cleared, a parade of waitstaff marched out of the kitchen, singing "Happy Birthday." A beautiful pink cake surrounded by sparklers was set up on a cart and rolled to the table. Many customers joined in the song, and Hannah looked very pleased as she blew out the candles.

"What did you wish for Hannah?" Carrie asked in a playful tone.

"Sorry, but I can't tell. If I do, it won't come true." She and Sophie exchanged a glance, then giggled in unison.

Carrie looked at Doug. "I think someone at the table has a good guess."

Doug laughed. "I think you're right. As it should be, between BFFs." His tone was serious, but his eyes sparkled with humor. Carrie had to smile. She knew plenty of men who were good dads, her own included on that list. But Doug was clearly a loving, watchful, and devoted father, and it was touching to see.

Hannah had opened her gifts from her father at home that morning. "She couldn't wait," Doug explained.

She only had one at the table, from Sophie. But she shrieked with delight worthy of ten surprises. It was just a t-shirt with a dancing pineapple on it she'd admired in a shop on Front Street.

Sophie had thoughtfully remembered and gone back to buy it for her.

"I love it!" Hannah declared. "Now you have to get one, too."

"Good idea. Maybe someone will surprise me. Hint, hint?" Sophie glanced at her mother.

"I'll spread the word. Maybe someone will."

Sophie had been so easy to deal with since her disappearing act. She did deserve a small surprise.

It was such a beautiful night they decided to walk on the dock after they left the restaurant. The girls ran ahead, eager to explore the shops and a video game arcade.

"I think this birthday is officially a success," Doug declared. "What do you think?"

"I think you're a wonderful father, and Hannah adores you," she said honestly.

He looked surprised by her blunt but complimentary appraisal. "Thanks. High praise, coming from a fellow parent of an adolescent girl. These years aren't easy."

"No, they're not, and it's going to get worse before it gets better," she warned with a wry smile.

"Once they hit high school, you mean. I'm bracing myself. I wasn't perfect, but I didn't give my parents much grief at that stage. I've heard girls can be tough."

"In our way," Carrie said knowingly. "My parents had to weather three of us in a row. But we all turned out fine."

"Absolutely." His soft smile made her feel self-conscious.

She didn't want to talk anymore about being a teenager or her high school years. Especially hers and his. She'd found Doug surprisingly easy to talk to. He laughed at all her jokes and found her amazingly clever. But she couldn't help thinking of him as the rich, popular boy who'd had never given her a second look when they were teenagers. It was so silly, and she tried to ignore it, but the feeling persisted, like a low-level hum in her head. She'd felt a bit on edge, as if she had to be on the top of her game when she was with him.

Which could be because you don't know each other, she reminded herself. *As much as you don't want to admit it, this is a lot like a first date—with two twelve-year-old chaperones.*

She never felt that way with Jack, she realized. She was just herself, warts and all, and rarely thought twice about what she said to him. *Maybe because you're his boss?* But it wasn't only that. It was just the way they were with each other, relaxed and authentic.

It seemed rude to think of Jack in the middle of a conversation with Doug. She quickly brushed the thoughts aside and gave Doug her full attention.

"Does Hannah's mother live in Boston, too?" she asked.

The personal question seemed to take him by surprise, but he didn't seem offended. "Yes, she has a condo not far from my house, and we share custody. When we can. Sara travels a lot for her work. She's an architect with a big firm that builds skyscrapers and hotels all over the world. She's working in Chicago for the summer on a building that will be even higher than the Sears Tower. That's why I have Hannah."

His ex-wife sounded highly accomplished and very successful in her field. Carrie hadn't even met her and felt intimidated.

"My ex-husband travels a lot, too. He and Sophie have a great relationship, but he's not around much. Which has pluses and minuses."

"I know what you mean. Sara and I make the big decisions about Hannah together, but I'm used to being in the line of fire day to day. Sara always spent time away from the family, even when Sophie was small. She's a good mother in her way, and I know she loves Hannah." He added, "It's just who she is. She's coming back to Boston for a few days in August to spend time with Hannah. Hannah is really looking forward to it."

"I bet," Carrie said simply.

The idea of fitting your daughter into a work schedule didn't sit well with her, but she knew it was unfair to judge. She knew nothing of Hannah's mother, except for the small bits Doug had just told her, and perhaps he was not completely unbiased.

"I know this time with Hannah won't last forever," he admitted. "She's growing up right before my eyes. Sometimes it's hard, but I wouldn't change a thing," he said with a warm smile.

"I wouldn't either," Carrie agreed.

The girls appeared, running down the dock. When they reached Carrie and Doug, they came to a breathless halt. "Can I have some dollar bills for the change machine, Dad? Sophie and I want to play the video games. They look really fun this year. There are a lot of new ones."

Doug glanced at Carrie. "Do you mind staying out a little longer?"

"Of course not." Carrie took out her wallet to give Sophie money, but Doug was faster.

"My treat, for Hannah's birthday. They need some amusement and are way too old for a piñata."

"Are you kidding? You're never too old for a piñata," Carrie insisted, making him laugh again.

They followed the girls to the arcade. Carrie's first instinct was to cover her ears with her hands, but she bravely pushed forward. Bells rang, lights flashed, and sirens whirred. Sophie and Hannah bought handfuls of tokens and led them to a game called *Galactic Warrior* that simulated steering a rocket through the dangers of outer space.

They all agreed Hannah should go first. She started well but couldn't make her way through an asteroid shower. Sophie did a little better but didn't last long, either. Doug urged Carrie to go next, but he looked so eager, she couldn't make him wait.

He swooped around the asteroids and sonic waves that threatened to melt the rocket. But he flew too close to a gravity field and crashed into a purple planet.

"Game over!" the screen screamed.

Carrie finally slipped into the seat. Her tailored dress bunched over her knees, and working the pedals in high-heeled sandals was hard. Once she focused, she surprised herself, deftly avoiding flying space debris, angry aliens, and flaming comets. Her audience oohed and ahhhed.

Until a black hole popped up, and she vanished into the abyss. Doug, Hannah, and Sophie groaned in unison, but Carrie was relieved.

"That was fun. If you want to have a heart attack." She needed Doug's help to get out of the seat, and Sophie had to retrieve a lost shoe.

"Nice driving, Carrie." Doug laughed in surprise. "You didn't mention that you're an astronaut in your spare time."

"Didn't I? It's just a hobby," Carrie replied with a shrug. "Well, it's getting late. You two have camp, and some of us have work tomorrow," she said to the girls.

"*It's so...annoying.*" Doug made a face and mimicked the girls, and they all laughed.

When they reached Carrie's house, Sophie and Hannah got out to retrieve something from Sophie's room. Carrie turned to Doug.

"Thanks again for inviting us. I had so much fun. I hope Hannah did, too."

"I'm sure she did. It was a birthday to remember. Much better than going out with just her stuffy old dad. I'm glad we got a second chance to meet and get to know each other a little. I know you're busy with the café, but I'd love to see you again. Without the girls, I mean."

Carrie was surprised by his words and flattered. She had a feeling he might ask her out but thought he'd play it a little cooler and call her in a few days. Or maybe not. He was very attractive, and she was sure he had plenty of women interested in him.

"Sure, I'd love to see you again, Doug," she said.

"Great." He looked pleased by her answer. "I'm having a party on my boat on the Fourth of July. It's at night, so that shouldn't be a conflict with the café, right?"

"Not at all," she assured him.

"Just a few friends. We'll go out into the harbor and watch the fireworks from the water. We do it every year. It's really fun."

"It sounds wonderful. I'd love to come."

"I'd love to have you there. I have your number. I'll call with the details."

The girls returned. Carrie said goodnight again and slipped out of the car. Doug waved goodbye with a wide smile as he drove away.

Had Doug Bolton, class president, captain of the Lacrosse team, actually asked her out? Carrie could hardly believe it.

She knew her mother and sister would grill her about the evening and decided to keep this unexpected punchline to herself for a while. Or she'd never hear the end of it.

* * *

Carrie felt tired, but it was only ten. She wasn't used to driving a rocket through outer space. That had to be it. Sophie went straight to bed; she had to get up early. Carrie walked back to the kitchen and found Brooke working on her laptop, surrounded by scraps of paper covered with scribbled notes, a mug of coffee within reach.

She glanced at Carrie, then back at her computer. "You look awesome in that dress. I hope *Hannah* noticed."

Carrie knew she really meant Doug. She gave her sister a look and put the kettle on for tea.

"Mom always said I clean up well." Doug had complimented her, but she wasn't going to admit it. "Where is Mom?"

"She just went up. She wanted to read in bed. How was your evening? Where did you go?"

"Who, what, where, when? Is that all you need to know, Lois Lane?"

Brooke grinned. "Exactly. In any order you please."

"Let's see...we went to Bolton's and sat at the best table in the house and were treated like royalty. The food tasted even better than usual. Maybe it's prepared a special way for the family."

"Definitely possible. Did you have a good time with Doug?"

Carrie poured hot water into her mug and let the bag steep. "It was a lovely evening. The girls are endlessly entertaining."

"There wasn't any time alone to get to know each other?"

Carrie dunked the bag more than necessary. If she confided that they'd talked without the girls, the questions would never stop.

"It wasn't a date. He invited me as the parent of his daughter's best friend."

"We both know he didn't have to do that. I think he likes you. Don't you like him? You keep saying he's a nice guy."

Carrie brought the tea to the table. "He *is* a nice guy. I like him fine. I thought he was snooty in high school, preppy and popular. But he's nothing like that now."

"And you're a grownup and you can see how silly that is."

It was silly to stick Doug with that old label. So why did she still feel like the unpopular girl around him? It wasn't anything he did or said. Just old tapes running in her head.

"Did he say he'll call you?" Brooke sounded hopeful.

Carrie looked away. "No comment."

"I knew it. He's perfect for you and a real catch. Successful, good looking, and his family has tons of money. You already said he's very nice."

Carrie stared at the ceiling. "There's nothing wrong with Doug Bolton. In fact, there's a lot right about him. But I'm not interested in getting involved with anyone right now. I have no time, even if I wanted to."

She had agreed to see Doug again, but a date here and there was one thing. She really was too busy for a real relationship.

"That's just an excuse. You can find the time. I wouldn't brush him off so quickly. How many guys with that many checks in the plus column have you met since you and Tim split up?"

The answer was zero, as Brooke already knew. Carrie took another sip of tea. She'd tried dating sites, but none of her matches lasted more than two or three meetings. Most were duds.

Jack was the only man she'd been attracted to in ages. She wasn't sure how many checks he'd tally on Brooke's scorecard, and she didn't care. The minuses loomed larger.

"It's hard to be on your own, working, caring for Sophie, and going to school." Brooke's tone was sympathetic. "I know you're strong and you do it all. But it doesn't have to be like that forever."

Carrie squeezed her sister's hand. "I'm not alone. I have my family. To tell you the truth, he did ask me out, and I'm going to see him again. Happy now?"

Brooke smiled and turned back to the computer. "That's all I wanted to know. 'You can't win it if you ain't in it.'"

"True." Carrie couldn't deny Doug suited her for a list of reasons. His dating site profile would pop up as a five-star match. She enjoyed spending time with him and found him attractive, too. Why did she still have reservations, the kind she could barely put into words? Maybe if they'd met this summer for the first time, without past history, she'd like him a lot. He seemed to like her.

A short time later, Carrie headed to bed. She'd just shut the light when she realized she'd forgotten to look over Jack's list of special dishes. She set an extra early alarm so she'd have time to do it before she left for the café. He'd made a real effort, and she didn't want him to think she didn't care.

She was in a deep sleep when the sound of Jack pushing his motorcycle up the driveway woke her. She checked the time, half past one. She had no need to watch from the window; she easily pictured him. Several nights a week, he came home this late.

Where did he go? Who did he see? He'd never mentioned a girlfriend and certainly didn't act as if there was one. But he'd easily misled them about his identity. Maybe he was fooling her about that, too. He had to be carousing or seeing someone to return so late, so often.

She recalled how he'd kissed her today, then felt annoyed for allowing it. And annoyed to feel so attracted to him, in a way she didn't feel for Doug. There had been plenty of chemistry with Tim, she reminded herself, and where had that gotten her?

Jack was another bad relationship choice. She had to remember that every time he reeled her in with those dark eyes. At first, she thought he was a rambling, irresponsible type who hopped from job to job, living in rented rooms, with nothing more to his name than a motorcycle. Landing in a place like Haven for the summer, and maybe Key West or Jamaica when winter came. That lifestyle clearly disqualified him.

Then she learned he was an award-winning chef, who moved in the highest strata of the culinary world. The very opposite of her first impression, but with a new set of disqualifiers.

The bottom line was, from now on, she had to keep things strictly business with the charismatic cook.

Brooke meant well, but Carrie knew she wasn't ready to date anyone. She had to get her life together before she could share it. The sensible thing to do was steer clear of both men.

Thirty-One

It felt like a long wait from Monday night to Wednesday. Tess tried not to get her hopes up and purposely didn't make any special effort when she dressed. She took care of morning chores and had her breakfast. When Ben's car drove down the lane, she was just going back outside.

She walked over and greeted him. As promised, he wore jeans and a t-shirt and carried work gloves. She noticed a pile of clothes and personal belongings in the backseat. Had he slept at the hospital again and not even made it home?

"I meant to get here earlier but got hung up in the ER again."

She was happy to see him but concerned about him, too.

"You must be exhausted. You should be home, sleeping."

"I'll crash later. Fresh air will be good for me." He gazed around and took a deep breath. "I'm actually starting to like the smell of manure."

"A lot of people say that...Never," she added with a laugh.

He smiled at her and swiped his hair aside with his hand. "Well, let's get at that hay. You want to move it, right?"

"Oh, I took care of that." With an inventive combination of ropes, pulleys, and the tractor, though not easily.

"There must be some job I can help you with. Any more pregnant goats around?"

Tess laughed. "The goats need to get their annual vaccination, CDT. It protects them from tetanus and overeating disease. There's a long Latin name for it, but basically, it's a bacteria that create toxins in their intestinal tract."

"Don't you have a vet come and do that?"

Tess shrugged. "Farmers need to be their own vets most of the time. As you saw with Daisy. If you don't want to do that, you could help me trim their hooves. It's sort of like goat wrestling without a referee."

He laughed and began rolling up his sleeves. "I'll go with the vaccination, thanks. I thought I'd get a break today from treating patients, but it seems to be my fate. Where do we start?"

Tess brought out the supplies, and they set up in the pen while Honey herded the goats from the grazing pasture. Ben took the medical end of the job, giving each their shot, while Tess held the goats steady. A few were troublesome. Duncan even kicked him.

"Do you need some ice?"

He rubbed his shin, frowning. "I'll be all right."

"I know it hurts, but it's better than being stuck by their horns."

"Sound like you speak from experience."

"You only need that to happen once. I'd like to get more goats. I mean, if I take over the farm. I've been reading a lot about making goat cheese and other products from the milk, like soap. It can be profitable." She caught Ethel in a tether and led her to Ben. "My father grew potatoes and cabbage, sometimes melons. Nothing else. Ever. I want to do things differently. Maybe plant some lavender. The sandy soil is ideal. Lavender farms do very well."

She didn't realize she was rambling until she caught his gaze. She felt embarrassed. "Too much information—sorry. I'm just thinking out loud."

"I love hearing your plans. Does this mean you decided to stay?" Ben's expression was serious, waiting for her answer.

"We're going to see Mr. Woods on Friday. He's drawn up the transfer. I have questions, but if it goes well, the deed will be signed over."

A wide smile lit up his handsome face, and she thought, for a moment, he was going to hug her. Maybe because she wanted to hug him. "That's big news, Tess. I'm really happy to hear it."

"Thanks." She shrugged, trying not to get ahead of herself. "It hasn't happened yet."

"Does your cousin know?" He set up the next dose for Ethel, his tone concerned.

"I don't know if my aunt told him. He hasn't called me." She pulled Ethel around to hold her steady. "He's visiting us on Fourth of July weekend. Maybe my aunt plans to tell him then."

Tess wasn't looking forward to that moment. Or seeing Richard again. But there was no way around it.

"He'll accuse me of going behind his back no matter what," she added.

Ben's expression grew serious. "As long as he doesn't stop you. Once it's done, maybe he'll just accept it. He has little chance of overturning his mother's decision."

Tess hoped so. She didn't want to talk about it anymore. They'd been having such a good day.

They took care of the rest of the herd without much more conversation. Her aunt had a book club meeting at the library and wouldn't return until the afternoon. But she'd left them sandwiches and lemonade, and they ate on the porch.

Tess thought Ben would leave after lunch, but he insisted on helping her weed the vegetable garden. As they tugged weeds side by side, he asked a lot of questions about farming, and she tried her best to answer.

They took a break in the shade of an apple tree and sipped cold water. "If farmers had degrees, you'd have a Ph.D."

Tess laughed. "You can get some letters behind your name if you study agriculture in college. But it's not the same as hands-on experience. I know a lot, but I'm always learning. Especially the past few weeks, running things on my own."

"You must have helped your father when you were growing up here."

"I had to," she said simply. "I enjoyed it, most of the time."

"I'm sorry your father didn't just leave you the farm in his will. That would have made everything easier."

Tess took a long cool drink. "If you knew my father, it's not surprising that his only legacy to me was difficulty."

Her words were delivered matter-of-factly, but she noticed a pained look on Ben's face.

"That wasn't a bid for sympathy. It's just the way he was."

"I remember that he wasn't at the trial, helping you. I thought he was angry at what you'd done, but it sounds like he'd never been a good father."

"He gave me food, shelter, and clothing. Made sure I did my

homework and went to church. That was more than some children get. I learned that from the women I met while I served out my sentence. He had a temper at times, but mostly, he just ignored me." She hesitated to tell Ben more. She didn't want him to pity her, but she wanted him to know her better. And she wanted to know him better, too.

"The thing is, my mother died right after I was born, and he blamed me. He never said it outright, but in his heart, I guess, I reminded him of all he'd lost."

"Maybe so. But it was wrong to blame a child for his grief. You were just a baby who lost your mother, for goodness sake. Didn't he think of that?"

Tess met his gaze and looked away. "I had Aunt Lila. She showed me what it was to be cared for and loved. As much he let her."

Ben didn't answer right away; his expression was soft but serious. "I've seen how close you two are. Now I understand why."

"I have a lot to thank her and my Uncle Will for. That's why it's been hard to decide if I should take the farm or not. I want to do what's best for her, too."

Ben smiled and brushed back some strands of hair that had come loose from her braid. "Accepting the gift she wants to give you will make her very happy. That's a gift to her, too."

Tess smiled, her thoughts muddled by his brief touch. "I never thought of it that way. Maybe that's true."

He rose and offered his hand, then pulled her up with a yank that made her laugh and made Honey bark.

"One last row," he noticed, gloves in hand. "Should we go for it?"

She'd never expected Ben to stay this long but was happy to

spend more time with him. "'No weed left behind,' that's my motto."

It was close to five when Tess insisted that they stop. "This isn't a hospital. We let the help go home at a decent hour."

He laughed and picked up the hoe and shovel, then followed her to the barn. She noticed her aunt's truck in the yard and was not surprised she'd left them alone, one of her matchmaking strategies.

Tess sat on a bale of hay and wiped the metal edges of the tools with a rag. Ben took a seat beside her to do the same.

"You'll sleep well tonight," she told him.

"I think so." He paused and glanced at her. "It isn't just night shifts that ruin my sleep. I still have dreams about the accident."

A ripple of tension washed through her. She wasn't sure what to say. "I'm sorry...I do, too," she confessed.

"You do?" He seemed surprised. "I'm not sure why, but I've never told anyone. I feel like I can talk about it with you, Tess."

"I understand," she said quietly.

"To this day, I don't remember much of what happened. Not after the impact. Even in my dreams, it's still foggy."

"Maybe that's a blessing." She remembered the scene too clearly. She didn't want to tell him that.

"At first, I did think that way. Now I'm not sure." He put the rake aside and turned to her. "Is it true you used a belt from your jeans to make a tourniquet for my leg?"

She swallowed hard. It was difficult to answer, but the conversation seemed important to him. "I knew a little first-aid. I did what I could."

"At the time, the doctors said it saved my life. I know now that's true. An important artery was severed."

She shrugged. "You probably would have been okay without it. I'm thankful if I was able to help you."

Ben met her gaze, then looked away. "Andy wasn't so lucky. So many advances have been made in emergency medicine—if the accident happened today, he would have survived."

"Is that why you became a doctor?"

"Yes, and I'm glad I did. It's a way of honoring him."

They worked in silence a moment, then he added, "I keep thinking about your testimony, when you said you weren't driving the car." Tess sat very still, wondering what he'd say next. "I didn't believe you, but I wonder now if it's true."

She stared at him and lifted her chin. "It is true. My aunt believed me. But no one else did. Not my father or even my attorney. I couldn't prove it without Zach Webster, and I can't prove it now."

There was a sharp edge to her tone that she quickly regretted, but his question had struck a nerve.

Ben leaned toward her, willing her to look at him. "If only there was a way. You must have thought that a million times."

"Of course I have. You sound like you might believe me, Ben. Or at least want to?"

"I want to believe that you weren't behind the wheel that night. Even if you were, I can see now that a single misstep shouldn't define a person and ruin the rest of their life. Anyone can make a mistake. Especially as a teenager. We were all very young."

"We were young. But there are some mistakes you can't come back from," she said with regret.

"I disagree. Getting to know you the past few weeks, I can see that you're a good person who tries to do right. You work hard and don't expect things to come easily. You're painfully honest and persistent to the point of pig-headed stubbornness." He gazed at her with an amused expression. "And you have a kind heart and a lot of courage."

Tess was touched by his words. So much so that she couldn't meet his gaze and was barely able to answer. "Thanks...but I'm not sure I live up to all those compliments."

"I think you do," he said quietly.

She felt him watching her as she collected a few hand tools and put them away. What was he trying to say? That he liked her, despite himself? That he was starting to have feelings for her...or maybe he could? She couldn't think of that now. It was too overwhelming. And very unlikely, she reminded herself.

"I do my best. Which isn't always enough. I can tell you what else I thought about a million times while in jail. I wished I could live that night over. I never would have gotten in that car. Everything would be different now."

"I've often wished that, too," Ben said sadly. He paused, and she knew he had something more to say. "I'm not blameless. I was at a friend's house that night, and my brother came to pick me up. I knew he'd had a beer or two. I could smell it on his breath, but he insisted he was all right. The alcohol in his blood must have shown up in the autopsy, but the police and district attorney downplayed it, or maybe even hid the information."

Tess found the admission shocking. No one had ever mentioned Andy Croft was possibly driving over the limit.

"I should have taken the keys. But Andy was my older brother, and he always got the last word. I should have been driving. Maybe we wouldn't have hit your car. Or, if we had, I would have been the one in the driver's seat."

And died instead of Andy, Tess knew he meant. An awful alternative to contemplate.

"You can't blame yourself for what happened, Ben. Zach Webster was drunk, and that's what counted most. As for the investigation, a lot of evidence was mishandled and conveniently suppressed, or even lost. My attorney was completely inexperienced. The police and prosecutor got away with a lot since there was never a trial. I've tried to make sense of it for years, and I've given up. My aunt says, 'You can't get anywhere in life looking in the rearview mirror. You need to focus on the road in front of you.'" She caught herself and winced. "Sorry for the driving metaphor."

Ben didn't look offended. "Your aunt is right. But we can't help looking back and wondering."

"No, we can't." Tess met his gaze and offered a wistful smile.

He smiled back and lifted his hand to touch her hair. "You have a few bits of straw in your braid," he noticed, gently lifting them out.

Tess felt awkward and tried to make light of it. "I always wear it like that. It's sort of a farm look."

He laughed softly as his gaze caught hers and held it. "I've noticed. It suits you."

She felt her breath catch as his fingertips traced the line of her cheek. His arm slipped around her waist, and she stepped into his embrace, warm and strong. She smelled the earth on him from their workday and the sun and fresh air. His face dipped down, and she closed her eyes, confused and thrilled and feeling a million emotions at once as their lips met.

He kissed her softly at first, exploring her mouth with his. "Tess...Tess..." he murmured. But didn't say more as he pulled her closer and stole her breath away, his embrace even more passionate.

Tess clung to him, unable to hold back the feelings she'd tried so hard to hide all day. She felt lost and overwhelmed and floating on a blissful cloud all at once.

She wasn't sure how much time had passed. Or how long her aunt had been standing in the yard, calling her.

"You'd better answer," Ben whispered as his embrace slipped away. He dropped one last kiss on her ear that tickled.

Tess walked toward the barn doors and out into the yard, feeling she'd just woken from a dream. She willed herself to seem normal, though her heart beat wildly.

"We just finished working."

"Good. I wondered if Ben would like to stay for supper."

Ben walked toward them and smiled. "I'd love to, Lila, but I've got tons of paperwork tonight. Can I get a rain check?"

"You come by any time," her aunt happily offered.

Her aunt was doing all she could to encourage the relationship. Was it as obvious to Ben? Tess had the urge to roll her eyes like a teenager but managed to resist.

Her aunt went inside, and Tess walked Ben to his car.

"Thanks for your help," Tess said, suddenly feeling shy.

"It was fun. Let me know how it goes on Friday."

He meant the appointment with Harold Woods. Did he really care that much if she stayed? It made her feel good, thinking he did.

"I will," Tess promised.

They said goodbye, and Tess watched his car until it turned onto the main road.

Their conversation had given her hope. He wasn't convinced she hadn't been behind the wheel that night, but he wasn't sure now that she had been. More importantly, he didn't define her by that single act anymore. She knew she'd replay every word he'd said in her head, many times over. At least she had his admiration and respect and some sort of pardon from him.

He may never believe you, she reminded herself, *or have real feelings for you.* The kind she was starting to feel for him. He'd kissed her, which was wonderful—and also an impulsive act she was sure he'd later regret, or at least question.

But she put her concerns aside and allowed herself to feel happy and encouraged at how far their relationship had come.

That was amazing enough.

Thirty-Two

By midday Friday, the village streets were filled with July Fourth visitors, with more pouring off the ferries every hour. The café was packed, and Carrie had the busboys set up extra tables under the awning in front. She was outside when Brooke arrived.

"Wow, nice crowd. Looks like your blueberry theme is pulling them in."

"The Fourth is always a crazy weekend, but the berry fest is drawing attention." Carrie didn't want to oversell it. The festival had only kicked off that morning.

"That banner helps. It's awesome." Brooke stepped back to take in the big banner that swooped across the front of the café. "Join Us For A Red, White & Blueberry Salute To July 4th! Delicious specials, and more!"

Carrie stared at her. "You should know. You put it there."

"I totally did not." Brooke looked confused. "What gave you that idea?"

"I just thought...well, it wasn't here last night, and I didn't put it there. Maybe Mom or Rebecca made it as a surprise?"

"It wasn't Mom. She's sending a balloon bouquet. Oops, sorry, I spoiled it. You better act surprised," Brooke added with a grin. "Our older sister is on Planet Rebecca as usual. She has no idea this is going on. Though I'm sure she'll give a full review when she gets here."

Carrie was stumped. While chatting with Brooke, she made sure tables were being reset quickly and the line moved along.

"Who could it be? This is a mystery."

"Maybe your not-so-secret admirer, Doug Bolton?"

Carrie ignored her teasing tone. Doug was a thoughtful guy and did go for the grand gesture, from what she'd seen so far. But she didn't think the banner was his style.

"I never mentioned it to him. Would he really promote Bolton's competition?"

"Ardent suitors have done stranger things to impress a fair maiden. Did you decide about going out on his boat Monday night?"

Soon after taking the girls out for Hannah's birthday, Doug had called with the details about his party. Guests were meeting on the town dock at six, then cruising past the jetty and tying up with boats owned by a few of Doug's friends. When the sun went down, everyone would watch the fireworks set off over the harbor.

"I said I'd go. I hope I don't regret it."

Brooke seemed puzzled. "Why wouldn't it be fun?"

"I won't know anyone but Doug, for one thing. I must admit, it sounds like an adult version of the sort of party he had with his high school crowd. That I was never invited to." She felt silly and even petty for admitting that, but it was her sister. She could tell her anything. Well, almost.

"You finally made the cut. You should be pleased."

"I guess so. Maybe he did put the banner up?"

As soon as she spoke, a light bulb went off, and she knew. And nearly laughed out loud at the revelation.

"It's Jack. He's the Banner Bandit," she decided. "He's the only other person who knew the plan and would do this."

Maybe even as a joke because I've been so obsessed with this marketing gimmick. I drove him crazy all week."

"It was nice of him, whatever the reason. For a temporary employee, he shows a big commitment."

Carrie didn't reply. Commitment was a tricky word when it came to Jack. She was interrupted and took down names for the waiting list.

"You're busy. I'll go. Holler if you need an extra waitress," her sister said.

"You don't need two jobs on a holiday, Brookie."

"I'd get good tips either way and would like to help the family if I can," she added. "I'm just going to grab an iced coffee. The twelve o'clock ferry is due soon."

"Already?" Carrie checked her phone. The day was flying by, a good sign. Maybe this blueberry gambit was the jumpstart the café needed to get going at full speed again.

* * *

The attorney's office was on the second floor of a large, old Federalist-style building on High Street, next to the post office.

Tess and her aunt gave the receptionist their names, and she told them to go right in.

As they walked through the office door, Mr. Woods rose from his chair. A gray suit and dark blue tie gave him a serious air. His thin gray hair was combed to one side, small brown eyes hidden behind thick glasses. A somber expression flashed to a warm smile as he greeted Tess's aunt.

"Good to see you, Lila," he said, shaking her hand, then turned to Tess.

"This must be Tess. I'm glad to meet you, finally."

She was relieved he hadn't said, "I've heard so much about you." That always unnerved her, since she assumed people had never heard anything good. But he seemed a genuinely warm and sincere man, just as her aunt had described.

"Thanks for meeting with us today," Tess said

"Happy to help. I know you have some questions. Take a seat, and we'll talk."

Less than an hour later, Tess's doubts were put aside, if not totally extinguished. Mr. Woods and her aunt made it clear there was no pressure to decide. She could take her time and return—or not—to have the deed signed over. But Tess did decide. After all the talk and explanations, it was not a logical conclusion that pushed her forward but a feeling deep inside. A clarity and sureness.

She knew it was the right thing to do. Without discounting Mr. Woods's learned advice and her aunt's support, she knew that Ben's opinion weighed heavily, too.

She signed the documents with a shaking hand, her first thought—that she couldn't wait to tell him.

Her aunt was bubbling with happiness as they stepped into

the sunshine. Tess felt stunned, but in a good way, and greatly relieved.

Lila handed her a crisp manila envelope. "This is yours now. Keep it someplace safe."

"I will, don't worry." The truck was parked down the street, and they walked toward it.

Tess stopped and took her aunt's hand. "I'm so grateful for this gift, Aunt Lila. With all my heart. I hope you know that." Before her aunt could answer, she added, "And I hope this doesn't mean you're thinking of moving out? I want you to stay at the farm for as long as you like. You'll always have a home there."

Lila squeezed Tess's hand, her eyes wet with tears. "Oh, my dear. . .that's so sweet of you. A time may come when I will go. Though certainly not far from you," she added.

Tess got the feeling she meant when Tess had a husband and a family. Maybe her aunt could imagine the scene, but she couldn't. Besides, she'd still want Lila there, more than ever.

"For now," her aunt concluded, "you're stuck with me, lock, stock, and barrel."

Tess laughed. "Just what I wanted to hear."

"And I'm so happy I could do a jig," her aunt declared, her tone a little giddy. She touched Tess's arm. "Let's celebrate. We should at least go out to lunch."

"Good idea. That would be fun." The scene at the café came to mind, and she suddenly felt wary.

"I know what you're thinking. But we haven't been bothered for a few weeks." *Ever since we met Ben at church*, she knew her aunt wanted to say. "Carrie Duffy promised she'd never allow anything like that at the Blue Sky again."

Carrie had said that, though Tess wasn't sure she could

prevent it. But her aunt had given her such a huge, life-changing gift; the least she could do was buy her a nice lunch.

"The café it is," Tess said.

* * *

Carrie was surprised to see Tess Hargrove and Lila Norton walk in. She was glad, too, and thought it was brave of her.

"Nice to see you, ladies." She greeted them with menus in hand. "I can seat you on the deck if you like."

There was a long wait list, but Carrie hoped no one noticed her jump Tess and Lila to the top.

"I love the deck, just what I hoped for." Lila's bright enthusiasm made Carrie and Tess smile.

"Right this way." Carrie led them outside to a vacant table in the shade with a clear view of the harbor.

"This is perfect," Lila said. "Thank you."

"My pleasure. In addition to our regular dishes, we have a special menu this weekend, featuring—"

"Blueberries?" Tess asked in an innocent tone.

Carrie grinned. "How did you guess?"

"Just a hunch. Truth is, I wanted to see what you cooked up with all the berries I delivered."

"Here's your chance. Lots of choices." Carrie handed down the menu, printed on light blue paper.

Lila adjusted her glasses and looked it over eagerly. "Everything looks so good. I can't decide."

"We're celebrating. We can order a few dishes and share," Tess suggested. "I didn't eat a bite this morning."

"You were nervous. Now it's done and dusted. We can relax

and celebrate." Before Carrie could ask, Lila said, "I just transferred the deed to High Meadow Farm to Tess. As it should be."

"I'm glad to hear it," Carrie said sincerely. "Congratulations, Tess. I wish you great success."

Tess thanked her with a wide smile. "It's taking a while for the idea to sink in."

"Some good food will help," Lila piped up.

"Always helps me," Carrie agreed. She took their drink orders. "I'll be back. Take your time deciding."

She headed for the kitchen, knowing that whatever they ordered, she would bring a few extra dishes. They could always take home the leftovers, and it would all be on the house.

Tess had made her way through a dark place. Seeing her reclaim what she'd lost and begin again was wonderful. Carrie wasn't sure she'd ever met anyone so quietly persistent. Today was a victory, one that Tess surely deserved to savor.

Thirty-Three

The café's booming business on Friday was no fluke. By lunchtime on Saturday, it was clear: the blueberry fest was a success. Carrie was surprised to see her family arrive around noon—her mom, along with Rebecca and Sophie. She thought they were headed for the beach.

When she'd told everyone at home about her plan, the reaction had been pleasant but tepid. A bit deflating, considering her high hopes. Now they could see for themselves that her idea, along with Jack's cooking, had the café filled non-stop.

"Love that banner. It's impossible to ignore," Rebecca said. "The line stretches down the sidewalk."

"I haven't seen a crowd like this since your father tried a giveaway with clam rolls," her mother recalled. "A lot of customers, but not much profit."

"Just the opposite today, Mom," Carrie assured her, but didn't say more.

She was careful not to overpromise. But if the momentum

kept up through Monday, the profits would put the café's accounts in the black again. She'd share the good news when she had hard figures but felt quietly proud of the achievement. She must have learned something in all those courses she'd struggled through.

A lot of credit went to Jack and his creative use of Haven Island's favorite berry. Even if she wanted to thank him properly, the place had been so busy the last two days, they'd exchanged only a few rushed words. She hadn't even thanked him for the banner, though she was almost positive he'd had it made and hung it there.

Which was fine with Carrie. She felt safer at a distance from Jack's charm and her attraction to him.

"I'd love to try one of the specials. If you can't find a free table, we'll order to go."

"Of course I can find a table for you, Mom." Carrie nearly laughed at the humble request.

It made her realize how much her mother's attachment to the café had changed in the past month or so. She'd been sketching and painting more and rarely mentioned returning to work. Carrie thought that was a good thing, though it put more pressure on her to untangle the financial problems and find a permanent manager by September.

She sat her family in a booth near the front window and handed out menus.

"Any recommendations?" Rebecca asked.

"It's all good," Carrie answered confidently. "But you better order fast. A few dishes are selling out."

The chalkboard by the kitchen already listed an 86 on the crepes.

"I'll have something that's selling out," Rebecca handed back the menu.

Carrie had to smile at her sister's logic.

"Baked Blueberry French Toast or Lobster Roll with Blueberry Slaw? Both are moving briskly."

"Lobster Roll. No question."

Her mom and Sophie both ordered the French Toast, and Sophie added a Three Berry Salute smoothie.

When Carrie put the order in, she caught Jack's eye through the pass-through window. "The Duffy women have landed. My mom loves everything, but you know how fussy Rebecca is. She ordered a lobster roll, by the way."

Jack peered into the dining room. "The food will be perfect. I'll give your sister a double helping."

"Don't be too generous. She'll get suspicious. Or tell me we should charge more."

He laughed. "It will be just the right amount, don't worry."

She knew she shouldn't keep Jack from his work but couldn't help adding, "They love the banner. I do, too. I meant to tell you."

He was preparing the lobster roll and kept his gaze on his work. "I'm glad. But why tell me?"

She was stumped a moment, and a little embarrassed, then realized he was playing her. "I know you put it there. It had to be you—unless the banner fairies are floating around Front Street in the middle of the night. Highly unlikely."

He smiled but still didn't look up. "I thought it would be fun. And I wanted to give your inspiration a boost."

The second reason snagged her attention, and she willed herself not to react. "It's been good for business. So, thanks."

She decided to leave it that.

A few minutes after her family was served, she dropped by the table for reviews. Her mother rolled her eyes with delight. "Tell Jack I said the French toast is absolutely yummy."

"It really is," Sophie agreed. Carrie noticed her dish was almost empty.

Rebecca patted her mouth with a napkin, making Carrie wait. "The lobster roll was excellent, as well. Very meaty, and barely any mayonnaise. But we usually serve a good one. I didn't expect to like the slaw, but it's actually very tasty, and inventive. The sort of side dish you'd expect in an urban, upscale place?"

She caught Carrie's gaze, and Carrie remembered Rebecca was the only other person who knew Jack's real identity.

"We'll have a Michelin star before you know it," Carrie joked. Then realized if Jack kept cooking for the café, that could happen.

They made a good team. Too bad he'd be gone in September, and she would, too, each headed in different directions. Until then, she'd do all she could to get the café back on track. That was her goal, Carrie reminded herself. There was no sense in speculating beyond it.

Richard arrived early on Saturday morning, then spent the day with his mother at the beach. Lila urged Tess to come, but she had a lot to catch up on. She'd missed the workday on Friday after meeting with Mr. Woods and eating a huge lunch. She wasn't good for much after that except for a nap on the porch with Honey.

She also hoped the time alone with Richard would make it easier for her aunt to tell him she'd transferred the deed. They'd discussed it on Friday, and her aunt promised she would let him know when he came. Lila didn't seem the least bit concerned that he might be upset. Tess acted as if she wasn't either, though privately, she dreaded his reaction.

Tess worked steadily and barely stopped for lunch. She was surprised when the truck returned, then realized it was almost five.

She came out of the barn to greet them. "How was the beach? Crowded, I bet."

"The weather was perfect. There was a lovely breeze all day." Lila held on to her big sun hat as she hopped down from the driver's side. She wore a flowered sun dress with a bathing suit underneath, along with rubber sand shoes. She looked a bit sunburned but happy.

"We found an out-of-the-way spot near Mariner's Point. A few other people did, too, but you have to share the shoreline on July Fourth weekend," Aunt Lila reported.

The hatch was filled with beach gear—an umbrella, chairs, and a cooler. Tess helped Richard carry everything to the porch.

"I picked up some takeout. Barbequed chicken and ribs, with all the trimmings," Richard announced.

"Sounds great. I've hardly eaten all day," Tess said.

"You work too hard, dear. But there's even less use telling you that now," her aunt said as she walked into the house.

Now that you own the farm, Tess knew she meant. She wondered if Richard had noticed. More importantly, she wondered if her aunt had told him the news.

He had his back turned as he took some paper bags out of the truck. "Here's the grub. I guess we can eat soon if you're hungry."

"I'll just take a quick shower. It won't be five minutes," she promised.

When Tess came down, the table on the porch was set with paper plates, plastic utensils, and takeout containers. Aunt Lila had brought out iced tea and lemonade.

"This food tastes even better because I didn't have to cook it." Aunt Lila helped herself to a square of cornbread. "There's nothing like the salt air to whet your appetite."

"Did you go swimming?" Tess asked.

"The water was too cold for me, but I waded a bit." Lila turned to her son. "Richard dove right in. Cold water never bothered him. I'll try again in August," Lila said with a laugh.

"It was a great day. I'm sorry you missed it, Tess." Richard glanced at her. She wasn't sure if his comment was sincere.

"I love a long beach walk, but I get restless quickly sitting there," she confessed. "You were better off without me."

"Our Tess is like a border collie. Not content unless she's got a job to do," Aunt Lila teased.

"Considering how I feel about dogs, I'll take that as a compliment."

"You can't run a farm without a solid worth ethic. Especially a woman on her own." Aunt Lila's fork was halfway to her mouth, and she put it down. She turned to Richard. "Which reminds me, we have some news. I signed the deed over to Tess. She wanted to wait, but I saw no need. I'm glad it's done. I feel relieved."

Richard had just taken a big bite of ribs. He coughed and covered his mouth with a napkin. When he sat back, his expression was composed. Tess could only guess what he was thinking behind his forced smile.

"That is news. When did it happen?"

"Just yesterday. We met with Harold Woods. It barely took an hour. We had lunch at the Blue Sky Cafe to celebrate. Tess has been selling them blueberries. They made a big special menu for the weekend. You ought to stop in while you're here, Richard. It was very good."

Tess could see that her cousin was not the least bit interested in the café's special menu. He was silent a moment, moving food on his dish. He looked up at Tess. "Congratulations. It's a big step. You must be very excited."

His gracious tone surprised her. "It hasn't completely sunk it yet. But I am excited."

He offered a tight smile. "As you should be." He sat back and sighed. "Well, I'm stuffed. There are plenty of leftovers for tomorrow, too."

Her aunt rose and began collecting the paper plates, but Tess urged her to sit. "I'll take care of the clean-up. You can both relax. Thanks for picking up dinner, Richard. It was great."

Before he could reply, her aunt said, "There's still dessert—pie and ice cream."

"I couldn't eat another bite," Richard said.

"Speak for yourself, son," Aunt Lila replied.

Tess laughed. "I'll bring it out. Just sit tight."

In the kitchen, Tess tossed out the paper goods and wrapped leftovers, slipping tasty scraps to Honey, who had waited patiently. She was glad for a moment alone to consider Richard's reaction. She'd expected worse. But Ben had predicted that once it was done, he'd probably give in and accept the situation. She'd have to tell Ben he'd been right. She was tempted to text or call and let him know that she'd taken his advice, but she wanted to give him the news in person, just to see his expression.

She felt relieved that Richard knew. And a little foolish for worrying so much. Whether his good wishes had been sincere or not, she had no regrets about taking ownership of the farm. She could see now it was the right thing for her to do.

Thirty-Four

No matter how many times Carrie watched a parade, she still felt a thrill as the marching band approached; the beat of the snare drums and lilting notes of trumpets and clarinets seemed to go right through her. It was impossible not to smile, hearing the big, white tubas and tinkling glockenspiels. The Grand Marshall, in a red hunting jacket and high black boots, rode by on a big white horse, and behind him a team of flag-waving high school students, Girl Scouts, Boy Scouts and dignified veterans, some in uniform.

The Coast Guard waved from their usual float, a patrol boat towed by a truck, followed by the island's bagpipe club, in smart berets, tweed blazers, and thick kilts, despite the temperature.

Mayor Lenhardt and the village trustees followed at a brisk pace, tossing candy at the kids on the sidewalk. The members of the garden club were on a flatbed decorated with blooming plants and even a few potted trees. The historical society strolled by next, in colonial dress, representing the island's first settlers. And at the very end, the Haven Island Fire Department proudly displayed their state-of-the-art equipment, along with an antique fire truck, with its clanging brass bell that always stole the show.

As usual, the parade traveled down Front Street, right past the café. Luckily, the customers were distracted enough so that the staff could take a break and watch, too. As the last police car passed with its siren whirring, Carrie looked up to find Jack beside her.

"You should have come out sooner. You just missed it."

"Not a fan of bagpipes. What about the pie tasting? Isn't that next?"

"The parade ends at the village green, and there are a few speeches. Then they taste the pies in the gazebo." She glanced at her watch. "It should happen in the next fifteen minutes or so."

"Don't you think one of us should be there to accept the award?" His wary tone contradicted his confident assumption. He was always so brash; Carrie wasn't used to seeing him uncertain.

He'd baked the pie very early that morning at the café, and Carrie had delivered it to the contest headquarters on the village green. She could tell he'd been waiting for the verdict ever since.

"Why don't you go? You baked it. You should get the honor," she suggested.

He pondered the suggestion, his brow furrowed. "You'd better go. This place is packed. I can't leave the kitchen."

Carrie knew that wasn't true. His excellent staff could cover for a few minutes. But she didn't argue.

"Okay, I'll go."

"And you'll text when they announce the winner, right? I want to know what happens. One way or the other."

She nearly laughed to see him taking the competition so seriously, but she didn't want to hurt his feelings. His pride was at stake. The great Jackson Gardeaux should have easily won best chowder. Striking out twice in this culinary backwater would be too humiliating.

"Right away. Absolutely. But it's just a little contest, Jack. We're doing a booming business. That's the main thing."

Carrie handed him her apron and headed to the green. "Tell Dory to keep an eye on things. I'll be right back."

By the time she reached the gazebo, the speeches were done. The judges sat at a long table, the pies displayed on another. An audience had gathered close to the stage, but Carrie found a shady spot on the fringe, and waited for the mayor to step to the microphone.

"I thought I'd see you here." Carrie turned to see Brooke beside her, her reporter's pad in hand.

"I snuck out for a minute. Jack is dying to know if we won. Are you here for the newspaper?"

"Just a fluff piece, but I couldn't refuse, or Jeremy will stop calling."

"Does he know you have a conflict of interest?" Carrie teased.

"He knows I'm a pro and totally objective. But I do hope we win."

The mayor stepped front and center, and Brooke began snapping photos. He welcomed everyone, introduced the judges, and announced the contestants.

The Blue Sky was matched against some impressive competitors, including Bolton's, Honey Bee Bakery, The Farmer's Friend, and Evaline Finch. The judges included Mayor Lenhardt, Burt Blackburn, who owned the hardware store and was the head of the Chamber of Commerce, and Frances Croft, who ran the newspaper.

Carrie felt nervous watching them taste the pies. It would help the café, but it wasn't the end of the world if they didn't win, she reminded herself. Just as she'd reminded Jack. But she would hate for him to be disappointed.

The ballots were turned in and calculated. Mayor Lenhardt took the microphone again, the decision in hand.

"Fingers crossed," Brooke whispered.

"Here we are, folks, the pies have been savored, and the votes of our esteemed judges tallied. I will say this year was a tough one. Each of the entries was tasty in its own way. But the panel has determined a clear winner. A crust above, you might say." He chuckled at his pun. "The winner of best blueberry pie on Haven Island this summer is…The Blue Sky Cafe!"

The audience applauded, and Carrie screamed, "Oh my gosh, I can't believe it!" Brooke jumped up and down, then hugged Carrie, her journalism ethics tossed aside.

The mayor spotted them and waved. "Come on up, Carrie Duffy, and accept your award."

"And smile for the photos," Brooke added. "You might make the front page."

"I sure hope that doesn't happen," Carrie murmured as she headed toward the stage.

She looked a sight after working all morning, but there was no help for it. She held her head high and marched forward. The mayor offered the plaque with a few words of praise, and Carrie gratefully accepted.

"Thank you, Mayor and judges. This is truly an honor, considering all the excellent entries. I must give all the credit to our wonderful cook, Jack...Dubensky," she added, nearly flubbing and using his other name. "We hope everyone will visit the café soon and find out why our pie is number one."

There was more applause as she handed the microphone back and stepped down from the gazebo. Brooke was nowhere in sight, but she was surprised to find Doug waiting.

"Congratulations, Carrie. Well done."

"Thanks, Doug. That's very gracious of you," she answered, gratified that the Blue Sky had beaten Bolton's this time.

"You win some, you lose some."

Cool and crisp, in a plaid sports shirt and dark blue shorts, he could have posed for a photo in a sportswear catalogue—the kind that features successful-looking, attractive men. He pushed his sunglasses up on his head and met her gaze, blue eyes crinkling around the corners when he smiled.

"I'm happy you're coming to watch the fireworks with us tonight."

"I wouldn't miss it." Carrie had been so busy the last few days that she'd almost forgotten about the invitation. But it would be great to have a break. "I've never watched the show while out on the bay."

"It's loud," he admitted, "but an awesome sight. We're meeting on the town dock at six. Is that enough time for you?"

Carrie recalled the timing from their phone call. Sophie was spending the day with Hannah at Hannah's grandparents' house, swimming in their pool and having a barbeque that night. Brooke had brought her there earlier.

Six o'clock wouldn't give her much time to shower and dress. But she didn't want him to change the plan just for her.

"I'll be there," she promised.

He seemed pleased. "I'm looking forward to introducing you to my friends. See you later, Carrie."

She held the plaque with both hands and watched Doug walk away. It sounded like she was Doug's unofficial date for the evening. Now she really had to look good. Carrie headed back to the café, fretting over what she'd wear and how she'd fix her hair.

She couldn't understand why Doug liked her so much, but as Brooke would say, "That's a bad thing?" Carrie smiled to herself. It was not a bad thing, not at all. Just...surprising.

Maybe she should try to get used to it.

Carrie entered the café through the kitchen door, stepping into a hectic scene. Jack stood with his head bowed, chopping something on a wooden block. He paused and looked up. "So... what's the verdict? You said you'd text, remember?"

Carrie felt bad. Doug had distracted her, and she forgot. "I'm sorry. But I wanted to tell you in person." She picked up a long stainless-steel spoon and struck a pot lid like a gong. "Attention everyone. I have an announcement—"

She pulled out the plaque which she'd hidden behind her back. "The Blue Sky Café has won the award for 'Best Blueberry Pie On Haven Island'!"

Everyone in the kitchen cheered. Joey, the busboy, thumped Jack on the back. Jack grinned and pumped the air with his fist. He laughed with relief, then smiled in his cocky way again.

"I'd like to add, all the credit goes to Jack. He baked a show-stopping pie. None of the others even came close." A bit of an exaggeration, perhaps. She hadn't seen the other pies, but she did know Jack's entry looked as perfect as a cookbook photo.

"No big deal." He shrugged. "I knew we would win it."

"You did?"

"I knew if we lost, you'd fire me. I couldn't let that happen."

They both knew she couldn't fire him and leave the café without a cook. Even if she wanted to.

"Luckily, it didn't come to that."

"Lucky for both of us." He held her gaze and smiled, dark eyes sparkling. She forced herself to look away.

She felt confused. She'd just been looking forward to Doug's party. But Jack's charm could sneak up on her like an ocean wave and knock her off her feet. Washing away all her good intentions about not getting involved with him.

She set the plaque on the stainless-steel table and stepped back. "Would you like to admire this awhile, or should I display it in the front window?"

"Front window, asap. It's excellent bait. The more customers we lure in here this weekend, the better. Back to work, gang. Show's over," he shouted to his crew.

Following the chef's orders, Carrie grabbed an apron and headed for the crowded dining room. Jack was clearly committed to the café's success. She not only appreciated that but knew his wholehearted effort was helping them dig out of the financial hole they'd fallen in. Perhaps someday, she'd thank him.

Carrie wanted to look her best for Doug's party, but that seemed impossible to pull off with such a tight schedule. Her hair, makeup, and nails—all of it needed major repairs. Not to mention pressing the long summer dress she wanted to wear. An organized person would have prepared last night. But she'd never claimed to be organized and had been so tired last night and the night before that she'd had no energy to even make a list.

A lot of people who'd grown up on the island came back to visit in the summer, especially this weekend. Former classmates might be invited, she realized. Which made her even more determined to look her best. Not like a frazzled, frumpy restaurant manager, which was what she felt like at the moment.

The cafe stopped serving at four, so they could close by five. With the high tide of customers, the staff would be stuck there even later. She could leave early, but she needed someone to close. Dory was the logical choice, but the waitress was hosting a family barbecue and had asked to leave a few minutes early.

That left Jack. She'd feel awkward asking him to stay while she ran home to fuss over her appearance. But the thought of looking anything but knock-out gorgeous tonight terrified her.

She found him walking out of the cold box with a carton of burgers. "I need to ask a favor, Jack."

The question snagged his attention. "Yes?"

Carrie felt nervous. "Would you mind closing tonight? I need to be somewhere by six, and I have to leave around four to get ready."

She could see that her vague explanation set the wheels in his head turning. "Somewhere like a party, you mean?"

"That's right." *Even I get invited to parties every decade or so*, she added silently.

He looked like he was going to ask another question, then stopped himself. "Sure, I can close, no problem."

She answered with a wide smile. "Thanks. I'll leave at four, but I'll let you know before I go."

He nodded but didn't reply, then headed to the kitchen.

Carrie felt relieved but also guilty, not just about Jack, but skipping out on the whole staff who'd been working so hard the last few days. She was sure they all had gatherings to attend tonight as well.

But you're the boss. You put up with all the headaches and responsibilities. There's got to be a few perks.

At one minute to four, Carrie pulled off her apron and picked up her purse. She walked into the kitchen and looked around for Jack.

He was nowhere to be seen, and chaos reigned...

Thirty-Five

Most of the kitchen floor was covered with water, a quickly expanding puddle fringed by mounds of soap suds. Joey and Luis attacked with mops and a bucket, but it kept spreading, fed by some invisible source.

"What is going on here? Where is that water coming from?"

Carrie didn't mean to shout but couldn't control her shrill tone.

"The dishwasher," Eddie answered. "We shut it off, but it keeps coming. Jack went down to close the water main."

Carrie was relieved to hear it. Then realized the café could not stay open a minute without running water. "Saints preserve me," she muttered under her breath.

Dory and McKenzie had come to the pass-through window to retrieve orders and stood mesmerized by the flood.

"Get out there and tell the customers there's an emergency," she instructed them. "We have to close immediately. Give them takeout boxes and no charge for the meals," she added.

She dropped her purse and headed for the basement, afraid of what she'd find. Halfway down the steps, she heard gushing water. She practically squeezed her eyes shut when she reached the bottom.

"Can't you shut it off?" she shouted to Jack.

"I found a faucet near the boiler that says, "Main Valve," but it didn't stop." He stared at her, looking flummoxed. He was soaking wet, from his head to his heavy black kitchen shoes. He smoothed his hair back with his hand.

Carrie stepped into the water puddled at the bottom of the stairs. "I just remembered. There are two valves. It's such an old building. The plumbing is totally quirky."

She ducked under the stairwell and frantically searched for the right faucet. She finally spotted it near the floor.

"Thank heavens, here it is."

She grabbed and twisted. It wouldn't budge. No one had touched it in years. "It's stuck, darn it—"

Jack ran over, his steps sloshing. It wouldn't turn for him either. Then he gripped it with all his might, the muscles in his forearm bulging. "Come on, buddy. Give it up," he mumbled. "And don't you dare break off in my hand."

Carrie nearly laughed out loud at his threats to the faucet. A few seconds later, the gushing water slowed to a trickle and finally stopped.

They stood side by side, watching the last few drips.

She gazed around the basement, stunned. "What a mess. It will take forever to clean this up. We'll have to throw out so much food. And stay closed for days."

She couldn't bear to think further. Just when the café was turning some profit, too.

The tall sacks of carrots, crates of apples, potatoes, and other long-lasting vegetables were stored in the cellar. Along with boxes, cans, and big bags of flour and sugar.

She tried to be stoic but felt close to tears as an onion floated by.

"A lot is ruined, no question. But we can salvage some. The cans are fine, and the jars, too. As long they stayed sealed," Jack pointed out. "We'll need to tape labels on so we know what's in them."

"Good point." Carrie had to smile.

"It could have been worse. And your insurance will help."

That was true, too. She had to call her agent first thing. "It's still an epic mess. How will I ever clean up this water?"

"One thing at a time. Let's go upstairs and make sure the kitchen didn't float away."

Carrie turned toward the steps and felt Jack's calming touch on her shoulder. She felt so grateful that he was there.

In the kitchen, the busboys and kitchen staff had used every mop and rag they could find to wipe up the flood. The dining areas were empty, and waitresses cleared tables.

"I'll call some plumbers I know, but no one will pick up on the Fourth of July."

Carrie's prediction was correct. She tried several numbers, leaving messages each time.

"Even if someone comes to fix the pipe tomorrow, we can't open with the flood downstairs."

Jack was staring at his cell phone. She wasn't even sure if he'd heard her. "You need a company that cleans up after floods and fires. A restoration service. This one looks reliable." He showed her the listing on his phone. "It says twenty-four hours."

Carrie doubted that included holidays, but she tried the number. She should know these things. Did her father ever call an outfit like this? She couldn't remember.

To her amazement, an operator answered. Carrie described the problem and was put on hold. A few moments later, she was told a crew would arrive at seven o'clock that night.

"They'll be here in about two hours," she told Jack as she ended the call.

"Great." Jack looked relieved. "Most of the water settled on one side of the cellar," he pointed out. "The machines they use will suck it up in no time."

He found a towel and wiped his face, then slung it around his shoulders. She thought he looked handsome, with his dark hair slicked back from his forehead. Then felt annoyed at herself for noticing.

"You'd better get going. It's almost five."

Carrie had not forgotten about the party but was surprised Jack remembered. Did that mean he didn't care if she was socializing tonight? She didn't want to get involved with him, but the idea still stung.

"The party is on a boat that's going to leave the dock in an hour. I'll never be ready in time."

"Won't they wait for you?"

She shrugged. She was disappointed to miss it, but the emergency had washed away her party mood. "I don't want to hold everyone up. I need to stay until the cleaners are done."

"I'll stay. It's no big deal."

Carrie considered his offer. "Thanks. But you must have plans tonight, too."

He smiled with a curious expression. "No one invited me to a party on a boat...Not even a backyard barbeque."

"Really? I'm surprised you don't have a date." She regretted the admission as soon as she'd said it. She was worn out and overwhelmed, and the filter between her brain and her mouth had obviously shut down.

"What makes you say that?" He looked even more intrigued and amused.

Carrie wished she'd never initiated the conversation but was in too deep to get out of it. "You're out almost every night. Sneaking in late, rolling the motorcycle up the driveway. I just assumed that you're seeing someone."

He crossed his arms over his chest. "I roll the bike to be considerate. I'd tell you where I go at night, but you won't believe it."

"Try me," she challenged him.

"I come back here and cook. The stove in that apartment isn't much better than a hot plate."

She knew that was true, but she wasn't sure she believed him. "Why would you cook here at night after working all day?"

"I'm writing a cookbook. I just nailed an awesome sea bass recipe. I went through twenty pounds of filet but finally got it right."

He looked so proud of the announcement, she couldn't doubt it. "A touch of coconut milk and curry?"

"Good guess, but it's smoked paprika."

Carrie nodded but didn't reply. She was relieved to hear he wasn't dating anyone. *But that still doesn't mean you should date him*, she reminded herself.

While Jack changed into jeans and a t-shirt he had stashed in a locker, Carrie dismissed the staff who'd stayed to mop up.

"Thanks for pitching in. We'll be closed tomorrow, but you'll all get paid. And a little extra for this job. With any luck, we'll open on Wednesday. I'll keep everyone posted."

She called Brooke next and reported the problem as succinctly as possible.

"What a disaster! I'll be right over. Rebecca should come, too. You shouldn't have to deal with all that alone, Carrie."

Carrie appreciated the offer, but there seemed no sense in having everyone run over. Her mother and sisters were going to a neighbor's cookout on the beach and would watch the fireworks from there. No need for everyone's night to be ruined.

"Jack stayed to help. Everything is under control. You'd better tell Mom, but try to be low-key?"

"I'll do my best," Brooke promised, "but she'll call with a million questions no matter what I say. I know this is the last thing you want to think about, but I need a quote for the pie contest article."

"Surprise me. Just make me sound smart and slip in a plug for the café."

Brooke laughed. "Will do. Let us know how it's going."

Carrie agreed and hung up. She stood by the rail of the deck and gazed at the harbor. It was a quarter to six. The inlet was filled with boats with more tied up at the dock. It looked like a huge parking lot at the mall during the Christmas shopping season. She'd have a hard time picking out Doug's cabin cruiser, even with binoculars, but she knew it was out there, and she couldn't help picturing his guests about to board.

She tried his number, and he picked up in one ring. "Carrie, how's it going? Is everything okay?"

"Not great. A pipe burst, and the cellar is flooded. I'm waiting for a clean-up company to pump out the water. I'm so sorry . . . but I can't make the party."

"I'm sorry for you. Sounds like a huge headache and very stressful." His sympathetic tone made her feel a little better.

"It is both of those things," she admitted.

"Any idea what time you'll be done? We're not going far. I can have a water taxi bring you out."

"That's so thoughtful, but I can't make any promises. You know how these things go."

"Sure, I understand. I hope they don't keep you waiting long, and it's cleaned up quickly." He did sound disappointed that she wouldn't be there. "Let's talk soon."

Was he annoyed that she wouldn't make the extra effort? "Let's talk soon" was a vague way to leave things.

"Thanks, Doug. Have a great night."

She'd just ended the call when Jack appeared, carrying a tray. "I thought we could use a bite to eat while we wait."

He chose a table with an excellent view and set down two dishes and place settings. Then he served them each a huge lobster roll, with a plate of the special blueberry slaw and a dish of fries to share.

Carrie took the seat across from him. "This looks great. I know some people can't look at food when they're stressed, but emergencies have a way of piquing my appetite."

"Mine, too," he confessed. "As my father used to say, 'No matter what, you still gotta' eat, kid.'"

Carrie laughed. Jack had already told her how his grand-mère had influenced his career path, but now she wondered about his father. "How did he feel about you becoming a cook?"

Jack prepared to pounce on his lobster roll. "He encouraged me to find a job I enjoyed, so it wouldn't feel like work. I always loved to cook, and I was good at it."

"You have a true calling, and you *are* very good at it." She forked up a bite of the slaw. If anyone had ever told her how tasty the combination of pungent blueberries with thinly shredded cabbage, carrot, red onion bits, and a light dressing could be, she never would have believed it.

"This is a great side dish. We should serve it for the rest of the summer."

"Duly noted." They sat without talking for a few moments, though Carrie felt it was a comfortable silence.

"You've heard about my humble beginnings," he said in a joking tone. "What about you, Carrie? You were eager to leave the island and live in the city. What were your plans?"

"Good question." Carrie put her fork aside, flattered by his interest but hesitant to confide. "My ambitions seem very naïve and impractical, looking back."

He sat quietly, waiting for her to continue, and she felt she had to. "I wanted to be an actress. In musical theater, to be precise."

He looked surprised, as she'd expected he would be. "I can see you up on a stage. You have a commanding presence around here, that's for sure."

She smiled. "I think you mean I'm bossy. It's not the same thing."

"It almost is . . . but that's not what I meant." He paused and dipped a fry in a puddle of ketchup. "You're certainly pretty enough. No question about that."

Carrie didn't agree, though she liked hearing him say that. She tried not to show it.

"I'd love to hear you sing sometime."

"I don't anymore, except when I'm alone in the car or the shower. I haven't practiced for years. I guess my voice was good enough when I was young. I had lead roles in the school musicals. All the attention raised my hopes. I doubt I would have succeeded, even under the best circumstances. Once Tim and I got married, there was even less chance. Launching his career as a musician always came first. It was hard to fit classes and auditions around my part-time jobs—and then Sophie came along," she recalled. "One of us had to be more practical."

"You were being responsible and mature and taking your role as a parent seriously. You should never fault yourself for that, Carrie. Who knows? Maybe someday you'll go back to singing or some other talent close to your heart. Sophie is a great kid," he added. "You should be very proud."

His words made her feel good about the choices she'd made. "It's not over yet," Carrie said, looking forward to the teenage years still to navigate, "but so far, so good. And a while back, I realized I do love the restaurant business. Maybe it's in my DNA."

"You're definitely a natural." He grinned, and her heartbeat quickened.

A breeze off the water blew his hair across his eyes. She was tempted to reach over and brush it back. Instead, she put her hands in her lap and looked out at the harbor.

It was a pleasant break to have the restaurant to themselves and enjoy the good food and conversation while a golden light dropped over the harbor.

Carrie rarely took a moment to appreciate the café this way, as if she were a customer. It reminded her why the Blue Sky was so special and people returned year after year. "The beating heart of

Haven Island," one food critic called it. Working at a hectic pace each day, she easily lost sight of the café's unique charm.

She heard a truck pull into the alley alongside the building and realized she'd almost forgotten the disaster zone in the basement and the party she was missing.

"The cleaners are here. I'll let them in," she said.

"Right on time. I'll clear this up and join you in a minute," Jack replied.

A short time later, the crew was in the cellar, setting up their equipment. She and Jack supervised a bit, deciding what to discard and what to salvage. Then they left the men alone to do their job.

As her father used to say, "It's always something when you run a business." At least Jack was there, his steady temperament a calming presence. Carrie was very grateful that he'd stayed.

* * *

Lila suggested a round of Scrabble to pass the time before the fireworks. Tess liked the game but posed no challenge to Lila's impressive vocabulary. Still, playing a game did limit the conversation, and Tess felt the less she talked to Richard, the better. So far, he hadn't said a negative word about her taking over the farm, but she still expected it.

Richard played well, but when the points were totaled, Lila reigned victorious. She gathered up the tiles and laughed. "Thanks for indulging me. Sorry I beat the stuffing out of both of you."

Tess grinned. "You don't sound sorry, Aunt Lila."

"That's okay, Mom. I don't mind letting you win once in a while," Richard teased.

"What a gentleman. One who was beaten fair and square," Lila added. "It's almost nine o'clock. Let's set up the chairs."

"Good idea." Tess picked up an Adirondack chair from the porch and carried it to a sloping spot on the lawn. Richard did the same. She was heading back for one more when her phone buzzed. It was a text from Ben, and she read it quickly:

Wanted to stop by this weekend but got stuck at work. Can I come tomorrow? I have some news.

Tess quickly texted back:

I'll be here. I have something to tell you, too.

Ben replied:

Now I'm curious. I'll come around noon, on my way to the hospital. Are you watching the fireworks tonight?

Tess replied:

Yes, from the farm, a bird's eye view.

Ben replied:

Wish I was there. See you tomorrow.

Tess answered with a smiley face and a thumbs-up sign. She wondered what he wanted to tell her. Good news, she hoped. She felt happy just to hear from him and knew the hours would pass slowly from now until tomorrow, noon.

"Just saw the first flare. It's about to start, Tess," her aunt called.

"Be right there." Tess grabbed the last chair. She hadn't watched fireworks in a long time and was looking forward to the show. But no matter how spectacular the explosions were in the sky, she doubted they could outshine how she felt inside, thinking about Ben.

The restoration unit was a practiced crew, faster and more efficient than Carrie expected. The water was removed, and fans and a dehumidifier were set up to dry out the lingering dampness. Carrie paid the bill along with a generous tip she felt was well deserved for a good job, and done on a holiday. Then she hung a sign on the front door, "Closed July 5th Due to an Emergency. Will Re-Open July 6."

She was ready to leave but couldn't find Jack. She wanted to thank him for all his help with the crisis, including their delicious, relaxing meal.

She called his name and heard him answer from the deck. "The cleaners just left. We can go, thank goodness."

"And miss the fireworks? It's just about to start." He pointed at the sky where Carrie saw a test flare arc above the harbor and explode with a boom.

She was exhausted. All she wanted was a hot shower, a cup of tea, and her fuzzy slippers. But before she could answer, another streaming light flew into the dark night and exploded into thousands of tiny red stars. Two more followed, creating fountains of golden glitter.

"You couldn't find a better place to watch than right here." *Not even some rich's guy boat*, she knew he meant.

Carrie walked to the railing where Jack stood. The glorious display instantly cheered her.

Three golden flares rocketed into the inky darkness. "Here they come," he whispered.

Moments later, spirals of silver sparks filled the sky, quickly absorbed into the night as whistling flares took their place, exploding with red, white, and blue lights.

"It's a perfect night for fireworks," Carrie murmured, staring at the show.

Jack slipped his arm around her shoulder. "It's a perfect night, period. Flood in the cellar and all."

When he pulled her closer, she didn't resist. She rested her head on his shoulder and he drew her closer. He turned and looked down at her. She felt his breath in her hair and couldn't resist meeting his gaze.

That was a mistake, a little voice warned. But she ignored it. She didn't care. She knew he was about to kiss her, and she ought to ease away. But instead, she turned and wound her arms around his waist. Despite the promises she'd made to herself, she had no resistance left after such a difficult day.

There was something irresistible between them. She might as well try to stop the bursts of color and light that filled the night sky.

The kiss deepened, and they held each other a long time, barely noticing the noisy grand finale.

Finally, the last few pops echoed, and the boats in the harbor "applauded" with a cacophony of tooting horns and clanging bells.

Jack lifted his head and grinned. "Now, that's hard to ignore."

Carrie also found the commotion a mood breaker, but an amusing one. His arms still circled her in a loose embrace, and she liked being close but knew it was really time to go.

"They'll clear out of the harbor quickly. And so should we."

He smiled as she stepped away, then followed her outside to her car, parked in front of the café. "Want a lift? You can leave the bike overnight. No one will bother it."

He smiled and shook his head. "No thanks. I'll ride. It clears my head."

She felt a bit muddled, too. She wasn't sure now how to act toward him.

"You've been working so hard. You ought to sleep late tomorrow," he said.

"Not a chance. I need to get a plumber over here."

She opened the car door and climbed in. "But you should use the free day to go fishing," she suggested through the window. "You've been working hard, too."

"We'll see." He stepped back and briefly waved. "Good night, Carrie."

She waved back and drove down Front Street, catching a last glimpse of Jack. He stood in the glow of a streetlight, arms crossed over his chest, his handsome face fixed in a thoughtful expression.

Everything between them had shifted. She felt elated and confused. And relieved to drive home alone. She needed time to orient herself to this new landscape, to understand what had just happened. If that was even possible.

Thirty-Six

Tess had just finished her early chores on Tuesday morning and didn't think anyone else was up. But she found her aunt and Richard in the kitchen. Her cousin held a cup of coffee in one hand and a piece of leftover cornbread in the other.

Lila was gathering her purse and keys. "Richard is catching an early ferry. There'll be a rush off the island today. It's the smart thing to do." Her tone was bright though Tess detected a note of regret that he wasn't staying longer.

"The boats will be crowded," Tess agreed. She poured herself a mug of coffee and took a sip.

Richard put his dish and cup in the sink. "So long, Tess. It was good to see you." He grabbed his duffel bag and opened the door without meeting her eyes. "We'd better go, Mom."

Lila followed. "I'll be out a while. I have errands in the village and a meeting at church."

Tess stood on the porch as Lila and Richard climbed into the truck. She waved goodbye, but Richard didn't wave back. She didn't care. She was relieved he hadn't confronted her about the deed. She hoped that meant he'd given up.

* * *

"Why did you let me sleep so late?" Carrie stumbled down to the kitchen, staring at her phone. She couldn't believe it was almost ten o'clock.

"Because you were exhausted." Her mother sat at the table, making a shopping list.

"When did that have anything to do with it?" Carrie poured herself coffee and took a huge sip. If she slept in every time she felt tired, she wouldn't have a life.

"Oh my gosh—" She slapped her forehead, and her coffee sloshed. "I missed the plumber! He was coming at nine. If he doesn't get in today to fix the pipe, we'll have to close again tomorrow and—"

Her mother raised her hand, like a referee calling time. "Rebecca is there. I'm sure she has everything under control."

Carrie had been at home with her mother and sisters the night before when a plumber finally called back. They'd overheard her make the appointment, but she never thought they'd remember and step in to take her place.

She took a carton of yogurt out of the fridge and found a spoon. "'Under control' is Rebecca's middle name. Clever of you and dad to choose it for her."

Her mother smiled as Carrie took a seat. "You should just relax and enjoy a day off. One day, in all the time you've been here." She paused. "I never meant that to happen when I agreed to let you take my place. It's been six weeks since my... episode." She'd paused to search for any term besides 'heart attack.' "It's time that I get back to work. I'm bored here on my own all the time, and way too young to retire. I'm going to tell the doctor next week at my checkup. But I don't care if he agrees or not."

Carrie wondered if her mother had shared this plan with her sisters. She was sure they'd feel the same way she did—alarmed.

"I'm not going to lie, Mom. Now that I've been at the café a few weeks, doing your job, I don't think you should ever go back. Not until we find a manager and you're just overseeing things. We all love the Blue Sky, but we love you more. We won't let you risk a setback. Not for anything."

Gena squeezed her hand. "You're very sweet. But you worry too much. You get that from your father," she added with a grin. "I'll need time to get my sea legs back. But I'll be fine."

Carrie doubted that. She'd often wondered how her mother had managed as long as she did, considering her compromised health. She was just starting to get strong again and back to her old self.

"Do you miss it that much, Mom? Honestly?" Before her mother could reply, she added, "You never worked there when Dad was alive. You never had much interest. Maybe you just feel obligated."

Her mother considered the question. "I think about your father all the time. He'd want me to take care of the business. I'm certain of that."

"Not at the cost of your health. Dad would never want that. I think Dad would say I was doing a darn good job."

Her mother's expression softened, her eyes bright. "I'm sure he's very proud of the job you're doing. We all are."

"Thanks, Mom. That means a lot to me," she said sincerely. "I balked a bit at stepping in, but the truth is, most of the time, I enjoy it," she confided. *Partly because of Jack.* She put that thought aside. "But I don't think you ever did."

Carrie hadn't meant to be so blunt; the words just came out. Her mother sighed and avoided her gaze. "I took pleasure in keeping your father's legacy alive. Our family's legacy," she added. "But I could never say I enjoyed the work the way I love painting and drawing."

"Then that's what you should do. If the doctor says it's all right, you should take classes and set up your studio again. There's no need to rush back to the café. I'll be here until September. That seems obvious. You should enjoy this time. Do things you love to do. That's the best way for you to get healthy again."

Tears welled up in her mother's eyes, and she whisked them away with her fingers. She smiled softly and rose to give Carrie a hug. "What did I do to deserve a daughter like you?" She pressed her cheek to Carrie's dark hair.

"I don't know, but it must have been good. You got two more in the bargain," Carrie said, making her laugh.

Tess was on the porch when she saw Ben's car drive down the lane. For once, he wouldn't find her covered with dirt from head to toe. She'd avoided the goat pen and fields all morning, taking care of paperwork instead.

She didn't want to look as if she'd spent too much effort on her appearance but still dressed with care in a pair of new jeans and a peasant blouse made of a gauzy fabric. She'd fixed her usual braid and, after deliberation, put on earrings and lip gloss.

When she opened the door and Ben's eyes swept over her, she couldn't have felt more self-conscious in an evening gown.

She thought he looked very handsome in a black polo shirt and jeans. There had to be plenty of women at the hospital who noticed him, not just his looks, but his kindness and intelligence, and what an able, caring doctor he was.

"Let's sit on the porch," she suggested. "I'll bring some iced tea."

"Sounds good. I'll help you."

A few moments later, they sat in the wicker chairs with a tray of iced tea and cookies on a low table.

"We both have news," Ben said. "You go first."

"I can wait. You texted me. It sounded important."

He looked away, a shadow crossing his sunny expression. "It's...complicated," he began. "I'm not even sure what to make of it. I remembered something about the accident." He paused and stared straight ahead, choosing his words carefully.

"I remember being on the ground and calling for help. Your car had hit a tree, and I was waiting to see if anyone got out. I don't know how long it took, but finally, I saw you come out of the passenger side door, and you ran toward me. And I saw a guy get out of the driver's side."

"Zack Webster." She hadn't meant to interrupt him. He was speaking so slowly, he almost seemed in a trance.

"Yes, it was him. He was yelling at you. But I don't remember what he said. I was in shock and in too much pain to understand him."

Tess dreaded revisiting that night. But she could hardly believe

Ben's memories had returned so clearly. "He didn't want me to help you," she explained. "Do you believe me now? That I wasn't the one driving?"

Ben nodded with a solemn expression. "I do. Without a doubt. I remember other details, too. Very clearly. I'm sure that my memories are valid. Not just because I want you to be innocent."

She met his gaze, then looked away, too moved to speak. If she could choose one person in the whole world to believe she was innocent, it would be Ben.

"That means a lot to me," she said finally. "I don't think I can find the words to tell you how much. It can't undo the past or what people think about me. But if it's changed your opinion . . . I don't need anything more."

Ben's eyes were soft with sympathy. He took her hand. "My opinion *has* changed, Tess. *Everything* has changed. You should never have gone to jail. You were totally innocent, just like you claimed. It will take time, but this is a start. It's something we can work with and build on."

"Go back to court, you mean?" Tess didn't intend to sound doubtful, but even though Ben's memory was momentous to her, it seemed slim evidence to overturn her conviction.

"I have a good friend who's a criminal attorney. I've asked him to review the investigation files. Maybe evidence to support your account of that night was overlooked or conveniently ignored. Along with what I remembered, maybe your name can be cleared."

The possibility was overwhelming. Tess rose from her seat and walked to the other side of the porch. Her aunt's flower boxes overflowed with purple petunias and trailing vines. She plucked spent blooms to give her hands something to do.

"It's tempting. But I'm not sure I can afford a lot of legal fees. I need to think about it."

Ben followed her. She could see her reaction confused him. "I'll talk to my friend about the fee. I'll pay it myself. That's the last thing you should worry about."

She turned; he stood very close, staring down at her. "What if it doesn't work out? I don't think I could stand the disappointment," she admitted.

"I'll be disappointed, too. But you have to try." He rested his hands on her shoulders, compelling her to meet his gaze. "What other choice do we have?"

She wasn't sure why he included himself in this question. She had a choice. And she could keep on as she'd been the past five years since her release, accepting that the world believed she was guilty of the crime and tolerating it.

"I appreciate the offer, Ben. I really do. But you, of all people, helping me clear my name? Are you sure you want to do this?"

"I didn't get it at first either. I told myself I just wanted to know what really happened. And maybe help someone who'd been treated unfairly. You said one thing, and the police said another. And I couldn't remember anything about that night. Now, I do, and I realize it's about more than finding the truth." He smiled softly and shook his head. "If anyone ever told me I'd fall for Tess Hargrove and go the limit to prove her innocence, I would have recommended a very thorough psychiatric exam. But that's what happened. If this is what crazy feels like, I'll take it."

Tess thought she was dreaming. That was the only explanation for Ben's words.

"Do you really mean that?" she asked him softly. "What if you hadn't remembered seeing me come out of the car—" She paused but forced herself to ask the question. "Would you feel the same?"

"I felt this way before I remembered. It just would have taken me a little longer to face it." His tone was solemn. "What about you, Tess? Can you look beyond the past? Or do I remind you too much of everything you want to forget?"

Tess was shocked that he thought she might reject him for that reason. She'd never seen Ben that way but realized now she could have.

"I think I fell for you the minute we met at the newspaper office; I just didn't know it. Even when I figured it out, it seemed so hopeless. I thought I was the last woman on earth you could ever let into your heart."

He met her gaze and held it, his arms winding around her waist. "You have my heart. Forever. We can't change the past, but we can move beyond it. I feel as if we already have."

Tess smiled softly but didn't need to answer. Ben pulled her closer, and they melted together in a sweet, hungry kiss. Tess still thought she had to be dreaming, and she savored every moment of the tender embrace.

They slowly parted, and Ben brushed her cheek with his hand. "I'd better go. I'm already late. . . But I just realized, you had something to tell me, too."

She took a deep breath and squared her shoulders. "Lila and I met with her attorney on Friday, and she transferred the deed to me."

Ben's face lit with happiness. "That's awesome, Tess. I was wondering. When you didn't mention it, I was afraid to ask. How does it feel to own this place, finally?"

"I'm a little nervous." She wouldn't have admitted that to everyone, but she could be honest with him. "It's a big responsibility. But I don't regret it. Not one bit."

"There's no reason why you should. Now you can follow through on all your plans, goat cheese and lavender. Who knows what else you'll come up with." He hugged her close. "How did your cousin Richard take it?"

"He wasn't happy, but he didn't threaten me again."

"If he makes one move in that direction, he has me to deal with now. Don't ever forget that."

"I won't," Tess replied quietly.

Ben dropped a kiss on her forehead and stepped back. "Let's talk tonight," he said, heading for his car.

Tess watched the Volvo until it disappeared. Her head was spinning, and her heart bursting with joy. She could hardly believe it—Ben remembered she wasn't driving Zach Webster's car. And he cared for her. Really cared.

This was either the best dream her head and heart had ever concocted. . .or the happiest day of her life.

Carrie's day passed in a long, lazy blur. Rebecca returned with a full report on the repair. Carrie and her mother had already packed lunch, and they walked across the road to the beach, where chairs and umbrellas were set up. In between short naps, Carrie read a book she'd been working on all summer.

After sailing camp let out, Brooke and Sophie joined them. Brooke proudly showed off a page proof from Wednesday's edition of the newspaper. Her article about the pie contest was on the front page, with photos. One showed Carrie accepting the award.

"Well done, Brooke. You finally nailed page one. Above the fold, too," Rebecca noticed.

"It's not hard news, but I'm getting there." Despite her nonchalance, she was proud, Carrie thought.

"It's an excellent article." Her mother had pulled out her glasses and read it quickly. "I'm very proud of you. And you, too, Carrie. That's a thoughtful comment."

"Thanks, Mom. What did I say?"

Brooke laughed, looking a little embarrassed. "She was too busy, so I had to make it up."

Her mother turned to Brooke. Carrie couldn't tell if she was scowling or laughing. "Is that true?"

Brooke avoided her gaze. "Publicists do it for their clients all the time. I worked in a nice plug for the Blue Sky."

"The publicity will be good for the café," Rebecca said.

"It will be," Carrie agreed. "I just hope that photo doesn't scare people away. I look a sight. I should have asked for approval."

"Next time you're on the front page," Brooke promised.

"You look lovely, dear. Like the hard-working businesswoman that you are," her mother said.

"That's a nice way to put it," Rebecca said. "It's so blurry, no one will notice."

"Thanks, that makes me feel loads better." Carrie glanced at her older sister, but she didn't notice the sarcasm.

In an obvious bid to change the subject, Carrie's mother said, "The water looks wonderful. Why don't we all go for a swim?"

The tide was high, but the waves were slow and gentle. The five women eased in, holding hands, and jumping up as the breakers rolled by, edged with foam as delicate as lace. Carrie realized she hadn't been swimming all summer and lingered with Sophie. Then took a long nap in her beach chair.

When they got home, the vote for pizza was unanimous. The sunshine and swimming had made everyone feel pleasantly worn out. Sophie headed for bed early, and Carrie soon followed. She never realized how much she'd needed a break to simply do nothing.

She hadn't caught a glimpse of Jack all day, not even going in or out of his apartment. It was just as well. They'd exchanged texts in the morning when she told him she wasn't coming in, but nothing after that. He probably wanted to be considerate about her day off. She welcomed a break from being around him, too. Their embrace during the fireworks had rocked her to her toes. Where would they go from there? If anywhere?

She was tired of resisting a relationship with him. Who was she fooling? It seemed they already had one, whether she admitted it or not. Maybe she should just relax and see what happened. If it only lasted the summer, was that the worst thing?

Carrie pondered the question as she drifted off to sleep.

All she saw was Jack's flashing dark eyes and renegade grin, challenging her to answer.

Thirty-Seven

"Hey, everybody, I have something to show you." Carrie arrived at the café at seven. The breakfast rush was just building, and the café was quiet enough to call the staff together. Since it was midweek after a big holiday weekend, many visitors had left the island, and the next wave had not yet swept in.

Once the group was assembled, she pulled out the newspaper. "'Blue Sky Cafe Wins "Best Pie" Honor,'" she announced. "There are more copies out front if anyone wants to read the article.

"Basically, it says our pie blew the competition right out of the gazebo. Owing to our chef and chief pie baker, Jack Dubensky."

Brooke had included high praise for him, which he certainly deserved.

"Yay, Jack! Way to go!" The staff clapped and cheered.

Jack nodded modestly. "I followed the café's traditional recipe *exactly*. With slight tweaks here and there. Maybe."

Carrie tried to look annoyed but couldn't manage it. "We'll discuss that later."

"We're back on top!" Eddie, the prep cook, pumped the air with his fist.

"You ought to frame that and hang it up front, where everyone can see it," Dory said. "Next to all the articles and awards your father collected."

"I'm going to do just that," Carrie promised.

"Thanks, everyone. Back to it." Jack tapped the service bell, announcing an order was at the window. The staff quickly scattered, and they were alone. He stood at the stove, swirling an omelet with one hand.

"Did you get some rest yesterday?" he asked.

"I was a total sloth. It was disgusting."

"Glad to hear it. You deserved a disgusting sloth day."

"You did, too."

"I had some fun."

She was glad to hear it. She felt less guilty. "Let me guess...you went fishing?"

He had the kind of tan fisherman get, his face and neck bronzed to the neckline of a t-shirt and the edge of shirt sleeves. It looked good on him, she thought.

"I started on the skiff you loaned me and met up with Finn, so we went out again at night. His boat has a stronger motor. And colder beer."

"Did you catch anything?"

"Finn talks so much, he scares the fish away. But I caught some beautiful flounder anyway."

Carrie laughed. "Sounds about right."

"Hey, why don't we celebrate the award tonight? We can have dinner out. Someplace nice." He asked with a questioning gaze and seemed unsure of himself—for once. It was sort of sweet.

"You mean...like a date?" Carrie felt embarrassed asking, but she didn't want to misinterpret.

"Yeah, a date. Any problem with that?"

If she wanted to pull the brake on this runaway train, now was the time to do it, a small voice advised.

Carrie shook her head, hoping she hadn't offended him. "Things are just so...I wasn't sure. But...yes. I'd like that."

"Great." He sounded happy and relieved. "We'll figure the place and time later. Don't worry, Carrie. My boat won't sail without you."

His reference to Doug's party caught her by her surprise.

He smiled, and she smiled back, then pushed through the swinging doors that led to the dining room. She set her expression in her "manager face," while inside, she felt as shaky as Jell-O.

She was going on a date with Jack. A real date. After all the weeks of meaningful glances and "hit and run" kisses, they were going to spend the evening together, like normal people, starting a new relationship.

Get a grip. It's only dinner. He didn't propose yet. It might be a big dud. But she knew that wouldn't be the case. They always found something to talk about. Even if it was just friendly bickering. The prospect of spending the evening with Jack felt scary because she liked him so much.

You can always say you have some prior plans you forgot, with Sophie or your mom. Carrie knew she wouldn't do that. She wanted to go through with this, even though it felt like a big, risky step.

For the rest of the day, Carrie forced herself to focus on any task at hand. When her thoughts drifted toward Jack, and she questioned keeping her promise, she pushed the doubts aside.

After the lunch service slowed down, she retreated to her office to make a schedule for the upcoming week, which was a lot like solving a Rubik's Cube, as she struggled to accommodate the special requests of the staff—to come in a little late one day, or leave a little early, or miss work entirely. She usually succeeded in keeping everyone happy. With finances improving, she'd hire another kitchen helper and waitress, making the workflow even more efficient.

Carrie stood by the printer, waiting for the schedule to roll out. It was half past four, and she'd head home soon. Jack had rarely seen her without an apron. She wanted to look nice. She'd decided on a white linen dress that had tan panels on the sides. It was stylish but simple, and the design did wonders for her shape. She wasn't sure what to do with her hair but would figure that out when she got there.

She took the schedules from the printer and noticed a few sheets of paper left on the tray. She leafed through, thinking they were drafts of old menus or inventory lists, but she didn't recognize the documents.

One was a page of email messages, a chain from and to Jack. He was corresponding with a large group. The subject line for all the messages was the same: "Proposed Gardeaux Venture—San Diego."

The correspondence was about plans for a new restaurant, she surmised. There was also a spreadsheet with categories like renovation costs, insurance, staffing, advertising, followed by dollar amounts with rows of zeros.

Jack's summer off the grid, or whatever he might call it, was obviously over. Or soon would be. He was planning a return to the bright lights and big city and sautéing for the stars.

Carrie sat at her desk, feeling as if she'd been pushed out of a plane without a parachute. Or maybe just pushed off the cloud she'd been floating on since the fireworks show.

While she pondered what to do about the information she'd discovered, she heard a knock and turned to see Jack in the doorway, as if summoned by her thoughts.

"We're ready to close if you want to go. I just need to take a quick look in the cold box."

He seemed excited about their night out, which made it harder to confront him. But she knew if she didn't do it now, it would burst out awkwardly while they were having dinner—and what sort of evening would that turn out to be?

"I was printing next week's schedule," she said in a flat voice. "And I found this. I think it's yours."

She handed him the page of emails and the spreadsheet, and watched color rise under his tan.

"Right. I'm sorry… should have asked to use the printer."

"As if I care one bit about that, Jack. You told me that you needed a break from the big leagues. But it seems you're jumping back in."

"It's only talk. Some guys in California got in touch. I'm just hearing them out."

It looked like more than that to Carrie, but she didn't want to argue.

"I won't leave before Labor Day, if that's what you're worried about."

"I know you'll keep your promise," she said quietly.

He looked relieved but still off balance. "What is it then? I know you well enough by now to tell when something is bothering you, Carrie."

"I was looking forward to our evening out. I really was. But now I wonder if there's any point. I mean, why start something when you and I are clearly going our separate ways? I'll leave Haven in September, too. But I'll still be in New England. You'll be in California, or wherever—a celebrity chef without borders. I was fooling myself by forgetting that. These pages are a red flag."

Jack forced a smile, but she could tell the conversation was hard for him. "There are planes. And email and FaceTime and all of that. A long-distance relationship is not impossible."

"It's not just that. You move in a different world than I do. When you're in your natural habitat, I mean. I Googled you," she admitted. "I watched videos on YouTube. You're surrounded by models and actors and rock stars. You're in New York one day, Hong Kong the next, cooking in castles and on yachts, living the lifestyle of the rich and famous," she confessed.

He shook his head and sighed. "You can't believe everything you see on the internet, Carrie. I thought you knew that."

"If even half of it is true, it still wouldn't work for me. I have a little girl. I'm trying to finish school...You know me, Jack. I'm like a bowl of plain old New England Chowder. I'd never fit in with all that, even if I tried."

"And you know me. I'm not that guy on YouTube, thinking I'm so special because I met a few actors or traded quips with some talk show hosts. Not anymore," he added. "Sure, I played the game, and I did it well. But I've had time to think. If and when I go back, it will be different."

She didn't know what to say. It seemed more a matter of when than if. He sounded sincere, but how could he make that promise? Who knew what the future would bring once he stepped through that door again?

"I'm not saying you should change, Jack. I wouldn't like it if you asked me to." She took a breath. "Maybe it would work with Jack Dubensky, but not with Jackson Gardeaux. We've both been through difficult breakups. Why set ourselves up for another one?"

"But it could work between us, Carrie. I know it could. Can you just take some time to think about it? Please don't pull the plug so rashly."

She met his pleading gaze and looked away. She couldn't answer. She knew if she did, she'd give in and put off the decision, and then...she'd chicken out.

"I know I wasn't upfront about my identity," he added, "but you can trust me," he promised. "I care for you."

His gentle defense tore her heart in two and nearly persuaded her she was acting from fear and insecurity. But she pulled back and held the line. She knew who she was and what she needed. It wasn't a celebrated, globe-trotting chef living in the fast lane.

"I care for you, too," she admitted. "But it's probably best if we let this go before we're more involved."

He looked about to argue but stopped himself. His expression was downcast, not angry but hurt, and she felt so bad to see him that way. She wondered if she'd done the right thing.

"If that's what you want," he said. "So...see you tomorrow."

"See you." She nodded and turned to her desk. Her eyes were filled with tears, and she hoped he hadn't noticed.

For goodness sake, there's no reason to cry about it. You hardly know the guy. It's not as if you're ending some long romance.

She knew that wasn't it. She felt sad to turn her back on something that felt so special, and all that might have been.

Thirty-Eight

"The attic is stuffy this time of year. We won't be long. I know what I'm looking for." Aunt Lila led the way up the narrow staircase, and Tess followed.

The sun had set, and even though it was cooler outdoors, the third floor of the old house trapped the heat. Tess quickly opened a window but still inhaled the scent of mothballs, moldering books, and dust motes.

Aunt Lila's church committee was holding a tag sale on the village green on the weekend, Saturday, July 16. All the items would be donated, and the proceeds given to families who needed help getting children ready for school—buying backpacks, sneakers, loose-leaf binders, and all the things needed in September. Tess thought it was a wonderful project. All she had to offer was vegetables, but Evaline would have a table selling flowers, baked goods, and honey, and she'd offer Tess's produce, too.

Aunt Lila wanted to give the group a few pieces of furniture.

Antiques, she claimed, though most of her possessions probably fell into the category by now.

"There's a piecrust table up here somewhere," she said, gazing around. "In good condition. Except for a little chip in the molding. And an alabaster lamp. It just needs a new switch. And a map of the island with a gold leaf frame. When I came to take care of your father, I rented my house and stored a lot of things up here. I can hardly remember all of it."

The attic was filled with old furniture, rolled-up rugs, and suitcases. Some boxes were marked, but most were not.

Tess found the double-tiered table easily. It was awkward to carry but not heavy. She left it in the hallway on the second floor and brought the lamp down next. It was Thursday night, which left her aunt only two days to brighten up her donations. Tess wondered if it was enough time.

When she returned, her aunt sat on a wooden chair, its broken cane seat barely supporting her. A shoebox was in her lap, and she'd slipped on her glasses to examine the contents.

Tess walked over and stood beside her. Her aunt held a photo of a young woman and a small child. It was summertime, and they stood in tall grass against a backdrop of bright blue sky. Tess recognized the barn in the background. The photo had been taken at High Meadow Farm. The young woman had dark-blond hair, parted on the side. Soft waves blew in the breeze around her pretty face. The child could barely stand on her chubby legs. She wore a sun hat and a pink dress. The woman was kneeling behind her and holding her up. She was kissing the child's cheek, her expression pure love.

Tess felt her breath catch as her aunt handed her the photo. She couldn't believe her eyes and squinted at it in the dim light.

"That's the same woman, the bride in the wedding portrait…That's my mother."

"That's correct," Lila quietly confirmed. "And that's you."

"How could it be? The little girl looks at least one. My mother died right after I was born."

"No, she didn't. Not then. Her name was Elizabeth, but we called her Liza. She was a gentle, sweet girl. She left your father. She had to. He was cruel to her. She ran away one night during a fight. An awful row. She came to us for help. She had bruises and was so frightened she could hardly speak." Lila suddenly looked up at her. "She tried to take you with her, but your father wouldn't allow it. He was stronger, and he didn't care if he hurt her. She was afraid he might hurt you, too. All she could talk about was coming back to get you. She wanted to return that night. Uncle Will and I told her to wait. It was so late, and she was in no state.

"The next day, we drove her here. We thought we could talk some sense into your father. A child your age needed to be with her mother; there was no question. When we got here, he was gone—and had taken you with him." Lila paused and took a breath. "I thought your mother was going to lose her mind. We could hardly get her back into the car."

Tess was overwhelmed, taking in a story that upended everything she'd been told about her childhood. She pictured the pretty young woman in the photo, so desperate and distressed to be separated from her little girl. *From me*, Tess realized.

I had a mother who truly, truly loved me. The realization was stunning. The memories she had, fractured bits, like shards of light, they were real, not just wishful fantasy. The space around her was suddenly spinning and she sat down on a big steamer trunk.

"What happened after that? Where did he take me?"

"I don't know. He never said. In about a week, he came back. Liza was staying with us, walking on pins and needles. She hardly spoke or ate and didn't sleep a minute. By then, your father had hired a lawyer, and he claimed in court papers that your mother had abandoned the family. Back in those days, it was hard for a woman to prove abuse. Women weren't believed. But your mother found a lawyer to defend her and fought to get you back. Or at least work out joint custody. But she died before the case reached a judge. She'd gone home to her family in the Midwest, but we were in touch almost every day. She kept complaining of a stomach problem. She hadn't felt right since she lost you and thought it was nerves. It turned out to be an ulcer. She'd ignored it too long, and by the time she went to a hospital, it was too late. She was so young. It shouldn't have happened, but it did."

"Aunt Lila...why didn't anyone tell me this when I was growing up? My father always said she died from complications after I was born. I thought that was why he hated me—because he blamed me for her death. I thought that my mother and I had no time together. That she didn't even know me. Now you say it wasn't that way at all. She dressed me up in sun hats and frilly outfits...She fought for me."

"I wanted to tell you, Tess. Always. But your father made me swear I wouldn't. I was afraid if I crossed him, he wouldn't let me see you. I couldn't have that."

Tess agreed. She didn't know what her childhood would have been like without her aunt and didn't want to imagine it.

"I don't know why he persisted in that lie. After a while, I think he believed it. He was badly hurt and humiliated when Liza left, even though he drove her away. It changed him deep inside. Maybe, denying the truth and making up his own version was the only way he could go forward."

Tess thought that might be true. She still couldn't forgive her father for treating her the way he had, but she could understand it a little better.

"He did tell me once she was buried in the place where she grew up, but never said where that was."

"A small town in northern Minnesota. I can't remember the name; it's in this box. Her family asked to see you, but your father wouldn't agree. After a while, they gave up."

She had another family. Other aunts, uncles, cousins. Maybe even grandparents who were still alive?

Lila studied her with concern. "Tess, you look pale. Are you all right?"

Tess nodded. "It's just a lot to take in."

"I know, dear. I've wanted to tell you ever since your father died. But not over the phone. Since you got back, there always seemed to be other matters." She reached up and took Tess's hand. "It's hard to admit I've known this for so long and kept it from you. I know it would have made a difference to you when you were growing up."

Tess nodded, reining in her emotions. "It would have. But it's not your fault. How could it be? I'm glad you made the choice that you did. It wouldn't have brought her back, and at least I still had you."

"You have a good heart, Tess. Just like her." Her aunt smiled. "There are more photos in the box and letters she wrote to me after she went home and was fighting for you. I've saved them, and now they're yours."

Tess took the box from her aunt in two hands, as if she'd been given a fragile heirloom.

"Let's go down. I need some fresh air." Aunt Lila stood up and smoothed her clothes. "I think we've done enough digging around up here for one night."

Tess agreed, knowing she'd come away with the most precious treasure of all.

Carrie kept telling herself that working with Jack would get easier, but over a week had passed since she'd found his restaurant plans and they'd had their heart-to-heart. The smallest interaction was still awkward and strained.

He acted as if he didn't care about what had happened between them—almost happened, she amended. As if he'd shaken the whole thing off, like a dog coming in from the rain.

He was either putting on a good show, which was annoying, or it really *didn't* matter. Which made her feel worse. Carrie did her best to act businesslike and pleasant, while keeping a distance. As if the whole thing didn't matter one whit to her, either. Which wasn't true. Though she was sure she'd made the right call for both of them.

Brooke stopped in for a bite to eat on Friday. It was late in the afternoon, and the café was almost empty. They sat on the deck.

Carrie enjoyed the break and the breeze, sipping a diet soda while her annoyingly slim little sister ate a huge cheeseburger with a double serving of French fries.

"Have a fry. It won't kill you," Brooke offered around a mouthful.

Carrie shrugged. "Thanks, I'm not hungry."

"Oh, I thought fry-envy was making you glum." Brooke glanced over her shoulder to make sure they had privacy. "What's up with you and Jack? Did you have an argument?"

Carrie sat up, suddenly alert. "What do you mean by that?"

"You've been acting strange around each other all week. Like you had a fight. But not exactly. More like something happened...and it didn't turn out well. Is that it?"

Carrie's mouth twisted to one side. "You are observant, Lois Lane. I'll give you that. Nothing happened," she added. "We almost had a date, but...I put a lid on it."

Brooke looked surprised. "Why? You seem to like each other. After some initial fireworks."

Carrie so wished she hadn't used that word. "We do like each other. But we're going in different directions soon, and I just didn't think it was worth getting involved."

"Because you'd end up liking him too much, and you'd get hurt," Brook summarized.

Carrie didn't reply. Her sister had hit the bulls-eye. That was exactly what she'd been afraid of.

"It was just...bad timing," she said finally, casting about for an excuse.

Brooke wiped her mouth with a napkin. "Maybe he's acting strange because you rejected him. His feelings are hurt."

Carrie had already considered that. "He'll get over it." There were a lot of gorgeous women in California who would help him forget. She remembered that Brooke didn't know Jack's true identity, and it didn't seem a good time to tell her.

"What about Doug Bolton?"

"You could say I missed the boat on that one, at the risk of a corny pun." Carrie smiled at her own joke. "He's been on a business trip. He told me he'd be back this weekend, but I haven't heard from him." She gave in and took a French fry.

"He's playing hard to get. You just didn't notice."

Brooke's theory made her laugh. "Possibly."

"I wouldn't count him out yet," Brooke said.

"I'm not counting anyone in or out. I'm not interested in dating, honestly. Half the summer is over, and I still have to find a job, a place to live, and someone to run the café."

Brooke sipped her iced coffee, her expression solemn. "That's a lot of plates to spin. No question. Did you apply for any jobs yet?"

"I saw a good one online this morning. An upscale restaurant is opening in Bar Harbor, and there are a few positions I qualify for. It won't open until mid-September, so the timing works out, too."

Brooke's expression brightened. "Sounds great. Send your résumé right away."

"It's polished and ready. I just need a cover letter." Carrie crossed her fingers under the table. She'd seen other postings, but this one offered the best salary and benefits.

"Sophie won't like leaving Medford," Brooke said. "Luckily, this summer showed her she can make friends in new places."

"I think it's been good for her to spend the summer here. She's less moody, and learning how to sail has given her confidence." Carrie checked the time. "That reminds me, I've got to leave soon.

Sophie is in a sailing meet. It's just a race around some markers close to shore, but she's very excited."

"How cute. Can I come? I'm on a break until six."

"Absolutely. She'll love a big cheering section. I'll meet you there in a few minutes."

Brooke had often driven Sophie to camp and knew where to go. Carrie went into her office to clear her desk. She decided to apply for the Bar Harbor job that night. As she slipped the information into her tote bag, Jack appeared in the doorway.

Thirty-Nine

"Hey, Jack. What's up?" Carrie forced a bland smile.

"Not much." He shrugged, his expression unreadable. "I know it might be hard to work this out. But do you think I could take a few days off, the first week in August? I have to go to California."

That made sense. Plans for the new restaurant were moving quickly. A week ago, he said it was just talk.

"We'll figure it out. Sounds like your new venture is moving along."

"There's a lot of ball game left, but it's taking shape."

She faced him, hoping to draw the meeting to a close. "Victor could come in. He told my Mom he's recovered from his fall."

"Perfect timing." He smiled but seemed put off that she could replace him so easily. She was about to leave when he said, "How's your job search going?"

She usually avoided talking about chickens before they

hatched, but she wouldn't be outdone by his progress. "Not bad. I found a good posting today. I'm sending my résumé asap."

"Good for you," he forced a smile. "Back in Boston?"

"No, in Maine. Bar Harbor." A location even farther from San Diego than Boston, and even harder to reach, underscoring her point about the futility of starting a relationship. At least, to her, it did. She had a feeling he saw that, too.

"Beautiful spot. But quiet in the winter, I bet. I hope Sophie likes it."

"Oh, it's too early to worry about that. I think she'll be fine. I think we both will." She wasn't sure why she said that. Just to needle him? Whatever the reason, she couldn't resist.

"Wherever you end up, you'll land on your feet, Carrie. You're the type who takes a lemon and makes a meringue pie. Look at this place. You've brought it a long way this summer."

She smiled at the compliment. "Thanks, Jack. I appreciate that." She stopped herself from saying more. And from holding his gaze. She hooked her bag over her arm. "Speaking of Sophie, there's an event at her camp. I'm leaving early to watch. Can you close?"

"No problem." He stepped aside to let her pass. "Have fun."

"Thanks. See you tomorrow." She headed for the dining room and the front door, forcing herself not to look back.

They'd finally had a civilized conversation, and she should have felt relieved. But for some reason, she just felt sad.

When Carrie reached the sailing school's dock, she found a crowd of spectators, mostly parents and siblings of the sailors.

Brooke stood on the edge of the audience, already taking

photos. Carrie was glad she didn't have to. She loved a record of Sophie's milestones, but sometimes she just wanted to be in the moment and enjoy it.

"Sophie's down there with her group. She just waved," Brooke said.

A floating dock was accessible by a metal ramp and large enough to accommodate the group of children in orange life vests waiting there. Carrie spotted Sophie with a circle of kids who looked her age. She stood beside Hannah, of course, but chatted with the others, too. An older group waited, while younger children boarded the small sailboats with the help of their counselors.

"Good luck, honey!" Carrie called down.

Sophie turned and smiled and waved back. She looked happy and excited, at ease with her new friends. She'd matured a lot this summer. Ending up on Haven had been a blessing in disguise.

"There's a decent breeze. Enough to keep from stalling out," Carrie noticed, "but not so much they'll have trouble out there."

"A counselor just told us the same thing," Brooke replied. "There are three groups, the Minnows, the Marlins, and the Sharks. They're split into two teams, red and blue, and have to sail around those markers." Brooke pointed to the bright yellow floats that bobbed in the inlet. Carrie also saw adults in rowboats out in the water in case the campers needed help.

Carrie and her sister watched the Minnows line up their boats as well as they could. An air horn sounded, and the boats headed out, each with a red or blue flag flying from the stern.

The youngest sailors wandered off course, but most rounded the marker and returned to the dock. One or two simply spun around and turned back or were towed by a counselor's boat.

A score for the two teams was posted on a chalkboard. The red team led.

Brooke squeezed Carrie's arm as they watched Sophie hop into a boat. "Looks like she and Hannah are on the blue team. Good luck, Sophie!" Brooke called.

As the little boats waited for the horn to signal their start, Carrie watched each sailor take control of the rudder and lines.

"Oh blast...did I miss it?"

She turned to find Doug Bolton standing directly behind her.

"Doug...hi...I didn't see you there."

"Hello, Carrie. Sorry to sneak up on you." He smiled into her eyes, looking pleased to see her. If he'd been miffed about her missing his party, he'd gotten over it.

"You're just in time. The Marlins are about to launch."

She made space for him to get a better view, though he was so tall, he could easily see over her head.

"There's Hannah. She must be wondering what happened to me." He waved and called to his daughter, and she waved back.

The air horn sounded again, and the Sunfish took off much faster and more efficiently than the first group. "The Minnows were cute, but this is a real race," Brooke said.

Doug laughed. "They look very serious out there."

Carrie realized Doug didn't know her sister and quickly introduced them. "Hannah's doing well. She's ahead of the whole pack," Brooke noticed.

"Go, Hannah!" Doug shouted proudly.

Carrie found Sophie in the middle of the group, but she wasn't last. "That's the way, Sophie! You can do it."

Hannah rounded the marker, and the rest of the boats followed. She came in first. Sophie came in fifth but still scored points for her team. They climbed out of their boats, and the older group took over. The two girls looked tired but elated.

Doug snapped photos, smiling with pride. He wore a gray suit, lightweight and well cut. A fancy silk tie hung loosely around his collar. It appeared he'd done some racing of his own, straight from his office to the ferry and then to the sailing camp. He looked very handsome in a suit, Carrie thought, though she wasn't surprised.

"The blue team is ahead. I hope they win," Brooke said.

"Win or lose, I promised Hannah pizza. Would you like to join us?" he asked Brooke and Carrie.

"Thanks, but I have to get back to work." Brooke looked at Carrie. *He's not giving up,* her glance seemed to say.

"Pizza sounds just right," Carrie replied. "Sophie and Hannah were probably cooking up the same scheme."

Doug laughed. "No doubt."

A cheer rose from the dock. Carrie turned to watch the Sharks deftly turn and head for the finish line. The last heat ended, and the campers climbed up to the main dock. As they joined their fans, the score was totaled.

A man in a t-shirt imprinted with a sailboat and the camp's name announced the results. "Thank you for coming out to watch our races. Cheers to our sailors. We've all had a safe, fun time."

He paused, and the audience applauded.

"The winner of tonight's meet is the Blue Team!" He paused again for cheering. "Great job, Blue Team. And great job, Red Team, as well. I saw some excellent sailing. Keep up the good work. Hope to see you all at our next meet in August."

Hannah and Sophie were dismissed and ran to join them. After the girls were congratulated, Brooke left for work. Hannah and Sophie loved the idea of pizza and picked a place in Mariner's Point.

"Why don't we go in one car? I can bring you back here later, Carrie," Doug suggested.

It did make sense, and Carrie agreed. He led them to his SUV, a large, black Audi. The fenders were so shiny, she could have tweezed her eyebrows in her reflection.

The girls climbed into the backseat, and Doug politely held the passenger side door open. The seats were smooth tan leather, and the dashboard looked like the controls of a space shuttle. Carrie sat back, taking in the new car smell.

"Off we go, Blue Team," Doug called out cheerfully.

She should have expected to run into him at the sailing meet. But she hadn't thought that far ahead. At least she'd worn a new summer dress today. For some odd reason, she'd been more careful about her appearance since she and Jack had hit a wall in their relationship. She couldn't say why, but the extra effort served her well today.

Doug turned and smiled. "I'm glad I ran into you, Carrie. I was going to call later when I got home. I'll be here for the weekend, maybe longer. I was hoping we could get together without the girls one night. What do you think?"

Carrie was surprised to hear him ask her out when they hadn't even had dinner. Surprised and flattered. She'd have to tell Brooke. This wasn't exactly playing hard to get. But she liked a man who didn't play games. Doug seemed sincere; she valued that quality.

"That sounds great. I don't have any plans. Except work, of course."

"I think you work too hard and don't have enough fun. I'm going to work on that if you'll let me."

She didn't answer, and he didn't seem to expect her to. He smiled and looked at the road. Carrie glanced out her window at the passing scene, the cliffs and rolling sea shadowed by the setting sun.

She thought of Jack, how sad she'd felt when he left her office. She reminded herself that she had done the smart thing in not getting involved with him. Whatever had almost happened between them was well and truly over.

As for Doug, she'd thought he was annoyed with her and she hadn't expected the evening to turn out this way. Now that it had, it seemed best to sit back and enjoy the ride, and the pizza. And not read too much into the invitation. She might go on a real date with him sometime, but if they turned out to be friends because of Sophie and Hannah, that was fine too.

Forty

On Saturday morning, Tess loaded the truck with Aunt Lila's table, lamp, and the framed map. Her aunt had polished and repaired the offerings, which made a big improvement since their liberation from the attic.

Tess had picked a load of vegetables—tomatoes, zucchini, and kale. She'd washed off the dirt and packed the bounty in baskets but knew Evaline would add her special touch.

Ever since Ben had confided his memories of the accident and how much he cared for her, they'd managed to see each other almost every day and talk on the phone every night. He'd visit the farm on his way to and from the hospital. Or they'd bring takeout to the beach and take long walks along the shore with Honey. She felt closer to him every hour and prayed they really did have the kind of future together he seemed to take for granted.

But when Ben tried to persuade her to stay at the tag sale, she balked. She planned to unload the donations and go straight home. She had a lot of work to do, she told him. Which wasn't entirely true. Finally, she admitted her real reason.

"It was fine to go to church that day. But a lot of people from town will be at the sale. I don't want a scene."

"I understand why you're wary. I do, Tess. But you can't live this way forever. It's been almost a month since there was trouble at the farm."

She knew he meant well and was trying to be positive. Thinking of her future and his, too. But Tess was not convinced the danger had passed. Maybe her nerves were still raw. But she knew it would take a long time to feel completely secure on the island. Longer than four weeks.

She knew why he wanted her to stay. Ben's mother had organized the event, which was why he'd volunteered to do some heavy lifting. His sister Jillian was visiting and would be there, too.

"What if you stay a little while and meet my mom and sister? Only the church members setting up will be there."

It was hard to say no, considering all he had done for her and all he meant to her. "Okay, I'll try," she said finally. "But if they don't want to meet me, I understand."

"Thank you, Tess. That's all I wanted to hear." He sounded satisfied, and she felt even warier. She hoped he was going to warn them.

She wanted to tell Ben what she'd learned about her mother, but there hadn't been a good time. She was still exploring the box of letters and photos Lila had given her, trying to take it all in. When she was ready, the right time would come. There was no rush. Tess was starting to see a long, lovely future unfurling in front of them.

Tess would not have normally worn a dress and good sandals

to load the truck on a hot July morning, but she didn't want to embarrass Ben in her scruffy work clothes. She felt a bit self-conscious, though she knew that what she considered dressed up were the clothes other people wore to the supermarket.

"Don't you look nice," her aunt said as she climbed into the passenger's side. Lila had noticed the blossoming relationship and thoroughly approved. But her aunt had the sensitivity and good sense not to ask a lot of questions, which Tess appreciated. She still pinched herself every morning, amazed at her happiness.

When they arrived at the village green, Tess saw a space in front of the gazebo cordoned off for the sale. Tables stood in a square under a bank of tall trees that would provide shade all day with their thick, leafy branches.

The furniture and large items stood in the middle of the square, and smaller pieces, vases, plates, and knickknacks, were displayed on the tables. Tess was emptying the truck when Ben appeared. She'd already brought out Lila's donations and was about to tackle the vegetables.

He put his arm around her and kissed her cheek. "Let me take that. You look too pretty to be unloading a truck."

"Haven't you heard the news? Women are strong, too."

He smiled and grabbed a basket with each hand. "You're the very definition of that, Tess."

They carried the load to Evaline's table, where she fluttered about in her usual way, unpacking jars of honey and tea made from dried herbs and flowers.

Evaline served the tea at little wrought iron tables and chairs set up behind her flower stand. It was shaded by a pergola covered with wisteria and climbing roses.

When a customer finished their cup, Evaline sometimes read

the leaves. Tess had never been tempted to visit for a reading, mainly because her future had always seemed so bleak. Lately, she'd wondered what Evaline would say. If she could even believe that sort of thing.

"What beautiful vegetables. Do you talk to them?" Evaline picked up a tomato and stared at it, as if it might reply before Tess did.

"Not too much." Tess laughed.

"It's a lovely donation, Tess, and will sell quickly. I have a few pretty cloths to line the baskets."

Tess had not thought of lining the baskets. She doubted there were any "pretty cloths" in the farmhouse, either, except for her aunt's fancy dinner napkins.

While Tess helped Evaline, Ben stood nearby with his mother. Tess recognized Mrs. Croft from the courtroom all those years ago. She hadn't changed much, still tall and slim. Her chestnut hair, the same color as Ben's, was now threaded with gray. Tess knew at a glance Ben's mother had never recovered from losing her child. *As if anyone could,* she reminded herself.

Their voices rose, and Tess heard Ben trying to persuade his mother to walk over to Evaline's table. A younger woman appeared. Tess guessed she was Ben's sister, Jillian. She hadn't been at the trial, but there was no mistaking the family resemblance. Jillian tried to calm her mother and seemed to be taking her side against Ben.

Tess stared straight ahead, unsure of what to do. Why couldn't Ben let it go? She felt so embarrassed, she could barely see straight, and it seemed as if everyone nearby stood quiet and still, watching the scene unfold. Including Evaline and her Aunt Lila, who now stood at her side.

Tess heard Mrs. Croft say, "How dare you ask me to meet her, as if she was . . .anyone. It's just . . .beyond belief. I can't keep you from seeing her, but it breaks my heart to think of you together. It breaks my heart every time I hear you say her name. You've betrayed your brother, Ben. You've betrayed your whole family."

Ben began to answer, but Tess called to him. "Ben, stop. Please. Stop right now." Her voice was low but insistent.

When Ben turned, she met his gaze a moment, then ran. She passed the ribboned perimeter and ran across the green, all the way to the truck. Then she climbed in and drove away.

Tears blurred her vision, and she wiped her eyes with the back of her hand. When that didn't work, she used the sash from her dress. She felt even more ridiculous wearing it now. Trying to look presentable for a woman who hated her with every fiber of her being.

Unfortunately, to Ben's mother and most of the world, Tess was still guilty. Even if Ben's friend found evidence that would clear her name, she doubted Mrs. Croft would believe it. Tess already knew that, but Ben's unfailing optimism had made her hope for a moment it could be otherwise.

The Crofts would never accept her. It was a cold, harsh truth that they both had to face. And she'd never want Ben pressed to choose between her and his family.

Forty-One

True to his word, Doug did his best to bring more fun into Carrie's life. She'd enjoyed Friday night's victory party with him and the girls; on Saturday evening, she and Sophie went out on Doug's boat.

The water was calm, and they cruised around the island and watched the sunset from Turtle Bay near the North Light. When Doug stood by her side and rested his hand on her shoulder, she knew the outing would have been very romantic if Sophie and Hannah were not onboard. He must have been thinking the same thing because he asked her out again for Sunday night, this time without their adolescent chaperones.

He made reservations at a small but exclusive restaurant at the edge of town called East Wind, a newcomer to the island's culinary scene and not to everyone's taste, with its spare décor of blue and gray and sophisticated menu.

"Thanks for choosing this place," Carrie said as she opened the menu. "I've wanted to try it but could never find the time."

The truth was, she'd pictured dining here with Jack. He would have relished the creative dishes and exotic spices.

Then she felt annoyed at herself and guilty for thinking about Jack at all when Doug had arranged such a nice evening. She not only liked Doug but also respected him and was determined to give him her full and complete attention.

"I've said it before, you work too hard. And you need to get out and sample the competition every once in a while."

Carrie peered at Doug over the menu. "We serve hot food at the Blue Sky, too. But I think the similarity stops there."

Doug laughed. "You're very funny, Carrie. I bet you hear that a lot."

She couldn't help liking a man who appreciated her humor. "I'm mostly just honest. Too honest sometimes."

"I remember that about you from school, the way you spoke up to Mrs. Braddock in history class. I was impressed," Doug said, looking back at the menu.

Carrie couldn't hide her surprise. "Oh, you mean, dear old Mrs. Haddock." That was the nickname she and her friends made up for their dry, dull, overly opinionated teacher. "What did I say? I don't remember."

"Nothing in particular. It was just your personality. You seemed so bold and sure of yourself."

"So were you. You were class president. A real leader."

"I acted confident. But mainly because it was expected of me. I didn't always feel that way. You were the real deal. At least, I thought so."

Carrie smiled at him, surprised by his memories and glad he'd shared them. "I was too sure of myself. I thought I knew all the answers, and nobody could give me advice at that age. I regret that now. I wouldn't have gotten married straight out of high school or had a child right away."

"We've all made choices we'd change if we had the chance. Life isn't a straight line. It's like sailing, you get knocked off course by the wind or the tide, and you adjust and keep going. You've done a great job that way, Carrie. Even if you are 'a know-it-all,'" he added with a smile.

"Thanks, that's nice of you to say. And I'm a *reformed* know-it-all, by the way." He'd given her a great compliment. A thoughtful one, too.

The rest of their conversation was lighter, with Carrie asking about his company and how he decided to become an accountant. He made her laugh with stories of his college years and pranks he and his buddies played, including hiding someone in a sleeper couch, which was accidentally carried out of the dorm and left on a curb during a frigid New England winter night.

"Students walking by heard this muffled voice calling for help but thought they'd imagined it."

Carrie laughed so hard she could hardly breathe. The shape garment she wore under her sleek dress didn't help.

The evening passed quickly. The restaurant was on the water, and when they left, they found a bench and took in the view.

Doug rested his arm just behind her bare shoulders. "Are you cold? There's a breeze out here."

"I'm fine," she said, but he took off his jacket anyway and slipped it around her. The fabric felt warm and smelled of his aftershave.

He put his arm around her again, and she leaned against him. "How am I doing with the more fun project? Did I make any progress?"

"I haven't had this much fun in months. Maybe years. I'm very impressed." She was teasing him but sincere, too.

He smiled and caught her gaze. "We're just getting started. Next time we're on the boat, you're going tubing."

Carrie knew other people thought it was fun, but the idea of hanging on to an inflated rubber donut and being dragged through the water off the back of a powerboat made her anxious. "Do I have to?"

She cringed, and he squeezed her shoulder. "You might like it more than you think."

He met her gaze and smiled, his blue eyes the same shade as the dark ocean. She liked him more than she expected. Maybe she'd feel the same about tubing if she tried.

"I know we got off track on July 4th," he said. "I hope we've made up for that this weekend."

Carrie wasn't sure how to answer. "Thank you for being so—"

"Persistent?" he finished. "I don't give up easily, Carrie. Not when I think the effort is worth it."

When she met his glance, he pulled her closer, and their lips met in a soft, sweet kiss. She didn't resist and kissed him back. He touched her hair and cupped her cheek with his hand as the kiss deepened.

A short time later, he leaned back, but still held her close. She rested her head on his shoulder and gazed at the dark sea and the star-filled sky.

It had been a lovely night. Doug made her feel special. It was hard not to like him. Why had she made it so difficult for him to get to know her? Whatever the reason, her reservations were fading.

* * *

Tess knew Ben would be at the hospital all weekend and would even sleep there. He sent her texts and left messages, but she wasn't ready to talk to him.

She guessed he'd stop by on Monday on his way home but had never expected him so early. It was barely light out, and she was busy with the goats when his car came down the lane.

Honey ran out to meet him and jumped up when he got out. He smiled but looked so tired that Tess thought the big dog might knock him down.

Tess stepped out of the pen and latched the gate, dreading their conversation. She'd faced so many difficult moments in her life, but none worse than seeing Ben this morning. Her heart had already broken a hundred times since Saturday.

They walked toward each other and met at the barn. Ben raised his hands in a gesture of surrender. "I just want to talk, Tess. Did you even listen to my messages?"

She swallowed back a lump in her throat and nodded. "I did. But I didn't want to discuss this over the phone."

"I'm so sorry for the way my mother acted. I expected more of her. She's a good person."

"I'm sure she is. And I don't blame her. It's too much to ask of anyone. How could she ever accept me? It was crazy to think she could."

"Maybe not now, but we'll prove you weren't driving. She'll hear the truth, and she'll have to change her mind."

"Will she? Even if your friend finds some overlooked evidence, there's no guarantee I'll be vindicated. It might take years. Will you be estranged from your family all that time? You might think you're willing to pay that price, Ben. But I'm not willing for you to do that. Your mother and sister have been hurt enough."

Ben's eyes grew wide, his expression, grim. What are you saying? You don't want to be with me anymore, just like that?"

"Your mother lost one son. I won't take the other from her. You heard what she said on the green." She paused, trying not to cry before she finished. "You have a loving, close family. I won't ruin that for you. I know the price you'd pay, even if you don't realize it."

"I can deal with my family, Tess. That shouldn't be your worry. You always put everyone ahead of yourself. Did you ever notice that? It's generous and noble, but I can deal with it my way. You don't have to protect me. Honestly."

She disagreed. She knew what it was not to have a family. He had no idea what he was setting himself up for.

"You're the most resilient, persistent person I've ever known, Tess. Why won't you dig in your heels about what we have? Isn't that worth fighting for? Why can't you have some hope?"

Whether by nature or just from her experience, she had learned to dig in her heels, be patient, and wait out the bad times to hope for something better. But this was different. Ben might be optimistic, but she saw little chance of a happy ending. Not the way things stood now. Maybe never.

She pushed herself to voice a deep fear. "All right. Let's say we ignore your mother's feelings and go on together, at the cost of you losing your family. In time, you might resent me. Have you ever thought of that? What if my name is never cleared? People will talk about you, too. You could end up regretting the choice you made, Ben. And I couldn't stand that. I don't know what I'd do..."

Ben's expression had gone from disbelief to pained, as if she'd landed a physical blow. "That would never happen, Tess. Not in a million years. The truth will come out. People will see how unfairly you've been treated, my family, most of all." He paused and caught her gaze. "I would love you anyway. Even if it had been true. I've told you that before, and I'll tell them too. But I guess...you don't feel the same."

"I love you more than I can say." She'd never told him that before, though she'd whispered it in her heart a thousand times. "That's why I'm doing this. I know you don't understand, but I won't hurt you. Or your family. Maybe, someday, things will be different."

Ben stared back with a grim expression, then dropped his gaze. "I don't want to wait for someday, Tess. But you clearly don't see it that way."

"No, I don't." Tess was relieved he'd stopped arguing but felt like she was falling to pieces. If he stayed another minute, she'd break down and give in.

"Goodbye, Ben," she said quietly.

He stared at her for a moment but didn't answer. Then he got in his car and drove away without looking back. The sun was rising in the east, the early morning light seeping into the dark sky like a curtain slowly lifting.

Tess felt so bleak and lost, it might have been the middle of the night. She told herself she'd done the right thing. Ben couldn't see it now, but in time, he'd realize she'd made this decision because she loved him. The thought was cold comfort. She hurt deep inside as if part of her had been torn away. She knew the aching emptiness would never stop.

Forty-Two

Carrie spent more time with Doug on Monday and Tuesday. There was mini golf with the girls and another outing on his boat. She somehow avoided tubing again but was secretly building up to it. She and Doug also enjoyed another dinner alone, but Carrie didn't mind when their time together included Sophie and Hannah. He was great with the girls, and she liked that about him, too.

She was happy to spend a quiet evening with her family on Wednesday and came home in a good mood. She'd received a response to her application for the job in Maine, and the company had asked her to do a virtual interview. Carrie hadn't shared the news with anyone and didn't plan to. It was only the first hurdle, but she was hopeful.

Little slipped by Brooke, born with a nose for news. They were finishing dinner when her younger sister said, "You're very chipper tonight. Does this have anything to do with all your socializing?"

"Maybe." Carrie shrugged.

Her mother was more to the point. "You've been seeing a lot of Doug Bolton. I thought you didn't like him."

"I never said that." Carrie knew she'd inferred it and felt a pinch of conscience. "We're just getting to know each other."

"Slow and steady wins the race," her mother offered in a sage tone. Carrie wondered what race she meant but didn't want to encourage the conversation.

At least Sophie wasn't around to overhear the speculation about a romance between her mother and the father of her best friend—a formula that would backfire in some embarrassing way if she were here. Sophie hadn't asked Carrie about her dinner dates with Doug, and Carrie hadn't felt the need to explain.

Sophie was on the beach across the road and well beyond earshot. She'd persuaded Jack to teach her how to surf cast, and he'd been giving her lessons in the spare hours between coming home from the café and sunset. He'd even fixed up an old fishing rod and tackle box for her that he'd found in the garage. Sophie had bragged she'd already caught a few fish. "But Jack said they were too small, and we had to throw them back. If I catch a big one, he's going to teach me how to gut it and cook it."

Carrie wondered about the fortitude of Sophie's stomach regarding the first step and was curious to see what would come of the second. She had to admit, Jack was very patient and a good sport, all things considered. He seemed to genuinely enjoy Sophie's company, and Carrie knew her daughter would miss him when the summer ended. She wouldn't even speculate how she was going to feel.

"In case you haven't noticed, Sophie considers herself an old salt these days. She wants to take Dad's boat out. I told her I would ask you, Mom, but it's fine if you don't want her to," she quickly added

Carrie had put off the question, worried it would upset her mother. Maybe she didn't want anyone to use their father's sailboat. It would bring up so many memories to ride in it again.

"Is she ready to handle a boat that size?" Brooke asked.

"The dinghies at sailing school are twelve and fourteen feet. Dad's is sixteen. That's not much different." Her father's craft was also a daysailer, without a real cabin or amenities for long trips. It was all about riding the water and wind. "I told her that if we put *Far Horizons* in the water, it would be for everyone, and she could never go out on it alone."

"I think that's wise," her mother said. "I'm fine with the idea. Your father would have loved seeing Sophie at the helm of his pride and joy."

"So I can tell her it's all right?" Carrie asked to be sure.

"Absolutely, dear. But how will you get it in the water? Will Doug help you?"

Carrie knew he'd happily help if she asked and would probably offer to dock it at his house so she wouldn't have to pay a fee.

"I'll ask Finn. He'll do it for a fair price and clean up the boat first, too. Sand and paint and patch any leaks, and all that."

Brooke looked excited by the idea. "Good plan. I can't wait for Sophie to take us out for a sail."

"I can't either." Carrie looked forward to using the boat herself. She hadn't sailed since her last outing with her dad, but guessed the skills would come back easily. And she'd have Sophie there to correct her.

Carrie was about to clear the table when her mother said, "I have some news, too." Her expression brightened. "Nadia is planning a show of local artists. She asked me to help with the preparations and hang the paintings. And she chose one of mine for the exhibit," she said proudly.

Brooke had been checking her phone. Her head popped up like a gopher from a hole. "That's great, Mom. When did this happen?"

"Just today. Another artist was going to help, but he dropped out. She's even going to pay me." Her mother shrugged. "I enjoy it so much, I'd do it for free."

"Isn't that what you told us, Mom?" Brooke asked. "Find something to do that you enjoy so much, you'd do it for free?"

"I'm taking my own advice, I guess. It's just for the next few weeks. In September, I'll go back to the café."

"But we're going to find a manager, Mom." Brooke glanced at Carrie. "Right?"

"Absolutely. If Nadia asks you to stay on, don't count it out." An art gallery was an ideal place for her mother to work. She already loved dealing with the public and would have plenty of time for her own painting.

Finding someone to run the Blue Sky seemed more important than ever. Especially if the job in Maine came through, or one like it. Carrie dreaded the idea of having to choose between staying on Haven or advancing her career. She promised herself it wouldn't come to that.

* * *

In the days after Tess sent Ben away, she moved around the farm in a fog. She would forget what she was doing in the middle of a task —why she'd gone into the barn or to the goat pen. She slept through her alarm, which had never been her way. She forced herself out of bed and threw herself into her demanding, physical work, trying to numb her aching heart and soul.

Her aunt didn't ask any questions when Ben stopped coming around. Tess was grateful. A witness to the scene on the green, Lila knew all she needed to. She acknowledged the situation in a quiet way, treating Tess with extra care. One night, just before bed, she leaned over Tess's chair and hugged her. "My dear girl. I wish there was something I could do for you. I wish there was some solution to all this."

Tess patted her hand. "I know you do, Aunt Lila. But there's nothing anyone can say or do."

Tess half expected Ben to text or call, and she checked her phone a hundred times a day. A week went by, and then another, and she found no message from him. Each time she was tempted to reach out to him, she forced herself to remember his mother's harsh words and realized how futile it would be for them to patch things up and try again. Parting a second time would only be harder. Tess didn't think she could survive it.

On Monday morning at breakfast, her aunt said, "August one. How did that happen? The summer is flying by."

"It is," Tess agreed.

"Did you say 'rabbit, rabbit' first thing?" her aunt asked playfully. Rabbit, rabbit was an old wives' tale. Her aunt had taught her to say the phrase first thing on the first day of the month and make a wish. Tess had tried for years but had never seen any results she could recall.

"I forgot," she admitted. "Did you?"

"Sure I did. I do it every time I remember." Her aunt rose from the table and poured herself a cup of coffee.

"What did you wish for?"

"If I tell, it won't come true." She added milk and sugar and stirred. "I find prayers work better," she added. "I can do that any day of the month I please."

Tess had to smile at Lila's logic. "That's very true."

She was in the barn, gathering her tools and gloves, when a mail truck pulled up. Tess came out and met the postman, Leo Tuttle, the same mail carrier they'd had for years. He held a thick, letter-sized envelope. "This is one's for you, Tess," he said. "Can you sign, please?"

"Sure." Tess scribbled her signature quickly and took hold of the envelope.

The return address was a law firm, and she guessed it held more documents about the deed transfer. But it wasn't from "Woods & Hildebrandt." It was from a firm in Hartford, Connecticut, and her pulse quickened, sensing it was not good news.

She walked into the barn and tore the letter open. She was so anxious, she could hardly make sense of the words on the page. It was from a lawyer who had been hired by her cousin. The attorney warned that his client planned on filing a lawsuit claiming she forced his mother, Lila Norton, to sign over ownership of High Meadow Farm.

His client had ample proof to present in court that Tess had harassed and pressured her aunt, taking advantage of her age and frail, unstable mental state. And that her aunt had transferred the deed out of fear for her safety.

The attorney warned that Tess's history—pleading guilty to a felony and serving a five-year sentence in jail—would weigh heavily against her in court.

The lawyer gave her ten business days to contact his office, or papers would be filed to initiate a suit. Tess calculated in her head. That meant an answer by Monday the fifteenth.

She stared into the shadows, panic building in her chest. It had taken nearly a month, but Richard had retaliated, like a bomb with a slow ticking fuse. She needed help but had no idea where to turn. Mr. Woods was a gentle man, a country lawyer comfortable with house closings and writing wills. She couldn't see him fighting this battle. Not successfully.

It had to be someone tough and sharp. Once she found the right attorney, how would she pay them? Borrowing against the property seemed the only solution, though she hated the idea of racking up debt when she'd barely gotten started.

Ben would know what to do. But she couldn't call him. Not even with this sword dangling over her head. She remembered how he'd said, "If Richard gives you any trouble from here on in, he'll have me to deal with."

Comforting words at the time, but no help to her now.

Richard could have gone straight to a lawsuit, but he'd fired a warning shot. He might be willing to talk things out. For a price. She wasn't completely naive; she knew that much. What would his price be? She didn't want to imagine.

Tess waited until Wednesday to call her cousin. She would have let him stew longer, but her aunt left after supper for her book club, giving Tess the privacy she needed.

Richard didn't bother saying hello. "I assume you got the

letter from my attorney."

Tess was shaking inside but forced herself to sound steady and calm. She wouldn't get anywhere showing fear to Richard.

"You mean your laundry list of lies? You won't prove any of it. I never asked your mother for the property. It was entirely her idea. She'll swear to it under oath. You must know that."

"My mother is an old woman, confused by her age and medications and easily influenced. Vulnerable to someone like you, an ex-convict, who arrived out of the blue and is living with her twenty-four, seven. Who knows how you manipulate her, Tess? Even threaten her."

His vicious accusations left her breathless. "I never once, nor would I *ever*, lift a finger to hurt your mother. And you know that. Her mind is sharper and clearer than yours. Obviously. You won't get anywhere with this pile of. . .manure."

"I have a specialist who will testify my mother is not competent to make these decisions. Or even a reliable witness to your behavior since you moved in with her."

"I have a doctor who's known her his whole life and will say the exact opposite." Tess recalled Ben anticipating this would happen. It would be hard to ask him for help, but she'd have to if it went that far.

"Sounds like you want to go court," Richard said calmly. "It will cost you. Money down the drain if you ask me. You'll end up borrowing against the property. A bad season or two and you'll be in trouble with the banks, and some developer will snatch up High Meadow Farm for a fraction of its value; a very nice sum they'd pay us tomorrow."

The word "us" infuriated her. "Me, you mean. If I want to sell, which I don't. There is no 'us' in the matter, last I noticed."

"That's just the thing, Tess. I'm offering you a way out—a profitable way out. I can arrange everything. Find the buyer, work out the terms, arrange to change the zoning, etcetera. All you need to do is sign on the dotted line, and we'll split the profit, fifty-fifty. A fair deal, considering my contribution. But we are family." He paused. "Otherwise, we sort this out in a courtroom. You may want to take that chance, owing to your temper and stubborn streak. But you'll lose. Then where will you be?"

"I think I'd win," she insisted, though she did worry about her track record with courts and judges, which wasn't very good.

"Don't answer off the top of your head, out of anger. Think about it. If you let me handle a sale," he continued, "you'll walk away with plenty to make a life for yourself somewhere else. It will be a lot more than nothing. Think of my mother," he added in a quieter tone. "You talk about her testifying. Do you really think she'll take your side against her own son? Even if she does, what will that do to her? She'll feel torn in two. It certainly won't be good for her health."

"It will be awful for her. We finally agree about something. But you're the instigator, Richard. If you were truly concerned about your mother, you wouldn't do this."

"I'm trying to protect her. That's what I told my attorney and will tell a judge. Of course, I must add that living with you creates a dangerous environment because of all the harassment and violence you've drawn to that place. That's another reason you should give in and sell out."

"That's over, Richard. No one has bothered us for weeks."

"Until the next time. There's no guarantee. It can happen again, Tess. You know that as well as I do."

When she didn't answer, he said, "The ball is in your court.

There can be peace in the family. It's up to you."

Tess sat at the kitchen table, feeling shaken. Honey rested her head in Tess's lap, and Tess absent-mindedly stroked her soft fur.

The most important thing now was to hide the situation from her aunt. It would upset her deeply if she found out.

Tess's first instinct was to fight Richard. He had no right to threaten and pressure her—the same tactics he'd accused her of using on his mother. The irony would have been amusing if the situation wasn't so serious.

She didn't trust her luck with the legal system. The idea of dealing with a lawyer, giving statements, and filing papers made her physically ill. Richard was counting on that, too. She worried about the cost, of course. But those issues paled next to her concern for her aunt. Maybe there was some way to convince Lila that she'd changed her mind about running the farm. Or she'd decided she couldn't make it work financially. Then she'd have an excuse to sell the property. She'd provide for her aunt from her share. She had no doubt of that, even if Richard didn't do the same.

But something inside Tess balked at that solution. She didn't want to give up and sell out. She had dozens of ideas about how she could make the farm a success. Tess doubted she could fool her aunt. As she'd told Richard, his mother's mind was sharp and clear.

Her head spun with questions and worries, and she stared at her phone, so tempted to confide in Ben. He would know how to handle her cousin.

But she couldn't. She had to sort this out on her own. Thinking about Ben only made the hollow place inside hurt even more.

Forty-Three

Carrie's weekend was very much like the last. Doug returned to the island on Friday night, and they took the girls out for Mexican food. There was another outing on his boat for Sophie and Hannah on Saturday and a dinner out for her and Doug that night.

On Sunday, she and Sophie were invited to a barbeque at his parents' house. Carrie was nervous about attending as his date, but Doug convinced her that any get-together of his big family was such mayhem, no one would notice her. It was mayhem, but in the nicest, warmest way, Carrie thought, with all the kids and dogs running around the pool and spacious property. His siblings and their spouses were very friendly, and his parents presided over the chaos with grace and charm.

When she was introduced, his father teased her about the rivalry between the Blue Sky Cafe and Bolton's.

"I heard that our Doug was charmed by the enemy, but now that I've met you, Carrie, I understand why."

"Dad?" Doug was embarrassed and blushed. "I never said anything like that," he insisted.

Carrie wasn't sure how to smooth things over. "That's a very nice compliment. Thank you, Mr. Bolton."

"Call him Jim," Doug's mother said as she handed Carrie a frosty glass of iced tea. "And please call me Marty. Everybody does."

The hours went by quickly, including a softball game after dinner on the spacious green lawn. Carrie hadn't played since high school but had been on the junior varsity squad and loved it. She and Doug were on opposite teams. He'd been a great athlete in school and was the pitcher for his team. He struck Carrie out easily on her first time at bat. She made contact at her second chance, but the ball was fielded quickly. In the last inning, with her team lagging by a run and one player on second base, she hit a solid fly ball over the short stop's head that landed in the outfield and bounced around crazily.

It should have been a double, but she somehow made it to third base while her teammate scored to tie the game. The outfielder fumbled with the ball, and her team screamed to go all the way.

She didn't mean to slide. It just happened. There was a messy, comic play at home base, but she was clearly safe and scored the winning run. Even players on the other team congratulated her.

Doug's team had lost, but he seemed proud of her victory and slung his arm around her shoulder. "You killed that sinker. I should have thrown my fastball."

"It was a lucky swing." A few men she knew would have pouted to be shown up by a woman, but Doug was a perennial good sport. He was comfortable in his own skin and didn't get ruffled by little slights, real or imagined. She liked that about him.

As Carrie was closing on Tuesday, Doug stopped in before he left on the five o'clock ferry. The café was empty except for the staff, still cleaning up. She led Doug out to the deck and brought out cold drinks.

"How's your shin?" Doug asked. Carrie had scraped her shin during her MVP play. There was still a small bandage.

"Coach says I'll be back in the lineup any day." She met his glance. "The barbeque was a lot of fun. Your family was so nice to me and Sophie."

"I'm still getting rave reviews. They want me to bring you back next weekend." He smiled into her eyes and took her hand.

Before Carrie could reply, Victor came out of the kitchen. "I just checked the cold box, Carrie. I left the inventory in your office."

"Thanks, Victor. We can talk before you go."

Jack had left for San Diego on Sunday. It was planned as a four-day trip, but he'd sent a text that morning, asking for a few more days. His meetings were taking longer than expected. She quickly agreed. What choice did she have?

"Did your cook quit? That tall guy with the dark hair? I don't know his name," Doug said.

"Jack, you mean," she filled in. "He's away. He had some personal business to take care of in California."

Like opening an exclusive, upscale restaurant.

"It's nice of you to give him time off in the middle of the season." Doug sounded as if he wouldn't have been so agreeable.

"Speaking of personal business, how did your interview go? You haven't mentioned it."

"Oh, I thought I did. Sorry," she said.

The interview had taken place via her computer. There were three executives on the other end, floating faces in little boxes, so it was hard at times to follow the conversation, but Carrie did her best and finished with a positive feeling.

"And?" Doug asked.

"I don't want to count my chickens, but I think I made a good impression. It's only the first round. They're going to sift out the candidates, and there'll be another virtual interview and then one up in Maine before they decide."

Doug seemed thoughtful. "I'm sure they were impressed with you. Who wouldn't be? I just wish Bar Harbor wasn't so far away. I miss you enough when I go back to Marblehead. It will be hard to see each other if you move up there."

Carrie knew that was true, but their relationship was so new, too new for her to make it a priority in this decision. She wondered how to explain that without hurting his feelings.

"We'll stay in touch with phone calls and FaceTime and all that," she assured him, realizing that she sounded a lot like Jack had when he tried to reassure her. "Besides, you'll be very busy in the fall with the new restaurants opening."

Bolton's was expanding, opening two restaurants on the mainland, one in posh, pricey Newport, Rhode Island, and another on the waterfront in Boston, not far from Faneuil Hall. Doug was very excited about the project but also loaded with extra work.

"That's just it. I won't have time to drive to Maine and back. And with a new job, you won't have time to come down here. I know we're just getting started, but I think we have a real future, Carrie. I thought you felt the same."

"I do," she agreed, though she sounded less sure than he did, she realized. "I really enjoy our time together, Doug. I like you, I really do," she assured him. "But making a good life for Sophie is my priority. It has to be. Tim is a good father in a lot of ways, but not when it comes to sending child support. This would be a great opportunity in a field I love, and the salary is double what I made at the college. I can give Sophie a good life in Maine. And..." she added, drawing out the word, "I didn't even get the job yet."

"I know. But I'm worried. I won't lie." He paused and caught her gaze. "I know how independent you are. It's one of the things I love about you. But if you'd accept a little help, we could find a great spot in management for you at one of the new restaurants. With an excellent salary, no question. You could make a good life for Sophie in Newport or Boston and be closer to your family here, too. It goes without saying, there'd be no strings attached. I'd like to help you, as a friend."

The offer was tempting. It would solve her problems in a snap, as if Doug pulled a rabbit out of a top hat. She could see him in the dapper tuxedo and cape, too. He was sincere and believed he offered the help as he would to any friend. But what if she did take a job for Bolton's and things between them didn't work out? It would be awkward, to say the least. She'd feel so beholden to him.

"My mother says not to fret about things that haven't happened yet," Carrie said brightly, hoping to shift the mood. "I might not get a second interview, much less get the job."

"Very true. Now you have another option. Just think about it, okay?"

"I will, I promise. And thanks. I appreciate it."

He finally smiled—a wide, warm grin. "My family would be lucky to have you. I'd be lucky, too."

As he leaned in for a kiss, Carrie knew he'd meant more than having her join the Bolton family business. The frank expression of his feelings made her a little nervous, despite how much she liked him. As she kissed him back, her hand resting on his solid shoulder, she told herself she was being silly.

You're just not used to a sincere, grounded guy like Doug, who's honest about his feelings and wants a commitment. That isn't a bad thing, Carrie.

The moment didn't last long. Victor appeared, making his presence known with some throat clearing. When Carrie looked up, he said, "Tess Hargrove is here with a delivery. She wants to speak to you."

"Oh, sure. Please ask her to wait a minute. I'll be right there."

Doug stood up and put his sunglasses on. "I'd better go. I'll miss my ferry."

They walked into the café, heading for the front door. "Have a safe trip."

"Thanks." He nodded. "I didn't know you did business with Tess Hargrove."

"Her berries and vegetables are great, and at a better price than suppliers on the mainland." She wasn't sure why she needed to justify dealing with Tess, but he looked curious. Even concerned.

"I doubt she's ever approached Bolton's. I'm not sure we'd deal with her."

Something in his tone was disturbing. "I guess if I ever work for Bolton's, I'll change that. I don't know anything about her guilt or innocence. I do know she served her sentence and is honest and hardworking. I don't believe anyone has the right to make her life any harder than it is already."

Doug offered a small, embarrassed smile. "That's what I love about you, Carrie. One of the many things. You call me out when I need it and show me a new point of view."

Carrie felt self-conscious, too, thinking she'd gone too far. "At least you listen. That's something I like about you."

After he left, Carrie headed for the kitchen. She found Tess watching Victor empty a crate she'd delivered.

"Look at this baby, Carrie." The cook held up a melon, fresh off the vine. "It's too pretty to eat."

Tess smiled, gratified by his praise. "The raccoons and rabbits don't agree. I'm happy to rescue a few for the humans."

"We're glad you managed to," Carrie agreed. "How's the goat cheese project coming along?"

Tess had mentioned she was studying up on making cheese from goat's milk and might have some to offer soon. Carrie wondered if that was why she wanted to talk.

"I have a ways to go, but I'm learning a lot. I wanted to ask your advice about something else." Tess glanced at Victor, and Carrie sensed she wanted to talk privately.

"Sure, let's go to my office." Carrie led the way. It was a tight fit for two, but Tess didn't fill up the space the way Jack did. Maybe that had more to do with her attraction to the to him than anything else, she realized, as she closed the door.

Carrie sat at her desk and found a chair for her guest. "What's on your mind?"

"It's a long story. Basically, I'm having a problem with my cousin, Richard. Lila's son. He didn't want his mother to give me the farm. Now that it's happened, he's very angry. He's threatening a lawsuit."

"That's awful." Carrie didn't know Richard Norton well, but he'd never made a good impression on her. There had always seemed something two-faced about him.

"What grounds does he possibly have for that?"

Tess pulled a letter from the back pocket of her jeans and handed it over. "It's a heap of lies. But you can read it for yourself."

Carrie quickly scanned the page. "He'll never prove this in court. He just wants to scare you. Have you spoken to him?"

"I called last week. He expects me to back down and allow him to sell the property. I'd try my luck in court, but there's my aunt to think about. She'll be forced to take sides. That will be a nightmare for her." Tess looked upset, foreseeing her aunt's distress. "Do you think your sister Rebecca would represent me or recommend a lawyer who would? Maybe I can sort this out with Richard without my aunt knowing. But I'll need a good advocate."

"I'll call her tonight. I'm sure she'll help." Rebecca loved representing female clients, mostly in divorce and custody cases and workplace situations, but she might take up Tess's fight. "He has no right to that property or any profit if you ever decide to sell. He wants to intimidate you and exploit your love for Lila. In the worst possible way."

"He knows my weak spot and went straight for it. I almost agreed. But something inside won't give in to this... bullying and intimidation."

"Good for you, Tess. There's no reason in the world why you

should," Carrie said as she stood up. "I'll give Rebecca your number and tell her to call right away."

"That would be great. Thanks so much. I didn't know who else to ask except for Owen Jessup."

"I love Owen," Carrie said. "But he's never mentioned any high-powered Boston lawyers in his family."

Tess smiled. "Not to me either, come to think."

They walked back into the kitchen. "I know it's not much, but the vegetables are on me for the rest of the summer," Tess said as she pulled open the door.

"No, they are *not*," Carrie insisted. "I'm happy to help any way I can, Tess. I mean it."

When she thought of her own tightly knit circle, she felt blessed. Especially compared to Tess, who had so few people in her corner.

Forty-Four

"That's all right, dear. Your work comes first. I understand."

Tess stood at the sink, washing the pots after Friday night's dinner. She scrubbed with extra energy, relieved to hear Richard tell his mother he couldn't come for the weekend as he'd planned. She'd dreaded being under the same roof as him. He was stuck in Hartford, unexpectedly, forced to attend a business conference. Tess wondered if the excuse was true. She distrusted everything her cousin said now.

Canceling his visit probably had to do with Rebecca Duffy's reply to his attorney's letter. Richard was probably surprised and definitely unhappy to learn he hadn't scared her into giving up the farm. And that she'd found a smart, tough advocate.

"Richard can't make it this weekend," her aunt said. "His boss wants him to attend a conference. A coworker was supposed to go, but she's come down with a bug."

"You must be disappointed." Tess could have danced around the room. But she put her feelings aside; her aunt looked so glum.

"I am. But he'll come see us soon. I already shopped, so we'll have to invite Evaline for dinner. Hardly the worst thing, right?"

"I'd love to see Evaline." Tess called Honey to her side. "Let's go, pal. Time for your last romp of the night."

Her aunt looked up and smiled. She was already calling her friend to make new plans.

* * *

Jack returned in the small hours of Saturday morning. Carrie heard a car pull up, stepped to her bedroom window, and then watched him carry a suitcase to the apartment. The clock on the nightstand read half past three. He'd promised to be back at work on Saturday, but it had been a long trip from southern California to Haven, and she didn't want him to fall asleep standing at the stove.

Despite the late hour, she sent him a text:

Just saw you get back. No need to work tomorrow. Victor can come one more day.

Jack answered quickly:

I'll be there, no worries. But nice to know you waited up for me.

His reply annoyed her. She nearly texted back, "I was *not*

'waiting up' for you. Your taxi woke me up." But she resisted trading barbs.

She slipped under the covers to catch a few more hours of sleep. She'd hoped the time apart would make her immune to Jack, like cutting sugar out of her diet. She hated to face it, but the detox hadn't worked. She'd missed him and was happy he was back. Though she'd never let him know that.

She cared for Doug; they had a great rapport and so much in common. There seemed to be a real future for their relationship. Doug was a solid, dependable guy, who wasn't going to move to the West Coast, or New York, or Barcelona out of the blue. She forced herself to focus on that.

Why did she still have feelings for Jack? *You're attracted to the challenge. The unpredictability.* It seemed more than that, but she was too tired to figure it out. The passing days would make the choice for her. By the end of the summer, both men might be out of the picture. The realization didn't make her feel any better.

It was almost noon when Carrie and Jack exchanged a few words beyond the briefest greeting. She walked into the kitchen during a lull between breakfast and lunch.

"How was California? Did you have a good trip?" She forced a friendly smile and casual tone. Somewhere deep inside, she wished it had been a fool's errand.

"It was great," he replied with a wide smile. He already looked different, with his thick hair cut in a sharp, new style and an expensive-looking sports shirt under his apron, instead of his usual rag-tag cooking clothes.

"The investors are all pros. They found a great location. Things are moving faster than I expected."

"Sounds super," Carrie replied through gritted teeth. She never used the word "super" – so corny. How had that come out?

"It worked out here, too. Victor can return full-time right after Labor Day. That's all set."

Jack didn't look happy to hear that. Or was she imagining that?

"You have it all under control, as usual, Carrie."

She wasn't sure why he'd say that. She was never able to control him.

"How's the job hunt going?" he asked.

"I interviewed for a position in Bar Harbor. There's a lot of competition, but I have a second meeting."

Jack's expression brightened. "Sounds promising. I'd be glad to give you a recommendation. I mean, I know a guy who's sort of well-known, and he would do that for you."

An endorsement from the famous Jackson Gardeaux would push her name to the top of any list, but she could never accept it.

He seemed so pleased for her. Too pleased. As if he didn't care that in three weeks, they'd go their separate ways and likely never see each other again. Unlike Doug, who was trying so hard to keep her close.

You were the one who decided not to get involved, remember? Just leave it alone.

"Thanks, Jack. But I'll sink or swim on my own merits."

"Which are impressive enough."

His dark gaze met her own. She looked away, trying to hide how unsettled he made her feel. "If the jet lag catches up and you want to leave early, let me know."

She headed to the deck to make sure tables were being cleared and customers were seated promptly. And settled her nerves after their encounter.

Just be professional and friendly for a few more weeks, and you'll have no regrets. Jack Dubensky—aka Jackson Gardeaux—will soon be a fond memory.

* * *

After decades of friendship, Tess wondered how her aunt and Evaline had anything left to talk about, but they kept up a lively stream of conversation for hours. Sometimes it seemed they forgot Tess was even there. Tess didn't mind being a fly on the wall as they traded recipes and the latest news circulating around town. Though not in a gossipy way, Tess thought. Mostly out of concern.

It was after ten when Evaline thanked them and headed home. Tess and her aunt watched from the porch as she drove away in her tiny car. They cleaned up the kitchen together and went upstairs to bed.

Tess tried to study her cheese-making text, but soon shut the light. She heard Honey pad into the room, then curl up in a ball next to the bed and release a long sigh. She dangled her hand down to touch the dog's soft fur, the last thing she remembered before she dropped into a deep sleep.

* * *

When Carrie got home from dinner with Doug on Saturday night, she made a cup of tea and headed up to her bedroom. The house was quiet. Sophie was sleeping at Hannah's, and she assumed her mother had gone to bed early. The art show was tomorrow, and Gena needed rest for her busy day. But Carrie saw a light on in her mother's bedroom. She knocked and entered.

Her mother stood in front of the mirror, wearing a navy blue dress with white trim around a boat neck, dark pumps, and small pearl earrings.

"Are you going out somewhere?" It was after ten, and Carrie thought that was unlikely.

Her mother glanced at her, then back at the mirror. "I can't decide what to wear tomorrow. Nothing looks right. I used to love this dress, but now it looks so...out of fashion." She glanced at Carrie. "What do you think?"

Carrie felt put on the spot. "It's. . .fine. If you're going out to lunch maybe—"

"With your accountant?" Brooke popped her head around the door. She'd obviously been eavesdropping.

Her mother made a face. "Very funny." She sighed. "It is a bit conservative for an art show, I guess."

"Dowdy is the word?" Brooke flopped on the pale pink satin comforter. "You're an artist, Mom. You need a hipper look."

"You've lost so much weight since you were sick. It doesn't fit well anymore," Carrie added, trying a softer approach.

Gena struggled with the zipper, and Carrie stepped over to help. "That's the problem. I don't have any stylish outfits. Much less 'hip' ones. I've barely bought new clothes since your father passed away. I didn't need to."

Carrie knew that was true. This exciting turn in her mother's quiet life had caught her unprepared. "Let me think. Maybe I have something in my closet that would work. Even though you're at least a size smaller. Or two."

"You're much taller, Carrie, and you have a large frame," her mom said in a loyal tone. Carrie had always been curvy, and never fit the female ideal found in fashion magazines, but her mother always made her feel perfect.

"I might have something that would work for you, Mom." Brooke hopped off the bed. "Let's ransack closets and rendezvous here in ten. Bring makeup and that blow dryer with the brush that makes your hair super smooth, Carrie."

"Girls? What are you going to do to me?" Her mother pulled on a robe and followed them out to the hallway.

"Sit tight. We'll be right back." Carrie ran up to her room, excited by the assignment. Her mother didn't know it, but she was about to get a makeover.

A short time later, her mother's bed was covered with clothes, the rug littered with footwear. Carrie had found a pair of wide-legged trousers made of a light, silky material. The champagne color was understated and classy, a perfect backdrop for the right top and accessories, she and Brooke decided.

Brooke donated a silky, kimono-style jacket printed with lotus flowers on a field of pale turquoise. Touches of black and cream in the pattern worked perfectly with the pants and a black tank top.

Gena loved the fabric. "This is beautiful. Why haven't you ever worn it?"

Carrie's sister shrugged. "It was waiting for the right occasion. Like tomorrow."

"Try it, Mom. Let's see how it looks," Carrie urged her.

Gena slipped on the kimono and checked her reflection.

"Wait . . .shoes. Try these sandals." Brooke offered a pair with wooden platforms that definitely made a statement.

Her mother eyed them warily. "They're so high. I might fall."

"They're perfect," Carrie insisted. "They give you that leggy look. And you won't need to hem the pants or roll the waistband. Otherwise, they'll be too long."

"Sit, Mom. Time for hair and makeup." Brooke coaxed their mother into the chair at her dressing table.

"Let's not fuss with that now. I need to go to bed."

"It's barely eleven. It won't take long," Brooke promised. "First, we'll put your hair back."

She pushed Gena's hair off her face with a wide headband and opened her makeup bag.

"You have great skin, Mom," Carrie said. "Not a wrinkle. I hope I got some of those genes."

"That's not true. I have plenty." Despite her denial, Carrie knew her mother was pleased by the compliment. "I don't use anything special. Drugstore potions. I've always been careful in the sun. Remember that," she advised.

While Brooke worked on makeup and hair, Carrie considered jewelry. The pearl earrings were all wrong, no question.

It was just about midnight when they were done. They were having so much fun, nobody noticed the time. Finally, Carrie and her sister were ready for their mom to see the results.

"You can open your eyes," Carrie said, positioning her mother in front of the full-length mirror.

"What have you two done to me?" Gena raised her hands to her cheeks. "I barely recognize myself."

She sounded surprised but not displeased.

"It's not so different from the old you. Just a bit updated and enhanced," Carrie said.

"And way hipper looking," Brooke added.

Brooke had applied the make-up with a careful, light hand, but their mother had never worn much at all, so of course, she was shocked. The highlighting of her lovely eyes and the soft lipstick was perfect and brought out her natural beauty. The hairstyle was not extreme either, but softer and more youthful looking.

"Think of it as the new, art gallery version," Brooke suggested.

"A version that's been itching to come out all these years," Carrie added.

Gena didn't answer for a moment. "Maybe," she agreed. "Someone has to help me do this whole routine tomorrow. I'll never get it right. Not even if you take a photo and draw a diagram."

Brooke laughed. "I'll help you, no worries."

"Thank you, dear." She gave her reflection one more look. "I'm just not sure about these dangling earrings," she added as she took one off and placed it on her dresser.

"Don't chicken out now," Carrie said. "'Fortune favors the bold.'"

"Very true." Their mother laughed and began to undress. "Thanks for coming to my rescue. I was in a state. I might feel self-conscious tomorrow, but at least I won't look as if I just met with my accountant."

Brooke laughed. "I doubt he'd recognize you."

Forty-Five

Tess dreamt that she sat at a bonfire on the beach. The smokey smell was pleasant, and sparks flew into the night sky. There were friends, maybe some farmhands she'd worked with last summer. Aunt Lila was there. It didn't make sense, like most dreams. She woke slowly and stared into the dark.

Honey was downstairs, barking her head off and Tess realized that she still smelled smoke coming from the open window in her room. She jumped up and checked the time, half past three. She ran downstairs barefoot, her heart in her throat. There'd been no trouble for weeks. Had the vandals come back?

Honey ran from window to window at the front of the house, whining and barking, and Tess heard the goats bleating wildly, a panicked sound. She stared out and saw a strange orange-yellow glow near the pen as a gray plume billowed into the night sky.

The shed next to the goat pen was on fire. She ran out to the porch and pulled on boots. She tried to make Honey go back into the house, but the strong, lithe dog slipped by her legs, determined to help.

They ran to the pen, and Tess pulled open the gate. Smoke filled her lungs and burned her eyes. She worried about Honey, but the dog seemed unfazed.

The goats huddled in a far corner, braying and jumping on each other, too frightened to run. Honey went to work. She poked, nipped their hind quarters, and danced around the group until the little herd began to move—and didn't stop until the last one was steered through the gate.

Out in the yard, the goats ran in all directions, and Tess turned back to the burning shed. Orange flames poured out the windows as the glass exploded from the heat and chunks of the roof caved in.

The barn stood a safe distance from the sparks, but the firelight danced on the building, illuminating words sprayed in green paint: KILLER! IT'S YOUR LAST WARNING!

Tess choked back a sob. She needed to call the fire department but couldn't pull herself away, as if keeping her eyes on the blaze would somehow magically contain it.

Her aunt appeared, wild-eyed, her white hair in disarray. "Tess! Are you all right? Come away from there." Her aunt tugged her arm. "I called the fire department. They're on the way."

The smoke was thick, and Tess could barely answer. Her eyes teared, and she lifted her t-shirt to cover her mouth and nose.

"Go back to the house, Aunt Lila. Please. I'm going to use the hose until they come."

Her aunt pulled her arm, coughing and shaking her head. She tried to speak but couldn't get the words out. Tess dropped the hose and put her arm around her aunt's shoulder, half-leading, half-carrying her back to the porch.

They heard the trucks roar up the lane, sirens screaming. Lila staggered and sat. "Thank God they're here. Thank God," she repeated, her eyes closed, her complexion ashen.

Tess squeezed her hand. "Don't move. I'll get help."

The trucks parked, and the firefighters ran toward the blaze, shouting at each other. An ambulance pulled up behind them. Tess reached the vehicle just as emergency workers stepped out.

"My aunt...She doesn't look well. She's over there, on the porch...help her, please..."

The EMTs, a man and a woman, had already grabbed medical bags and jogged to the porch. Tess ran ahead, even faster.

Forty-Six

Tess was allowed to ride with Lila in the ambulance, though she had to sit by the rear doors while one of the technicians attended to her aunt and the other drove. Wires attached to Lila's chest kept track of her heart rate, and an oxygen mask covered most of her face. She couldn't speak. Tess didn't want her to try.

The ride to the medical center seemed endless. Finally, Lila's stretcher was unloaded and rolled into the ER. Tess followed, but a nurse soon blocked her path as Lila disappeared through swinging doors

"I want to stay with my aunt...Please..."

"I understand, but she needs to be examined now and treated. You'll see her in a little while, I promise." The nurse caught her eye. "What's your name?"

"Tess. Tess Hargrove." Tess watched the woman's face for a reaction, but her expression didn't change.

"Okay, Tess. While you're waiting, we'll get some information and see how you're doing, too."

Tess nodded. She didn't see any choice and felt so overwhelmed, she thought she might fall down if she didn't find a chair.

She was led into a curtained cubicle, where she sat on the edge of an exam table while the nurse took her blood pressure and other vitals. The nurse asked questions, and she answered with a word or two. She'd already filled in the EMTs about her aunt's age, health issues, and other information.

"Your oxygen level is a little low," the nurse said. "Other than that, you seem fine. You're lucky."

That was the understatement of the year. She thought about her poor aunt, older and weaker, who had also inhaled the acrid smoke.

The nurse took white towels from a closet. "You can clean up at that sink. Would you like some help?"

"I'll be fine, thanks." Tess hadn't caught sight of her reflection yet, but her hands were black with grit. She imagined her face was, too.

A small mirror above the sink framed her reflection. She looked a sight, as if she'd dressed as a coal miner for a costume party. While Lila was loaded into the ambulance, Tess managed to find a big denim shirt on the porch and pulled it on over the t-shirt she'd worn to bed. She wore pajama bottoms and her work boots. Her hair had come loose from a ponytail, and her face was coated with black grime. She pulled her hair back tight, then scrubbed her hands and face with the soapy cloth. Most of the soot washed off, but her nose was still filled with the smell.

She heard the curtain slide open as someone entered the cubicle. "I'm almost done," she said, assuming the nurse had returned.

"No, rush. Take your time."

She found Ben's reflection in the mirror, and her breath caught. She struggled not to show a reaction.

"I heard there was a fire at the farm. Is that true?"

She turned slowly, drying her face on the towel. Of all the doctors here, he'd have to be on duty. "The shed near the goat pen. Thankfully, it didn't spread. Have you seen my aunt? Will she be all right?"

"She has smoke inhalation, but she should be fine. We'll keep her a day or so to make sure." He moved closer but stopped. "Are you okay? No burns? Nothing like that?"

Tess shook her head, avoiding his gaze. "I'm all right. But it was frightening," she admitted. "I need to call my cousin. If my aunt gets worse. . .if she has a heart attack or something. . .it will be my fault. . ."

She met Ben's expression, full of sympathy and concern.

He rested his hands on her shoulders. "Of course, you were frightened. Thank God you're all right."

He pulled her close and pressed his cheek to her hair.

She couldn't help herself and rested her head against his shoulder as tears began to flow.

"There was another message on the barn," she told him. "It said this was my last warning. Richard is right. I can't stay here. It's very selfish. I've put my aunt in danger. She could have died. He'll certainly use this against me if we end up in court."

"Lila will be fine, I promise." Ben pulled back and looked into her eyes. "What do you mean 'end up in court?' Did Richard sue you?"

"Not yet, but he plans to."

Tess told Ben about the letter and the claims he'd make against her. She also explained the deal her cousin offered.

"I hope you didn't agree to anything." Ben looked shocked and angry.

"I stood up to him, and I hired Rebecca Duffy to deal with his lawyer. She wrote a letter, fighting back. But I'm afraid now that he's right. Maybe I should give up and buy land somewhere else. It's not worth risking Aunt Lila's life. Or my own."

Ben gripped her shoulders. She had the feeling he wanted to shake her though his touch was gentle and comforting. "He's trying to manipulate you, and he's succeeding. You're very upset right now. You're not thinking clearly."

Tess met his gaze but didn't reply. Even in a clearer moment, she'd come to the same conclusion. But she didn't want to argue.

She took out her phone. "I have to tell him that his mother is in the hospital. Then, I'd like to see my aunt if I could?"

"Of course, you can. It will do her good."

"Thanks for helping me. I know you took an oath and all that but...thanks for just...being here and listening."

Ben's eyes were bright. She wondered if she'd upset him. "I'm always here for you, Tess. No matter what. As for your cousin, I can hardly wait to meet him."

Richard would rush to the island once he heard, and Tess dreaded facing him. It was good to know she wouldn't have to do that alone.

"How about this—tell Richard about the fire, and I'll fill him in on his mother's condition. Then you can see Lila for a few minutes, and I'll take you home. I just finished my shift. You'll have some time to yourself before he gets here."

Tess wasn't used to anyone making an agenda for her, but this time, it felt good to let someone step in and take care of her. Especially Ben.

She dialed Richard and braced herself. She expected him to be angry and emotional when he heard the news, but his reaction was even worse.

"Is this enough proof for you? People on that island hate you. There's no other way to say it. My poor mother is paying the price for your infamy and selfishness. Can you finally face the facts?"

Tess didn't know how to answer his outburst. Ben signaled to her and held out his hand. "Aunt Lila's doctor is here, Richard. He wants to speak with you."

By the time Ben was done talking to her cousin, she'd calmed herself, though Richard's accusations echoed in her head.

Her visit with her aunt was brief but reassuring. Lila still needed oxygen, and Tess didn't want to tire her by talking.

"I know you feel awful, but Ben said you're not in any danger and you'll be better in a few days. Richard is on his way. He should be here in three or four hours."

The news brightened Lila's expression. She offered Tess a small smile, then closed her eyes again to rest.

The sun was just rising as they reached the farm, and the early morning sky promised a fair day. But when Ben pulled into the yard, Tess was glad her aunt was at the hospital. The scene was deeply disturbing. The shed was reduced to a charred black skeleton surrounded by puddles of water. The goat pen was empty, the yard filled with deep ruts from the fire trucks and a smokey scent hung in the air.

Worst of all, horrible words screamed at her from the side of the barn. In her mind's eye, Tess could still see the dancing orange flames that had terrified her.

Honey ran out of the barn. She rose on her hind legs, licked Tess's chin, and then sat very still so Tess could pet her. Her fur was full of soot, and she needed a good bath.

"Honey was a real hero. She wouldn't give up until she saved all the goats." She surveyed the scene again and sighed. "I guess we were lucky the fire wasn't close to the barn or the house."

"I think it was more than luck. Whoever set it wanted to cause damage and frighten you, but they didn't want to put you and your aunt in real danger."

Like they will the next time, Tess almost replied. "The fire chief told me they'll be back to investigate. It seemed obvious to them that the fire was arson. But I don't know what they can find beyond that."

Ben gazed at her with a serious expression. "I have a confession to make. Remember when I came on my day off to help you here?"

Tess was confused. "Sure, I do. What of it?"

"I was determined to find out who was vandalizing your property. You already told me that you wouldn't ask the police to look into it or even get a security camera. But I was still concerned that it reflected badly on my family. I realize now, I was also concerned about you," he added. "When you left me to work alone, I put up a security camera tucked above the barn doors. I've never looked at the images. There was never any need. I forgot it was even there until this morning."

Tess stared at him in disbelief. "How could you do that without asking? It was so...high-handed."

"It was," he agreed, his expression apologetic. "I didn't know you well, and I overstepped, totally. But I have to admit, now I'm glad I did."

"I guess I am, too," she admitted. "How can we watch the video?"

He looked relieved. "My laptop is in the car. Let's see if there's a recording from last night."

A few minutes later, they sat together at the kitchen table. Ben was happy to see the camera had not been knocked out of place and had been recording.

He brought up the video from Saturday night and hit fast-forward. Tess saw Evaline's car zip out of the yard, then nothing but animals skittering in the shadows. The timestamp in the corner of the screen approached three a.m., and Ben slowed the film speed.

A figure in a hooded sweatshirt appeared near the goat pen. There was no car, and Tess guessed he'd walked from the road. He carried a bucket and walked around the side of the barn. He was gone for a few minutes, and Ben sped up the film again. "He must be spray painting. Too bad there's no audio. Wait...there he is, checking his handiwork."

Sure enough, the hooded stranger stepped back into the frame. He stared at the barn in full view of the camera.

The picture was grainy, and Tess could barely make out the man's face until he took out a flashlight to check the contents of his bucket.

She gripped Ben's shoulder. "That looks likes Richard."

Ben reeled back and froze the frame where the flashlight came on, then zoomed in. "It *is* Richard. I can't believe it," Tess whispered.

Ben sighed. "I can."

Tess leaned back in her chair to watch the rest. Richard headed for the shed and went inside. A few moments later, the shed's windows glowed with a flickering light. He ran out and disappeared across the field behind the goat corral as the image grew blurry from the smoke and the fire grew bigger. Ben stopped the tape and turned to her.

"I hope your cousin found a good lawyer. There's enough here to send him to jail for a long time."

Tess was so stunned she could hardly speak. "Do you think it's been him all along? Those other times, too? Maybe there isn't anyone on the island trying to chase me away."

"We'll have to ask him. I'm sure the police will."

Ben's last point was jarring. "If they see this recording. I have to think this through. My aunt will be crushed if she learns Richard set the fire and may have been harassing us all along. If he gets arrested. . .I can't even think about it. Despite what he's done, I don't know if I can let that happen."

Ben met her gaze. "I had a feeling you'd say that. You'll let him off too easily, Tess."

"Maybe, but my aunt's peace of mind is more important to me. Especially in the state she's in right now. I'll take a shower and get rid of this smoky smell. Then I'll figure out what to do."

"I have a few suggestions when you're ready." He reached across the table and took her hand. "First, I'll make us some breakfast. Coffee, scrambled eggs, toast?"

"Yes, to all the above." Her stomach was so empty it was rumbling. Had he heard it? "There's probably bacon in the fridge, too. Someone told me even doctors eat that once in a while." She glanced over her shoulder and smiled. "Please make enough for Honey. She deserves a good treat."

Forty-Seven

As Tess devoured the big breakfast Ben had cooked, they discussed a strategy for dealing with Richard. After that, Tess needed a nap. She'd been up all night and couldn't keep her eyes open.

She returned to the hospital with Ben at noon, feeling refreshed and ready to face her adversary. Her cousin had arrived about an hour earlier, and a nurse told her he was visiting his mother.

She'd nearly reached the room when he walked out. He met her with a dark look, and Tess steeled herself. She knew his true colors now. Nothing he said could undermine her.

"Hello, Richard. How is Lila doing?"

"How should I know? I've barely seen a doctor or nurse since I got here. They say she doesn't need to be air-vacced to Boston, but I'm still looking into it."

"Dr. Croft will be here soon to speak with you." Ben had to check in with the staff but would catch up. Despite Richard's complaints, Tess knew her aunt was closely monitored. Ben had called at least twice from the farm and heard she was stable and out of the woods.

"Croft?" Richard frowned. "Isn't that the same family—"

"Yes, it is," Tess replied in a curt tone. "Did you speak to her? Was she awake at all?"

"She told me everything. She's traumatized, for pity's sake." He scowled with disgust. "You're heartless, just like your father—selfish to the core. As soon as she gets out of here, I'm moving her off that farm. If she'd died last night, it would be on your head. Another life that you ended, Tess."

His vicious insults could have cut deep, but she focused on what she knew.

"We were lucky the fire wasn't closer to the house." She paused and looked him in the eye. "But you already know that."

"What do you mean?" He feigned confusion. "Lila told me about the message on the barn: 'your last warning.' Are you really willing to take that risk?"

The hallway was busy with passing medical staff and visitors. Tess wanted to finish the conversation privately.

"Good question. There's a meeting room down the hall. Let's talk in there."

Without waiting for Richard to reply, Tess walked to the room. When he entered, she shut the door.

There was a couch, armchairs, and posters with seagulls and daisies meant to be uplifting. Tess thought the décor ironic, considering the circumstances.

She stood and faced him. "If your mother was badly injured or even lost her life, heaven forbid, that would be on your head, not mine. I know you left the graffiti and set the fire."

He turned red-faced with anger. "Are you crazy? I was at a conference in Hartford all weekend. How could I possibly have done that? *Why* would I ever do that?"

"The second question is easy to answer. To scare me off the land and let you profit by a sale. The first isn't much harder. Haven is only three hours or so from Hartford and can be reached even faster in the middle of the night. I'm sure the hotel has security cameras that can be checked and the ferry stations, too, come to think."

Richard laughed. "You're a detective now? That's rich, all things considered. You can't just accuse someone of arson, Tess. I could sue you for that, too."

Tess was about to reply but heard a knock on the door. She saw Ben in the window and waved at him to come in.

"It's Doctor Croft. He spoke to you on the phone," she reminded her cousin.

"Can you come back in a few minutes, Doctor? My cousin and I are working out a family matter."

"He can stay," Tess said in an even tone. "We have something to show you, Richard. There was a security camera on the farm. It captured a clear image of you setting the fire."

Richard went pale as a bedsheet. He stared at Tess, then back at Ben. "This is a hoax. You patched together some video to get me in trouble."

"Why don't you watch it before you accuse us of anything?" Ben glared at him, then pressed a button on the computer.

The video of Richard filled the screen. A few moments into it, Ben paused the recording and magnified Richard's face, illuminated by his own flashlight.

"Are you still going to deny what you did?" Tess asked. "The police can easily analyze these images and confirm the video is real. I'm a farmer, not some tech guru."

Richard's face flushed. "I'm not confessing to anything. Are you going to turn me in? You'd love that, wouldn't you?"

"That's what I should do." Tess barely managed to tamp down her temper. "I'm a lot more concerned about Lila than you are, obviously. She's the only reason the police aren't here. I won't give you up if you agree to a few things."

He smirked. Was he relieved at her reprieve? She knew he had to be. "Go on."

"You pay for all the damages to my property. Including the prior vandalism."

"The prior incidents?" He looked angry again, but she called his bluff.

"I didn't have a camera up, but I'm sure it was you."

If she'd had any doubts, his reaction confirmed her accusation. "Guess I'm stuck with the bill, either way. Is there more?"

"You drop all legal action against me and never attempt it again. Rebecca Duffy will draw up a letter for you to sign."

He crossed his arms over his chest. Defeat was a bitter pill, but he was getting off easy, Tess thought.

"What else?"

"That's it."

"That will be plenty if you keep your word and leave Tess alone." Ben had urged her to be harder on her cousin but had accepted her decision. "If you don't, I promise you'll regret it."

Richard suddenly seemed to notice him. "I thought you were my mother's doctor. How did you get involved in all of this?"

"It's a long story. But you can expect to see more of me."

Richard heaved a defeated sigh. Tess guessed he'd spent a lot of time fantasizing about how he'd spend the money he expected to make from the real estate deal. He'd need another way to make his fortune now—while he "could still enjoy it."

"I'll check on my mother, if you don't mind," he announced in a sarcastic tone.

"I'll be by in a few minutes," Tess said. "Oh, better book a room in town. I don't want you at the farm."

He answered by slamming the door. Tess turned to Ben, feeling limp as a rag. "That's over with, thank goodness."

"You were awesome. I was so proud of the way you stood up to him."

Tess grinned. "I enjoyed it. After I got past my nerves. Being tough takes a lot out of you."

Ben stepped toward her and took her in his arms. "It's over now. You can relax. There's nothing to fear. I was psyched to put him in his place, but you didn't need me at all."

"I'm not so sure about that. I do need you, Ben. Now, more than ever," she confessed. "What you said to Richard, that you expect to be around—does that mean you forgive me for breaking up with you?"

"Breaking my heart, you mean." His tone was sterner, and she felt she'd misjudged what was going on between them. Maybe this wasn't a reconciliation after all?

"I always understood that you had good intentions, Tess, and believed you were making a sacrifice for me. But I've told my mother and sister about the memories that came back, and about my friend looking into your case. I think that in time, they'll accept you. They can see how miserable I've been. I can live without you. But not happily. I think they'll try, if you will."

She knew what he was asking. She felt like she was at the very tip of a high diving board, pushing herself to jump into thin air. "I will try, for you. I've missed you so much. I was practically walking into walls."

He laughed. "So you could come to the ER and see me again, you mean?"

"Maybe." She wound her arms around him even tighter. "I love you, Ben. With every fiber of my being. I don't know how you found it in your heart to forgive me...and believe me."

"You were easy to forgive. Once I put aside the hateful image that had lived in my head all those years, and saw who you really are." Ben's expression turned thoughtful. "I've heard forgiveness can work miracles. Now I know it's true."

Without waiting for her reply, he gathered Tess in his arms, and they melted together in a long, deep kiss that Tess wished would go on forever.

Forty-Eight

Carrie was the last of her family to arrive at the Firefly Gallery. A sign out front said, "Art Show Today! Meet Haven Island's finest local artists." There was a list of names, including Gena Duffy, and she stopped to take a photo. Her mother was so modest, she probably hadn't thought of it.

The artwork was set up indoors and along the sidewalk, her mother's clever idea, which had helped attract a crowd . Carrie quickly greeted familiar faces as she made her way inside.

Looking every inch an artist and a gallery owner, Nadia Popova stood in front of a large abstract canvas, discussing it with an older couple. The mustard-yellow jumpsuit with a halter neck and large earrings that looked like mini-mobile sculptures made for a striking combination, but she wore it well. Her Mom's borrowed kimono and silk trousers seemed tame in comparison.

The gallery was in a wide storefront with two rooms, every inch inside whitewashed, including the floor and ceiling. Carrie spotted her family at the back of the main room, near French doors that led to a courtyard garden filled with sculptures.

"Congratulations, Mom. What a turnout!"

"I'm surprised by the crowd myself," she admitted with a radiant smile. "We put announcements and flyers around town, and Brooke helped me do social media. She's writing a story on the show for the newspaper. Nadia's very pleased," she added in a quieter tone.

"Some of this stuff is surprisingly good," Rebecca said. "I might even buy a piece."

Rebecca had arrived a few hours earlier. She'd come for the show and was staying over to meet with Tess. Her sister would have probably helped as a favor, no matter what. But once she'd heard Tess's story, she sank her teeth into the case. *Heaven help Tess's cousin,* Carrie thought.

Sophie tugged on her grandmother's sleeve. "Where's your painting, Grandma?"

"Nadia chose three. I still can't believe it," she admitted. It's a series, studies of the same rock formation at the beach near our house. I finished the last one just in time. The paint might even still be damp."

Her mother led them to the second room, where three vivid watercolors hung across a wall. The paintings were each stunning in their own right, the bold strokes and deep colors unusual for her work.

Each captured the same rough-edged granite boulders piled at the water's edge. The first, on a bright day, touched by the foamy edge of a blue wave; the next on a cloudy day, beaten by wild white caps; and the last, with a night sky in the background and moonlight reflecting in the tidepools where sea life teemed. Each was signed in the lower right corner with block letters, "G. Duffy."

"These are amazing, Mom." Carrie was always impressed by her mother's talent but today stood in awe.

"Thanks, dear. That's sweet of you," her mother replied.

"We're not just being nice. These are really good," Rebecca insisted. "Look, a red sticker. You already sold one."

"I did?" Her mother stepped closer to the scene of the rocks at night, then stepped back with a proud smile. "For goodness sakes. . .it *is* sold."

"That's awesome, Grandma. Now, you're famous."

"Not quite, honey. But if I ever am, I'll be another Grandma Moses."

Sophie frowned. "Who's that?"

Her grandmother laughed. "Just a lady like me who loved to paint but took her sweet time getting around to it."

"Let's take a picture." Brooke waved her hands, directing them. "Mom, in the middle. Everyone else, squeeze around."

Carrie herded her sister, mother, and daughter together while Brooke stepped back to take the shot.

"You have to be in it, too, Brookie," her mother said.

"Selfie, selfie!" Sophie called out. "I can do it."

Carrie thought a selfie would be cute, but the moment called for something more formal that would also include her mother's artwork.

"There's Nadia. I'll ask her," Carrie said.

The gallery owner was strolling in their direction alongside one of her guests. His brown hair turned silver suggested the late fifties or early sixties, but he looked very fit and well-dressed in a navy linen sports coat, khaki pants, and a crisp, light blue shirt.

Before Carrie could ask Nadia about the photo, the man with gallery owner stepped forward. "Gena Martone? Is that really you?"

Her mother stared at him, wide-eyed. Then smiled. "Jonathan—it can't be. What are you doing here?"

"Enjoying the show. I just bought a painting."

"One of yours," Nadia said. "Mr. Borden asked me to introduce him to the artist but it seems that's not necessary?"

"We were in college together," Gena explained. "I'm surprised you recognized me."

"You haven't changed a bit. You look wonderful."

Especially after last night's mini-makeover, Carrie thought. Her mother held her admirer's gaze a moment, then looked away. Carrie saw her blush.

"You haven't either," she said. "Before you ask what I've been up to all this time, these are my daughters, Brooke, Carrie, and Rebecca, and my granddaughter, Sophie," she added proudly.

Gena's old friend smiled warmly and shook each of their hands. "You have one amazing, Mom. I hope you realize that."

"She surprises us every day." Rebecca gave their mother a look that said, "You never mentioned this former beau. He's clearly still smitten."

"It was nice of you to buy my painting," her mother said.

"Nice? I love it. It's the best work here, in my opinion, and a good investment. I might take the other two. By the way, ladies, your mother was always the most talented—and the most understated—in our group. I can see she hasn't changed in that respect either." He turned back to Gena. "My daughter rented a house on the island for the summer. I'll be visiting for a while. Can I call you? We can catch up."

"Please do. That would be fun." Gena gave him her number as Carrie and her sisters exchanged looks.

"I'm so glad we ran into each other. And now I own an original Gena Duffy. Isn't that something?"

After he left, Nadia said, "How about a photo in front of your mother's wonderful artwork? It's been a big day."

Carrie and her sisters lined up in front of the seascapes, with their mom in the middle. It wasn't the time nor the place to fire questions at her. But Carrie was sure that before too long, they'd know more about her college days and Jonathan Borden.

* * *

Carrie woke before the alarm on Monday morning. She remembered her interview at ten o'clock and felt an anxious knot in her stomach. When they got home the night before with Mexican takeout—to celebrate her mother's success—grilling her about Jonathan Borden had been more fun than a review of talking points about restaurant management.

"He was just a friend," her mother insisted. Even Rebecca's courtroom techniques couldn't coax out more than a few memories.

"There was a group of us, art majors, taking the same courses. We hung around together. We even took a trip out to Haven Island one summer. One of the girls knew about the place, and we chipped in to rent a cottage. I'd just finished my junior year," she recalled wistfully. "But we were all just friends."

Carrie wasn't convinced. "Jonathan really likes you. Are you sure nothing was going on?"

"Maybe he had a little crush on me. He took me out once

while we were here. I guess it was a date. I can't say for sure. We went to the Blue Sky for lunch. That's when I met your father. You know the rest of the story," she'd summed up with a laugh.

Brooke listened intently. "So, Dad stole you away from Jonathan before he could declare himself? Is that what happened?"

"You make it sound so dramatic. I doubt he was heartbroken. I heard he married one of the other girls in the group a few years later."

"He doesn't seem married," Rebecca remarked. "I didn't see a ring."

"What does that matter? He might not even call. He's visiting family. He's probably too busy." Her mother's tone was offhand, but some note suggested she cared if he called more than she wanted to let on.

"Busy or not, you'll hear from him," Brooke said.

"I bet he calls tonight," Rebecca predicted. "Wait, that looks very uncool. Tomorrow, definitely."

Carrie's mother shook her head. "You're all being very silly. We'll chat for a while, and that will be that. He already knows how many kids and grandkids I have. Most of the conversation is covered."

Carrie had a feeling there would be more to it than that.

Carrie would have loved an extra hour of sleep, but she was wide awake. She decided to use the precious quiet time to review notes she'd made, guessing possible questions. Via her computer, she'd meet with the Vice President of Operations for the restaurant group, Lynda Novak. Carrie had searched the executive online and found her bio and photo, surprised to see she was only a few years older.

But had obviously made different choices to go so far so quickly, Carrie thought with a twinge of envy. She shook her head to dislodge the "stinkin' thinkin'" as the life coaches advised.

You can't change the past, but you can create the future, she reminded herself. *Even if you don't get this job, you're moving in the right direction.*

"It doesn't matter how slow you go, as long as you don't stop," she said aloud, recalling another favorite motto.

She was taking the meeting in her office, as she had for the other interviews. Those meetings had been scheduled after five when the café was empty. It would be hard to focus with the place bustling just outside the office door, but she was eager to get it over with.

She left the house extra early so she'd have time to pick up an order at Evaline Finch's roadside stand, a short distance outside the village. Evaline made her rounds through town with deliveries once a week, but the café was unexpectedly low on her quality jams that tasted like fruit right off the vine. Carrie didn't want to serve an inferior backup if she could avoid it. People really noticed the difference.

It was not quite nine, but Evaline was already open for business, arranging bouquets of fresh-cut flowers that would sell out quickly. The counter was covered with an enticing array of baked goods, from chocolate zucchini bread to peach and plum tarts. Carrie had already eaten breakfast, but the choices piqued her appetite.

There was also a basket of fresh baked breads and cupcakes covered with pastel icing and real flowers dipped in fine white sugar. Shelves behind the counter displayed Evaline's famous jams and bags of her herbal teas. A collection of China teapots and elegant cups were ready for use in the garden behind the stand.

"Hello, dear. What brings you out here so early?" Evaline wore a canvas apron over a flowery summer dress and a big floppy hat tied under her chin. She smiled at Carrie but continued arranging bottles filled with golden honey.

"Your delicious jam. We must have used double the last two weeks. We're nearly out."

"Sounds like you're doing a brisk business," Evaline said. "Good for you. What do you need?"

"Strawberry, raspberry, and peach—six jars of each. If you have it."

"I do. But I need to go up to the house if you can wait a minute. There are plenty of jars already boxed, and I won't need to clean out the stand." She glanced at the pyramids of colorful bottles balanced on the doily-trimmed shelves.

"Sure, I can wait." Carrie dreaded the interview and didn't mind dragging her heels.

"Let me pour you a cup of tea." Evaline turned and filled a teacup covered with pink flowers from a matching pot. Carrie was more of a coffee person in the mornings, but it felt rude to refuse.

"Sit back here. It's nice and shady. I won't be a minute."

Carrie followed Evaline down a short stone path behind the stand to a stone patio covered by a trellis dripping with wisteria and climbing white roses in full bloom.

The space was edged with thick banks of flowers, tiger lilies, hydrangea, fragrant sage, and bright black-eyed Susan. Bees and butterflies had already begun their workday, and a tiny goldfinch hovered above a bank of pink cone flowers, making a breakfast of the seeds in spent blooms.

A few small tables were set up in the shade of the thick vines. She took a seat and sipped her tea—a hibiscus and orange blend that needed no sweetening. Carrie took a deep breath of the cool fragrant air and closed her eyes a moment.

The self-help books she read often advised a quiet time in the morning for meditation or journaling. Especially before an important meeting. Carrie thought this unexpected visit to Evaline's garden was just as good, if not better. How fortuitous to find herself here right before her big interview.

She hoped to get the job, but if she didn't, it wouldn't be the end of the world, she reminded herself. *Sometimes when things don't work out, it's for the best, and something even better comes along.* She had to remember that if the meeting turned out disappointing.

Evaline appeared just as Carrie was finishing her tea. "I left the boxes on the counter. Give me a shout next time you run low. I'll make a delivery to the café anytime."

"That's all right. Stopping here was a great way to start the day. I can't remember the last time I came by." She sipped the last drops in her cup and came to her feet. "What do I owe you?"

Evaline bustled over. "Oh, you can't go yet. I haven't read the leaves."

Carrie had forgotten Evaline's special talent and the extra service she offered to some guests of the garden. Carrie didn't go in for horoscopes or tarot cards, but she was curious.

"All right, if you really want to."

"I do, for you. There are questions, like little birds, swooping around you, Carrie."

Carrie wouldn't have put it quite that way, but she knew very well what Evaline meant.

Evaline rested her reading glasses at the tip of her nose and sat in a chair. Carrie sat across and watched as the older woman squinted at the cup, turning it to one side and then the other as she studied the bits left at the bottom.

"Interesting," she murmured.

"In a good way?" Carrie asked.

"Well… I see dark clouds; I won't deny it. Some flashes of lightning, too."

"That doesn't sound good." Carrie laughed, making light of the prediction. This was exactly why she didn't like this stuff.

"It's a brief storm. You manage fine," Evaline assured her. "You're very strong and able. Brave," she added, seeming surprised. "You get what you think you want," she said, making Carrie feel good. "But you'll throw it back. You pull in a big catch. It fills the boat." She looked up at Carrie with a delighted grin. "It's the real prize."

"I didn't realize I was fishing," Carrie replied, feeling as if the conversation was making less and less sense.

"Neither did I." Evaline gently placed the cup back on the saucer. "I don't think you set out to. But there you are. A prize catch. You never know."

She looked at Carrie as if she'd delivered very good news. Carrie smiled and came to her feet. "Thank you, Evaline. The tea was delicious, and this secret garden is a treasure. I have to come back soon."

Evaline walked Carrie back to the stand. "Please do, dear. Let me know if the leaves were right. I have a good feeling about it for you."

Carrie left some bills on the counter to pay for the jam and took the boxes. "I will Evaline. You'll be the first to know."

"No, you'll be the first," Evaline corrected. "As it should be."

A few minutes before the meeting, Carrie checked the dining room, kitchen, and deck to make sure everything was in order. Then she asked Jack to keep an eye on things while she "took care of something in the office."

He replied with a wink. "Sure thing. Hope you get the job."

"Is it that obvious?"

"Well, you're jumpy as a cat and all dressed up—what can be seen of you from a computer screen."

She didn't need to look down at herself to know that was true. She'd done her hair and makeup with a sleek, professional look and wore a pale pink silk blouse and small pearl earrings. Her gray linen blazer hung on her office door. The rest of her was covered by a denim skirt and the comfy slip-on sneakers she wore for work.

"Is that lipstick and mascara?"

"Is that what it's called? Brooke loaned me a bunch of tubes. I wasn't sure what went where," she replied tartly. "Just hold down the fort, okay?"

"Will do." She heard him chuckle as she turned away and had to smile. Trust Jack to break her concentration, but he'd also lightened her mood.

Carrie stuck a "Do Not Disturb" sign on the door and brought up the virtual meeting room a few minutes in advance. She felt on edge, staring at the restaurant logo. When Lynda Novak suddenly appeared, Carrie heard herself speed talking. But the executive's relaxed manner quickly put her at ease. She was also very complimentary about Carrie's résumé, and Carrie felt well-prepared to answer all of her questions.

The Vice President of Operations asked about the Blue Sky and the challenges of running a small, family-owned restaurant. Carrie was well versed now on the topic and also able to apply what she'd learned the past weeks while wrestling with the café's finances to a larger operation.

They covered other topics, and Carrie asked Lynda questions, too.

"It's been great talking with you, Carrie," Lynda said at last. "The team has been very impressed with your interviews. I can see why. It's not my usual style, but why wait? I feel sure you'd make a great manager of the Arcadia Table."

Carrie was stunned. She'd expected it to take a week or more to hear the decision. "Thank you so much. I don't know what to say. This is amazing."

Lynda looked pleased by her response. "Take some time to think about it. Maybe you can give us an answer by the end of the week?"

"I don't need time. I happily accept."

"I heard that you were decisive. I like that." Lynda laughed. "Stephanie Burns, in Human Resources, will be in touch about the salary and benefits. We'd like you to come up sometime soon and meet everyone. My assistant will reach out. I look forward to seeing you in Bar Harbor, Carrie."

"I look forward to being there. Thank you again."

The screen returned to the restaurant logo. Carrie sat back, feeling stunned. And then elated. For months, her future had seemed like a dark tunnel without a flicker of light in sight. She'd worried endlessly about finding a good job so she could take care of Sophie and rent a nice place for them. She dreaded ending up in another dead-end situation just to make ends meet. But she would have done it, if necessary

This was the huge break she'd been waiting for and had worked hard for. A position with limitless opportunity for advancement. In time, she could be an executive like Lynda Novak. Anything was possible. It seemed like a dream.

She wanted to do handsprings across the café, then call everyone in her family. Instead, she took a deep, steadying breath, not quite ready to share the news.

Forty-Nine

Carrie opened the office door a crack and pulled the sign off. Then snapped it shut again. The café had survived for an hour without her attention. She slipped a blue apron over her fancy blouse and stashed the pearl earrings in her pocket. She was just about to emerge when she heard a light tap.

Jack poked his head around the door. "How did it go?"

She bowed her head to tie her apron and avoid his gaze. "It was good... Better than I expected."

He stepped in and faced her. "Should we buy you a going-away gift? Lobster crackers and a big pot?"

She tried to hold a poker face but couldn't suppress a victorious smile. "That might come in handy."

"Congratulations, Carrie." His tone was warm but emphatic. "Speaking of lobster, I have an idea. I want to cook a nice dinner for your family to thank you for being such great people to work for and for all your hospitality. I was thinking, it's time I came clean with them about Jackson Gardeaux. And apologize, especially to your mother."

She wondered what had brought on this bout of conscience. Maybe he expected to be back in the trade news with his new restaurant? Or he had to leave sooner than expected?

"You did trick her in a way. But I'm sure she won't mind. She'll be too excited when she realizes a famous chef has been working at the café all this time."

"Well, this famous chef is going to make the Duffy women a five-star gourmet meal. There's a lot to celebrate."

He meant her new job, but there was also her mother's success at the art show, and Sophie was graduating from sailing camp this week. And maybe he meant the kickoff of his new restaurant, too? His generous offer was a bittersweet reminder that the summer was winding down.

"If it's all right, I'll cook here after we close and serve on the deck. How about tomorrow night, around seven?"

"I think that would be fine. I'll send everyone a text and let you know for sure."

"Just enough time to plan the menu and catch the entrée. Finn said the striped bass are running. If I can catch a few, you can preview a recipe from my new cookbook."

"We'll be beta taste testers?" she quipped.

"I was thinking focus group, but that's a good one." He laughed. "What's your boyfriend going to say about you moving to Maine?"

"Doug, you mean?" She didn't bother denying that he was her boyfriend. She didn't put Doug in that category but knew everyone else did. Doug included. "I haven't told him yet."

She had a good guess of what he'd say but wasn't going to

confide in Jack about her relationship issues. Doug would stop in at the café before he caught the five o'clock ferry today and would surely ask about the interview.

"I haven't even told my family," she added.

"I'm honored to be the first then."

"Because you wormed it out of me," she reminded him.

"Didn't take much. I thought you were better at keeping a secret."

She pulled the clipboard of receipts off the wall and flipped through the pages. "I can when I really need to."

Like keeping my feelings secret from you, she silently added.

"We need you, Jack," Eddie called from the kitchen.

"Coming," Jack called back. In a quieter voice, he said to Carrie, "I love Eddie, but he still hasn't learned how to make a decent omelet. Cooking school 101."

Maybe because his former boss and mentor, Victor, can't either, Carrie almost replied. Even if the Blue Sky customers didn't miss Jack's cooking, Carrie knew she would.

* * *

Carrie had long ago removed her apron but couldn't decide about the earrings—on or off? She decided to put them back on. She'd feel more confident facing Doug if she already looked the part of a manager at an upscale restaurant.

She was glad to see the cafe empty by five. Even Jack had left to fish for his dinner ingredients. Doug found her behind the counter, emptying the register.

He leaned over and kissed her hello. "You look so polished and professional. Like a stockbroker."

Carrie laughed. "I need a few more finance courses to go in that direction."

He sat on a stool and watched her sort out piles of bills. She knew he was about to ask about the interview.

"Can I get you a cold drink? Or a sandwich for the ride?"

Distracting him with food? You're only avoiding the inevitable.

"No thanks. I'm fine. How did your interview go? It was this morning, right?"

"Bright and early." She gathered the money in a single pile and shoved it into an envelope. She'd count it later. She couldn't concentrate.

She looked up and gave him her full attention. "It went very well. The VP who interviewed me offered me the job...and I accepted."

She hadn't intended to be so blunt, but it seemed senseless to drag out the punchline.

"You accepted, just like that?" He snapped his fingers. "I thought you'd think it over a bit. And we'd talk about it?"

"I thought I'd do that, too. I didn't even expect to get a decision. But when I was offered the job, I knew that thinking it over wouldn't make a difference. I'm sorry if you're disappointed."

"I am happy for you, Carrie. I'm also proud of you. But it sounds like our relationship didn't factor into your thinking at all, and that makes me unhappy."

He seemed sad and hurt, and she felt helpless to make it better. She couldn't deny what he was saying.

"I care for you, Doug," she said carefully. "We get along great, and we've had a wonderful summer. Why does all that have to end when I move to Maine? It's not the North Pole," she added, trying to lighten the mood. "We can still see each other."

"We can say that now, but I've had long-distance relationships before. It's not as easy as you think. Phones and computers aren't the same as spending time together and really being part of each other's lives. I know that we haven't been dating long. But I thought there was a real future here. I feel like you're throwing that away."

Carrie knew what he said was true. It was an effort even for couples who had been together for a long time to keep a relationship going after they moved apart. "I don't mean to throw it away. I don't want to," she insisted.

She'd ended things with Jack because he was not only moving far away but also returning to a high-flying world where she'd never fit in. A world with different values and priorities.

She and Doug were cut from the same cloth—single parents who valued family ties, leading conventional lives perhaps, but people you'd find cheering on soccer games or watching a school play. Not traveling the world, chasing fame and the spotlight.

Maybe fireworks didn't go off when they were together, but fireworks streaked across the sky for an instant and disappeared into thin air, she reminded herself.

"Can't we see how it goes before we decide it won't work?" she asked.

"I know you're sincere, Carrie. But I need to think about it. We'll both be so busy in the fall. You'll be immersed in your new job, and I'll be opening the new restaurants. Even with the best intentions, I doubt we'll have the time or energy to hold things together when we're so far apart." He sighed and took both of her hands in his. "To be honest, being apart a lot was one reason my marriage unraveled," he reminded her. "I'm not sure I want to go through that dance again. Or feel any more disappointed about our relationship than I do already."

Carrie was surprised by his reply. He had told her about his marriage, but she didn't think this situation was the same. He wasn't ending things but seemed headed in that direction. She felt her eyes fill with tears and nodded. "I'm sorry, Doug. I never wanted this decision to hurt you or ruin things between us."

"I know you didn't," he assured her. "It's no one's fault. Like you said, we had a lot of fun. I hope that whatever happens, we can stay friends."

"I'm sure we can." Carrie wondered if they should have aimed for friendship from the start.

He leaned over and kissed her cheek. "Congratulations on your new job. When I get back, we'll celebrate."

"Yes, let's do that." She forced a smile.

Logically, she knew he would return in a few days, and they would get together, if just for pizza and mini golf with the girls. But it felt as if they were saying goodbye forever.

* * *

Doug wasn't the only hurdle Carrie faced after accepting the position in Maine. She still had to tell Sophie; she thought her daughter should know before anyone else in the family.

Earlier that week, Carrie had mentioned the opportunity and the long list of reasons she wanted it. Sophie had asked questions but didn't seem upset about the possibility of moving to Bar Harbor in September instead of returning to Medford. Carrie and Tim had taken her there on a vacation one summer, and she had good memories of the place.

Of course, living there full-time was far different than visiting. But so far, she hadn't objected, which boded well. Living on Haven Island had been a positive experience for her daughter. It had opened her mind and made her willing to try new things. Carrie hoped those life lessons would kick in when Sophie learned they were moving to another unknown territory.

She'd promised Sophie that if she got home early, they would go sailing for a few hours before sunset. Carrie hurried to keep her promise; it would be a good time to talk to Sophie about the new job and the move.

She found her daughter in the kitchen with her grandmother. Sophie was making a smoothie, as usual, and Carrie's mother was on the phone. She smiled and waved but seemed intent on her conversation and walked into the dining room.

"It's Jonathan," Sophie whispered with a mischievous grin.

Carrie wasn't surprised. "Let's give her some privacy. Do you still want to go sailing?"

Sophie's expression brightened. "Can we?"

"Sure, there's plenty of time before dark. Why don't you pack some drinks and snacks? I'll run up and get changed."

"Why are you dressed up? Did you have another interview?"

"Yes, I did. I'll tell you all about it on the boat," Carrie promised, heading to her room. She crossed her fingers for smooth sailing with Sophie in every way.

Carrie drove back to the village, and they walked down the town dock and climbed aboard the *Far Horizons*, then pulled the equipment out of the storage space in the hull, life jackets and other necessities. Sophie needed no instructions to get the little daysailer ready, Carrie noticed.

"You're the captain tonight. Just tell me what do," Carrie told her.

Sophie seemed surprised by the role but quickly assumed the title. "All right, swabbie. Untie the sails while I check the rigging."

"Ay-ay." Carrie followed the request with a smile.

She kept an eye on Captain Sophie as she carried out her tasks. She wanted to see how well she'd learned her lessons.

The boat had a small outboard engine, and they motored into open water before raising the sails. Sophie was at the helm, steering their path around the colored buoys that marked traffic lanes in the water. The small cove was a sheltered spot, and a good place for a novice to sharpen her skills.

"I think this is a good spot to raise the sails," Sophie said, cutting the motor.

Carrie didn't disagree. There weren't many boats out, a few motorboats and sailboats skimming along the water.

"It was so sunny when I left the café. Seems to be clouding over a bit out here," Carrie noticed.

"There's no forecast for rain," Sophie replied. "At least there's some wind. I thought we were going to be stuck."

The wind had picked up. Carrie thought if they hadn't been able to sail, they could have dropped anchor to swim. And then have their talk. But they'd have the conversation when the time was right, she reminded herself. She'd promised Sophie a sail and was glad they were out here.

"All right, Captain. Show me your stuff," Carrie said.

"Help me raise the mainsail, and let's get underway."

Carrie helped raise the big sail, pulling on the line and securing it. Next, Sophie did the jib in front, very ably.

Sophie sat at the back of the boat again, holding the rudder with one hand and controlling the mainsail with the other.

Carrie sat beside her, and they were soon underway. The main sail caught a strong gust, and they flew along, heeling at a slight angle, enough to push them shoulder to shoulder.

"I'll sail up to that jetty," Sophie said, "then turn around."

"Good plan." The jetty marked a point where the harbor opened to rougher water. Carrie approved of Sophie's prudence.

They approached the jetty, and Carrie readied herself for the boat to turn. "Coming about," Sophie called as the boom swung to the other side of the craft. The sail flapped, slack for a moment as Carrie did her part, pulling the line until the fabric grew taught again while Sophie steered, quickly catching the breeze.

"Nice work," Carrie said sincerely.

"Just doing my job," Sophie replied.

"Speaking of jobs, I want to tell you about the interview I had," Carrie began. "Do you remember the one in Maine I mentioned?"

Sophie did remember and listened as Carrie related how well the talk went and how she was offered the position on the spot.

"I decided to accept. I'd already thought so much about it, the pluses and negatives, too. It's a great opportunity and a good salary. It will be a great place for us to live."

It was hard to gauge Sophie's reaction, she was so focused on handling the boat. Maybe telling her here wasn't a good idea?

"I know it's a lot to consider. But I hope you'll try to see the positive side for us and give it a chance. The company wants me to visit soon. I thought we should go together and look for a place to live and see where you might go to school up there."

Sophie glanced at her. "I thought that's what you were going to say, and I thought I'd be upset to hear for sure that we won't go back to Medford," she admitted. "But I had a meltdown when we had to stay here, then ended up liking it. I guess I can give Bar Harbor a chance. It's probably a lot like this place."

"Very much so," Carrie agreed, relieved that her daughter was taking the news in such a reasonable way.

"And maybe we can find a place to live where you're allowed to have a dog?" she added in a hopeful voice.

Carrie laughed. Sophie had a talent for seizing an opportunity, didn't she? That would come in handy later in life.

"We'll definitely keep that mind," Carrie promised her.

A gust of wind pushed the boat, and Sophie eased the line. Before Carrie could remark, they heard a distant but definitive rumble. The sky above was blue, but a short distance away, mounds of dark clouds moved their way, like a stain spreading on a cloth.

"That weather looks ugly. Let's head back," Carrie said.

"Hey, I'm the captain. I'm supposed to decide," Sophie reminded her. "And I totally agree. We'll go faster if we sail with this wind. That outboard stinks."

Carrie couldn't argue with that. "All right, we can drop the sails later if we need to. Here, put your windbreaker on, Captain," Carrie added in a deferential tone.

They both had on lifejackets and took them off briefly to put on windbreakers Carrie had packed at the last minute. Carrie made sure her daughter put her life jacket back on and did the same.

They weren't that far from the dock. Carrie thought they'd be all right. She wished now she had more covering than a thin nylon jacket and a baseball cap, but the forecast had not called for any precipitation, much less a sudden squall.

Sophie deftly turned the boat again, and they headed for land. Carrie noticed that every other craft was doing the same, though there were very few left in view.

Carrie felt as if the storm clouds were chasing them. The sky grew darker and darker. There was another rumble and a streak of lightning in the distance. She didn't like that but tried not to panic.

They were about halfway to the dock when Sophie shouted and pointed off the starboard side of the boat.

"Mom, look out there …Isn't that Jack?"

Fifty

Carrie turned and caught sight of a small dark green boat, exactly like the skiff Jack was using to fish. A man was hunched over the motor, yanking the cord without success. Carrie heard it sputter and stall out.

The man stood up, and she knew Sophie was right. "It is Jack. He's not even wearing a life jacket."

The waves were getting rougher, and Jack's boat rocked from side to side.

"We need to help him," Sophie said.

Carrie could tell she was afraid. She'd just learned how foolhardy it was to stay on the water one more second than necessary in weather like this, but she'd never leave Jack out here to fend for himself. Neither would Carrie

"Yes, of course. But quickly," Carrie said. "Help me drop the sails."

Sophie let the lines loose, and Carrie helped push the sheets aside. "I'll take the helm now," she said. "Let's hope this puny motor is up to the job."

Sophie looked scared but tried her best to put up a brave front. "I'll wave. I hope he can hear us."

It was too rough to stand, so Sophie called out from the side of the boat. Jack didn't notice them at first. But finally turned their way and waved back.

He looked relieved even from a distance. They weren't far apart, but Carrie suddenly felt fat, cold raindrops strike her face and bare skin.

"Oh blast...here it comes."

The thunder sounded closer, and out on the horizon, another sizzling crack of lightning zipped across the sky.

Sophie hunkered down and put her hands over her ears. "Mom, I'm so frightened. We shouldn't be out here."

"Hang on, honey. We'll pick up Jack and head straight to shore."

That seemed a doable plan as the rain pattered on the deck and hull. Carrie saw Jack try to start the motor again, a futile effort. He stood up to give the string a good tug just as a wave knocked the skiff and sent it rocking.

He did a jig, trying to keep his footing. Then flipped overboard, arms waving in the air before he hit the water.

Sophie gasped. "Oh, no, Mom! Jack fell in!"

"I'm sure he can swim. We're almost there." Carrie tried to stay calm and keep their boat aimed for his. She searched the water, waiting for him to come up, her heart wildly pounding.

She had the urge to scream his name but knew that was no use. She couldn't get hysterical. It wouldn't help him, and she didn't want to scare Sophie. What if he'd hit his head and was unconscious? She didn't want to even think that.

"Do you see him?" she called out.

"Not yet," Sophie answered in a quavering voice.

"Get the life preserver. Make sure the rope is tied on tight. Stay low, or you'll be knocked overboard too."

The sailboat's little motor struggled to progress against the rising waves and wind. Carrie didn't want to cry. There was already enough water blurring her vision.

Jack, you idiot. Why didn't you put a vest on? Too sissy for you? Where are you? Come up where we can see you, for goodness sakes, she railed at him in her head.

Please come up, Jack. Please, God...make Jack come up. Let us see him...

Sophie returned with the life preserver. "He's over there." She pointed, and Carrie saw his dark head bobbing in the waves. He stared around, looking disoriented. He was treading water but mostly with one arm.

Sophie called to him. "Jack, over here!"

He turned and began swimming. Carrie aimed their boat at him, praying they'd meet quickly. He took a few strokes, then leaned back in the water. He seemed to be in pain.

"Please God, let us reach him in time." The motor sputtered. Finally, they were close enough.

"Sophie, take my spot. Try to steer closer."

Sophie nodded and took over. "You're going to toss the life preserver to him?"

That was Carrie's initial intention, but Jack looked injured. She wasn't sure he could hold on to it.

She slipped off her sneakers, the floating device in hand. "I'd better bring it to him. Then we can pull him in."

Sophie looked shocked, then nodded. "Okay, Mom. I'll try to hold the boat steady."

"Good girl." Carrie dropped the life preserver over the side, then followed. It took her a moment to bob up, and she pushed herself to move quickly in the cold water.

Her life vest made it hard to swim, but she dragged the floatation device and moved toward him. She'd been a lifeguard all through high school and was a strong swimmer, but the water was rough, and it was slow going. She saw him go down again, slipping under the surface. What if she didn't get to him in time? She felt herself crying as she swam.

When she finally reached him, he was trying to float on his back. There was a streak of blood in his hair, and he looked exhausted. "Can you grab this?" she shouted.

He nodded and held out his right arm. "On this arm. I hurt the other side."

"Just hold on. I'll get onboard, and we'll pull you in."

Carrie helped him grab the donut and then dragged the rope behind her as she swam back to the boat. Sophie had maneuvered it closer, which was a huge help.

Sophie pulled her up on deck while Jack floated beside the boat. "He can only use one arm, but we have to get him up."

They worked together and finally tugged Jack over the side. He huddled against the hull, exhausted and clutching his side. Carrie saw blood on the back of his head. She didn't have any blankets, so she covered him with a tarp. He seemed to be in shock, and she knew it was important to keep him warm.

She felt shaken as she knelt by his side, silently thanking heaven that he was alive. Thunder rumbled, and rain poured down, but she barely noticed, realizing he could have gone under. She could have lost him forever.

She tucked the covering around him, and he reached up and gripped her hand. "Carrie...thank God you were out here," he mumbled.

Carrie's heart was in her throat. "It's over. Everything's all right. You're all right, Jack," she repeated, reassuring herself.

While she took care of Jack, Sophie turned the boat toward the shore. "Where should I go in, Mom?"

"Anywhere. Look for a dock. Just don't hit any rocks." A crash landing was all they needed.

Carrie looked down at Jack again and tucked a cushion behind his back. He blinked and coughed. "You saved my life."

"Barely. Why weren't you wearing a life vest?"

He started to smile and coughed. "I should have been. You're right." His expression grew serious. "You're amazing, Carrie...just...amazing. I thought I'd never get the chance to tell you."

Carrie swallowed back tears. When he'd gone under the water and she didn't see him come up again, she regretted not saying many things, too.

"Jack..." She shook her head and pressed her hand to his chest. "Just rest. We'll be in soon."

Sophie spotted a private dock and aimed straight for it. As she steered the sailboat in, a couple ran down to meet them, an older man and a woman, dressed in matching yellow rain slickers. With the hoods pulled up, Carrie could barely see their faces until they were very close. Then she recognized Mayor Lenhardt and his wife, Eileen.

Carrie tossed George Lenhardt a line, and he secured the boat to the dock. "We saw you out there, Carrie. We called the marine constable, but he couldn't find you. Thank God you made it back."

Sophie hopped out first, and Eileen Lenhardt wrapped her arm around the girl's shoulder and led her to the house. "What a fright. My granddaughter's just your size. We'll find you some dry clothes right away."

George climbed into the boat to help Carrie get Jack out, which was no small feat. Blood matted his hair, and he winced every time he tried to use his left arm.

Once inside, Eileen gave everyone towels and dry clothes. Carrie found her cell phone, sealed in a dry bag in her pocket, and called Brooke. Her sister was so upset, she could hardly speak.

"We called and called, and you never answered. Mom called the Coast Guard. They're out looking for you."

"I hope they found the marine constable at least," Carrie said, trying for a lighter tone.

"What?"

"Never mind. Sounds like everyone was looking for us. Let them know we're safe and pick us up right away. Jack is hurt. He needs to be checked out, but he won't let me call an ambulance," she added in a whisper so that he couldn't hear.

Carrie had already explained that the Lenhardts had taken them in, and Brooke knew the way.

A short time later, wearing borrowed but dry clothes and full of hot drinks, Carrie, Sophie, and Jack piled into Brooke's van. Jack looked a bit better, but Carrie was sure his arm was sprained if not broken, and a head injury was not to be taken lightly.

They sat together in the back seat, side by side. Sophie sat up front with Brooke. Carrie held Jack's hand, to reassure herself that he was all right, she told herself. He didn't seem to mind.

Jack only noticed Brooke had taken them to the medical center when they pulled up the circular drive at the Emergency Room entrance.

"Hey...what are we doing here? I just need an ice pack and some aspirin."

"And an X-ray of your arm and one of your head. They won't find any common sense. I know that already." Carrie was still upset from the misadventure and, instead of crying, felt mad at him. "Just humor me, please?" she asked in a gentler tone.

He looked at her and sighed, then got out of the van. "All right. I'll let you know how it goes."

Carrie got out as well, surprising him. "I'll keep you company." She was concerned and wanted to make sure he had a full examination. He was so ornery; he might not go in if he was left there on his own.

She leaned into the car and spoke to Sophie. "I'll be home soon, honey. Brooke and Grandma will take care of you."

Sophie had seemed shaken earlier but was now energized by the adventure. "I'm fine, Mom. Aunt Brooke is going to interview me for the newspaper. 'Dramatic Rescue in Piper Cove.'"

"Let's talk about that when I get back." Carrie didn't want any attention for the incident and was sure Jack didn't either. But there was no stopping Brooke when she'd caught the scent of a story.

* * *

Carrie took Jack's hand again as the van drove away. The storm had cleared as quickly as it swept in, and her eyes blinked at the late-day sunlight and blue skies. It suddenly felt as if the dark drama on the water had been a frightening dream and she had just woken up.

"Let's get this over with. I hate to waste a doctor's time. There are sick people in there who really need attention," he groused.

As they walked toward the entrance, Carrie led him to a courtyard on one side of the building. It was filled with large stone planters; the blooming flowers and leaves sparkled with raindrops. She found a bench and sat. "It looks busy in there. I need a moment to collect myself."

"Good idea." Jack sat beside her, his injured arm folded across his chest.

"Does your arm hurt?" she asked.

"It's just a sprain. I'll be fine in a day or two."

She guessed it might take longer than that but would leave a doctor to decide. "Why didn't you wear a vest, Jack? Is that too wimpy?"

He offered a small, embarrassed smile. "I've been on boats all my life. I've never gone over the side. Not once, even in choppy water."

Carrie's throat got tight remembering the sight. "When you fell in and didn't come up...I...I...didn't know what to do. I thought I'd lost you," she confessed. "And I knew what a fool I'd been not to give us a chance. I know what I told you. But I realize now I was afraid I wouldn't fit in with your other world. You'd see I was just an unsophisticated hometown girl who ran a little café for her family, and you'd decide that you made a big mistake falling for me. And that...well...that would hurt worse than anything," she confessed. "I knew I couldn't risk it."

He stared at her, shocked by her words. Then he put his good arm around her and kissed her as if he truly was a drowning man, and only she could save him.

When they parted, he said, "I was totally thrown when you said you didn't want to get involved. I stomped off to San Diego in a black mood, determined to shake it off.

"I had a lot of time to think," he added. "When I got back, I wanted to tell you about a crazy idea I got out there. But I kept losing my nerve. You seemed so cozy with Doug Dolt-on."

"Don't call him that. He's very nice." Carrie could hardly hold back a smile at the nickname.

"But not for you, thank goodness," he reminded her. "Here's what I wanted to say. I love you, Carrie Louise Duffy. Bossy, brave, beautiful, sassy, sweet, and everything in between. I'll be any guy you want. If I can be near you...and cook.

"I don't need to go to San Diego and be Jackson Gardeaux. I don't want to be him anymore, anywhere. I want to stay on Haven Island or go to Maine, or wherever you and Sophie go. Could you see yourself with that guy?"

"I love you, too, Jack. Just the way you are."

He pulled her close, and they met in a long, sweet kiss. Carrie lost all sense of time and place. When they parted, she rested her cheek on his chest, and he tucked her head under his chin. The embrace felt so natural, right where she should be.

Jack seemed to share her thought. "I feel so much better. I think we should go home."

"Glad to hear you're coming around. But you're going in there to see a doctor." Carrie lifted her head and caught his eye. "Did you think I'd fall for that?"

He laughed. "I'd better step up my game. I've met my match."

"Yes, Jack, you finally have," she happily agreed.

He squeezed her closer. "You're some catch. Do you know that?" he whispered.

She smiled at the compliment, then suddenly remembered Evaline's tea leaf reading and nearly laughed out loud. "No, you are," she whispered back. "I didn't mean to go out fishing today, but I ended up with a prize catch, one that filled the boat."

The nonsensical words made him laugh, a warm, deep beautiful sound she hoped to hear forever.

* * *

"I'd like to make a toast." Jack lifted his glass. "To the Duffy women, with my deepest gratitude."

Carrie sat with Jack and her family at a large round table on the deck of the café. Even Rebecca had arrived on time. She rarely came to the island on a Thursday night, but after the close call at sea, she wanted to see Carrie, Sophie, and Jack.

It was almost seven, and the clouds at the horizon over the harbor were touched with pink and gold. They had just finished dinner, a wonderful meal Jack had prepared, despite one arm in a sling. To his regret, he hadn't caught the fish for his entree, but had transformed Finn's catch of flounder into a deliciously sublime dish from his unpublished cookbook.

"You're an amazing group," he added. "I don't know where I'd be without you and my summer on Haven Island."

"That's very sweet," Carrie's mother said after a sip of wine. "But you rescued us, too. You took over the kitchen like a pro and won the blueberry pie contest."

"Carrie inspired me." He glanced at her and smiled. "After the chowder flop, I was afraid of what she'd do if I blew that one, too."

"I liked your chowder," Brooke said. "It tasted very... sophisticated."

Jack met Carrie's glance, and she knew what he was about to say. "Thanks, Brooke. Since you mentioned it, there's a reason for that. The thing is, most people in the restaurant business call me Jackson Gardeaux. It's sort of a stage name."

"Jackson Gardeaux?" Brooke's eyes grew wide. "Wait...I've seen you on cooking shows. You have a glitzy rooftop restaurant in New York City, Gardeaux's."

"*Had* a restaurant," he corrected her.

"Even I've heard of that place." Gena stared at him. "Why didn't you tell us?"

"It's a long story."

"We've got time," Brooke broke in. "Tell us everything."

She wasn't recording him on her phone, but Carrie could see her absorbing the information.

"I do owe you all an explanation. Here goes," Jack began.

Jack told them the story he'd told Carrie, how his wife and partner had an affair and caused his restaurant to close and how they cheated him of his rightful share. And how he was hounded by social media and reporters.

"I had offers to headline other famous restaurants or open a new one. But I wanted a break from the pressure. I also needed to go off the grid and escape my alter ego. I saw your ad," he said to Gena, "and I knew in my stock bones, this was the place for me. It was my lucky day."

"Goodness—I never suspected a thing," Gena said.

Rebecca rolled her eyes. "No comment."

Sophie pulled out her phone. "It's so cool that you're famous. I'm going to Google you."

"Carrie smelled something fishy from the start, if you'll excuse the pun," Rebecca told them. "I had one of the snoops in my office check Jack out, and they uncovered his alias."

"You knew all this time?" Gena asked.

"Yes, Carrie did, too," Rebecca replied.

Brooke looked annoyed. "That's not fair. Why didn't you guys tell me?"

"Because Jack wanted his anonymity, and I knew you'd be dying to to make a newspaper story of it," Carrie said.

Brooke frowned but couldn't deny the accusation

Gena turned back to Jack. "So in September, you'll turn into Jackson Gardeaux again. Is that the plan?"

"It was." Jack glanced at Carrie and took her hand. "Until I had some sense knocked into my thick skull. Carrie and I have been talking."

"And Sophie, too," Carrie looked across the table at her daughter, who replied with a wide smile.

"We've decided to stay here, on Haven. At least for the time being. I had plans to open a restaurant in San Diego, but I can do the same on the island. Nothing that will compete with the Blue Sky," he quickly added. "But not nearly as over the top as the sort of thing Jackson Gardeaux used to put his name on. I'm thinking of a casual but classy spot with great food and excellent service. Most of all, an authentic atmosphere." He put his arm around Carrie's shoulder. "I'll be in the kitchen, and Carrie will run the front of the house."

"That sounds wonderful. I'm so happy for you." Gena's warm gaze took in all three of them. "I've grown so accustomed to having all of you here, I dreaded the day you had to go. It's like a wish I didn't dare hope for coming true."

Rebecca squinted at Carrie. "I knew you had a thing for Jack. You always found something to argue with him about, but I saw through that ploy."

Carrie blushed. "We argue because one of us is impossible." She meant Jack, of course.

"—But she's trying to be more flexible. Aren't you, honey?" He graced her with a trademark, mischievous grin.

"Good luck with that," Rebecca advised.

"I think this family is very fortunate and blessed," Gena said. "The summer didn't start on the most promising note. But look at us now."

Carrie knew she meant her heart attack and the café's financial problems. Carrie could say the same. No job, no place to live—her life was a trainwreck the night she and Sophie had arrived. The clouds had taken time to clear, but she felt grateful and even amazed to see how everything had worked out. More wonderfully than she could have asked for or even imagined.

Carrie heard a knock on the side door, and her mother rose and headed for the kitchen.

"That must be Jonathan," she called over her shoulder. "I had to cancel our dinner plans, but I asked him to drop by for dessert. I hope no one minds?"

"Of course not," Carrie said, though her mother hadn't waited for an answer. She and her sisters shared a look.

"This is getting interesting," Sophie whispered with a giggle.

"Isn't it?" Carrie whispered back.

Epilogue

It was Aunt Lila's idea to have a party. Tess was in favor, but she'd never given one and didn't know where to start. She kept her concerns to herself and let her aunt take charge. Once Lila got going, she was like a runaway train. When Ben heard the plan, he happily jumped on board.

They were out with Honey, picking apples from the cluster of trees that edged the property, a job Tess had always loved as a child. Her father would let her climb the branches to pick the ripest fruit that hung just out of reach, and she enjoyed doing just that today.

The day was warm and sunny, though the date and the task marked summer's passing. She might have felt bittersweet about the change of seasons, but lately, every day seemed to bring more happiness. Sometimes she wanted to pinch herself to make sure she wasn't dreaming. But it was true; this was her life.

"I should get a ladder, Tess," Ben called up through the branches. "You're really out too far now."

"'If you want the sweetest fruit, you need to go out on a limb,'" she called back. She wasn't sure where she'd heard that advice, but it seemed to fit the moment. "I'm almost done. Here come a few more. Watch out."

She tossed the apples she'd picked down to Ben, and he caught each one, then placed them in a bushel that was already full.

"Coming down," she told him as she abled through the branches.

"I hope so. I don't want to see you in a cast for the party."

Tess laughed. "I haven't even agreed yet."

He stood by the trunk, ready to help her. She jumped, and he caught her in his arms. "We absolutely need to have a party, Tess. We have so much to celebrate. So much to be thankful for. When do you want to do it?"

She stared up at him, her arms circling his broad shoulders. How could she say 'no'? They did have a good reason. It was true.

"Aunt Lila picked next Sunday, the first weekend of fall."

"Perfect, I'll spread the word."

"Feel free." She knew he meant he'd invite his family to the farm, his mother, sister, and aunt. An idea that was positively unthinkable a few short months ago.

Tess smiled as she stepped from his embrace and dropped a few more apples into the basket. A deep sense of joy and peace welled up inside. She'd never felt so happy and secure. A few days prior, Ben had rushed to the farm with news too important to tell her over the phone.

Examining the files from the car accident, the attorney helping them had found evidence that had somehow been ignored in the investigation--blood and hair on the passenger's side of the dashboard, and fingerprints on the passenger's side door as well. There were photographs, and hair strands had been preserved. The prints were already matched to Tess, and the rest would surely be confirmed by a DNA test.

It was enough to ask the court to overturn her sentence. Or at least grant a re-trial. Her name would be cleared, for once and for all.

To Tess, the news was mind-boggling. She could finally step out of the shadows and start a new life.

In the past weeks, she'd waivered about contacting her mother's family in Minnesota, though she had researched them online. She wanted so much to meet them and learn more about her mother. But each time she considered what to say about her own history, she froze. It seemed dishonest not to admit her past, but how could they ever believe she hadn't deserved her imprisonment? Now she could connect to a whole family she'd never even known existed.

The attorney's discovery had smoothed the way with Ben's family, too. They had tried hard to put aside their reservations and get to know her, for Ben's sake. But any time Tess spent in their company had been strained and awkward.

The solid proof that Tess had not been driving the car on that fateful night stunned them. But they accepted that it was true, and that Ben had been right; Tess could not be blamed for Andy's death. His mother and sister had even apologized for treating her so harshly. Tess assured them that she understood and was simply grateful for their change of heart.

Aunt Frankie had always been friendly. When she heard of the new evidence she told Tess that she wanted to put a story in the newspaper about the dramatic turn of events. "Once the new evidence is confirmed and the motion filed for your conviction to be dismissed," she clarified. "Everyone remembers this case. They should know mistakes were made and the injustice that you endured."

Tess cringed at the idea of being in the public eye again, but she wanted the truth to be known even more. She knew that if Ben had his way, he'd ride around the island on the back of her truck with a megaphone and nearly laughed out loud at the thought.

She owed him so much for putting his pain and resentment aside when they first met. And opening his mind and heart. For believing in her innocence and their future, even when she'd lost hope. Most of all, for loving her. But she felt sure now she had a lifetime to make it up to him, and then some.

The day of the party, the air held a crisp hint of fall, though it was mild enough to entertain their guests outdoors as they'd planned. Evaline was the first to arrive, her little car filled with cakes and breads and decorations for the tables, beautiful arrangements of majestic dahlias and colorful mums mixed with cat tails, greenery, pomegranates, and sugar pumpkins.

Tess and Lila had set a long table on the porch and smaller tables on the lawn, covered with bright cloths that lifted in the breeze like the hem of a long dress. Lila had been cooking for days while Tess chopped and cleaned up. Honey had helped by eating all the tasty bits that dropped to the floor.

"The table pieces are a work of art, Evaline. You've outdone yourself," Tess said as she helped empty the car.

"It's a happy occasion, dear. I was inspired." Evaline gave her a hug and then lifted a cake box from the front seat.

Owen Jessup and his wife, Florence, arrived next. As Tess greeted them, the Duffys drove up. First Carrie, Jack, and Sophie in Carrie's SUV. Sophie had brought her new puppy, a yellow, retriever mix she named Ruby. Honey was delighted to have company and quickly introduced herself. Carrie's sisters, her mother Gena, and Gena's friend, Jonathan arrived next.

Tess was especially pleased to see Rebecca and thought it was nice of her to come. Tess was sure Rebecca had more exciting things to do on the weekend than visit a farm, but she seemed very pleased to be there.

Richard had arrived the night before. He and Tess managed to keep up a pleasant front for Lila. Tess felt sure he'd never bother her again and maybe, even felt ashamed now of what he'd done. Though Ben said she was giving him far too much credit.

"Carrie, Jack. . .thanks so much for coming." With Ben at her side, Tess greeted her guests with warmth and a special affection for each one.

"We wouldn't have missed it," Carrie assured her. "I know you said you didn't need anything, but I couldn't keep Jack out of the kitchen."

"She did try," Jack confirmed. "But it didn't feel right to come here empty-handed."

He took a big pot from the trunk of the SUV. "Just some fish chowder, for a starter. A traditional Duffy family recipe." He glanced at Carrie. "With a few small changes."

"I helped catch the fish," Sophie said.

"Wow, that makes it extra special," Tess told her.

Her aunt and Ben had been right – it felt good to gather their friends and family and celebrate all the blessings in their lives.

* * *

It had been a beautiful afternoon at High Meadow Farm. The party was winding down, with everyone content and full of the good food Lila had served and Evaline's scrumptious desserts.

Carrie gazed around at the guests. Rebecca sat on the porch with Tess and Ben, deep in conversation, along with Ben's mother and his sister, probably advising them about legal matters the family faced. Tess seemed to have the Crofts in her corner now, and Carrie was sure that meant the world to her. It might take time, but Carrie had a feeling it would all work out in Tess's favor.

Brooke was at the other end of the porch with Frankie Croft. Her tenacious younger sister had been stalking the publisher since the party began and had finally cornered her prey. Carrie guessed Brooke was pitching a story. Luckily, Frankie looked interested.

Her mom and Jonathan sat at a table on the lawn with Lila, Evaline, and the Jessups. Her mother had mentioned a new project during lunch—she was going to paint the portraits of longtime island residents. Practically all the guests seemed flattered when she asked if they'd sit for her, though Owen seemed the shyest about having his portrait painted.

Her mother dug out a sketch pad and charcoal from the car and was already working on a rough draft of Evaline, who kept asking the others, "Is this my good side?"

Carrie glanced around for Tess's cousin, Richard, then remembered he'd left early in a taxi. He'd been quiet, lingering in the background most of the day.

Carrie knew a little from Rebecca about what he'd put Tess through, and thought Tess was a generous soul to allow him on the farm at all, much less invite him today. But no doubt that Tess had been thinking of Lila. Tess had a good heart, and Carrie was glad to see her and Ben so happy.

"Let's take a walk. It's so pretty here . . . and I think I ate too much," she said to Jack.

"Lila is some cook. I have to get her recipe for that stuffed squash. It would be an interesting dish for our new place."

"Yes, it would be." In addition to the other hundred dishes he'd so far jotted down in his idea book.

It would all get sorted out, and they'd have great fun—and a few debates, she was sure—while deciding.

Carrie smiled as Jack took her hand and led her down a path that crossed an open field of tall grass, golden in the fading sunlight.

"I've never been up this way. The view is breathtaking."

"Isn't it? You can see the entire island from here." Carrie spun around, and Jack caught her, his hands on her waist.

"Can you see where we should open our restaurant?"

They hadn't found the right location yet, but there were some good possibilities. "I'd need a telescope for that. And a crystal ball."

"We'll figure it out. I've already got the perfect name. We could call it 'Carrie's'. . . What do you think?"

"Very catchy. I'll add it to the list." She turned to look out at the view, and he put his arm around her shoulder and pulled her close.

"I'm a lucky man. I have a beautiful view no matter where I go. As long as I'm with you."

"I'm lucky, too. More than I can say." Carrie tucked her head against his strong shoulder, her heartbeat quickening. She'd always feel this way about Jack. She had no doubt. "Who would have guessed the tall, dark, cranky guy who bit my head off the first time we met would turn out to be the love of my life?"

He winced. "I wasn't that bad, was I?" When she didn't answer, he added, "You held your own, as I recall. You didn't let me get away with much, Carrie."

"I didn't. And I won't," she warned in a playful tone.

"Point taken. We're a good match. At least that's one thing we can agree on...Oh, and this." He pulled her close and kissed her.

Carrie smiled and wound her arms around his broad shoulders, basking in his warmth and strength. And his love. A love that had taken her by surprise and unfurled a future ahead, as far as she could see; a long, beautiful road, bright with possibilities.

Dear Readers, I hope you enjoyed your visit to Haven Harbor.
The best way to thank an author is to post a review!

Please share your thoughts about this new series with a review at
Amazon, Barnes & Noble, Goodreads
and other book sites.

Your opinion counts and will help new readers discover
Haven Harbor!

Don't miss the next book in the Haven Harbor series!

Coming in 2023

Join Katherine Spencer's email list for advanced news and special offers!

Contact her at: anne@annecanadeo.com

Made in the USA
Middletown, DE
17 February 2023